I0819675

THE FINAL TARGET

Also by Nora Roberts

Hot Ice • Sacred Sins • Brazen Virtue • Sweet Revenge • Public Secrets • Genuine Lies • Carnal Innocence • Divine Evil • Honest Illusions • Private Scandals • Hidden Riches • True Betrayals • Montana Sky • Sanctuary • Homeport • The Reef • River's End • Carolina Moon • The Villa • Midnight Bayou • Three Fates • Birthright • Northern Lights • Blue Smoke • Angels Fall • High Noon • Tribute • Black Hills • The Search • Chasing Fire • The Witness • Whiskey Beach • The Collector • Tonight and Always • The Liar • The Obsession • Come Sundown • Shelter in Place • Under Currents • Hideaway • Legacy • Nightwork • Identity • Mind Games • Hidden Nature

2-in-1s by Nora Roberts

Entanglements • Pride and Passion • Welcome Home • The MacGregors: New Beginnings • Western Stars • Irish Pride • Small Town Dreams • Heart and Soul • True Horizons • Graceful Hearts • Without a Doubt • Bright Stars • Heart of the Game • Summer Shadows • Blue Skies • A Christmas Promise • Force of Nature • Meant to Be • Here's to Us • Danger Zone • Starlight • Moondance • Royal Secrets • Irish Secrets • Royal Destiny • Close to Home • Playing with Fire • Perfect Strangers • Winter Wonderland

Series

Irish Born Trilogy
Born in Fire • Born in Ice • Born in Shame

Dream Trilogy
Daring to Dream • Holding the Dream • Finding the Dream

Chesapeake Bay Saga
Sea Swept • Rising Tides • Inner Harbor • Chesapeake Blue

Gallaghers of Ardmore Trilogy
Jewels of the Sun • Tears of the Moon • Heart of the Sea

Three Sisters Island Trilogy
Dance Upon the Air • Heaven and Earth • Face the Fire

Key Trilogy
Key of Light • Key of Knowledge • Key of Valor

In the Garden Trilogy
Blue Dahlia • Black Rose • Red Lily

Circle Trilogy
Morrigan's Cross • Dance of the Gods • Valley of Silence

Sign of Seven Trilogy
Blood Brothers • The Hollow • The Pagan Stone

Bride Quartet
Vision in White • Bed of Roses • Savor the Moment • Happy Ever After

The Inn Boonsboro Trilogy
The Next Always • The Last Boyfriend • The Perfect Hope

The Cousins O'Dwyer Trilogy
Dark Witch • Shadow Spell • Blood Magick

The Guardians Trilogy
Stars of Fortune • Bay of Sighs • Island of Glass

Chronicles of The One
Year One • Of Blood and Bone • The Rise of Magicks

The Dragon Heart Legacy
The Awakening • The Becoming • The Choice

The Lost Bride Trilogy
Inheritance • The Mirror • The Seven Rings

eBooks by Nora Roberts

Cordina's Royal Family

Affaire Royale • Command Performance • The Playboy Prince • Cordina's Crown Jewel

The Donovan Legacy

Captivated • Entranced • Charmed • Enchanted

The O'Hurleys

The Last Honest Woman • Dance to the Piper • Skin Deep • Without a Trace

Night Tales

Night Shift • Night Shadow • Nightshade • Night Smoke • Night Shield

The MacGregors

The Winning Hand • The Perfect Neighbor • All the Possibilities • One Man's Art • Tempting Fate • Playing the Odds • The MacGregor Brides • The MacGregor Grooms • Rebellion/In from the Cold • For Now, Forever

The Calhouns

Suzanna's Surrender • Megan's Mate • Courting Catherine • A Man for Amanda • For the Love of Lilah

Irish Legacy

Irish Rose • Irish Rebel • Irish Thoroughbred

Jack's Stories

Best Laid Plans • Loving Jack • Lawless

Summer Love • Boundary Lines • Dual Image • First Impressions • The Law Is a Lady • Local Hero • This Magic Moment • The Name of the Game • Partners • Temptation • The Welcoming • Opposites Attract • Time Was • Times Change • Gabriel's Angel • Holiday Wishes • The Heart's Victory • The Right Path • Rules of the Game • Search for Love • Blithe Images • From This Day • Song of the West • Island of Flowers • Her Mother's Keeper • Untamed • Sullivan's Woman • Less of a Stranger • Reflections • Dance of Dreams • Storm Warning • Once More with Feeling • Endings and Beginnings • A Matter of Choice • One Summer • Summer Desserts • Lessons Learned • The Art of Deception • Second Nature • Treasures Lost, Treasures Found

Nora Roberts & J. D. Robb

Remember When

J. D. Robb

Naked in Death • *Glory in Death* • *Immortal in Death* • *Rapture in Death* • *Ceremony in Death* • *Vengeance in Death* • *Holiday in Death* • *Conspiracy in Death* • *Loyalty in Death* • *Witness in Death* • *Judgment in Death* • *Betrayal in Death* • *Seduction in Death* • *Reunion in Death* • *Purity in Death* • *Portrait in Death* • *Imitation in Death* • *Divided in Death* • *Visions in Death* • *Survivor in Death* • *Origin in Death* • *Memory in Death* • *Born in Death* • *Innocent in Death* • *Creation in Death* • *Strangers in Death* • *Salvation in Death* • *Promises in Death* • *Kindred in Death* • *Fantasy in Death* • *Indulgence in Death* • *Treachery in Death* • *New York to Dallas* • *Celebrity in Death* • *Delusion in Death* • *Calculated in Death* • *Thankless in Death* • *Concealed in Death* • *Festive in Death* • *Obsession in Death* • *Devoted in Death* • *Brotherhood in Death* • *Apprentice in Death* • *Echoes in Death* • *Secrets in Death* • *Dark in Death* • *Leverage in Death* • *Connections in Death* • *Vendetta in Death* • *Golden in Death* • *Shadows in Death* • *Faithless in Death* • *Forgotten in Death* • *Abandoned in Death* • *Desperation in Death* • *Encore in Death* • *Payback in Death* • *Random in Death* • *Passions in Death* • *Bonded in Death* • *Framed in Death* • *Stolen in Death*

Anthologies

From the Heart • A Little Magic • A Little Fate

Moon Shadows

(with Jill Gregory, Ruth Ryan Langan, and Marianne Willman)

The Once Upon Series

(with Jill Gregory, Ruth Ryan Langan, and Marianne Willman)

Once Upon a Castle • Once Upon a Star • Once Upon a Dream • Once Upon a Rose • Once Upon a Kiss • Once Upon a Midnight

Silent Night

(with Susan Plunkett, Dee Holmes, and Claire Cross)

Out of This World

(with Laurell K. Hamilton, Susan Krinard, and Maggie Shayne)

Bump in the Night

(with Mary Blayney, Ruth Ryan Langan, and Mary Kay McComas)

Dead of Night

(with Mary Blayney, Ruth Ryan Langan, and Mary Kay McComas)

Three in Death

Suite 606

(with Mary Blayney, Ruth Ryan Langan, and Mary Kay McComas)

In Death

The Lost

(with Patricia Gaffney, Ruth Ryan Langan, and Mary Blayney)

The Other Side

(with Mary Blayney, Patricia Gaffney, Ruth Ryan Langan, and Mary Kay McComas)

Time of Death

The Unquiet

(with Mary Blayney, Patricia Gaffney, Ruth Ryan Langan, and Mary Kay McComas)

Mirror, Mirror

(with Mary Blayney, Elaine Fox, Mary Kay McComas, and R. C. Ryan)

Down the Rabbit Hole

(with Mary Blayney, Elaine Fox, Mary Kay McComas, and R. C. Ryan)

Also Available . . .

The In Death Cookbook

(by Theresa Carle-Sanders with Foreword by J. D. Robb)

The Official Nora Roberts Companion

(edited by Denise Little and Laura Hayden)

THE FINAL TARGET

NORA ROBERTS

ST. MARTIN'S PRESS
NEW YORK

This is a work of fiction. All of the names, characters, organizations, places, and events portrayed in this work are either products of the author's imagination or used fictitiously.

First published in the United States by St. Martin's Press, an imprint of St. Martin's Publishing Group

EU Representative: Macmillan Publishers Ireland Ltd, 1st Floor, The Liffey Trust Centre, 117–126 Sheriff Street Upper, Dublin 1, D01 YC43

Printed in the United States of America. For information, address St. Martin's Publishing Group, 120 Broadway, New York, NY 10271.

www.stmartins.com

Endpaper art by Ervin Serrano

Design by James Sinclair

The Library of Congress Cataloging-in-Publication Data is available upon request.

ISBN 978-1-250-41358-1 (hardcover)
ISBN 978-1-250-41359-8 (ebook)

First Edition: 2026

10 9 8 7 6 5 4 3 2 1

To women
We're stronger than we look

BOOKS

PART ONE

Shattered

Like one, that on a lonesome road
Doth walk in fear and dread,
And having once turned round walks on,
And turns no more his head;
Because he knows, a frightful fiend
Doth close behind him tread.

—Samuel Taylor Coleridge

Chapter One

The back room of Next Chapter bookstore tended toward organized chaos. The small space held a counter, a couple of stools, shelves crammed with books. Boxes of books yet unopened were stacked along one of the short walls.

Arden knew where everything was, down to the extra pens, the rolls of tape, the box cutters, the printer paper, the Sam's Club M&M's. And all the rest.

She'd worked part-time in the bookstore since she'd moved from the Columbus suburbs to the Short North with her college degree hot in her hand.

Considering her major in English lit, most expected her to go into teaching.

Instead, she'd written a book.

It had taken her more than a year, juggling her college, then her work schedule and what barely passed as a social life, but she'd done it. It took months more to find an agent who'd take her and *Whispers* on. More months before the agent performed the miracle of selling the manuscript.

Now, two years and nine months after she'd sat at the keyboard and faced the first blank screen, she'd accomplished what she'd set out to do.

She held on, gratefully, to the fact no one could ever take that away from her. Whether or not she sold a single copy, whether or not everyone who bought or borrowed it thought it stank, she'd sold and published a book.

The proof stood in stacks on the counter of the back room of Next Chapter.

Where in about five minutes, she'd face her first event.

She knew how signings and readings worked. As a bookseller, she'd helped run plenty of them. But now instead of managing the line or ringing up sales, she'd be the one sitting at the table, signing a book with her name on the cover.

Whispers by Arden Bowie.

Because it made her giddy, Arden picked up a book from the stack just to look at it again.

Her name on the cover, her words inside.

She had friends and family coming, so she would sign at least a handful. Amazing, she thought, and after giving the cover a stroke, set it back down again.

In a few minutes, she'd be the one smiling and chatting and pretending she knew what the hell she was doing.

She felt a little bit sick.

She'd handle it. Maybe she'd been born an introvert, but she'd taught herself to be outgoing, she reminded herself. A good thing, as she'd been taller than most of the boys her age, and gawky with it.

Tall, gawky, with hair just red enough to make her feel awkward? A natural outcast if she hadn't pushed herself.

Then when her parents hadn't come home from their date night, when they'd been two of the fatalities when a sixteen-wheeler had skidded on icy roads, she'd been the orphan. The fourteen-year-old orphan who'd had to move from Brooklyn to Columbus, Ohio, and the home of an aunt and uncle and two cousins she barely knew.

She'd been the angry, grief-soaked kid without a choice.

She hadn't made it easy for them, but gave herself a break there. They certainly had given her one.

They were out there now. Her aunt Jen, uncle Doug, her cousins Zoey—and her fiancé, Boone—and Travis and his wife of eight months, April.

They'd given her back what that terrible night in February had taken away, and she'd never forget it.

She opened one of the books stacked on the counter to the dedication page.

To family, lost and found.

She thought of her parents, hoped they'd be proud she'd done what she'd wanted and needed to do.

Then closed the book.

Terri, the manager and five-foot-two powerhouse, stepped in. "About ready?"

"Yeah, sure."

Had to be, wanted to be, would be.

"We've a nice crowd."

Arden had stuck to the back room because she hadn't wanted to see. "Really?"

"Eighty-six by my count."

"Really?" Arden repeated. She'd have done a tap dance for half that number. "That's a solid number for a Tuesday night, and a weight off. I know what it takes to put one of these on, and I'm so grateful."

"You know we enjoyed every minute. It's the first time we've done an author event for one of our own. And I told you I loved the book."

"You have to say that."

"I don't have to mean it, but I do." Terri reached up, patted her hands on Arden's cheeks. "And you look great."

"Thanks."

She'd bought the short, simple dark green dress because she'd wanted new for this first time. And thought it looked professional but not stuffy paired with tights and boots—also new. Flat-heeled, as at five-eleven she didn't need the height.

"Hair okay?" She patted at the hair, freshly bobbed at her jawline.

"It's perfect. Lana's warming them up. I'm going to introduce you, then it's off and running. You're going to have fun."

If she didn't babble, or freeze or choke.

But Arden stepped out, plastered the welcoming smile—she'd practiced—on her face.

The little-bit-sick ebbed when she saw people in the event area. And went away altogether when she found her family.

Terri stepped up. "Welcome, everyone. Some of you already know

Arden Bowie, as she's part of the team here at Next Chapter. And we're excited to have her here tonight signing her debut novel, *Whispers*. Trust me, reading it's going to keep you up late tonight. Arden's going to give you a little preview of why you'll need an extra shot of coffee in the morning. Let's give a Next Chapter welcome to our own Arden Bowie."

They applauded. Really, Arden thought, what choice did they have? But she appreciated it, even the hoots her cousin Travis let fly.

"Thank you, Terri, and thanks to my teammates at Next Chapter, the best independent bookstore in Ohio."

She heard her voice carry through the room, relieved that it sounded strong and clear.

"And thanks to all of you for coming out on this cold Tuesday night, giving some time to a new author and her first book. I'll add I hope Terri's right and *Whispers* costs you some sleep. It seems only fair, since it cost me plenty of sleep to write it."

She took a breath, scanned the room, made eye contact here and there as she picked up the book on her table.

"*Whispers* is a story about a woman leading a quiet, even ordinary life who finds that life turned inside out. To survive, she'll have to peel away the ordinary and reveal who and what she really is. This is the beginning.

"'She shouldn't have been there,'" Arden read, "'at that time, in that place. If she hadn't stayed behind, worked so late, if she hadn't given in and laid her head down on her desk, she'd have been home. Home in the quiet and the safe.

"'But by the time she woke, annoyed with herself, gathered her things, switched off the light, it was already too late. The voices came, hardly more than whispers in the quiet that would never be safe again.

"'And she heard.'"

As she read the opening chapter, Arden saw it as she had when she'd put the words on-screen. For that space of time, it became her reality, replacing the bookstore with its colorful stacks, the rows of chairs she'd helped arrange only hours before.

For those few minutes, she let herself live it, so when she reached the end, closed the book, the applause jolted her back.

Her quick laugh was breathless and genuine. "Thank you."

"And thank you, Arden, for putting us all on the edge of our seats."

Beaming, Terri stepped up again. "And since we are, Cassie and Drake will help you form a line to have your book signed."

Her family got there first, and Douglas Rogan laid down a stack of seven books.

"Uncle Doug, really?"

"All called for, right, Jen?"

"Absolutely. You were wonderful, honey. We're so damn proud. Now, there's one for each of us, one for Doug's dad, one for your grandmother."

As Jen rattled off the names, Arden just grinned at them. She'd heard her uncle called a handsome son of a bitch. He really was handsome, with his wavy brown hair, bold blue eyes, and wide rubber grin. And with Jen—tall, lean, chestnut hair—they made a handsome couple.

Another stack for Travis and his new bride, and double that for Zoey and Boone.

"I've got a big family, and I get to brag my sister-in-law is a big-deal writer."

"'Big deal' is yet to be determined."

"You are to us." Zoey reached out to grip Arden's hand. "The biggest."

For months after Arden moved in, she and Zoey had butted heads, and hard. Then, though neither could say just when, how, or why, they'd bonded like glue.

"Drinks at Barney's after you're done. Mom and Dad already have it set up, so no argument or excuse."

"None."

"Now get to work."

She smiled at the first unknown face, and got to work.

She lost track of time in the wonderful weirdness of signing her book, handing it back to people she didn't know.

Some she did—regular customers, friends, even a smattering of people from her high school years.

She talked, laughed, signed, and felt very much as if she stood to one side watching it all in amazed amusement.

When the last in line stepped up, her smile came as easily as it had with the first.

"Hi. Thanks for waiting."

"Oh, no problem. I really liked your reading."

"I hope you enjoy the rest of the book."

"I read a little more online. Totally hooked. I just moved here a few weeks ago, and this is my first book signing."

She knew the value of making a connection, so warmed up her smile a little more. "You'll love living in Short North. It's a great neighborhood. Who can I sign this to?"

"For Dustin. For me. You probably hear this a lot, but I'm trying to write a book, too."

"That's great."

He beamed at her, a man with a solid build, dark blond hair pulled back in a short tail. He had a pleasant-enough face with deep-set brown eyes that lingered on hers.

"Any advice?"

"I'm barely off the ground here, but if I have any, it's don't give up. If it's something you want, something you love, you don't quit. Quitters don't win, even if it's just doing something you love for yourself. That's a win."

"That's really good advice. Thanks."

She offered him the book. "I hope you enjoy the rest of the book."

"Oh, I know I will. You know, you have hair the color Titian painted."

She'd heard that a time or two, and just kept smiling. "Red hair's a Bowie trademark."

"And amazing eyes. Like bluebells. My grandma, she loved bluebells. It makes me feel like I kind of know you."

"Dustin." Terri slipped smoothly forward. "Cassie will ring you up. I hope you'll come back. Did I hear you say you've just moved to Short North?"

"Yeah, just a few weeks ago." He glanced back at Arden over his shoulder as Terri guided him away.

And when they shut the door with the CLOSED sign out, the staff cheered.

Cassie held up a hand. "And let me announce, with that last sale? One hundred and sixteen copies of *Whispers* have walked out the door."

"A hundred and sixteen?" Arden danced in place. "Holy crap! Well, my family bought half of those, but still."

"They did not buy half." On a laugh, Cassie threw her arms around Arden. "Congratulations."

"You've all made this the best night of my life."

"It's just starting," Terri reminded her. "You've got the Friends of the Library talk, the signing at More Books in Clintonville."

"I wouldn't have any of those if you hadn't twisted arms."

"I didn't have to twist, just tap shoulders. Go, your family's waiting for you."

"I'll help break this down first."

"You will not. Drake, you walk over with her. That last one might be lingering out there. He was hitting on you, Arden."

"Oh, he's trying to write so he wanted to talk. He wasn't any trouble."

"Maybe not, and maybe I'm old enough to have two grandkids—God knows how that happened—but I still know when a man's got the hit-on in his eyes."

"How about this? I help break down. It won't take long. Then everybody walks over and has a drink. Best night of my life," Arden reminded them.

"I vote yes, Grandma." Cassie grinned at Terri.

"All right, all right. Then let's get it done."

He had lingered, and hadn't felt the cold. When, from the shadows, he saw the whole group walk out together, saw the others form what seemed like a wall around Arden, he felt that cold.

And with it a bitter disappointment.

When Arden woke in the morning, she decided she'd make this the second-best day of her life. Since she tended to wake early, she rolled out of bed in the dark, hit the lights, then made her way into her kitchen.

She'd chosen the small-scale two-bedroom apartment for its location. Just over a block from her part-time job. And the two bedrooms gave her a dedicated office.

The kitchen, tiny compared to the space in her parents' home, in her aunt's, suited her. Its galley style meant everything was close at hand when she had the urge to cook.

In her flannel pants and T-shirt she made herself her version of a latte, which she'd been told—often—was coffee-flavored frothed milk.

But that suited her, too.

Wednesday mornings meant the gym. Weight training—because otherwise her arms went to toothpicks and her legs to spaghetti. Her yoga class, then home before ten. A shower, a midmorning smoothie.

And all day, all second-best day, to write.

Gulping her latte, she went back to the bedroom to make her bed. Then nodded in satisfaction. The bedroom reflected her—the calm blues and greens, soft fabrics, pretty pillows, the fluffy hand-knit throw she'd found in a local shop.

In the bathroom, where the size alone required everything be organized and stowed, she pulled her hair back into a stub of a tail. And thought, again, she missed the nearly fourteen inches of hair she'd had cut off because she thought the shorter style was more sophisticated.

It *was* more sophisticated, she reminded herself. It was just that the rest of her really wasn't. Plus, it seemed to her the style made her chin look more pointed than it already was.

"It'll grow back," she muttered. "Eventually."

She brushed her teeth, went through her morning skin-care ritual, even though since it was a gym day, she'd repeat that routine after her shower.

She could still hear her mother's voice.

You have such beautiful skin, Arden. It's like porcelain. You need to take care of it.

She hadn't paid much, if any, attention at the time—what young teen did? But in the years following her parents' death, in a kind of homage, she'd become religious about it.

After changing into black yoga capris and a tank, she pulled sweats over them. The app on her phone told her the weather would be cold and clear, so she'd walk the four blocks.

Bundled into her coat, knit cap, and scarf, she headed out the door, jogged down the two flights.

Dawn had broken, and the app hadn't lied. The cold hit her face and did more than the latte to wake her fully.

She walked the block to High Street with its metal arches. Traffic, still light at this hour, cruised along. She passed shops and restaurants, still closed. In the next block, she spotted a local walking his corgi.

"Hi, Mr. Grassley. Hi there, Jimbo." Crouching, she gave the wagging dog a rub.

Grassley, short and stocky like his dog, pushed up his glasses. "Gym day?"

"That's right."

"Don't work out too much or there won't be anything left of you."

"I work out to put it on, not take it off."

"Well, you looked real nice last night."

"Thanks. I appreciate you and Ms. Grassley coming."

"The wife started on your book when we got home. Said it's good so far. She'll pass it over to me when she's done." He gave Arden a wink. "I'll let you know what I think."

Arden lifted both hands, fingers crossed. "See you later."

Buoyed by the *good so far* she quickened her pace to the fitness center.

She spent thirty minutes between the machines and free weights, and pleased herself by working up a sweat. And from there to yoga, where she felt buoyed again by a couple of members congratulating her on the signing.

As she walked home she wondered if it would ever get old. And hoped it wouldn't.

Along the walk, her phone signaled a call. When she saw UNKNOWN NUMBER on the display, she ignored it.

By ten-thirty, she sat at her desk and did what she'd resisted the night before due to the time she'd gotten home. She texted her agent.

> Signing successful! 116 books sold! Thank you again for helping me get here.

On a long sigh, she booted up her computer. She opened the fat manilla folder where she kept her notes and research. For a moment, she closed her eyes to help put herself back into the story and the people in it.

The bass intro to Queen's "Another One Bites the Dust" rocked out of her phone.

Jolted out, she glanced at the display and this time saw her agent.

"Yvonne, hi!"

"Congratulations, Arden. Your first signing, and a really strong showing."

"I had a lot of friends and family there, and it sure didn't hurt."

"You take your bows," Yvonne said, with warmth in her clipped native New Yorker voice. "You did the work, and you wrote a good book. Now I'm going to say you wrote two good books. Your publisher made an offer on *Rebound*."

"You're kidding. You're not kidding?" She already pushed up from the desk. "Holy shit."

She'd written it during the months and months of hunting for an agent, of hoping for a sale. Then had kind of torn it open and reworked it.

"Do you have time to talk about the offer?"

"Oh, I think I can definitely make time for that. Just hang on one second."

After muting the phone, Arden threw back her head, let out a war cry.

Then she breathed in and out before sitting at her desk again. Unmuted the phone.

"I'm back."

After the call, she sat. She'd expected to bask. Instead, she felt the jitter of nerves and an urge to weep. Once she'd given in to both, she went to the kitchen to drink a glass of water, to settle herself again.

She took an orange out of her little fruit bowl, peeled it more for the smell than the taste. The scent brought her father there, right there.

Basking would wait—she'd give herself that later. All of that was down the road, and the road could and did take sharp turns.

"I did it twice," she murmured. "And that matters. What matters more, right now, is doing it again."

She went back to her office, sat, put everything out of her mind but the story and the people in it.

And got to work.

The next day, she put in six hours at the bookstore and had the strange delight of ringing up her own book for customers, twice.

She put in another four hours at Next Chapter on Friday—three sales!—then rushed home to change for her second-ever book signing.

When she stepped out of the back room, she had the surprise of seeing Zoey and two of her cousin's bridal attendants in the front row.

And a second surprise when, as she began to speak, scanned, she saw the man who'd been the last in her line at Next Chapter.

As she spoke, part of her brain searched for his name, but couldn't quite find it.

After her reading, she sat, picked up her pen. Then rolled her eyes at Zoey.

"Are you stalking me?"

"I certainly am." Zoey tossed her wavy brown hair, wiggled brows over golden-brown eyes. "A twice-published author gives me the hots."

"You already bought the book—and that's after I gave you one of my author's copies."

"I did, and I'm buying this one for my new boss."

The new boss brought it home, again, that in just under two months, Zoey and Boone, the newlyweds, would relocate to Oregon for career opportunities for both too good to dismiss.

"It's for Carmen." Because they both knew the move would be hard, Zoey laid a hand over Arden's and squeezed.

"She'd better appreciate you. Valley Vineyards better appreciate you. Oregon better appreciate you."

"I'm going to make sure of it."

If anyone could, Arden thought.

"We're so excited for you, Arden." Cecily, Zoey's friend since high school, passed over her book. "After this, margaritas at Ranchero."

Even as Arden opened her mouth, Allison, the second attendant, held up a hand. "Single. One drink. You're driving, so one and nachos and wedding talk to soak that up. We'll save the multiples for the bachelorette party."

"I can agree to that."

"We're going to browse around first. It's a cute shop. And we'll meet you there when you're done. You're doing good," Zoey added.

When she reached the end of the line, she still hadn't jogged the last reader's name loose. But she smiled up at him.

"Hi. It's nice to see you again."

"You did great. You look great, too. That blue dress really brings out your eyes."

Hitting on her? Yeah, maybe. But she knew how to block a hit.

"Thank you."

"I read your book. I thought it was terrific, start to finish. And what a finish!"

"I'm so glad you enjoyed it."

"Loved it. I literally couldn't put it down. The way you described things? It's like I was right there, living it. Plus, all the details about bioweapons, the FBI. I mean, wow. You must've done so much research."

"Thank you, that's so nice to hear. You're buying another copy?"

"Oh, yeah." He gave her a big, wide smile. "For Dustin."

It shook loose—Dustin—so her polite smile went puzzled.

"Um. My grandfather. I was named for him. Even signing all these books for people, you remembered my name. Anyway, I know he'll love it as much as I did."

"I hope so." She began to sign.

"I'd really like to talk to you about your book, your process. How you research."

Those deep-set eyes stayed latched on hers and she felt her spine start to itch.

"Oh, I imagine everyone has their own process, don't you? I'm so new at this, and hardly an expert. And I'm—"

"I'm really interested in yours. Your advice the other night really hit home for me. Don't quit until you get what you want. Don't let anything or anyone stop you. That's exactly how I feel, so we've got a similar mindset."

Had she said that? She didn't think she'd said exactly that.

"I hope you'll keep writing. You have to love it to stick with it."

"Exactly. When it's meant to be, you know it. We need to talk more. Could I buy you a drink, or a late dinner?"

"Thanks, but I'm meeting some friends when I'm done here." She handed him the book. "It's really sweet of you to buy the book for your grandfather. I hope he enjoys it."

"No question about it. Listen, I'd love to get together sometime. It'd be awesome to talk to somebody who's done what I'm trying to do."

She wanted to get up, stretch her legs, relax her smile muscles. But she kept her smile in place as she put her pen away.

"I know what you mean, but I'm really busy right now. With all this, the writing, and my cousin's getting married in a couple weeks. I'm maid of honor and in charge of her bachelorette party."

She rose now, hoping it would signal the bookstore manager. "You might consider joining a critique group."

"I'm not about groups, you know? All those opinions and agendas. I'm better one-on-one."

"A critique partner then."

His eyes seemed to sparkle. "You'd do that?"

"Oh, no, sorry, I really can't. You should talk to the manager." A little desperate now, Arden lifted a hand, waved her over. "I bet she can give you some names or suggestions. Thanks so much for coming."

She slipped into the back room, took a breath. Maybe not hitting on her so much as a woman, she decided, but as a published writer.

She needed to get better at giving good, broad-based advice, she thought. Obviously, she'd made hers too personal, given him the wrong idea.

And he'd gotten a little spooky.

After she said her goodbyes, she went out to her car to drive the handful of blocks to Ranchero.

She didn't notice the car following her, or pulling in a few parking spaces away. And when she came out an hour later, laughing with her friends, hugging goodbye, she didn't notice the car that followed her home.

Chapter Two

Always at home in a library, Arden didn't stress her library event. After all, she'd be speaking to librarians, readers, and patrons. Plus, she had Zoey.

"You're driving to the library where you spent hours and hours in high school. Not to study or hunt up books this time, but as the featured speaker. Doesn't all this feel a little weird and unreal?"

"No, it doesn't feel a little weird and ureal. It feels an entire crapload of weird and unreal."

"Okay." Zoey shook back her hair. "Just checking."

When Arden's cell phone rang, Zoey glanced at the phone in its holder. "Unknown number."

"Hit ignore. I've been getting a couple of those a day."

"You have heroic willpower. I know better, but can never resist."

"And it's always a bullshit solicitation or something about a car warranty or student loan. Possibly a deal on a cemetery plot."

Zoey sighed, hit ignore. "It always is."

"To wind back? You're getting married in two short weeks. Barely a month after that—and after two weeks of lots of honeymoon sex in Hawaii—you're moving across the country and into a house you and Boone bought on a whirlwind five-day trip. A few days after that, you'll be marketing manager of Valley Vineyards while Mr. Boone Yeoh does what none of us really understand as VP of operations at Security One.

"Doesn't that feel weird and unreal?"

"Hmm? Sorry, I was still on the *lots of honeymoon sex in Hawaii*. What it feels is bizarre. Wonderful, scary, exciting, and seriously bizarre."

Zoey reached over to pat Arden's leg. "I think I'll miss you most of all, Scarecrow."

Because she loved her cousin, Arden put her personal loss aside. "You may not be leaving Oz, but you're having a hell of an adventure, Zoey."

"We both are. Just think," she added as Arden navigated into the library's parking lot. "You're about to go in and blow away any socks worn in the library. And after that, we're going for the final fitting of my incredibly awesome and spectacular wedding gown."

They got out of the car into a brisk March wind. Since the lion roared, Arden hoped, for the bride's sake, April produced a lamb.

"Want more weird?" Zoey asked.

"Always."

"I already feel married."

"You've lived together for the best part of a year, after you dated exclusively for over six months."

"It's not just that. I told you how, the first time I met Boone I was like, oh no, I'm not ready for this, but there he is. He's the one. And he was, he is."

"So you got ready." As she often did when they walked, Arden looped an arm around Zoey's shoulders.

Since Zoey wore heels that added three inches to her five-five, Arden didn't feel like she towered over her cousin. Too much.

"I did get ready, and fast, and it was easier than I thought. It could happen to you."

"I don't think that's how it usually works. Plus, I'm younger than you."

Zoey added an elbow jab with her laugh. "You used to hate when I hit you with the two years older."

"I know, but now, and forever after, I gloat."

Inside, Arden shook hands, introduced Zoey. They turned over coats, scarves, shook more hands.

Rachel Fines, the head librarian, kept Arden's hand clasped in hers an extra moment. "We're awfully proud of you, Arden. I can't tell you how satisfying it is to shelve a book from someone we know. We have a waiting list for *Whispers*."

"Well, I can't tell you how satisfying that is. You were always really kind to me, Ms. Fines."

"And you always studied quietly and brought back your books on time. Now, if you're ready, we'll get you started."

"I'll go find a seat, and count socks."

"Socks?" Rachel said when Zoey walked away.

"Family joke."

It felt the same, Arden thought, like every library—however small, however large—she'd ever stepped into. Like countless open doors waiting for her to choose which one she wanted to go through at that moment.

In the first weeks and months after her parents' deaths, the library had been sanctuary and escape. There, she could do and be anything she wanted inside the pages of a book.

Inside the library, inside those pages, she'd realized what she wanted to do and to be. She wanted to write her own pages, her own stories. She'd wanted to be a writer.

While she waited for Rachel to introduce her, she looked over the audience. She found a face that brought that itch between her shoulder blades.

The guy, she thought . . . Dustin. Again? Sitting there, hands folded on a copy of her book.

She couldn't say unreal, as there he sat, but she considered it several clicks over weird, and yes, into that spooky she'd felt the last time.

He wanted to write, she understood that, and how lonely it could feel. But to show up at all her events? Just a little too obsessive for comfort.

She decided she needed to ease off the friendly there, and stick with professionally polite.

Regardless, before she found that line, she had a job to do, and intended to do it well.

She stepped up to the podium.

"Thank you all for coming. We're all privileged to be here, inside a library where we only have to reach onto a shelf for knowledge, for entertainment, for adventure, for solace. We might come to check out a book or spend a quiet hour right here reading. We come to study for an exam, to research a term paper, to bring our kids to Story Time. All that and so much more is right here, open doors for us to walk through."

She wound it around to her own doors, her own path toward writing.

Her talk would run sixteen minutes—she'd timed it.

Three times.

Afterward, she'd take questions. And hoped she had answers. The unknown of that worried her a bit, but she liked the span of the audience, from retirees to a few teenagers.

When she finished to polite applause, she braced herself.

"If anyone has any questions . . ."

It surprised and nearly unnerved her when several hands shot up.

Where do you get your ideas?

"Well, given inflation, ideas are a dollar a dozen. The answer, for me, is to make the idea work, to care enough about the story and the people in it to make it work."

Where do you find the time?

"Where do we find the time for anything? We make it and we take it. I was still in college when I started writing, trying to. I missed a lot of parties. I had to keep my grades up, too, and I worked part-time in the college bookstore, so it takes a lot of juggling and shuffling."

She answered more, thought—hoped—she found a rhythm.

Then she smiled and nodded at the girl who'd been busy typing on a MacBook.

"How do you know it's a good idea?"

"You don't, until you take the leap."

"So you should write what you know?"

"I don't think so. I mean to say, write what you know if you want to write what you know. But? Right here?"

She spread her arms. "You can find out a lot you didn't know when you walked in. Why not write what interests or intrigues you enough to find out?"

Dustin's hand shot up.

She gave him the same smile and nod. "Dustin?"

"You told me once not to give up. When you want something you keep working until you get it. That's not just true for writing, is it? But for just life."

"I'd say yes, unless what you want is to rob banks. I think it's believing in yourself, then putting in the work. The time, the effort, making the sacrifices. Maybe you want to run a marathon. You can't do it by wishing. You have to gear up and train. You have to run, even if you can only make it a quarter mile the first time. If you want it, you'll keep running. Eventually, you'll cross the finish line."

"Life's a marathon, isn't it?"

"Most of us hope it's a really, really long one. So let's keep running. Thank you again for coming. And remember to support your local library."

She exhaled quietly, then braced again when people moved forward to speak to her.

She shook more hands, answered more questions.

Dustin worked his way up.

"That was really . . . it was just great. The marathon thing? It's given me a lot to think about." He held out the book. "Would you just sign this one? I haven't decided who to give it to."

"You keep buying my book, you'll end up an honorary member of the family."

As soon as she said it, she mentally kicked herself. Friendly knee-jerk needed to stop with this one.

"I'd love that! You're a celebrity."

She had to laugh. "Not even remotely."

"Sure you are! I read the article about you in the paper. Anyway, I know you're busy, but—"

"I really am. In fact, I've got to take my cousin for her final wedding dress fitting shortly. We're approaching that particular finish line."

She shifted her gaze and, relieved, greeted a familiar face.

"Ms. Cauder! Thank you, Dustin."

She handed him the book, stepped away, and hugged her high school English teacher.

"When I saw you, I had a flashback to fourth period, senior year."

"You did me proud."

Because her eyes teared up, so did Arden's.

"I couldn't make either one of your signings. Parent conference for one, babysitting my grandbaby for the other. But I bought this."

She pulled the book out of her bag. "I want my former, very talented student to sign it for me."

Arden wrote what she felt. *Thank you for helping me make the right turns.*

"I don't think there's anything a teacher wants to hear more from a student. I'm trying to help this one now. Arden, this is Danica, fourth period, senior year, and she's decided you're her midterm project."

"Oh. That's a serious first for me."

The girl was cupcake pretty with golden-brown skin, razor-sharp features, and wide, gold-flecked brown eyes.

"I want to be a writer. A novelist. I like finding out about things I don't know. Ms. Cauder told the class about you, so I put my name on the library list, and I've already read your book. I really liked it."

"Thanks." Arden angled her head. "I bet you write every day."

"At least in my journal if I can't make or take that time for more. Ms. Bowie, if I could have some time now, or when you can spare it, I'd like to interview you for my assignment."

Arden glanced at Zoey, who'd come over to join them.

"Go ahead. We've got a good twenty minutes."

"Is that enough time, Danica?"

The girl lit up. "Twenty minutes would be super."

"Let's find a spot."

It took less than five minutes for Arden to realize she'd enjoy this interview more, and find it more challenging, than she had her interview for the local paper with a professional journalist.

Dustin watched her from the stacks. Anger nearly choked him. She'd blown him off—again—and here she sat, giving some stupid kid the time that *he* was entitled to.

He got playing hard to get—women did that, a kind of power play. And to his mind they used that tactic when they wanted the guy to keep coming back, to push a little more.

It's why she didn't answer her phone when he called. Why she made excuses when he asked her out.

And all the while he gave her compliments on how she looked, on her stupid book.

He looked down at the book in his hand and had to fight the urge to crack the spine, tear out pages.

Instead, he rubbed the leather bracelet on his left wrist. A reminder to keep calm, carry on.

No, she just had a big heart, that's all. A big, naive heart. She'd felt sorry for the kid—and the old bag had pushed the kid on her anyway. And the cousin, the whole wedding thing sucked up her time.

He could wait. He knew by the way she smiled at him she wanted him to wait.

Quitters don't win. Take what you want or someone else will. How many times had his father said that to him? And Arden had said the same thing.

A marathon, he reminded himself. So he'd keep running. And when he reached the finish line, she'd belong to him as she was meant to.

Days rushed by. Fittings, seating arrangements, a party filled with women and margaritas, gifts arriving, a music list to help curate. Wedding favors, a rehearsal dinner.

Manis, pedis, hairstyling, makeup.

Then after the blur, Arden stood in her spring-green column, wearing the necklace with the interlocking rings Zoey had given her, and looked at her friend, her cousin, her sister, in her wedding gown.

Bridal white with its sparkling strapless bodice giving way to a full skirt of frothy layers, like flower petals, of silk and tulle. Rather than a veil, she'd crowned her upswept hair with the sparkle of a tiara.

Zoey's mother's eyes glistened with tears as Jen adjusted it.

"My baby, you're so beautiful."

"I feel beautiful, Mom." Zoey wrapped around her. "I feel . . . everything. Thank you for being . . . for being Mom."

"Okay, that one did it." Jen turned away to grab tissues. On a watery laugh, Zoey turned to Arden.

"What do you think?"

"I think you look like a fairy tale. You look like happy ever after."

"We're going to have that. Boone and I are going to have that. Arden, I couldn't have gotten here without you. All the work you did. The details you picked up so I didn't have to."

"Were genuinely a pleasure for me."

"When you're ready, I'll do them for you."

After a light knock, the wedding coordinator opened the door. "Now, there's a breathtaking bride. Are you ready?"

"I've been ready since he said: *Hi, I'm Boone*."

"Then, Jen, your son's waiting to escort you down and seat you."

Jen laid her hands lightly on Zoey's cheeks. "I love you, Zoey."

"I love you, Mom."

"I'll give you a minute. I'll be back when it's time." The wedding coordinator closed the door.

Zoey said, "Here we are. I'm with my best friend in the last minutes before I become a married woman."

"You're not even a little nervous."

"Not even a little. Just the next step—and, come on, let's be honest, I look totally amazing."

Arden laughed. "You really do."

"So do you. I'm going to send you pictures from Hawaii. You send me some from New York."

"You may be too busy to look at pictures from my three-day trip to New York next week."

"No, I won't. I'm never going to be too busy, and neither are you." A little teary, Zoey reached out both hands, took Arden's. "Promise?"

"Promise."

She stood watching Zoey and the man she loved exchange vows, exchange rings, and felt content. The next step, she remembered. Just the next step. And the right turn on the path.

To make up for the time off for the wedding, and her upcoming trip to New York, Arden put in two full days at the bookstore. After ringing sales, taking orders, stocking shelves, she figured she'd throw something together, quick and easy, for dinner, then squeeze in a couple of hours at the keyboard.

She still had to pack, but she'd take care of that after a full day of writing—after the gym. Then she'd will herself to get a good night's sleep before she drove to the airport and flew to New York.

Water the plants before she left, she reminded herself, check the weather forecast one last time—pack an umbrella no matter what it said.

And going over her checklist, she all but ran into Dustin.

"Hi!" He put a hand on her arm when she pulled up short, and left it there. "Where were you?"

"Too many places, sorry."

"Wedding planning?"

"What? Oh no, the newlyweds are enjoying sunshine and island breezes in Hawaii."

"That's great. I've always wanted to go there. Listen, since you're not wedding planning, how about I buy you a cup of coffee?" He gestured, as they stood directly in front of the café.

She really wanted to just get home, but he had that hopeful smile on his face.

She'd probably looked the same way when she'd talked to one of the featured authors at Next Chapter.

And making another excuse felt rude, and a little mean.

Ten minutes, she thought. Fifteen tops. What could it hurt? And then she'd be done and guiltless.

"Sure, I've got a little time. Just a little."

"Super!" He kept his hand on her arm as he turned to the café. "You keep really busy, don't you?"

"I like busy. Still, the last few months have been packed."

"You shouldn't work so hard. Maybe it's vacation time."

"Actually, it's not vacation so much, but I'm going to New York on Thursday, for a few days. I still have to pack and take care of loose ends, so just a quick coffee."

"Exciting!" Inside, he steered her to a two-top, then put his hands on her shoulders.

She stiffened, started to turn.

"Let me help you off with your coat."

She ordered herself to relax. "Thanks."

As she sat, the server strolled over.

"Hi, Arden. We don't see you in here much this time of day."

"Hi, Macie. How are things?"

"Better than average, and I'll take it. The usual?"

"Yeah, thanks."

Macie turned to Dustin. "What can I get you?"

Dustin didn't spare the server a glance. "What's the usual?" he asked Arden, but Macie answered.

"For Arden, that's a café latte, heavy on the latte."

"That sounds perfect. Make it two. You want a muffin or something?"

"No, just the coffee, thanks."

"I'll get that right out to you."

"So, New York," Dustin said as Macie walked away. "I guess it's business." He smiled. "Work, work, work."

"Mostly. Some meetings. And my publisher actually managed to get me a signing at a downtown bookstore."

His eyes widened. "A New York signing. Wow. That's the big time."

She laughed, relaxed as she decided he was just strangely starstruck.

"It's a little independent on the Lower East Side, but it's big time for me. Are you looking for that critique partner?"

"I've got some names, and I'm thinking about maybe hooking up online. I just have to get up the nerve to make contact. It feels . . . Well, it's scary to think about showing my work to a stranger, you know?"

"I do know. But that's the actual goal, isn't it? For strangers to read your work."

"Did you have that? I mean the critique group or partner?"

"I took writing courses in college, so I had professors and classmates." She looked up as Macie came back with the drinks.

"Thanks, Macie."

"All in a day's. Let me know if you need anything else."

"I was really shy in school," he told Arden. "My dad died when I was eight, so—"

"I'm so sorry."

"Yeah, he was a firefighter, went down in the line. It was rough. My mom had to move for work. New place, new school, no dad. I guess I escaped into books. Then Mom got sick. I'd just turned thirteen when I lost her."

Heartsick, knowing how that deep a loss felt, she reached over to take his hand.

His eyes, full of emotion, clung to hers as he clung to her hand.

"You understand. I read that you lost both your parents when you were fourteen. I guess that's even harder, losing them both at once. You moved here, right? To live with your aunt and uncle?"

"Yes. Did you have someone?"

"Grandparents. They were great, but, you know, another new place, another new school. They did their best for me, and it couldn't've been easy for them, at their age, right?"

He drank some latte, looking around at the other tables where people sat talking, or others worked on laptops, scrolled on their phones.

"Thinking about retiring, maybe getting an RV and traveling, and bam, you've got a teenager." He smiled a little. "A moody one, too, who just wanted to sit up in his room and read. They loved me, and made sure I knew it. They did their best. Then Gamma died when I was in college, so I came home. My grandfather needed help. They'd looked after me when I needed it, so I looked after him."

"I'm sure that meant a lot to him."

"I think it did. I know it did," Dustin corrected. "And to me. We had nearly five years, the Dubecki men, before he passed. Just a few months ago."

"Oh. I thought I signed a book for your grandfather."

He looked blank a moment. "Yeah, yeah. My other grandfather—my mom's dad. He's still around. A regular powerhouse, too. After Grandpa died, I thought about moving closer to him—we always got along great. But I wanted . . ."

He sighed, leaned toward her. "I wanted to find my own place, you know? And Gramps doesn't need me like Grandpa did. This feels like my place, for now. I guess it feels like yours, too."

"It's a good place, a good neighborhood, and my family's here. I'm going to miss Zoey like a limb when she and Boone relocate to the Pacific Northwest. But we won't lose touch."

"That's a long way."

"It is, but the move's a career boost for both of them. Everyone has to find their place."

"Mine's the mountains. A good cabin in the mountains, solitude, scenery." He laid a hand over hers before she could move it. "You could really write in a mountain cabin. No distractions, someone to take care of you."

She slid her hand free. "I've been a city girl my whole life. What do you do now, until you try out that mountain cabin? For work?"

"Right now I'm stocking shelves at Costco." He shrugged. "Grandpa left me everything he had, so I've got a buffer, but a man's got to keep busy, right? Got to work and provide. And I use that time to think about the story I'm writing. People-watch, you know?"

"Yes." She finished her latte, nudged the cup away. Before she could speak, he did.

"Listen, I feel like I've spent this whole time talking about me. Why don't I take you to dinner so we can talk about you?"

"First, you didn't. And second, I really have to get home. I have a million things to do before I leave on Thursday." Standing, she took her jacket from the back of the chair. "Thanks for the latte."

"My pleasure." He got up quickly, helped her on with her jacket. "You don't need it, but good luck in New York."

When he moved in, she shifted her face just enough so his lips met her cheek.

"Make that contact," she advised. "If nothing else, you could make a writing friend."

"I feel like I already have one."

She smiled. "Thanks again."

She went out, quickened her pace to make the Walk light at the corner. The attempted kiss shouldn't have surprised her. And meant she'd have to go back to making excuses. Or worse, telling him outright she wasn't interested.

It seemed to her he mostly wanted a mentor, and she simply wasn't qualified. Or wired for it either. And if he looked for more, a relationship didn't fit into her short-term plans.

Plus, he just didn't stir anything up in her but sympathy for the losses he'd suffered. And a feeling there was something off about him, maybe due to those losses.

Coffee was as far as it would go, and she'd avoid a repeat there.

She put it out of her mind as she walked into her building. Her downstairs neighbor—wife, expectant mother, physician assistant—had grocery sacks over each shoulder as she dug for her keys.

"Monica. Let me give you a hand."

"I'll take it. Whew." She blew out a breath that fluttered the fringe on her short brown hair. "Long day, and John's having a longer one."

Arden carried one of the sacks into the apartment with nearly the same footprint as hers. But where she had calm, quiet colors, Monica and John Betz went for bold.

In the kitchen, they set the grocery bags on the counter. Then Monica rubbed a hand over her baby bump. "Twelve more weeks to go, and this is one of the days when I feel like I've been pregnant for five years. Maybe six."

"How about I put this away and you sit down?"

Monica tapped up the blue-framed glasses that had slipped down her nose.

"You know, Arden, you're the queen of upstairs neighbors. We rarely hear you up there. No stomping around, no loud music, no wild parties. And the few times you've had a party, you invited us. You watered our plants and got our mail when we were on vacation, and had fresh fruit and milk stocked when we got back. And you'd put my groceries away."

"You had a long day, and you've got twelve weeks to go."

"Very true, but I've got this. You'll end up organizing my refrigerator again, like you did when we were on vacation."

Arden winced. "I can't help myself."

"I've learned that in our—what is it?—eighteen, nineteen months of living above and below each other. Why don't you have the glass of wine I can't while I put this stuff away?"

"I'd love that, but I'm already behind schedule. Which reminds me, I'm going to be in New York for a few days. Leaving Thursday, back Sunday."

"Water your plants?"

"It's just a few days, and I'll do that before I leave. I just wanted you to know I wouldn't be here. I'm not expecting any deliveries, but—"

"If something comes, we've got it."

"Thanks. I'll see you later."

She went upstairs, then let out a long breath. Home, alone, quiet. At last.

The first thing she did was change out of her work clothes. It was, to her mind, never too early for pajamas. Though she wasn't particularly hungry, she ate her classic quick and easy meal. A cup of tomato soup from a can, a grilled three-cheese sandwich. And since Monica had put it in her mind, had a glass of wine with it.

Then with three Double Stuf Oreos—fresh from her organized fridge—on a saucer, she went into her office.

Two hours, she told herself, and booted up her computer. And if she hit a roll and went for three, who's counting?

She didn't look out the window. Even if she had, it was unlikely she'd have noticed the man sitting at a window table of Amigos, drinking a Dos Equis with his chile relleno.

He'd seen her lights go on before he'd gone into the restaurant. From his seat—booked the day before—he'd watched her move from room to room. She had shades on what he assumed was her bedroom, but the rest weren't blocked.

He'd ordered, waited, watched.

He considered himself a patient man.

A man with a plan!

The lights came on in another room, and he saw her walk across the window. Then he couldn't really see her.

Working, he thought. Writing. Yes, that's what she did now. He knew it. He knew because they were connected.

A harmless hobby, he decided. He'd allow it, for a while. For as long as she didn't neglect her duties once they had their place in the mountains. But he'd provide—the roof over her head, the food she'd cook, the clothes she wore.

And she'd be grateful. They'd be happy, the way it was meant.

So he ate and he drank. He watched and he planned.

Chapter Three

She made it to the gym, did her circuits, took her yoga class, and nearly made it home before the rain started. She jogged the last half block, and rushed in, only slightly damp.

Monica and John came out of their apartment as she shoved a hand through her hair.

"In and out, in and out," Monica said with a grin. "Did you forget something this morning?"

"No. Why?"

"We heard you go out. Baby check this morning." She patted her belly. "So we're both going to work late."

"Gym days. Mondays, Wednesdays, Fridays." John, a high school teacher, pointed at Arden. "You're like clockwork. Except this morning."

Confused, Arden lifted her shoulders. "I left when I always do."

"Then came back, like five minutes later," Monica said. "We hardly ever hear you up there, but slow morning for us, so we did."

"I didn't come back. I left before eight, and I've been at the gym this whole time."

"But we heard you, walking around upstairs," Monica said as John lost his easy smile.

"Honey, go wait inside, okay? I'm going to walk up with Arden."

"Someone was upstairs. Someone was in your apartment, Arden. We *heard*."

"We're just going to go take a look." John gave Monica a little nudge. "Go on back inside."

"Should I call the police?"

"Let's just go take a look. We heard what we thought was Arden leave again, so we'll just check."

"I'm sure it's fine," Arden said as she started upstairs with John. But she wasn't. "How long did you hear someone?"

"I can't tell you exactly. Half hour, maybe a little longer. Why don't you give me your key, stand back? We heard someone leave, but how about I go in first?"

"You know what? I'm not going to argue with that." She handed him her key as she nodded at her door. "If someone broke in, they didn't actually break in."

He unlocked the door, opened it.

"Everything looks as usual to me. I'm just going to do a quick walk-through while you wait."

But she came in behind him.

"It's not."

"Not what?"

"Not as usual. The throw on the couch. That's not how I left it." Her heart began to hammer in her throat. "Neither are the pillows."

"Okay." He rubbed a hand on her arm. "Is anything missing?"

"I don't know, I . . . Yes. A picture of Zoey and me, on that shelf. It's not there. A candle. I just bought last week. I had it on that table. It's gone."

When it struck her, she ran to her office.

"Someone sat at my desk. I always push the chair all the way in. It's not. And things on the desk, they've been moved. God, my flash drive's gone. My backup."

"Go on and check your computer. I'm going to call the police, and text Monica. I'm going to stay with you."

Her fingers trembled as she booted up her machine. "You have an appointment."

"We'll reschedule."

"It's here." She breathed out. "It's all here. You need a password to open anything. I started that in college, and it's a habit now. It's all here."

"Have you got any cash, any jewelry?"

"I always keep two hundred right here." She opened a desk drawer.

"And there it is, but . . . John, this is crazy, but I had a box of pens in here, and they're gone. Who'd take pens and leave cash?"

"You've got me. You should keep looking around, make a list of what's missing. I'm going to make those calls."

A half hour later she sat on the couch, flanked by her neighbors, and spoke to Officers Uli and Jamison.

"I left at seven-forty-five—or very close to it. I spent the next ninety minutes at the fitness center and got back just as it started to rain."

"We heard her leave," Monica put in. "Arden leaves about that time on Wednesdays, and Mondays and Fridays. Then we heard her come back—or we thought it was her. We laughed about it because Arden's so organized."

"We heard someone walking around," John added. "Arden's so quiet you forget someone lives up here, but we heard someone walking around, then leaving again. It had to be at least a half hour. At least."

"This is a four-unit building," Uli began. "The other tenants?"

"Jim Fetteral up here," Arden told him. "He lives alone, travels for work. He's away now. Downstairs, ah, Karen and Mike Angelo."

"They both work," Monica put it. "They're usually gone by eight-thirty."

"You said you have things missing," Officer Jamison said.

"Yes, I made a list. It doesn't make any sense. The only things of real value, to me, are my flash drive, a pair of heart-shaped gold stud earrings my parents gave me when I got my ears pierced. And especially my mother's locket. My grandparents gave it to her when I was born. It had a baby picture of me and a lock of my hair in it."

When tears burned her eyes, she pushed them back.

"Do you have a photo of the earrings, the locket?"

"I have one of the locket. My mother wearing it."

"If we could have that. We'll get it back to you."

Rising, she handed over the list she'd made. "There are other things, odd things. My hairbrush, my shampoo, a half-empty bottle of hand lotion, things like that. I'll get the photo."

Uli glanced up from the list as she came back with the photo. "A box of pens?"

"In a drawer of my desk where I had two hundred in cash. The cash is still there, the pens aren't. Who takes pens, or a half-empty bottle of hand lotion, a hairbrush, a used candle, a tube of lipstick, things like that?"

"Who else has a key to your apartment?" Jamison asked her.

"My aunt and uncle. That is, they keep a key for emergencies. They've never used it."

"A boyfriend?"

"No. I'm not involved with anyone. I haven't been for . . . I haven't even dated for close to a year. I've been focused on work. I haven't broken up with anyone, and I've never given my key to anyone other than my family."

She answered questions, but none of them lessened the sick feeling in the pit of her stomach.

Someone had come into her home, pawed through her things, taken away personal items.

When the police left, she just felt lost.

"How about I call the locksmith for you?" John gave her hand a squeeze. "The cops were right. You need to change the locks, add that dead bolt."

"No, I'll take care of it. You've both done enough. More than. I'll have the locks changed, add the dead bolt, and a nanny cam on top of it. But they're not going to find my things."

"They'll do what they can, Arden, including going around the neighborhood to ask if anyone saw someone come in, or someone just hanging around the building."

She nodded at Monica. "I'd say it had to be kids, just doing the stupid, but the cash? That makes no sense. Thanks for sticking with me. I'm okay. I'll call about the locks, and I'm ordering that stupid camera."

"If you need anything, we're here. And while you're in New York, we'll keep an eye and ear out."

"We'll let the other tenants know," John added. "More eyes and ears. I'm really sorry, Arden."

"Me, too."

She had her locks changed, a dead bolt added. Though she tried to work, she got up from her desk again and again to check those locks, to look out the windows.

When she finally gave up, she packed. After going through her travel checklist—twice—she went to bed.

Minutes later, she rose. Even as she told herself she was overreacting, she picked up one of her dinette chairs and hooked it under the doorknob.

And still barely slept.

Once, Arden had imagined herself living in New York again. Not Brooklyn this time, but Manhattan. A writer of searingly controversial novels, she'd live in a loft in SoHo and fashion herself a studio where she'd work surrounded by books and art.

She'd frequent trendy coffee shops where she'd sit with interesting, erudite friends for hours discussing the mores and foibles of society at large.

She'd host interesting cocktail parties and sleep with quirky, interesting men.

Then she'd realized she actually didn't want to sit around coffee shops for hours, had no talent or desire to host cocktail parties, and just wasn't built to sleep around.

She absolutely didn't want to or have the chops to write searingly controversial novels.

What she wanted was the work. She wanted to tell stories and know that some outside her family would read and enjoy them. She liked the routine she'd fallen into. Friends, family, work.

She didn't need to be important. Or famous. She'd rather have a seat in the audience than stand in the spotlight.

Because her parents had left her financially secure—the college fund, their life insurance, their savings and investments, the house in Brooklyn—she'd been able to take and make the time for her writing.

Her other jobs had always been more about discipline, socializing, and pushing herself out into the world.

She liked her simple, organized life, its lack of chaos, even its predictability. Knowing a large part of that was rooted in her world shattering at fourteen, finding herself tossed into the unknown—however warm and loving—didn't change the fact of it.

Now, after a smooth flight, after unpacking, she stood at her hotel window and once more considered moving to New York.

Not for the lofty café conversations or sophisticated parties. Certainly not for the men she'd take to her bed, then flick away with a careless smile.

(Although maybe just once or twice on that one.)

But for the energy and color. The unapologetic *life*.

As she watched the traffic, the people swarming the sidewalks, she had to smile, shake her head.

Yes, for a few days, maybe a week or so, she could embrace and absorb all that movement, that life. And after a few months—if not sooner—it would exhaust her.

But she'd lived a few subway stops from this area for the first fourteen years of her life, so she knew it. She'd take some time to embrace and absorb before her first meeting.

In the bathroom, she opened her travel kit, touched up her makeup. She knew what she was doing there, so did what she could to erase the signs of a sleepless night.

And after years of hit-and-miss, she knew what looked good on her. Simple lines, forget the frills, and go for strong colors.

When she shopped, as she had for this trip, she leaned toward classic instead of trendy.

She liked the fit and feel of the chocolate-brown pants in a velvety suede, paired with boots of the same color. When you had a yard of leg, play it up rather than hide it. The spring-weight coral V-neck celebrated being a redhead, with a trio of thin-chained necklaces layered in the V for a little dash.

Simple gold hoops, another trio, as Zoey had convinced her they needed to get that third ear piercing.

She topped it with the thigh-length leather jacket, a sort of cognac color she'd treated herself to when she'd sold *Whispers*.

Add a scarf that played with those tones, and because the April day was breezy but bright, sunglasses.

She strapped on her cross-body bag, gave her reflection a nod.

Angling her head, she realized she'd have to decide whether to keep the shorter hair or let it grow back.

A decision for later, but for now?

"Yeah, you'll do. No one would guess you're still not sure all this is actually happening."

Could be the Matrix, she thought as she checked her bag for her hotel key before leaving. And all this? Programming.

On the street, she walked, flowing along with the river of tourists and natives.

Where did she fit there? she wondered, and supposed she straddled the bridge over that river.

She'd walked these same streets with girlfriends, poked into some of the shops, sat over pizza or tacos or ice cream and bitched about clueless parents, whined about teachers, talked endlessly about boys.

When it came to the boys, Arden remembered, she'd been the one the others had confided in. Mostly because she had nothing much in the area to confide herself.

She'd been a listener, a watcher—a seat in the audience.

It paid off, she thought now, and gave in to the urge to stroll into a bookstore.

It took some wandering, some hunting, but she found her book—two copies. And took that glow with her to her meeting with her agent.

The first time she'd ridden this elevator to the twelfth floor to meet Yvonne Siscal, she'd been terrified, as she'd meet, for the first time, the woman she felt held her dreams in her hands.

The second time, after the sale of *Whispers*, she'd felt giddy, with a side of terrified.

Now she took stock and decided she toggled between happy and anxious.

The agency's lobby always struck her as library-esque with its oversized leather chairs in a classic claret, its crowded bookcases, its sleek reception desk.

Before she could speak, she was struck dumb when the receptionist rose, smiled, and remembered her name.

"Ms. Bowie, so nice to see you again. I hope you had an easy trip in."

"I did, thanks. It's Arden."

"Yvonne's expecting you. I'll just let her know you're here. Oh, here's Elle now. You remember Elle, Yvonne's assistant."

She was memorable—young, gorgeous, about five-two, and a fast-talking, fast-moving dynamo.

"Right on time." Instead of offering a hand, Elle offered a hug that made Arden feel like a giant. "Just give Yvonne a buzz, Luce. I'll take Arden back. So how was your flight in? No problem getting to the hotel, right?"

Even with a yard of leg, Arden had to quicken her pace to keep up as Elle breezed through a door, then down a corridor lined with offices and books, books, books.

"The flight in was quick, and the hotel's perfect."

"They've got a great bar. Like a speakeasy. You should definitely go in for a drink. Your first week on sale's numbers are in. Solid. Yvonne will talk to you about that. And the podcast."

"The—"

Yvonne's corner office door stood open, and Elle strode straight in.

"Coffee, tea, water—flat or sparkling."

"Oh, water's fine. Flat," she added as Yvonne stood from behind her desk.

She always gave Arden a flash of Meryl Streep in *The Devil Wears Prada*. The silver wedge of hair, the strong cheekbones, and just the air of being in charge and knowing exactly what to do next.

She crossed to Arden on black heels—probably Pradas—and took both of Arden's hands in hers.

"It's so good to see you."

"It's really good to be here."

"Take off that gorgeous coat that I'd steal if I were five inches taller, and have a seat. Tell me how you're feeling."

"Good. Overwhelmed, grateful, and good."

Arden took one of the leather chairs—these the same color as her pants—while Yvonne took the other. And Elle dashed in with tall glasses of water on ice.

"Let me know if you need anything. I'm on the move."

"Isn't she always?" Arden murmured when Elle dashed off again.

"In the nearly four years she's been here, I've yet to see her battery run down."

"Yvonne, let me go back to that gratitude. I'm so grateful. I know you took a chance on me."

"I have a good sense of what and whom to take a chance on. You didn't break my streak. You wrote a good book, Arden, and in my opinion, you wrote an even better one with *Rebound*. You're young, and building your foundation and career. My job, our job, is to help you with that.

"Let's talk foreign rights for a start."

"Foreign rights?"

"We have some offers. They're low. We'll negotiate, get them up a bit, but not by much."

"We have offers from other countries?"

Yvonne smiled, sipped. "I'll be almost sorry when you lose that wonderment. Selling your book is what we do. Justin in our foreign rights department is shepherding *Whispers* through the process. We'll get you the numbers and details when we finalize them, then you'll decide whether to take the offers."

"Yvonne, if they offer five bucks and a cookie, I'm taking it."

"Yes, I'll be sorry when you lose that. We'll get you more than five bucks, and you'll buy your own cookies. Now, you have the signing at Pages and Pages on Saturday, and we'll talk about that later. Another opportunity opened up. It's last-minute, and your publicity department's really high on it. Gracie Ullman's podcast, *Gracie's Book Club*."

"Elle mentioned something about a podcast."

She'd never heard one, and wondered if she should confess that.

When she wrote, she wrote in the quiet. And when she read, she read in the quiet. Otherwise, music or TV.

"I'm sorry, I don't know who that is."

"A lot of other people do. She has a very popular podcast, and she's based in New York. She had a last-minute cancellation, and publicity jumped on it. It's good exposure, a chance to reach potential new readers, and she does a fun interview."

"I've never done a podcast."

"You've never had a book published before."

"Right. Well . . . when would I have to do it?"

"At four-thirty."

Arden just gaped. "Today?"

"Last-minute cancellation, and your opportunity. I hope you'll take it, Arden. I'll go with you, and so will your publicist. It runs ninety minutes, so after, I'll take you out to dinner. We'll celebrate. Tomorrow,

I'll pass you to your editor. Diane will show you around, introduce you to that team."

"Ninety minutes."

"Gracie Ullman's good at what she does, and so are you. They'll hype your book signing. You say yes, publicity will let the bookstore know. Advice?"

"Yes, please."

"Hit while it's hot, Arden."

It made her queasy, but she nodded. "All right, of course."

"Great. Let me tell Elle to get the ball rolling, then we'll walk over to foreign rights so you can meet more of your team."

Team, Arden thought. That meant being a team player, even if you had to do a ninety-minute podcast when you really weren't entirely sure exactly what that meant.

So she did it, and it wasn't as horrible as she'd feared. Basically, she'd had a long conversation with an energetic woman who loved books. Despite nerves and outright dread, she had some fun.

When they sat in the restaurant, snugged at a table with voices all around, Yvonne lifted a glass of the wine she'd ordered.

"First, I'll say it again. You were good. Quick, funny, entertaining, and honest."

"Thanks, again. And again, I barely remember anything I said."

"Including telling Gracie you'd be happy to come back when your next book's released?"

"She threw me off by asking if I would. I'm definitely not going to think about that now."

"All right." She clinked her glass to Arden's. "Here's to you, Arden Bowie, and your future."

She spent the next day meeting people, thanking them. She signed books for various accounts at a big conference table where they'd brought in pretty cupcakes and champagne.

After dinner with her editor, she slid into bed for the second night and slept like the dead.

When she woke, she lay there, listening to New York push its energy against the windows. And took stock.

Yes, she was enjoying herself, and learning as she went. So much to learn. But one more day of meeting, greeting, smiling, talking? Probably about her limit.

Unlike Elle, Arden needed her batteries regularly charged.

She got up, pushed herself down to the hotel's fitness center. Back in her room, she showered, indulged herself with a room service breakfast. Since lattes weren't on the menu, she took her caffeine with ice in a Pepsi.

Finding she had a few hours to spare, she sat down with her laptop and added to her work in progress.

There, she thought as she dressed, an hour in the gym, a nice breakfast, and a little time to write.

Batteries recharged.

She'd chosen a dress of deep blue, belted at the waist, with a straight skirt. She'd planned to wear her mother's locket with it, and the memory of that brought on a pang of regret. Instead, she went with the interlocking rings Zoey had given her. And checking the time, decided to walk the eight blocks to the bookstore.

Though it proved breezy again, Arden walked in springtime. It certainly showed itself in the daffodils, the tulips in flower stalls, the tender green leaves on trees. She heard it in the shouts of kids in a little urban playground, in the singing—wonderfully off-key—of a woman who washed her third-floor apartment windows.

She took her time, strolling, window-shopping—and decided she might do actual shopping after the signing. Then she stopped, let out a half laugh because she stood in front of the pizza place, a favorite of hers as a teen. Surprised and pleased to find it still in business, she vowed to stop in on the way back to the hotel for a slice of nostalgia.

When she reached the bookstore, she set the past aside. Squared her shoulders, put on her best smile, then walked inside.

"Welcome, welcome! Glenda Durning." The woman with a flood of gray-streaked black hair shot out a hand. "I'm the manager. My, you're a tall one. We're so happy to have you. We had a lot of calls after your podcast—you were wonderful, by the way! We ordered more stock. I'm going to whisk you into the back room. We have some online orders we need you to sign before we start."

Arden wondered if Glenda and Elle were somehow related, as the woman chattered all the way during her fast-clipped pace through the store.

Smaller than Next Chapter, she noted, but with shelves and tables cleverly arranged to allow room for browsing.

And people did just that as Glenda did indeed whisk her back to the tiny, crammed room where a dozen—no, fourteen—copies of *Whispers* were stacked on a counter amid the expected chaos.

"Thank you for having me today," Arden began.

"Oh, we're delighted. We love highlighting debut authors, and you're essentially a local. Brooklyn born. Now, as we related, this will be a straight signing. We do occasional readings on a weeknight, but Saturday afternoons are too busy, and we don't have the space."

"That's fine."

"Now, we have pens—oh, I see you have your own—and the books are flapped. Those requesting personalization have the name highlighted. Can I get you something to drink?"

"Just water, thank you."

"That's easy! We had an author in last month—I won't name names! And she insisted on ginkgo tea with brown sugar. I'll go get your water. You go ahead and start signing the orders, and I'll be right back. Oh, restroom's just over there."

She whisked out as she'd whisked in, and Arden began to sign.

While she feared the humiliation of sitting at a signing table, trying to look pleasant because no one had bought her book, at least she'd sold fourteen copies.

Thirty minutes later, when she sat at the corner table and saw she actually had a short line snaking through tables and shelves, she put away her fears.

When a number of people in the first group mentioned the podcast, she decided lesson learned.

When your agent and publisher want you to do a podcast, or anything else, do it.

Smile in place, she reached for the next book, and caught a movement out of the corner of her eye.

She sat a moment, book still in hand, leaning to try to see around a bookcase.

"It's for Mike."

"Oh, sorry. I thought I saw someone I know. I hope you enjoy the book, Mike."

"Heard you on *Gracie's Book Club* the other day. It sounded like something I'd like. From Brooklyn, are you?"

"Originally, yes."

While she carried on the conversation, she had to resist looking past him.

He'd been wearing sunglasses, a ball cap, and for a minute she'd thought she'd seen Dustin. But that was crazy. And since she didn't like the feeling it gave her, she dismissed it.

Instead, she looked at the next person in line. Her smile turned into a gasp of surprise before she sprang up.

"Kyra!"

"Yes! I wasn't sure you'd remember."

But Arden had already wrapped her former schoolmate in a hug. "Of course I remember." She pulled back. "You cut your hair."

Gone were the teenager's beaded braids. The woman wore her hair in a pixie cut of curls with a few of the curls twirling down to her big, dark eyes.

"You, too. I couldn't believe when I heard you on *Gracie's Book Club.* I had to come, see you, get your book. I know you're busy. I don't guess you have time to catch up."

"Damn right I do. I passed Lombardi's on the way over, and I thought of you. How about Italian sodas after this? Cherry for you, right?"

"And lemon for you. God, the things we remember. I'd love that, Arden. Girl, I've missed your face! Sign my book. I'm going to do some shopping, and I'll come back in an hour."

"Perfect. I'm glad you came, Kyra."

When she ran out of line, Glenda had her sign stock, then copies for staff.

"This was great, Glenda. You have a wonderful store, a wonderful staff."

"Customer service, number one. You did really well. We'd love to have you back for your next book."

"I'd love to come back."

"I see your friend's waiting. We just need a picture with the staff for our website before you go."

The minute they were outside, Arden hugged Kyra again.

"I can't believe we're here. When I walked over, I thought about how we'd come downtown, haunt the shops, get pizza or ice cream, talk and talk. You, me, Bonita, Kelly."

"Our own melting pot. The redhead, the Black girl, the Latina, and the Asian."

"How are they? Have you kept in touch?"

"Bonita went into international finance. She's based in Milan. English." As they walked, Kyra ticked off fingers. "Spanish, Italian, French. Four languages. So far. She's studying Japanese now."

"Wow."

"We email now and again. If and when she comes to New York, we try to get together. Kelly's in Harvard Law."

"One more wow."

"We like to talk—actual phone calls every two weeks. And she comes home to see her family, so we get together. Wait until I tell her about this! Arden Bowie, author."

"How about you?"

"Kyra Brightstone, RN. Surgical nurse, Brooklyn Hospital Center."

"And the wows keep coming."

They sat, as they once had, in the busy restaurant over Italian sodas.

"I don't want to dredge shit up, but I want to tell you, I wish I'd known better what to do after you lost your folks. It was all so fast, and you were gone, and I didn't know what to say, what to do."

"There really wasn't anything. I shut down, closed off, and made it hard on my aunt and uncle for a while. But they were patient, and just kept loving me anyway. I cut you off, I closed out everything from before. I shut that door, you didn't."

"You needed to then."

"Maybe I did. But I'd like, very much, to keep it open now."

Kyra took out her phone. "Number, email, address, in my contacts list."

Arden took out her own. "Same."

"Girl, you ghost me, I'll be pissed."

"Won't happen."

Thumbs flying, Kyra put in her data. "Why don't we do something else we used to? Order pizza and talk about boys. And something we didn't used to. Have a bottle of wine with that."

"I'm in. But I don't have much to talk about in the boy-slash-men area. You?"

"I've been seeing Denzel for about eight months now. We're making noises about moving in together."

"I want to hear all about it," Arden said as she signaled the waiter.

"Oh, trust me, you will."

They sat another hour. As she walked home in the evening bustle of downtown, Arden thought how easily friendship came back, how a broken connection could link again, if you let it.

He followed her. He had to see her safely back to wherever she was staying, didn't he?

Maybe he'd lost his nerve in the bookstore, and after, she'd gone off with that woman, so he'd lost his chance to surprise her. To take her to dinner. To, he'd imagined, take her back to her hotel, have her invite him up.

And spend the night showing her what they were to each other.

He had to wait, just a little longer, for that. But it didn't mean he'd shirk his responsibility. She was just a woman, alone and vulnerable in New York, so he'd see her safely back.

Chapter Four

With her return to Columbus, Arden fell back into routine. Part of that routine included a monthly family dinner at her aunt and uncle's. And that included a celebration of Zoey and Boone's return from their honeymoon.

As usual, Arden came early to help cook.

"I was counting on you." After a hug, Jen pulled back. Frowned. "Honey, you look tired."

"I worked late the last couple nights." And still, even with new locks and a dead bolt, didn't sleep well in the apartment. "I've gotta roll when it does. Not working today, so I'll have a fabulous dinner and go to bed early, or at least on time."

"Good. Now, I want to hear all about your trip to New York. I feel like we haven't really talked in weeks."

"Things will slow down now. Sales are good—better than I expected, and truthfully, I really didn't know what to expect. And though they've been cheerleaders, I think better than the publisher expected."

"Then you, and they, didn't expect enough. And you can tell me everything while you make scalloped potatoes. Yours are better than mine."

They'd been one of her father's favorites, and at twelve she'd wanted to please him, so she'd learned. Of course, when she hit thirteen he and her mother had become idiots, and often enemies.

She'd started the circle around that, and hadn't quite completed it when she'd lost them.

"Dad loved them."

"Always did. Our mom would make extra, but there were never

leftovers when Evan was around. I wondered if you'd go over to Brooklyn while you were in New York."

"No. I didn't need to." Arden got out potatoes, the peeler, sat to work. "But part of Brooklyn came to me. Kyra Brightstone, an old friend. We went to school together."

"Oh, Arden, that's just great."

"It was . . . well, pretty much everything, Aunt Jen. After the signing, we went to this Italian place we used to hang out in, and we just picked it all up again. Like basically a decade hadn't happened."

"As real friends can and do. It's good to hear that, Arden. I hope the two of you keep in touch."

"We absolutely will. I told you about the podcast."

"Yes, and we've listened to it. You were terrific. Smart, friendly, and just sassy enough."

"She—Gracie—made it easy. The whole thing? The whole three days was like—almost—being someone else. I was in there, but gawking and stammering and stumbling. The rest was Author Arden."

"That's who you are."

"Yeah, but most of the time I'm just Arden, or Writer Arden. It's different. I like it, but it's different. I also realized I was right about not moving to New York."

Jen slid the pork roast she'd marinated into a baking dish. "I didn't know you'd thought about doing that."

"Thought about it. I had a whole bohemian Arden—bohemian-yet-sophisticated Arden—holding court. Probably in SoHo. In an art- and book-filled loft over a snooty coffee shop where people read weird poetry and had intellectual conversations over tiny cups of espresso."

Jen snorted. "Yeah, that's you, all right."

"Yeah, no. I realized I wasn't, and didn't want to be, bohemian or sophisticated. And this trip reminded me. I really enjoyed my three days, but New York's too fast and full for me at this stage. I need, and I want, a slower pace."

"You, my darling, are anything but slow." Jen put the roast in the oven. "I'm going to make that quinoa dish Boone likes so much. With the broccoli and cheese."

"Sounds good."

"I can't wait to see them. They didn't get in until late last night. Well, you know, you were on the group text. They sent so many fabulous pictures. Honeymoon in paradise."

"The way the two of them glowed, you almost needed sunglasses to look at them. I've earmarked three photos, and still need to choose which one to have framed for them for Christmas."

"Arden, it's not even May."

Arden shook her peeler in the air. "Preplanning eliminates impulse and panic."

"Some of us like impulse and panic. And damn, that's a good idea."

"Who doesn't like photos, especially when they look fabulous? I need to ask Zoey if she still has that one of us on spring break."

"Don't you have that framed, in your living room?"

"Did. I can't understand why anyone took it."

"Took it? Who took it?"

Arden didn't bite her tongue, but she thought about it. She hadn't mentioned the break-in, and wasn't sure she intended to, ever.

She carried the peeled potatoes to the sink to wash.

"Somebody got into my apartment. I think—"

"Got in? Broke in? Well, God, Arden, when?" Alarmed, Jen put one hand to her heart while the other shoved at her hair. "While you were in New York?"

"No, just before that. I think it had to be kids. They took silly things. My hairbrush, an open box of pens, hand cream, things like that."

"Did you report it?"

Arden got out the mandoline, a cutting board, and began to slice potatoes. "Yes, and the police came. Not a lot they could do. I had the locks changed, added a dead bolt, but honestly, what they took wasn't valuable. The only things I really miss are that photo, my mom's locket, and my heart-shaped earrings."

"Oh, Arden, your locket. I'm so sorry." Crossing over, Jen wrapped her arms around Arden, swayed. "I know how much that means to you."

"The police have a picture of it, so if it shows up . . ."

"I hate that this happened. I'm glad you weren't there when it did, but I hate that it happened at all. And why are you just telling me now?"

"Because it was more irritating than scary, and we've all been busy. And I knew you'd get that look in your eye."

"What look?"

"The worried-about-you look."

"Worrying about you, Zoey, Travis, now April and Boone comes with my job description. Don't screw with my job. Have you been seeing someone? Maybe someone who wanted some, I don't know, souvenirs?"

"No. And no one had a key. The locksmith said the old lock was, well, crap. Now I have better. I honestly think it was a kind of dumbass scavenger hunt."

"Maybe. Kids can be morons. And you've been front and center around here for a few weeks. But I don't like it."

"Neither do I. But they didn't take the cash in my desk drawer. Took pens, but not cash. So what I think? They figured who's going to notice or care if they can't find their hairbrush or some pens? And if they do, how much would the cops push it?"

It helped Arden to think it.

"So a couple of teenagers—most likely—think, *Hey, let's break into that author lady's place, make a bullshit list, and see if we find it.*"

"Moronic but, as I've had experience with teenagers, not outside of the realm. But be careful, honey."

"When am I not?"

"Be extra careful for a while."

Arden had just put the casserole in the oven, set the timer, when the front door opened.

"Aloha!" Zoey called out.

They looked golden, Arden thought as Zoey put a lei around her mother's neck, then one around Arden's. Golden and glowing and next to giddy.

"We have one for everyone! And presents! And more pictures! Where's Dad?"

"He's over at Travis's. They needed something or other installed, and he's the man with the tools. They'll be here soon. But we're not waiting for him to open some wine! Oh, you both look . . . perfect." Jen hugged them both again. "Just absolutely perfect."

"We had an amazing time, in an amazing place."

"We have jet lag from hell," Boone added, "but it was worth it."

"Sit, just sit. I'm going to open that wine. Then you'll tell us everything."

Zoey smirked, raised her eyebrows. "Everything?"

With a mom look on her face, Jen took out a corkscrew. "Up to an R rating."

Doug came in, let out a whoop, then plucked Zoey right off her stool. "There's my baby. She may be your wife, Boone, but she's still my baby."

"She's my wife because she was your baby first, so I'm good with that."

Zoey took out another lei, ringed it around her father's neck. "I'm always going to be your baby."

Arden saw Jen pause with the wine to brush away a tear.

Family, she thought. And when that door had brutally slammed on hers, they'd given her theirs.

Then Travis and April came in and made it complete.

Zoey presented more leis while Jen poured wine.

"None for me, thanks," April said. "I'll have some of Doug's favorite ginger ale."

"I'll get that for you." After giving April's hand a squeeze, Travis walked over to take a glass from a cabinet.

He added ice, poured as Zoey began pulling out gifts that ranged from a grass-skirted dashboard dancer, to yarn for April from a Hawaiian sheep, to a South Sea pearl pendant.

Arden immediately exchanged her earrings for the plumeria-shaped dangles.

"We're definitely going back." Boone sipped some wine. "Everyone needs to see Hawaii at least once. When we're in Oregon, it's an easier flight, so you guys can come to us, hang for a couple days, then we'll all go together."

"You'd love it, Mom. Volcanos, rainforests, beaches, sunsets you have to see to believe. And, April, plenty of hiking for you."

April smiled into her glass. "Well . . ."

"We actually have a little news." Travis slid an arm around April's waist.

They nodded at each other, spoke together.

"We're having a baby!"

"Oh. Oh" was all Jen could manage as she set her wine aside to wrap her arms around April, then burrowed into Travis.

"A *little* news?" With a laugh, Arden rose to join the hug.

"I'm going to be an aunt." Zoey bounced in her seat. "Dad, you're going to be a grandpa!"

"I'm getting that. I'm processing that." He shook his head, let out a baffled laugh before moving to his son for a hard hug. "Good work, kid." Then folded himself gently around April, kissed the top of her head.

"When? God, my brain's just fuzzed. When are you due? How are you feeling?"

"I feel great. I feel, I'm going to admit it, smug. No morning sickness—yet, which if it comes will pop that smug bubble. And I feel stupid happy. December second."

"You're going to be a father," Zoey murmured as she took her turn burrowing into Travis.

"We should have champagne." Tears flooded her eyes as Jen threw up her hands. "Doug, why don't we stock champagne in this house?"

"We will from now on."

"Good, good, that's good. December second—Sagittarius."

Now Doug turned to his wife, gave her a smacking kiss. "You would."

"I would. An optimist, a bright-sider with an adventurous spirit. Oh boy! December second," Jen repeated. "You're a couple months along."

"Seven weeks, so we're keeping it to family." April reached out to Zoey. "I took a test right before the wedding, but we didn't want to step on your and Boone's big day. And I wanted to get the you're-absolutely-pregnant from the doctor."

"Then we decided we'd hold on to it until you got back. Full family announcement."

"I'm making a human." Laughing, April hugged herself. "Of all the things I love making, this is the biggest and the best."

"It's perfect." Jen let out a long sigh. "It's just absolutely perfect."

While Arden celebrated in the kitchen, Dustin rearranged his shrine. He didn't think of it as a shrine, but simply his tableau.

He'd bought a display stand for the locket, and often opened it to study and smile at the baby picture, the lock of hair.

When they had a child, he'd buy Arden another to put their baby's photo, a lock of her hair in. Like a family tradition.

He'd set out her hairbrush, her lotion because she'd want those when she came to live with him. A woman was meant to live in the man's home, under his roof, under his protection.

He'd stocked his kitchen with what he'd found in hers.

He had a copy of the local article about her, a recording of the podcast, copies of the web page from the bookstores' announcements of her signings, and of course her own web page.

He'd set out her pens. Obviously, she'd want those, too, but he'd taken one for himself, enjoyed holding it.

He'd used it, carefully copied her handwriting to add his name and a sentiment onto the book he'd had her sign but not personalize.

Now it read:

> *To Dustin,*
> *The only man I've ever loved or ever will love.*
> *Yours always and forever, Arden*

He had her candle, and had set out two others with a small vase—hers—of fresh flowers. He had photos he'd taken of her at signings, or walking home from the bookstore.

But his favorite was the one of her he'd taken from her apartment. He'd spent a lot of time working on that, using Photoshop to replace the other one—the cousin—with his own image.

Maybe it didn't look quite right, but it would do for now.

Wouldn't she be surprised when she saw how he'd taken so much time and trouble to arrange things for her?

He'd even cleaned his apartment—women's work, but he didn't want to bring her home to anything less than perfect.

There were times he thought of her, of what they had together, and couldn't bear it. He could light her candle, spray one of the perfume samples he'd found in a drawer, and imagine her with him when he took his release.

A man had needs, and a woman was made to meet them.

He understood the flirtation, and a woman's tendency to pretend, and he'd been patient. For weeks!

Looking at his tableau, seeing her smiling out at him from the photos, he knew it was time to step up his game.

So he showered, groomed, splashed on some Eternity aftershave because that's what he and Arden would have together.

Eternity. And it would begin tonight.

When Arden got back, still glowing from what she rated the happiest family dinner in the history of family dinners, so did Monica and John.

"Hi, neighbor."

She grinned at Monica. "Hi, neighbors. Been out on the town?"

"So to speak. My husband took me to dinner."

"Somebody really, really, *really* wanted chicken parm."

With a laugh, Monica rubbed her belly. "Somebody really did. Is that a lei you're wearing? Oh wait, your cousin—Zoey—they're back from honeymooning in Hawaii?"

"Just. We all had dinner."

"That's not only beautiful, but it smells amazing. You should look up how to preserve it."

"Already on the list. Tonight, it goes in the fridge because I'm freaking tired. It's going to be pj's and fall-asleep-over-a-book time for me really soon."

"I hear that."

"No word from the cops?" John asked her.

"No. I've firmly decided it was teenage assholes playing some stupid game. See you later."

And she'd sleep tonight, she told herself as she went upstairs, because nothing else made sense. Anyway, she had sturdy locks now, she thought as she unlocked them.

Then locked them again behind her.

After some last sniffs of her lei, she laid it in the fridge—which reminded her she needed to do her weekly grocery shopping before her afternoon shift at the bookstore.

Gym, groceries, she thought as she took off her earrings on the way to the bedroom. Squeeze in some writing time, go to work. Home, dinner, pj's, more writing time.

Maybe it was still a little shy of eight, but she ordered herself to stay out of her office. If she told herself to take just an hour, she wouldn't. She'd get caught up, then it would be after midnight.

Taking the night off, she thought as she changed into her usual sleepwear of cotton pants and a roomy T-shirt. Reading someone else's book, and the way she felt, she'd likely be out for the count before ten.

As she started toward the bathroom to take off her makeup, someone knocked on her door.

"Really? Tonight?"

Maybe her across-the-hall neighbor had returned from his most recent trip and needed or wanted something. Whatever, she hoped it proved quick and easy.

She glanced through the peep, saw Dustin Dubecki—with a big smile and a bouquet of flowers.

And just laid her forehead on the door.

Why?

Then she took a breath. Gone too far, way too far. Time to set some serious boundaries.

She opened the door. "Dustin—"

"I had to run out for a couple of things, saw these, and thought of you." He pushed the flowers into her hand. "They're almost as pretty as you are."

"Thanks, really, but—"

"What a great place!" He just slithered right by her. "It's really calm. I bet you need that for writing. Calm and quiet, yeah? You'll really like my cabin in the mountains. Calm and quiet. No distractions."

"I'm fine right here. Dustin, I've had a long day, and I'm not—"

"You work too hard." He laid a hand on her cheek, and his eyes flickered when she stepped back out of reach. "You need somebody to look out for you. Take some of the load off. You shouldn't have to work at the bookstore."

"I can look out for myself, and I like working at the bookstore. Now, I need you to listen, I need you to hear me. You can't—"

"Women working outside the home causes so many problems. I mean writing, you're right there, and can still do all the things you're supposed to. Like keeping a calm, clean place like this, making good meals."

Temper—she'd been told she had a slow burn that ended with a hot and deadly flash—simmered so simple irritation threatened to boil up to mad.

Boundaries, she thought again. And if she hurt his feelings, he'd have to deal with it.

"First, my work, my life are no business of yours."

"Now, Arden." He smiled, indulgently. "Of course they are. You don't have to worry."

"They're not." At her limit, she snapped it. "And I don't appreciate you coming to my home, uninvited, and telling me what I need or how I should live my life. Second, you've crossed a line coming here at all. You need to go."

His face turned to stone. His eyes burned in it. "You need to calm down."

"Do I?"

"You do. Calm down and show some respect. Bitchy's not a good look, and I don't like bitchy women. I've been patient, Arden, but it's time to stop playing games. I brought you flowers. You need to put them in water, in a nice vase. And you haven't even offered me a drink. That's rude."

Had she thought something was a little off with him? More than a little, she decided. And she wanted him gone.

"That's rude? Are you just clueless? The only game I've played is being polite and professional with you, and that's done. Take these ridiculous flowers, your lack of all boundaries, and get the hell out."

She shoved the flowers at him, started to turn to fling open the door.

The backhand shot across her face, drove her back. Her head hit the door with a crack as her feet left the floor. Stars exploded.

"You need to learn a lesson, that's what you need. Need to learn your place. With me! That's what I want, that's what's meant."

Dazed, limbs rubbery, she tried to get her legs back under her, tried to scream.

Then he squeezed a hand around her throat, cutting off air as his other slapped her, back and forth, back and forth, until she tasted blood.

She struggled, flailed, but her lungs felt scorched; her vision grayed. Red streaks shot through the gray as she felt herself going, going . . .

Then she could breathe again. With a sound like a thin whistle, she sucked in air. It hurt, God, it hurt, but greedy, she struggled for more.

As her desperate lungs filled, she realized he'd pulled off her shirt, and his hands gripped her breasts. He squeezed, squeezed so her gasp of shock raked claws down her throat.

"Take what I want, bitch. You want it, too."

She tried to shove at his hands, and one pushed under her pants, the other clamped over her throat again.

His fingers jammed into her as she fought to breathe again.

No air, all pain, all fear.

Dying. Everything started sliding away because she was dying.

His mouth clamped brutally over hers, and his tongue rammed inside.

She bit it, and raked her nails down his cheek.

He yowled, jerked back, and weeping, she tried to push him away.

"You think you can play me like this, fucking whore? Look what you're making me do."

His fist slammed into her face, into her belly, stealing the air she'd just found again.

Help! She tried to shout it, but could only wheeze. *God. Somebody help me.*

He dragged her by the hair, knocking over a table so the lamp on it shattered.

"Learn a lesson. In bed. You want it rough, you'll get it rough. You got that nice bed, all those pillows. We'll do this right, and you'll learn." Using her hair, he rapped her head twice on the floor as he dragged her.

The scream sounded piercing in her head, but only came out as a croak as the room spun and swam.

"Calm and quiet, soft and soft. I left the candle on the nightstand so we could light it when we made love here. I love you, and you love me. Always and forever. It's time to show it. Show love and fucking respect for the man who's going to provide for you."

She heard, far away, banging and shouting. The burning in her scalp eased even as her head hit the floor again.

"This is your fault." He dragged her up to her knees, pushed his face into hers. "You ruined it. But I'll fix it." He pressed his mouth to hers again. "That's what real men do."

When he let her go, she tried to crawl.

"Arden, Arden, it's John. Oh God. Here, here, I've got you."

She could barely see him, but lifted a hand as he gathered her up in his lap on the floor. "Cops are coming, and an ambulance. Monica's getting her medical bag."

"He—he—"

"He's gone. I should've stopped him, but I saw you on the floor. You're going to be okay. Monica—"

"That's right, you're going to be okay." Monica whipped the throw off the sofa, laid it over Arden. "He's gone. We're here. I know it hurts. Can you tell me if he hurt you anywhere but your face, your throat?"

"Don't know." Arden blinked against the light Monica shined in her eyes.

"John, go down so you can show the police and the ambulance where to come. I'm right here, Arden. I'm going to look, okay? Help's coming, but I'm going to look. I want you to try to stay awake, okay? Who was he?"

"Dustin. Ah . . . Can't 'member. Dustin something. Can't see right. Blurry, and . . . Cold. It's cold."

"You're in shock, and you've got a concussion." And bruising on her breasts, her inner thighs. "Arden, can you tell me if he raped you?"

"Tried. Don't think . . . His hand, his fingers." The tears hurt, but she couldn't stop them. "On me, in me. Dubecki," she said as the tears flowed. "Dustin Dubecki."

"Okay. They're coming. Hear the sirens? What's your name?"

She swallowed on her raw throat. "Arden Bowie."

"That's right, that's good. Stay awake now. They're coming, and they'll take you to the hospital. They'll take care of you. John and I will be there. We'll be there. We'll call your family."

"Learn a lesson."

"What?"

"He said, learn a lesson. Knew the bedroom. Broke in before. Knew."

"All right. Don't worry." With some effort, Monica pushed herself up when the paramedics rushed in.

"I'm a PA. She's in shock, concussed, suffered head and face injuries. She's been choked. I don't know if she lost consciousness. But she's responsive and lucid. She'll need a rape kit. Her name's Arden, Arden Bowie."

As they got to work, Monica rattled off the statistics she knew—age, height, approximate weight—while John spoke to the responding officers.

"We heard thumping, like someone falling, and banging around. I came up—she had a break-in about a week and a half ago, so I came up. I could hear—I'm not sure what—but I pounded on the door, called her. He came running out, plowed right into me, and kept going. I'd have gone after him, but I saw her on the floor."

"Can you describe him?"

"White guy, light brown or dark blond hair. Mid-twenties, I think. I'm not—"

"Dustin Dubecki." Monica stepped up. "She told me his name, and was able to tell me he was the one who broke in last week. John, I'm going with her. I'm a physician assistant," she told the officers. "I'm going to stay with her. She's been beaten, choked, sexually assaulted. She can't tell me for certain if she was raped."

Arden heard them talking, vague sounds, drifting words. Everything hurt, but even that floated under a cloud. Then she was lifted, rolled, and the room swam again so she feared she'd be sick.

Someone took her hand. "Arden, I'm right here. It's Monica, and I'm right here with you. You're safe now."

Safe. She clung to the word, clung to the hand, and closed her eyes.

Chapter Five

By the time he got home, Dustin had calmed down. Though his hand hurt a little—bruised knuckles—he rubbed his leather bracelet.

Just a lovers' spat, couples had them all the time.

Really, they added the spice to a relationship. A little spice, a little heat.

He'd give her time to calm down, too. Women were so freaking emotional. Jesus, you looked at them sideways, they got hysterical.

He went into the bathroom, examined the scratches on his cheek, stuck out his throbbing tongue, and considered them evidence of her passion for him.

No question she'd wanted it, and wanted it rough. If they hadn't been interrupted . . .

No, he had to admit it. He'd panicked. Hearing that shouting and banging on the door had scared him. Instead of telling the asshole to fuck off, he'd cut and run.

That wouldn't happen again.

He winced at the sting as he washed the scratches. Man! She'd really dug in! After smearing some Neosporin on them, he decided on ice cream for his tongue.

He'd never forget that kiss.

And the way she'd looked at him when he'd had his hand around her throat. Bluebell eyes so wide, so focused on his. Paying attention, as if he were the only man in the world.

Thinking about that, about the sounds she'd made, how her body had bucked under his, made him hard again. He decided to take a shower, take his release before ice cream.

By the time Dustin relaxed with TV and a bowl of Nutty Coconut, Arden lay in an exam room. The man—doctor—had gentle hands, but she still cringed from them.

"Arden, can you tell me if you're on any medication?"

Because her throat burned, she just shook her head. Because the lights hurt her eyes, she kept her eyes closed. When she had to speak—so many questions—the buzzing in her ears got louder, louder than the hoarse whisper she could manage.

When they used the rape kit, she couldn't stop the tears, and even the tears hurt.

They ran tests, but it all mixed together with the questions, the voices, the hands on her body, on her face. She tried to go somewhere else, anywhere else, in her head, but every attempt flashed her back. Pinned under him, his hand squeezing her throat, his fingers jammed inside her.

So she pushed herself back into the exam room, the too-bright lights. Safe, Monica said.

But she didn't feel safe.

They took her to a room. More lights, more hands on her body, more voices murmuring against the buzzing in her ears. A headache that felt like it might split her head in half.

Then Jen's lips, tender on her cheek.

"We're here, honey. We're all here."

Despite the pain, the burning throat, the buzzing, she could weep. At last, in arms she knew, safely held, she could weep out the fear and the shock.

Dustin had nodded off in front of the TV, so the knock on the door jolted him. Nobody ever knocked on his door.

He had a secure apartment, best that money could buy, and nobody came knocking.

He considered just ignoring it, then it struck him.

Arden. She'd come to make up! To tell him she was sorry, ask his forgiveness.

He started to rush to the door, then reminded himself a man shouldn't seem too eager. Forgive her? Sure. But he needed to make her work for it some.

Only when he opened the door, it wasn't Arden. A man and a woman stood there.

"Dustin Dubecki?" the man asked.

"Yeah, how can I help you?"

The man, and the woman, held up badges.

"Detectives Venmar and Brill, Columbus PD. We'd like to come in, ask you some questions."

The woman was on the short side. Up until Arden, he'd preferred shorter women.

Redheads, he had a thing for redheads, but until Arden, petite ones.

And this woman had a sour look about her.

"What questions?"

"Better all around if we ask them inside." The man, probably in his fifties and carrying an extra ten around the middle, glanced over his shoulder at the door across the hall. "Unless you want the neighbors in on the conversation."

"You've got some nasty scratches there, Mr. Dubecki."

Glancing back at the woman, Dustin shrugged. "No big deal. What's this about?" But he stepped back to let them in.

He liked keeping a low profile.

The woman, Brill, looked around the living space.

"Nice place." Nodding at his big black leather sectional, the eight-foot wall screen. "I guess you're a minimalist."

He shrugged again. "I only moved in a couple months ago, and I don't like a lot of clutter anyway. Is there trouble in the building or something?"

"Not that we know of." Venmar did his own survey of the room with its excellent view. "Can you tell us where you were about eight-thirty this evening?"

"Just hanging out."

"Here?"

"Here and there. What's the problem?"

"Would the *there* be Arden Bowie's apartment?" Brill asked him.

Stupid cops, he thought. But rubbed the leather on his wrist. He didn't want cop trouble.

"So what? I can't go visit my girlfriend?"

"Is that what you call it?" Brill's eyes drilled into his. "A visit. Do you often beat, choke, and attempt to rape a woman when you visit?"

He let out a sound of disbelief. "That's bullshit. Who said that? That's crazy."

"Arden Bowie says that. As does the witness who saw you run out of her apartment, leaving her lying on the floor, bleeding, half conscious."

"Well, that's nuts, okay? We had a little spat, that's all. I guess she's still pissed at me, so she's saying crazy stuff."

"Your little spat put her in the hospital."

Shock reverberated through him, jumped into his eyes. "Arden's in the hospital. Where? I have to go be with her. She'll need me."

"That's the last thing she needs. You're going to need some shoes, Mr. Dubecki."

"Why?"

"Because we're going to have a longer conversation at the station. Detective Venmar, why don't you go with Mr. Dubecki to get his shoes, a jacket. It's a little cool out tonight."

"I'm not going anywhere with you, and you need to leave. I know my rights!"

"I haven't read them to you yet. Let me fix that. Dustin Dubecki, you're under arrest for assault, for attempted murder, for sexual assault, for attempted rape. You have the right to remain silent."

"This is insane. Arrest? Bullshit. Arden and I love each other. We're devoted. She's just upset. I need to talk to her and straighten this out."

"Let's get your shoes," Venmar said as Brill continued the Miranda. "Bedroom?"

He wanted to punch them both, toss them out. But there were two of them. The man might have a spare tire, but he looked tough.

Cooperate, he told himself. Everything would work out.

"Yeah, yeah. Look, you have to take me to the hospital. I have to see her. She needs me to look out for her. She's got some emotional issues."

Venmar followed him out of the living area, past a kitchen/great room area, and into a bedroom.

"Hey, Brill, you should see this."

"I set that up to surprise Arden," Dustin said as he got shoes out of the walk-in closet. "To show her what she means to me. Those emotional issues? She needs lots of reassurance, attention."

"I bet it's a surprise, seeing how she reported this stuff missing after a break-in at her apartment last week."

Cold sweat pearled on the back of his neck, but he let out an easy laugh.

"Boy, do you have it wrong. We've been seeing each other for months." Dustin shook his head. "She likes to play games. She's a writer, you know, so she makes stuff up, all the time."

"Right." Brill took out her handcuffs. "Hands behind your back."

He sneered at her. "Look, I'm not letting some woman playing cop put handcuffs on me. I've had about enough of this, so back off now. Do you know who the hell I am?"

When he shoved her back, she shot Venmar a look that had him lifting his hands so she could muscle Dustin around, snap on the cuffs.

"I just love playing cop. We'll be adding breaking and entering, theft, assaulting an officer, and resisting to your menu of charges."

He submitted, completely and all at once. He couldn't fight two of them. But it would all work out. It always did.

"This is a terrible mistake. Arden will tell you. It's just one of her games."

When Arden woke, the headache pounding, her throat aching, Zoey leaned over to take her hand.

"I'm here."

For a moment everything stayed blank, then it came in drips and trickles. "Hospital," she whispered.

"That's right. And you're going to be okay. Here, try to drink a little."

When Zoey held it for her, Arden tried to sip from the straw. "Hard to swallow."

"I know, but that'll pass."

"Time is it?"

"It's just after seven. In the morning. You got some decent sleep, and they said that's key. Rest and more rest." She stroked Arden's hair. "More water?"

When Arden shook her head, Zoey set the cup down. "You'll want it straight. He hurt you. You've got a concussion, needed a few stitches. You've got a bruised trachea, but it's not broken or crushed."

She stopped because her voice had cracked. Zoey swallowed, then continued.

"You've got a pair of black eyes, some facial cuts and bruises on top of that. Other bruises where you fell—your hip, your shoulder. He sexually assaulted you, but the rape kit was negative."

She lifted Arden's hand to her face, then pressed her lips to the palm. "They took a bunch of tests, and they'll do more, but there's no sign of cognitive damage, no brain bleeds. They're probably going to want to keep you today, get you up to walk, that sort of thing. Then you can go home. Tomorrow. To your place or to stay with Mom and Dad for a couple days."

She held up a hand before Arden could speak.

"The only reason we won't argue if you decide your place is because you have the magnificent John and Monica downstairs."

"They were there. John, at the door."

"That's right. The bastard ran off when John pounded on your door. And Monica rode in the ambulance with you, stayed with you. They are now my favorite people in the world.

"The police have him, Arden. They arrested him."

Arden inhaled in shaky, multiple gulps. Closing her eyes, she began to shudder.

"Easy now. I'm here."

"Locked up?"

"Yes, yes, he's locked up. He can't hurt you or anyone now." Gently, she brushed at Arden's hair. "That's really all I know about that. I know the police came by last night, but you were sleeping. They're going to come back to talk to you, when you're up to it."

Arden nodded. "Need to tell them." She gestured toward the cup. "More?"

She sipped slowly, willing herself to swallow.

"Tell them to come."

"All right, but first I'm going to ask your nurse to come in. And we'll clear it with your doctor. Then you can talk to them. I need to call the family. And the magnificent Monica and John."

"Bookstore. Supposed to work today."

"I'll take care of that, too. Let me get the nurse, then you need to rest again."

"Tired."

"I bet. I'll be right outside. And one of us will be here as long as you are."

She went through more tests, and though she didn't want to go back to sleep, fatigue simply took her under. When she woke again, Jen sat with her.

She had soup, Jell-O, and told herself swallowing wasn't as hard or painful now, but she really wasn't sure.

She needed to go home, she thought. She needed to prove to herself she could live and eat and sleep in her own apartment.

When the doctor came in, she hoped he'd tell her she could.

First she had to give him the date—day, month, year—count backward from twenty, name the months of the year—backward.

"I know it probably feels otherwise, but you're doing very well."

"I'd like to go home."

"We're going to give it another day, and if you're still improving tomorrow, we'll move in that direction. I want you to consider, seriously, therapy. Nonfatal strangulation causes psychological damage as well as physical, Arden. As does sexual assault. Someone will be in to talk to you about that.

"You may have some memory gaps, and that's normal."

"I don't. I did, sort of, but I don't now. I remember it all. The police. I want to tell them."

"Then I'll clear that. Don't talk any more than you have to for another day or two. And rest, Arden. No physical exertion for a couple of weeks, plenty of sleep and rest. If the headaches persist after a week, or recur, you need to come back."

"All right. Thank you."

She drifted in and out with an audiobook, then set it aside when her nurse came in.

"The police are here. Do you want to talk to them now?"

"Yes, I do. Can I sit up a little more?"

"Let's get you comfortable. Now, if you're done, and they're not? You signal me, and I'll move them out."

Arden took several deep breaths to prepare herself.

She saw a woman, late thirties with a compact build and a brown ponytail. A man, maybe a dozen years older, on the chunky side, with gray threaded through dark hair.

"Ms. Bowie. I'm Detective Brill, and this is my partner, Detective Venmar. Are you up for some questions?"

"Yes. My voice." She brought a hand to her throat. "I can't speak up, I'm sorry."

"Don't worry about that. You know who did this to you?"

"Yes. Dustin Dubecki."

"How do you know him?"

"He came to my book signing, my first, at Next Chapter in Short North. Then he came to my next signing, and the talk I gave at the library."

"Did you go out with him socially?" Venmar asked.

"No—well, we had coffee once. He kept asking if he could buy me coffee or a drink, after an event, and I had plans. And I didn't want to. But I finally had coffee with him once."

"Did you have a romantic or sexual relationship?"

She shook her head, but that hurt. She breathed through it.

"Absolutely not. I only saw him at those events—he said he was trying to write—wanted to talk. Then the time we had coffee. I ran into him after work—at the bookstore—I didn't have an excuse handy, and felt I couldn't keep making them. And I felt sorry for him, especially after he told me about losing his parents, and living with his grandparents, then losing them."

Brill's eyes narrowed. "He told you he'd lost his parents, lived with his grandparents?"

"Yes. My parents were killed in an accident when I was fourteen, so I know how it feels."

"Ms. Bowie, his parents are living. They divorced when he was thirteen, but they're very much alive."

Arden closed her eyes. "He played me. He tapped that tender spot and played me."

"He had one of your books in his apartment," Venmar said. "Signed, and written 'To Dustin, the only man I've ever loved or ever will love. Yours always and forever, Arden.'"

Arden opened her eyes again as her heart began to pound, and her breath to hitch.

"I didn't write that. I never wrote that. I signed three books for him. One 'Best wishes,' one he said was for his grandfather—same name, he said he was named for him. I think I signed 'Happy reading.' The last, just a signature. He said he wasn't sure who he'd give it to."

"Why don't you tell us what happened last night? What you remember."

"I'd had dinner at my aunt's. Family dinner. I got home just after eight, I think. Monica and John—downstairs neighbors—had been out to dinner and got back at the same time. We talked downstairs a few minutes. I went up. I was tired, planned to make it an early night. I got ready for bed, figured I'd read for a while, and he knocked on the door."

"You let him in?"

She looked at Venmar. "I looked through the peep, saw it was him. He had flowers. I felt tired, irritated. And I thought, how the hell did he know where I live? And I need to set some boundaries.

"I opened the door, and he was all smiles, saying he'd seen the flowers and thought of me. I told him I'd had a long day, I was tired, but he kind of pushed past me and came in."

"You didn't ask him in."

"He just pushed the flowers at me, came in. And I tried to get him to go, but he just kept talking. What a nice place I had. He went on about how I should have a place in the mountains or something. I shouldn't be working outside the home. He'd take care of me. Writing was fine for a woman, if she did it at home. I'd had enough, and got mad. Not his business, my life, my work. I told him he'd crossed a line coming to my home. I told him to go.

"He said I was rude, and I'd led him on, and he'd been patient. I shoved the flowers back at him. I started to turn to open the door, and he hit me."

She pressed a hand to her face. "Hard. Hard enough I fell back, and my head hit the door. I saw stars. I never knew that was literal. That you literally see stars. Then he was on me. He was on me, and . . ."

Despite her best intentions, the tears started.

"Arden." Brill spoke gently. "Take your time. How about some water?"

With a nod, Arden took the cup. "Still hurts to swallow. He was on me, and the room was spinning, and I couldn't breathe. He was choking me with one hand and slapping me. Everything slipped away, then I could breathe again. He was squeezing my breasts, and I tried to fight. I couldn't scream, I couldn't get the sound out. But I tried to push him away. He put a hand around my throat again, and then he shoved his hand under my pants, jammed his fingers in me. He had his mouth on mine, he stuck his tongue in my mouth.

"I bit it, hard as I could. I scratched his face."

"Good for you," Brill murmured. "We can pick the rest of this up later," she added when Arden closed her eyes.

"No. Want it over. Need a minute."

"Take your time."

"I bit him. He yelled, but he didn't stop. He let go of my throat, so I could breathe, and he hit me. Punched my face, my stomach. He dragged me by the hair, started dragging me. He said I needed to learn a lesson. Learn my place. In bed. In my nice bed with all the soft pillows, and the candle on the nightstand. I needed to learn a lesson. He hit my head on the floor, so the stars came back, and I couldn't stop him. He was killing me, but I couldn't stop him. I tried to scream, but I couldn't. In my head, I was screaming, but it wouldn't come out.

"Then John was there, and Monica. I forgot—he had to be the one who broke in. I reported it. He took things from my apartment, and he knew things about it when he came last night. After the break-in, I changed the locks, and I got one of those nanny cams. It looks like a picture frame. I put it on the shelves in the living room."

"Can we have your permission to retrieve that? To view the recording?"

"Yes. Please. You'll see . . . I don't want it back. I don't ever want to see."

The thought of reliving it through the recording had the air in her lungs shutting down again.

"Arden." Brill reached down, gripped Arden's hand. "He can't touch you now."

"Is there anything else you remember?" Venmar asked. "Anything you can tell us."

"I don't think . . . Yes. I went to New York about two weeks ago. I had a book signing. I thought I saw him, then I thought that would be crazy, so I dismissed it. But I think he was there."

"We'll look into that," Venmar assured her.

"My cousin said you arrested him. He's in custody. He's in custody?"

"Yes, and we found the things missing from your apartment in his. He had photos of you," Brill told her. "At your events, on the street in Short North. One obviously doctored that has you with Dubecki."

"My locket? My mother's locket?"

"Yes, and we'll get it back to you as soon as we can. Arden, you should know, it looks like he's been stalking you for a few weeks at least. In our interviews with him, he's adamant everything that happened was consensual, that the two of you are in love."

Instead of panic, she felt the rage.

"Look at the recording and see if you judge anything to be consensual. Look at my face, and tell me I wanted him to beat me, choke me, try to rape me."

"That's not what we're saying."

"I met him four times, five if last night counts for that. The longest conversation we had was over that damn coffee, and that couldn't have been fifteen minutes."

"He'll be examined by a psychologist," Venmar told her. "We want you to be informed and prepared. His very-much-alive mother hired a legal team. There's a lot of family money. He has a trust fund."

Closing her eyes again, Arden nearly laughed. "He—he said he was stocking shelves at Costco."

"No. He's been living off his trust fund."

"He wanted me to feel sorry for him, to relate. An orphan, losing his parents as a teenager, trying to write."

Panic bubbled up again, so her voice came raw with fear as well as pain. "Will he get out? Lawyers, expensive lawyers, will he get out?"

"We're going to get that recording. In addition to that, we have solid evidence, including the photographs the officers who responded last night took of your injuries. Your medical reports. Your statement, your neighbors' statements. We'll do everything we can do to make sure he goes to prison for a long time."

She looked at Brill, wanted to trust that. "I thought he'd kill me. Rape me, then kill me. He wanted to. That's what was in his eyes."

As they walked out, Brill looked at her partner. "She's not wrong."

"Then let's keep his ass where it belongs. Let's go get the recording."

Because rest and more rest, tests and more tests were the orders of her stay, they limited Arden's visitors. But not her flowers.

She sat in the hospital bed, hoping she'd passed the morning's tests and could go home. Surrounded by flowers. From her family, from her neighbors, from her coworkers, from friends.

And stroked the little purple dragon Zoey had brought her. Her support animal. Though Arden had laughed it off at the time, she had to admit, it worked. So did the flowers.

Maybe she'd be stuck here another day, but she had the comfort of knowing people cared. When the anxiety crept in, or more often flooded over her, she needed to remember that.

Arden put on a smile she hoped looked genuine when Zoey came in.

"No word yet on my parole," Arden began.

"Actually, there is. Mom's out there dealing with your discharge papers. You're going to have a long list of dos and don'ts." She handed Arden a protein drink. "Protein's one of the dos. Drink."

"Are you serious?"

"Yes, drink it."

"I mean, I can go home?"

"You're sprung. The doctor will be in soon to go over the dos and don'ts, which you'll promise to do and not do."

The relief was so huge, her insides trembled with it.

"Solemnly. I'm going to get dressed, see if I can do something with my face."

"Arden, get dressed, but as your loving cousin and best pal, I'm going to tell you there's not enough makeup in the world, there are no sunglasses big enough to cover your face at this time."

As she'd seen her face, she knew her loving cousin and best pal spoke truth.

"Maybe I could borrow that thing Uncle Doug uses to spackle."

"Not even then." Zoey gave Arden's shoulder a gentle pat-pat. "I could run out, buy one of those hats with the long, thick black veils."

"I bet the vintage shop would have one. How long would it take you to get it back here?"

"Oh, it shouldn't take longer than never."

"That works."

She got out of bed, slowly, as recommended. They'd already brought her fresh clothes, just sweats for comfort.

"I'm skipping the bra."

"With those little girls, you could skip the bra daily and no one would notice."

"You just like to brag because you actually have tits."

"I do, and they're fabulous. Here, let me help. Your shoulder still has to hurt."

"Not much."

Zoey thought the ugly rainbow of bruises there, the other splotch on Arden's hip indicated otherwise, but said nothing.

"You're starting to sound like yourself again."

"Nearly there. To my ear it just sounds like I smoke a couple packs a day. Swallowing's getting easier."

When Zoey just put her arms around her, held on, Arden wondered who comforted whom. Then understood they comforted each other.

"Have you heard anything about him?"

"They had a bail hearing. Denied," Zoey said quickly, when Arden went stiff. "Dad went, and said the bastard's mother was there."

Arden only sighed. "That would be the mother who died of cancer years ago."

"Yeah, that one. I know they ordered a psych eval. I'm not going to tell you not to worry about him, but I am going to tell you to focus on yourself, your health and recovery."

"That's the plan."

Jen came in with the doctor.

"In a hurry to leave our fine establishment?"

"I'd hate to overstay my welcome."

"Why don't we sit down, discuss your parting package?"

"Zoey and I will go load up your flowers while you talk to the doctor."

"Thanks."

Arden sat on the side of the bed, took a breath. "So what are my orders?"

"First, you've got family support. Use it."

"They don't give me much of a choice."

"And that's not going to change," Jen said as she and Zoey carried out the first load.

"Good for them. Now, walking's fine. Walking's good. The same goes for soft food. No strenuous or impact exercise for the next ten days. Your aunt scheduled your follow-up, so we'll reevaluate in ten days."

As the doctor went over Arden's discharge instructions, Theresa Lester sat on the other side of the glass from her son.

A slightly built woman, she'd dressed in a gray Armani suit and styled her pale blond hair in a smooth twist. She wore her wedding ring set with its flashing diamonds—she'd found what she'd wanted and needed with her second husband.

On her right, she wore the square-cut emerald he'd given her for their tenth anniversary only the month before because he said it matched her eyes.

She loved her son, and though she believed she'd done her best for him, she knew she'd failed. She'd failed the demanding child, the surly teen, and the troubled young man who smiled at her through the glass.

Nothing had worked. The attention, the rewards, the discipline, the counseling, the schools, the privileges, or the removal of privileges.

She'd had one job as a mother: to raise a happy, healthy, responsible human being. And had failed utterly.

She couldn't fail him now.

"Is there anything I can do for you, Dustin?"

"I told you. How many times do I have to tell you? You need to talk to Arden."

"Your lawyer has told me, adamantly, not to do that."

He scowled. She knew that look. She'd seen it on his face all his life. She'd swear even as an infant he'd looked at her with that same annoyed disgust.

"Who's more important to you? Me or the lawyer?"

"You are, Dustin. But the lawyer's looking out for your best interests. He thinks—"

"You need to talk to Arden. She has to tell them the truth. I don't like it here. I'm not going to stay here. Make her tell the truth."

"Dustin, you hurt her. You—"

"She made me! She wouldn't stop playing games. She had to learn a lesson. She knows better now, so you go tell her she needs to stop this shit. I forgive her."

It chilled her. How often had Dustin's father insisted she had to learn a lesson? He hadn't taught those lessons with his fists, but his words, oh, his words had bruised and battered.

Abuse cycled. She knew it, she knew it very well. And she'd do anything to save her son, her only child, from perpetuating that cycle.

"Dustin, the most important thing now is to get you the help you need. Your lawyer's arranging for you to speak to a psychiatrist."

"I already talked to a stupid shrink. I want—"

"This would be ours, an expert, and we believe we can have you moved to a place where you can get help, and you'll be safe."

He leaned forward, and yes, she'd seen that look in his eyes before. That hard, glittering, frightening look.

"Fuck you. You never gave me what I wanted. You never loved me. You sucked as a mother just like you sucked as a wife. If you'd learned *your* lesson, you'd have stayed married to Dad, you'd have known your place, you'd have taken care of our family."

Theresa didn't defend herself—she knew the futility of that.

"I'll do everything I can to get you into a safe place."

"My place is with Arden. If you want to make up for breaking our family, for always putting yourself first, go talk to Arden, tell her I forgive her, and I'm going to take care of her."

Now his eyes shined with tears.

"Please, Mom. You'll see how special she is. You'll see how we're meant for each other. I need her, Mom. I can't live without her."

"I'll do the best I can for you."

Tears still shining, he smirked. "Your best never measured up. Do better."

The sinking sensation in her heart, in her belly stayed with her when she left. She hadn't just failed as a mother, she thought.

She'd raised a monster.

Chapter Six

When she got home, Arden found her apartment sparkling clean, and a new lamp on her end table.

"The other one was broken," Jen told her as she and Zoey placed flower arrangements. "I couldn't find an exact replacement, but it's pretty close."

"It's even better, thank you."

She looked at the floor, remembering how he'd dragged her by the hair. There would've been blood.

"You cleaned."

"Honey, you keep a clean place, but we weren't going to have you come home to any sign of what happened."

"I don't know where I'd be without you."

"I put one arrangement on her desk," Zoey said as she came back in. "Since the doctor said you can write as long as you rest, and stop if you get a headache. I'll get the last of them, Mom."

"Nothing like flowers to perk everything up," Jen said as Zoey went down again. "We stocked your fridge and so on. Plenty of eggs for scrambling, milk, yogurt, ice cream—you can make smoothies. And April made you potato soup. Doug made his famous bread pudding, no raisins for you this time. I made spaghetti sauce, and that's in the freezer when you want it. You need to cook the pasta until it's soft. Then—"

Arden just put her arms around her aunt.

"We want you to feel comfortable, feel safe, heal."

"If I don't, it's my fault, not yours. You've sure handed me the keys to it."

Jen laid her hands, gently, lightly, on Arden's face. "I want you to promise me you'll call if you need anything. Even if it's just to talk, or to have someone here for a while."

"That's the easiest promise I could make or keep."

"You know one of us, we'll take turns, is going to check on you every day."

"You'd hurt my feelings if you didn't. But I can tell you." She glanced over and smiled as Zoey brought in the last of the flowers. "I'm going to be okay. I'll rest, mostly because I get tired. And since I can't go back to the bookstore looking like this, even if they'd cleared me for that, I'm going to use this as an opportunity to write."

"Stop when it gives you a headache," Zoey added.

"Stop when and if it does. I'm going to get back to my life. I won't let him take that from me."

"Okay then. How about I heat up some of April's soup for you?"

"Actually, Burnie and I are going to lie down for an hour, then I'll heat it up."

"Burnie?"

Arden pulled the purple dragon out of her purse. "With a *u*, like *burn*. Dragon, dragon fire, burn. Get it?"

Zoey laughed, gave the stuffed dragon a quick tap. "You and Burnie take a nap. Text later, okay?"

"I will. Thank you, everybody, for everything."

She knew they left because they understood her, and that she needed to be alone. She could be grateful for that, too.

She turned the dead bolt, then stood, took stock.

Feel safe? Maybe not all the way, but nearly. He'd never have gotten in if she hadn't opened the door. Now she'd locked it. Now he was locked up, and if there was any justice, he'd stay that way.

"Come on, Burnie, let's lie down. Fifteen minutes, unless we conk."

She rested, ate soup—so soothing. Since she didn't want to go outside and frighten small children with her face, she took laps around the apartment.

Then, she tried the next step. She sat down at her desk, opened her work in progress.

"He can't take this away either."

She read back a few pages, nodded.

Yes, she remembered where she'd wanted to go.

And went there.

Just over an hour in, she felt the headache starting. Instead of stopping, she tried closing her eyes first. Since she could see the scene, she'd try writing it with her eyes shut.

With that method, she managed another hour, and accepted she'd done enough for one sitting.

She shut down, then did some more laps while trying to decide if she'd have more soup at dinnertime, try the spaghetti, or just scramble a couple eggs.

At the knock on the door, panic shot straight up from her toes, through her belly, and into her throat.

"It's Monica and John."

One slow breath didn't do it, so she took two more before she went to the door, then couldn't stop herself from checking through the peep.

When she opened it, Monica reached for her hands.

"We heard you moving around. I should've texted instead of just coming up."

"I'm so glad you came." She drew them both inside. Locked the door behind them.

Then she turned, hugged John. "Thank you for saving my life."

"Oh, I didn't—"

"You did. If you hadn't come, he'd have killed me." She said it flatly—fact, not speculation. "And you." She held Monica. "I can't tell you what it meant to me to hear your voice. You stayed with me, and I needed that so much.

"Come in, sit down."

"We don't want to tire you out," John began.

"You're not. I have wine—and I have soda for you. I'm going to have a glass of wine," Arden decided.

"Meds?"

She smiled at Monica. "I haven't needed any pain meds today. So wine works."

"Then I'd love a pop, and I'll envy you and John and your wine. Let her do," Monica murmured when Arden went to the kitchen. "It's good for her."

"You heard me moving around because I'm supposed to walk, and I'm not ready to take that show outside until my face heals up more. But I'm following the rules. Rest, walk, eat, exercise the brain."

She brought out John's wine, and a ginger ale on ice. Then went back for her own.

"You've got some beautiful flowers here."

"The ones you sent are in my office. They brightened it up while I did a little writing today. Exercising my brain."

"Not to diminish that, but put them all together, they still don't match up to the enormous and gorgeous arrangement your family sent us."

To prove it, Monica took out her phone. "I took pictures."

"Well, whoa."

"Right? The delivery guy could barely get it in the door," John told her. "Luckily I'd just gotten home from school or we'd have blocked the hallway with it."

"We'd met them before, but spent a lot of time with them that night. You have a great family, Arden, one that loves you."

"I do."

"How are you feeling?"

"Better. The buzzing in my ears is gone, and that's a huge relief. It's easier to swallow, and I don't have a constant headache. A little sore, but really better.

"They denied him bail."

"We heard," John said. "Your aunt's keeping us informed. And I'm going to say good. He shouldn't be out on the street. Sick, violent bastard."

Arden saw Monica rub a hand on John's thigh as if to bring down the temper.

"No, I feel exactly the same. I can't express it like I want to, as I'm not up to yelling and shouting yet. At first, lying in the hospital, I tried to think of what I'd done to make him think I was interested in him."

She shook her head before Monica could speak.

"Nothing. None of this was on me. I never did anything to make him think that. And even if I had—which again, fuck no—I didn't deserve this. No one does."

She sipped some wine.

Monica gave her hand a squeeze. "No, no one does."

When they left, Arden decided to go back to the soup, then had to admit fatigue was setting in, and just a touch of a headache.

She readied for bed—checked her door locks again—then cued up an audiobook. Listening, with Burnie tucked into the crook of her arm, she let herself drift away.

While she slept, Dustin lay on his cot.

He hated lights-out. Hated not being able to stretch out, watch TV, play some video games. He hated being in a cell, not having good sheets, a decent goddamn pillow.

And the slop they fed you? Disgusting. He'd considered a hunger strike, but a man needed to eat.

When he got out, he'd see to it Arden cooked all his favorites. It was the least she could do.

Still, even after all this, he'd forgive her. Women were weak and emotional, and just fucking stupid in a lot of ways.

She needed him to take care of her, to make sure she lived as she was meant to do.

He'd known the first time he'd seen her, walking into that bookstore, so tall and slim, her hair shining in the sun. He'd known even before he'd dreamed of her that night.

She knew, too. He'd seen that by the way she'd looked at him, the way she'd smiled at him.

When he got out, they'd pick up where they'd left off.

They'd need to move, of course. Somewhere quiet, a little remote. No more city life—too many bad influences and distractions for her.

Probably one of those bitches she hung around with had told her to string him along for a while, to play hard to get. He'd just get her away from those bitches.

A spacious cabin in the mountains, he imagined. A big kitchen for her to cook for him. She'd take care of the house, he'd take care of the yard, like things were supposed to be.

She could have a space for writing, that was fine.

Until the first kid came along. Then she'd need to give that up, concentrate on being a good mother.

More than his ever did.

They'd have plenty of kids. She'd take care of them; he'd take care of her.

He knew he'd have to teach her another lesson, but if he did, he did.

Once he got out, he thought, and turned on his side to try to sleep, things would be fine. The way they were meant to be.

He slept, and he dreamed of her.

Determined it was the best way to heal in every way, Arden pushed herself back into routine. Or what she thought of as her interim routine.

She had to skip the gym and working at Next Chapter for a little while, but she could and would fill in that time.

Considering the condition of her face, she stuck to her apartment. Maybe she slept a little later in the morning, but since she woke multiple times in the night, it didn't matter.

So she set an agenda.

Get up, have coffee, do laps around the apartment for fifteen minutes. Make and drink a protein smoothie. All of it. Dress for the day. Write until one o'clock. Make lunch, eat lunch. Another fifteen minutes of laps. Back to work at two, break at five to deal with any emails, texts, or return phone calls.

Make and eat dinner.

Laps.

Continue research or read or watch TV. Add in a morning shower or evening bath as mood directed.

She considered it a good agenda, and felt it would carry her through until she could get back to her normal life.

She got up on what she considered Day One and followed the agenda smoothly.

Until she sat down at her desk to write.

The door was locked, she *knew* the door was locked. Still, she couldn't concentrate until she got up, checked. She sat again, tried to put herself into her work. And constantly found her gaze drifting to the open office door.

On a frustrated breath, she rose, closed the door, locked it.

Minutes later, with her mind scattered on what-ifs—someone broke in the front, lay in wait? Or broke through the office door?

It wouldn't happen, of course it wouldn't happen, but what if? She shouldn't have been attacked in her own home, but she had been. It could happen again.

She couldn't calm herself, couldn't find her way back into the story she wanted to tell. Giving in, she got up again, went out to check the front door lock again. And this time hooked a chair under the knob.

She carried the second chair into the office. Locked the door behind her, hooked the chair under the knob.

She stood, waiting to see if she'd feel closed in, claustrophobic. Instead, she felt relief.

"Whatever it takes then," she murmured.

Over the next days, she followed the agenda, which now included the locks and the chairs. The bruises began to fade, but since she wasn't ready to face the stares or second looks, she had groceries delivered.

From her windows, she watched spring hit its mid-season stride with leafy green trees, barrels of flowers shining in the sunlight. People walked in light jackets or shirtsleeves. Cars drove with windows open to the air.

She'd just broken for lunch when the knock on the door froze her blood, stole her breath.

"Hey, it's Zoey! Open up!"

She pressed the heel of her hand against the pain in her chest. Breathed slowly in and out as she removed the chair, set it back at the table.

Then pushed a smile on her face as she unlocked the door.

"Hi! This is a surprise. You got the day off work?"

"Arden, it's Saturday."

Arden managed a half laugh as she closed, and locked, the door behind Zoey. "I lost track."

"I'm here to get you back on it. It's not only Saturday, but it's gorgeous out. Let's go grab some lunch, then you can help me find something amazing for Mom for Mother's Day. I want to give it to her—whatever it is—before I leave for Oregon."

Arden's hand went instinctively to her face. "Oh, well, I'm . . ."

"Looking a lot better—sounding better, too. When's the last time you've been out of this apartment?"

"Ah . . ."

"Exactly. Go put on some makeup, change out of those sweats. I say we have a glass of wine with lunch—my treat." Because she knew her cousin, Zoey added a hug. "I've only got nine days left before we go. Spend some of it with me."

"I'm not being vain—much. I just want to avoid the looks that say: *What happened to you?*"

"Screw them. And it's better. I wouldn't tell you that unless true."

Nine days, Arden thought, then she wouldn't be able to have an impromptu lunch with her best friend, or prowl the shops with her looking for a gift.

"Screw them. But I'm covering up whatever I can."

Maybe it wasn't as bad, Arden thought as she dealt with the sickly yellow, the fading mauve. For the most part, she'd avoided looking at her own face because it brought back that night too clearly.

Makeup helped. Maybe she'd add that to her daily routine.

"So, looking and sounding better," Zoey said as Arden changed into jeans. "How about feeling?"

"Better. I think I'll get the all clear at my follow-up, but right now I'm taking advantage of enforced captivity. I'm getting a lot done on the book."

"I'm going to ask, then we'll put it away. Have you heard anything about what's going on with Dubecki?"

"Not since they denied him bail."

Arden put on sunglasses. "Are you sure I look reasonably okay?"

"You look more than reasonably okay. Let's eat, drink, and shop."

Whatever jitters she felt she locked down just as she locked the door to her apartment. And told herself to enjoy the fresh air, the steady march of spring after the long winter.

Her heartbeat skidded the minute she stepped outside the building so she felt almost dizzy. The world, this outside world, seemed too bright, too hard, too *full.*

Then Zoey had her hand, tugged her along.

"It's a lot." Zoey tightened her grip, all reassurance. "But we're not going to let it be too much."

"It's easier to stay inside. Don't let me."

"Let's just walk, then we'll have big, crazy salads and a glass of wine. A totally girl lunch."

"Good. That sounds good."

At first the restaurant seemed too loud, too crowded, but she focused on Zoey, on the moment, and found her balance.

"We'll come back for the baby, then for Christmas."

"Back-to-back events."

"I might be able to work remote for a couple weeks—Boone can. If we figure that out, we'll just stay. Meanwhile, you'll come this summer, won't you?"

"That's a plan. No regrets, right?"

"No. Nerves, but no regrets. That trip we took out there to finalize all this, to find the house? We both fell in love with the area. It really was like, oh, here it is. Our spot in the world. But we'll come back here and all of you will come out there."

"We'll text, we'll FaceTime. And I definitely want a video tour of the house when you've set it all up."

"Guaranteed. Now, we've completed the eating and drinking portion of the afternoon. Let's shop."

Arden knew Zoey's shopping style. Window-shop, browse. See everything, twice, narrow the choices, consider again, second-guess, waffle, look one more time.

So it surprised her when Zoey zoomed in within twenty minutes.

"That's it!" Zoey pointed to a necklace in a jewelry display case.

"Really? You're sure?"

"I was." Zoey's bright look dimmed. "You don't like it?"

"It's gorgeous, and very Jennifer Rogan. It's just that you never decide on first look."

"I wanted something special, and sentimental, and meaningful all at once. See the three hearts? That's me, Travis, you. We're her heart, and we're interlocked—even when we're not together, we are."

"Oh, well. Bull's-eye. She'll love it. I was thinking of giving her that gorgeous hummingbird feeder, but how about those earrings? Little double hearts—four hearts, so that adds Uncle Doug in. It's not so matchy as a set, but, well, sets a theme."

The bright look returned, and bumped up to incandescent.

"I call brilliant. And that bracelet, all those little hearts? I'm going to take a picture, text Travis. It adds Boone and April, and he can say future grandkids.

"Naturally, I get credit for inspiring the brilliance."

"Naturally."

Zoey smiled at the clerk. "Can we see these three pieces? Oh, and that pendant—the moon and stars. Mother-in-law. She's always saying her kids are her moon and stars. I'm going to send a picture to Boone, but he'll go for it."

Arden just stared. "Who are you?"

"I know! I may never repeat this decisiveness again, but I'm taking it now." Zoey slid an arm around Arden's waist, tipped her head toward Arden's shoulder. "You brought me luck. Now you can help me find the perfect bag for my first day on my new job."

Since the decisiveness didn't extend to bags, Arden got home tired, but upbeat. She'd been out for hours, and really hadn't felt self-conscious. At least not as much as she'd assumed she would.

She'd add to her daily agenda, she thought as she tucked the earrings away for Mother's Day. A daily walk outside. No more apartment laps.

And she'd stop in the bookstore, make some plans with friends for drinks or dinner, or both.

She celebrated the process with a pizza delivery, and later with a bowl of popcorn and streaming a couple of movies.

She made it until nearly four a.m. before she gave up and put the chair under the door.

If she had to force herself to go for the morning walk outside, she pushed through it. At first her heart beat too fast, so she kept her pace slow until she felt steady.

She promised herself it would get easier, and she'd start to enjoy it rather than tough it out. And so what if she needed to add a chair under the door to perfectly good locks?

It made her feel safe.

By Monday, she believed she'd turned a corner. She'd walked outside twice, had stopped into a local café that morning for a latte and a muffin despite the healing bruises.

Now she'd work, and when she broke off in the afternoon, she'd drop in at the bookstore. She could see about getting back on the schedule after her doctor cleared her.

And this time when she sat down to work, she didn't feel the need to lock the office door, add the chair. In fact, she opened her office window enough to let in the spring air and the sounds of the neighborhood.

Definite progress.

"Give me a couple more weeks, maybe I'll throw a party."

Maybe she would. Something fun and simple. Food, drink, music, friends. She missed people, conversations, and feeling wholly like herself.

Make it a week, and she could have a going-away party for Zoey and Boone.

Plan it later tonight, she told herself. Work now.

Less than an hour later, the knock jerked her out of the story and closed her throat.

"Stop, God, just stop. He's locked up."

She went to the door, looked through the peep before she removed the chair—she hadn't quite turned that corner yet.

And saw Detectives Brill and Venmar.

Quietly, she removed the chair, set it back at the table. Her hands trembled, but she opened the door.

"They—they let him go. He made bail after all?"

"No," Brill said quickly. "Can we come in?"

"Yes, yes. Come in, sit down. Sorry, when I saw you, it was the first thing I thought. Ah, do you want coffee?"

"We're fine," Venmar told her. "Why don't we all sit down?"

"Why do I feel you're not bringing good news?"

"It may not be all we want," Brill began, "but Dustin Dubecki will do time. He's been examined by two psychiatrists, and while there's not full agreement, there is considerable overlap. With these evaluations, the prosecutor and the defense attorney have agreed to a guilty plea."

"Oh." Relief simply poured over her. "That means no trial? I won't have to testify? He'll still go to prison?"

"The plea is based on irresistible impulse."

Arden blinked at Venmar. "I'm sorry?"

"Basically, his mental disorder made it impossible for him to resist what he did even though he knew it was wrong."

"How can . . . He found it impossible not to attack me, to sexually assault me, to strangle me and try to rape me?"

Before Venmar could speak, Brill held up a hand. "I'll tell you straight out, it sucks. Dubecki's family has a lot of money, a lot of influence, and the lawyers pulled out all the stops."

"On the other hand," Venmar began, and Brill nodded.

"There is another hand. No trial, no putting you through that. He's admitted, on record, what he did to you. He'll be transferred to a psychiatric facility, full security."

To hold herself in place, Arden gripped her hands together. "For how long?"

"The judge ruled a flat five years. That means he can't and won't be released before five years."

"Five years," Arden murmured. "Then they just let him go?"

"He'll receive treatment throughout his sentence," Venmar said. "And as part of the deal, will need to be evaluated annually, and be determined mentally stable, and no longer a danger to society, before his release."

Venmar leaned toward Arden. "He's a sick son of a bitch, Arden, but sick's part of it. The law, the courts, have to factor that in."

When anger bubbled up, she didn't bother to subdue it. "Basically, it's *I beat her, choked her, rammed my fingers in her, but I just couldn't help it*? If John hadn't come, I guess he would've raped and killed me because he just couldn't help it. And his family's money and influence help him land in some—some rehab center."

"It's not a rehab center where he can come and go, where he can choose to leave. And," Brill added, "it probably doesn't help that I'm pissed, too."

She looked at Brill, saw the frustration eking through. "Maybe it helps a little."

"It won't be a day at the beach," Venmar assured her. "Money and influence or not, he didn't draw the cushy card. He's locked up, regulated, monitored." He spread his hands. "This being his first offense counted."

"The first you know of."

Eyes on Arden's, Venmar nodded. "Yeah."

"He didn't believe it was wrong," Brill said flatly. "And that sticks in my gut. He believes he was justified in what he did to you. He's just saying what the lawyer told him to say to make the deal. We know it, but . . . we couldn't make it stick. I'm sorry."

"Okay. Okay. It's better to know. I appreciate you coming to tell me."

"We'll keep tabs on him." Venmar rose. "We can do that much, and if you want to know anything, if you have questions, you can contact us."

"Five years. At least five."

"Yes."

"I need to know when—if—he gets out. I need to know."

"You will." Brill moved to her. "Arden, we won't stop keeping those tabs in five years."

She let them out, closed and locked the door, then replaced the chair.

Because her legs felt weak, she sat again. She stared at the locked door, imagined him behind one.

And all she could think was every day that passed brought her closer to the end of that five years.

Chapter Seven

The minute Dustin saw the room, he began to fight. When they'd unshackled him, he believed all the bullshit was over.

He'd done the rehab, therapy, mental health crock of shit before, and prepared himself to do it again.

But they'd taken him to a windowless room, a room with dull beige walls, a narrow bed with a single pillow, and a toilet right there! Right out in the open.

Unacceptable.

He'd repeated that opinion over and over as he'd taken a swing at the guards. As he'd spat and kicked and screamed.

Unacceptable, unacceptable, as they'd muscled him inside, as they'd jabbed a needle into him.

And he muttered it as the drug took him under.

He dreamed of a house in the snowcapped mountains, one with sweeping views from where he sat in a big leather chair by a roaring fire. Outside, snow fell in soft, steady flakes, perfect little stars, to add more layers of white to the towers of pines and the jagged peaks.

The fire snapped at logs he'd split himself, and with the satisfaction of a job well done, he sipped the old-fashioned she'd mixed for him.

A man's drink.

In the dream, he'd built the house with his own hands, three soaring stories of wood and glass with all the luxuries he wanted.

The steam showers, the sauna, the hot tub in the glassed-in sunroom off the main bedroom. He saw it all perfectly. The game room, because a man needed to relax; the home gym, as a man needed to keep in shape.

The wide deck on the main held an outdoor kitchen, another fireplace so she could cook there in the spring, the summer, even the fall while he relaxed, unwound from the rigors of the day. As he sipped his evening drink.

He'd designed an open floor plan so he could always see her whether she polished the wide-planked floors or washed the wide windows to keep his view perfect.

And her hair glowed, like the firelight.

She sang as she worked in the kitchen, a happy, female sound. He saw to it she was happy because he treated her like a woman, because he provided.

The scent of the bread she'd baked wafted to him, along with the aroma of the hearty stew she stirred in the pot.

Earlier, while he'd been out splitting wood, she'd baked his favorite red velvet cake.

She loved cooking and baking for him. He heard the love in her song. Just as she loved keeping the house sparkling. Of course, he provided her with the best tools because he enjoyed spoiling her.

He sipped his drink while he watched her set the table. The woman did like to fuss with her flowers and candles. Didn't he always bring her flowers?

Of course, in the spring, she'd tend the garden as meticulously as she did the house. He'd watch her then, too. He'd sit on the deck after mowing the grass, sipping the fresh lemonade she'd made, or in the evening, maybe a gin and tonic she'd brought him.

He'd watch her, keep her safe. Always.

Watch her while she washed the windows of the house he'd built for her. While she scrubbed floors or planted flowers. While she prepared food he'd provided. While she sat and knitted in the evenings.

While she slept.

She needed him to watch her, to provide, to tend. Otherwise, she'd slip back into her old ways.

Unacceptable.

But she'd learned her lesson, he thought, and smiled as she took off her apron. She'd learned it well.

If she forgot, as women would now and again, he'd simply remind her. For her own good.

Gracefully, her lovely red hair framing her sweet face, she stepped around the big white marble island and smiled at him.

"Dinner's ready, darling, unless you'd like another drink first."

"No, I'm ready to eat. It smells great."

He set his empty glass aside, walked across the shining wood floors he'd laid and she kept polished. Sliding an arm around her waist, he yanked her against him.

"But I want dessert first."

Her voice came breathy with anticipation. Those bluebell eyes deepened with desire.

For him. Only him.

"Oh, Dustin."

He shoved her against the wall he'd built. She liked it rough, and he wanted to give her what she liked.

He tossed up the skirt of her dress—he only bought her dresses. They were more feminine and offered easy access.

She was wet, of course. She stayed wet for him, only him.

She cried out when he rammed into her. Cried out his name, over and over, as he watched her, as he pounded. Harder, faster, until she screamed.

He liked to hear her scream. And if he didn't want that, he could squeeze his hand at her throat until she stopped. He liked that, too.

So he took her, the way a man takes his woman, hard and fast against the wall while the fire roared and the snow fell outside the house he'd built to keep her safe.

When he'd finished, when he'd proven his manhood, and his ownership, he kissed her lightly.

"Let's eat."

As he'd taught her, she served him first, then took her place beside him.

"Do you love me, Arden?"

"You're the only man I've ever loved or ever will love. You are my world, Dustin. I'd be lost without you. I wouldn't want to live without you."

"That's how it should be."

He gave her hand a pat, then spooned up some stew.

He woke not to the scent of freshly baked bread or hearty stew, but to the smell of his own sweat. He woke not in the house he'd built, but in the horrible room with beige walls.

Tears stung his eyes as he realized that perfection had only been a dream. She'd betrayed him, the woman he wanted to devote his life to.

They'd all betrayed him.

He felt like they'd wrapped a thick, wet cloth around his brain. They'd made him weak, stolen his freedom.

He wept first, hot, bitter tears of grief and fear. The mix of them left a rancid taste in his throat. They'd tried to erase his manhood.

Then those tears, hot and bitter, washed away all but a deep, ferocious anger.

They'd lied to him. The fucking lawyers, his stone-cold bitch of a mother. They'd held up the terror of two decades in prison and contrasted it with the promise of a treatment center.

He didn't need treatment, but he understood sometimes you had to play the game. So he'd chosen to play along. Therapy—been there, done that, so could do that again. He could put on the contrite and open to help. Christ knew he could walk the walk, talk the talk with the best of them.

He'd have a private room, and that had weighed heavily in his agreement. He'd seen it as an extended stay in a hotel.

They'd let him believe that, and they'd pay for it.

He'd find a way out, and they'd pay.

The lawyers, his mother, the cops who'd put him here.

Arden.

He'd forgiven her, and he'd even forgive her for this. But there would be consequences. She needed to be punished. Otherwise, how would she learn from her really fucked-up mistakes?

She needed to learn a lesson.

He'd figure it out. He'd need to hide his very justified anger and outrage and play the game.

And for every day he spent in this nasty room, he'd levy a price.

He could spend those days deciding on the weight and shape of that price, and just how he'd collect it.

Arden didn't throw a party, but she earned her all clear at her follow-up. With the caveats that she start with moderate exercise, rest when tired, and report any recurring headaches, any dizziness.

She'd recovered—or nearly—physically, but when she couldn't stop herself from locking herself in the bedroom at night, when she continued to make excuses to skip going out, she made an appointment with a therapist.

She wouldn't live like this, couldn't allow Dustin Dubecki to steal her life, so she'd fight her way out of it.

She hadn't told anyone about the plea bargain, hadn't told her family about what could happen in four years, eleven months, and twenty-four days.

The therapist, with her calm brown eyes and quiet manner, listened. When she probed, it was so gentle it didn't feel intrusive. Maybe she did feel better, at least for a while, after her two sessions.

She tried the meditation, the yoga—at home for now—and found she could venture out for walks when she listened to music. At Dr. Wren's suggestion, she visualized. Working at the bookstore, going out with friends. Putting her mind into places and activities that made her happy, fulfilled.

She didn't throw a party, but she went to a family dinner on the night before Zoey and Boone's departure. And surrounded by people she loved, people who loved her, she found the voices in her head—the ones urging her to close herself in, stay safe—quieted.

"I tried making your angel food cake, Jen." Boone accepted a generous slice. "Zoey warned me it wouldn't be the same." He ate a bite. "She was right. I'm going to miss this damn cake."

"Maybe I'll send you one for your birthday."

"Don't toy with me, Jennifer!"

"You could come out for his birthday, make one in my fabulous new kitchen. We'll be settled in," Zoey said, "and have the guest rooms fluffed and ready by August."

"I'm pretty sure we'll be racking up those frequent flyer miles. But." Doug held up a finger. "That doesn't get anyone out of actual phone calls, and a monthly family Zoom."

"We're there. And you guys." Zoey nodded at Travis and April. "You have to text the next ultrasound picture of our niece or nephew when you get it."

"We're thinking of doing eight-by-tens and framing them for everybody."

April rolled her eyes at Travis. "No. But we will share."

"And you." Zoey pointed at Arden. "You text, day or night, the minute you finish your new book."

"How about I do that when"—she crossed her fingers—"my editor says it's a go?"

"That, too. So both. I'm taking *Whispers* to read on the plane."

"You've already read it."

Head angled, Zoey flipped back her hair. "But now I can show it off to the flight attendant and other passengers while casually mentioning my cousin wrote it. Then I bask in the reflected fame."

Arden sampled her slice of cake and decided angels couldn't bake one better. "Fame's a big reach."

"Not for me. And you're talking to the marketing girl here. I bet I get you some sales."

"Who could argue with that?"

As the evening wore down, Jen caught Arden's eye.

"Parting gifts." Arden brought out a bottle of champagne. "For you to open on your first night in your new home. To toast yourselves, your new beginning, and of course, your incredible family back east."

"A candle"—April set the large stained-glass jar on the counter—"I made specifically for you to light your new home, your new memories."

"Cuttings, ready to plant, from the peonies you love. Something from your home here to your home there." Jen put the bag with the other gifts. "We love you."

Zoey started to speak, then just buried her face against Boone's chest.

"You have to know." He stopped, let out a breath, swallowed. "How much we love you back. How much we'll miss you."

"Mom." Zoey pulled away to wrap around her mother. "I love you so much, love you all so much."

"You'll call the minute you land in Oregon." Jen drew Zoey's face up, kissed her cheeks.

"Promise. I'll call so much you'll get sick of me."

Laughing, Jen kissed her again. "That hasn't happened in twenty-five years."

"We're proud of you. Both of you." Doug opened his arms, took his daughter in. "And you know, if you need something fixed, I make house calls."

"Careful," Boone said, "we could hold you to that."

"We want to see all the ultrasound pictures of the baby." Sniffling, Zoey hugged April. "And weekly pictures of the bump. Promise."

"Consider it done."

Blinking at tears, Zoey turned to Travis. "I'll probably miss you, you jerk."

"I might miss you, pest."

"Arden, God, I'm going to ugly cry! No, I'm not. But I'm going to text you multiple times a day."

With Zoey in her arms, Arden laughed. "Which means nothing changes."

"Look out for them for me," Zoey murmured in her ear, then pulled back. "Don't think you can get another best friend just because I'm a couple thousand miles away. I'm it, and don't forget it."

"Same goes."

Arden cried a little, and cried more when she got back to her apartment. Then her phone signaled a text.

Consider this the interim continuation of multiple texts a day.

So she followed another of Dr. Wren's suggestions, and laughed.

When she didn't feel compelled to lock the bedroom door that night, Arden thought of it as family healing.

In the morning, she talked herself out of the apartment and aimed for the gym. Maybe she'd go in, maybe she wouldn't, but she'd take that direction.

So she put on her workout gear, and since her hair had grown enough, she tied it back. Awkward length now, she thought, needed a trim, some styling.

But she couldn't begin to face going to the salon.

Tie it back, she thought. Let it grow.

She grabbed a ball cap as she went out.

On the way, she saw Mr. Grassley and Jimbo.

"Arden! Looking good, and good to see you."

"Feeling good." So far. She bent to pet the dog, offer the treat. "He didn't forget me."

"'Course not." He gave her hand a squeeze. "We're both glad to see you. Is it a bookstore day?"

"Not today." Soon, she promised herself.

"Well, enjoy your workout."

"Thanks."

She kept walking. Nerves bubbled up as she approached the fitness center, but she told herself she could handle them. Would handle them, and took a moment to visualize herself doing circuits on the machines, taking the yoga class.

Normal, normal, normal.

And reminded herself she could walk out anytime she wanted or needed.

She went in.

"Arden!" The woman on the desk radiated smiles as she clapped her hands together. "We've missed you around here."

The pressure on her chest released a little. "I've missed being around here."

The truth of that helped her regain her inner quiet.

She paced herself through her circuits, used the music she'd programmed to keep her steady and calm. Steady and calm enough she tried her yoga class, where she again felt welcomed back.

Flushed with success, she checked the time. The bookstore wouldn't be open yet, but someone would be in there, getting the coffee going, checking emails, completing the daily opening routine.

Using one of the recommended breathing techniques, she crossed the street. If they still wanted her, she'd get back on the schedule. She could try. If she found she wasn't ready, she'd step back again.

They weren't just coworkers but friends. They'd been there for her—sending flowers, food, calling, texting, dropping by.

She wasn't walking into a group of strangers or desperate for a job. She wanted to see her friends and reconnect.

So she visualized that as she walked up to the door.

She peeked through the glass, then tapped on it.

At the checkout desk, Cassie looked over. Her face lit, her hands flew up, and she rushed to the door.

Before Arden could speak, she was enfolded, squeezed, bounced.

"Tell me you're coming back! We miss you. Oh, you look good. You've been to the gym. How do you feel? Terri should be here any minute. She hired another part-timer to fill in, but oh, Jesus, major fail. Who knew? Anyway, didn't last two weeks. Let me fix you a latte."

"I'll fix it. Make sure I haven't lost my touch." She walked to the coffee station. "I know I thanked you for the flowers, the brownies, Terri's homemade lasagna, and everything. I just want to thank you again for looking out for me when I was down."

"We were worried about you, and so damn angry for you. That fuck-faced prick."

Eyebrow lifted, Arden looked over. "That's some mouth this morning."

Cassie shot a finger at the Closed sign.

"We're not open yet, so I'm getting any fuck-faced-prick comments out. You really do look good. You look like yourself, and that's good."

"I'm feeling like myself. Or more like me." The scent of coffee, of books, of Cassie's spring-in-the-garden scent, the sound of the machine frothing milk all added up to the more like her.

"You've been writing, right? The last time we talked, you said that was going really well."

"Yeah. It's . . . It's my safe place. Outside of that, I've been feeling nervous, anxious, out of myself. Too much. And with Zoey leaving . . . Their plane's about to take off."

Sympathy covered Cassie's pretty face. "I know you'll miss her something fierce."

"I will. I already do. But I need to pick up my own life. Can't let the fuck-faced prick win, right?"

"Damn right."

When she heard the back door to the store open, Arden's breath hitched.

"There's Terri now! Terri! Look who's here."

"The dog puked on the rug, and I barely got out before . . . Arden!"

Welcome came again to quiet the nerves. Ten minutes later, as the store opened for the day, she was back on the schedule.

As she walked home, Zoey sent a text.

> Taking off and heading west. Send good vibes our way. Love you!
>
> **Vibes heading up and streaming west along with you. Be happy.**

She added a trio of heart emojis.

A good day, Arden decided. And a kind of new beginning for her, too.

It took two weeks in the hellhole before his mother visited. They told him that was protocol, but Dustin knew it for more bullshit.

But he'd just smiled and said he looked forward to seeing her when she could come.

He was in the long game now.

So here she was, with her perfect hair and quiet suit. She didn't have to shower in some echoing tank, with a guard practically under the water—not hot enough either—with him. She didn't have to wear cheap pants, a crap shirt, shoes without laces.

The visitor's lounge? More bullshit. No security glass like jail. A couple of hard chairs, and no privacy with guards close by.

When she hugged him, he imagined plowing his fist into her stomach—and that fist held a long, jagged knife—but he just patted her back.

"Macaroons," she said, smiling as she picked up a box. "They said you could have them. I know they're a favorite."

Cookies, for God's sake. The best she could do was buy him cookies.

"Thanks, Mom. These'll be a treat. The food's okay here, just not what I'm used to."

"But you look well, Dustin. How do you feel?"

"I don't want to be here." That smashed the smile from her face. "Nobody does. Maybe I did something wrong, but I couldn't help it. If I couldn't help it, it wasn't my fault, right?"

"You're here to get treatment so you will be able to help it."

"I know that, just like I know this isn't the right place for me. I think I'd be better if I could go somewhere else. Like back to the rehab center from when I was a teenager. You know, where I could walk outside, or play games, watch TV."

He tried the practiced puppy dog eyes.

"Jesus, Mom, I can't even shower in private here—it's so humiliating. And I can't have a computer here. I really need one."

Theresa took his hand, gripped it in both of hers.

Looking down at them, all he could see was the flash of diamonds, the gleam of the emerald.

Symbols, he thought, of her betrayal of their family.

"I know it's not easy, Dustin. I think they said you'd be able to use one of the computers here after a while, and you can earn other privileges."

"Right. But I don't belong here, so you need to get me moved somewhere better."

"I can't. The judge—"

"Mom." God, she was an idiot. He kept his smile on, used his patient voice. "Come on now. You just pay him to change it, that's all. I can do the stupid therapy, do the circle talk crap and all that. I don't want to do it here. If you can't fix it, tell Dad to deal with it. You got me into this pit."

She'd hoped, how she'd hoped, to see some progress after these two weeks. They'd warned her not to expect it, but still she'd hoped.

She wanted to stroke his hair, urge him to be patient, tell him it would get better. But knew from the look in his eyes, he'd just slap her hand aside.

"Dustin, this isn't something we can fix or change. There was only this, or a trial and prison. You'll earn privileges as you go, and—"

"Fuck that." He said it softly, for her alone. "You need to make this right."

Slowly, pain in her eyes, she drew her hands away.

"I'm sorry, there's nothing I can do. Even if there were, I feel this is right. I'm going to visit as often as possible. In fact, I'm buying a house nearby so I have somewhere to stay when I come see you. You can live there after your release for as long as you need or want."

"You've got a house, and I get a cell. Yeah, that's fair."

She, too, spoke softly. The pain in her eyes echoed in her voice.

"I didn't put a woman in the hospital."

He leaned forward. "She asked for it. Now I'm telling you, fix this mess you got me into. It's *unacceptable*. If you can't or won't fix it, just fuck off."

She rose. Theresa had promised herself, and promised her husband, she'd hold firm this time.

"I hope you'll get the help you need. I'm your mother, and I love you. I'll visit as often as possible. If there's something you want that I'm allowed to bring, you only have to ask. I'll be back next week."

Goddamn it, he needed her. So he brought on tears.

"I'm sorry, I'm sorry. I'm sorry! Don't leave me. I didn't mean it. I'm just scared. I'm so scared, Mom."

She did exactly what he'd known she'd do. She came to him, knelt down, and folded him in. Stroked his hair while he wept on her shoulder.

"They make me take medicine, Mom! And I don't know anybody. I'm alone, and locked in that awful room. Sometimes I hear people screaming. I don't know what they're going to do to me. I didn't mean all those things, but I'm just so scared. Don't leave me here alone."

"I know you're scared. I know how hard this is for you. But it's going to be all right," she murmured. "I promise this is the best place for you right now. It's going to take time, baby, but it's going to be all right. You'll be safe here. You'll get better here."

While he clung to her, he imagined throttling her.

One day, he would.

Chapter Eight

Four Years Later

Arden hadn't made the decision lightly or impulsively. She simply wasn't good at light or impulsive. She'd thought it through, weighed the pros and the cons.

Just as she'd done when she'd bought the nice little house in the suburbs nearly three years before.

It had seemed right at the time. Had been right, she determined, as she did one more walk-through of what had been her home.

She'd needed to get out of the apartment, and the temptation that dogged her to lock herself into it. She'd given up walkability, but then she'd given up her bookstore job to focus on writing. And with the house she could, and had, set up her own home gym.

Then again, she could walk the handful of blocks to her aunt and uncle's. She had a little yard, and enjoyed taking care of it. After a year or so she'd decided to share the house and yard with a dog.

For the companionship, for the pleasure of having a pet to love, and who loved her. With his stuffed llama in his mouth—the current favorite—Zorro walked through with her.

She'd chosen a Lab, as her research assured her of the breed's loyalty and sweet nature. Good with kids, with families. Since her two cousins had four kids between them, and her neighborhood had plenty of children, she'd required kid-friendly.

"It's a good house, right?" She trailed a hand over Zorro's handsome black head. "Just the right size for the couple who bought it. It worked okay for us. But this is a good change."

And they couldn't stay here.

Dustin Dubecki could, and likely would, get out within months now. So she needed to be somewhere else. And Oregon worked. She'd loved the area every time she'd gone out to visit.

No, not impulse, as she'd thought about it for years now. Thought about it long and hard enough that she'd started looking at houses in the Willamette Valley.

She'd wanted to be close to Zoey, but not too close. Secluded but not isolated. Roomy but not too overpowering. A view, if she could get one, and—essentially—a yard for Zorro.

And on her last trip west, she'd found it near the big town/small city of Riverbend. The location suited, she assured herself as she set the welcome basket she'd bought for the new owners on the kitchen island.

She'd live an easy twenty-minute drive from Zoey and her family, just over an hour from the coast, and ten minutes from Riverbend.

Zorro would have a yard to play in, and she could play in the already established garden. She'd have a nice, updated kitchen, a semi-open floor plan. The space the previous owners used as an office she'd make into a library.

Eventually.

She'd have office space on the second level—or would when she converted what had been a playroom—and four bedrooms, including her main with an en suite.

A family home, she thought. Well, she hoped, one day, she'd have one of her own to fill it. But until then, she and Zorro would enjoy the added space.

The lower level needed some work, but it was fine as is for storage and her gym equipment.

Though she promised herself she'd join the local gym.

Eventually. Maybe.

What she would do, absolutely? She'd make the house hers.

She could afford it. She was working on her fifth book, and the last one had crept onto the bottom of the *New York Times* list, for two weeks.

She couldn't claim to be a household name, and didn't aim to be. She wanted to make her living telling stories, and that's what she was doing.

But she needed to do it somewhere else.

Zorro barked seconds before the knock sounded on the door. And she hated the way her chest clutched at the sound.

She'd cycled out of that, out of the anxiety, the nerves and ugly dreams. Over the past year, despite therapy, she'd cycled back in again.

She glanced out the window, saw her aunt's car.

She opened the door and received a nice long hug.

"And one more for you," Jen added, then bent to hug Zorro.

When she did, he sang his happy song. The series of doggie woos and subtle yowls never failed to bring smiles.

"Oh, I'm going to miss that tune." Jen straightened. "And you. I stopped by to see if there was anything left to do, but I figured there wouldn't be. Ms. Efficient."

"I just did the last walk-through. All done except taking Zorro for a walk before we head to the settlement. Want to go with us?"

"Yes."

Arden got her purse, her jacket, the leash. She took one last look behind her, then closed and locked the door.

"I know you have it all timed out, have your stopping points, but traffic happens. You'll text when you stop for the night."

"I will. New car, good driver, no hurry. It's a girl and her dog adventure. You and Uncle Doug will be heading that way in a couple of years."

"We will." Jen took Arden's hand as they walked. "After Travis took that position in Northern California last year—and now April's got her craft shop out there—all our grandchildren are there. Now you."

She gave Arden's hand a squeeze.

"We'll retire a little sooner than we thought, and move west."

"Where Uncle Doug will probably start up a handyman business."

Jen sighed, laughed. "Yes, he probably will, which means I'll be drafted as bookkeeper."

"Nobody does it better. And you'll both love it."

"No question about it. We thought we'd work on talking you into doing the same, but you beat us to it."

"I haven't told you why, not altogether. I miss Zoey, but that's not really why."

"Not altogether."

"No. It's like I stopped working at Next Chapter to focus on writing, but that wasn't all of it. Maybe not most of it."

She glanced at her aunt, saw so much of her father there.

"You knew it wasn't all."

"I knew you didn't want to talk about it. Do you want to now?"

"I do."

Maybe more importantly, Arden finally felt she could.

"You've probably figured out most of it anyway. I just wasn't ready to say it. I do talk about it with Dr. Wren, and I really thought I'd gotten through it. I look back, and yes, I was hurt, but I wasn't shot or stabbed. I wasn't raped."

"Don't minimize what he did to you, Arden."

"I'm not. I can't."

And on this quietly breezy day, she could bring back every second of the assault if she let herself.

"Too often, I think I do the opposite, and I don't like giving him that power. I stopped working at the bookstore because I didn't want to leave the apartment. I used various techniques to go out, but that was something I could stop and have a reason to justify it. I bought the house because I felt closed in, and it was another reason I didn't have to go out, to work, to the gym. I even let my hair grow back because I couldn't face the idea of going to the salon every few months."

"I love your hair." Jen ran a hand down Arden's long, thick braid.

"Yeah, well. A few months ago, I started closing myself in again. Locking the door on my office when I was in there, locking myself in the bedroom at night. Getting my groceries delivered. I could feel myself sliding back to where I'd been in the weeks and months after it happened."

"I wish you'd talked to me."

"I was so angry, Aunt Jen, at him, at myself, and I didn't want to live like that. Don't want to live like that. I can't stay where I know he can find me. Or," she corrected, "I don't feel safe staying where I know he can find me."

"I've never been hurt the way you were, but I can understand."

"I thought about moving to New York, but I don't want that, not really."

"It's not for you," Jen said easily. "You need your family."

"Yes, and my family's going to be in Oregon, or close. I want that. I don't want to be alone, and here, even with you and Uncle Doug nearby, I feel alone.

"I'll be in a new place, a couple thousand miles away. He won't know where I am."

"You're going through this again because he could get out in another year."

"Ten months, one week, three days." Heart heavy with that burden, she looked at her aunt. "I hate that I know that. I want to put all that away, and start this next part of my life fresh."

"Then you will. I've never known anyone more determined or focused. You'll make the life you need."

"I'm sure as hell going to try. I feel . . . calmer when I think of that, and when I can reassure myself he won't know where I am. He may not even think of me anymore. I want to stop thinking about him, the way I can when I write. I want to live the rest of my life with that peace of mind."

"I'm listening to you, and one thing I hear is you think you're weak. And, Arden, you're not. I watched you, just a child, fight your way through the grief, the anger, when you lost your parents, your home, your sense of security, and your innocence."

"You gave me all of that again."

"You needed to be strong to take it, to thrive, and you've thrived. I've watched you become a writer, successful and happy, because it's what you wanted most. And I've watched you come back from the trauma that son of a bitch put you through."

When Arden started to shake her head, Jen stopped.

"Don't do that. So you locked doors—it's what you needed. You got the help you needed with Dr. Wren, and that takes strength. You're about to drive cross-country with that sweet dog, and that takes courage. You're going to build your life there, and you won't let him stop you. You won't let anyone stop you."

"I'm working on believing that." Arden looked in Jen's eyes, so like her father's. "It doesn't hurt a damn thing that you believe it."

"You can trust me, someone who knows and loves you. Believe it. And in a year and a half, since you're so good at it, you can help me and Doug find a house that's somewhere around a two-hour drive from all our kids."

"I can do that. I'm going to miss you, so those two years to retirement better go fast."

"We'll be out for Christmas for certain. Hopefully later this summer if we can juggle enough."

They'd circled back to the driveway and Arden's car.

"God, okay. Text, text, and text. Drive safe."

"Always." Arden hugged, held on before she opened the rear door for Zorro to jump in. "Okay. Here we go."

"Text!"

"From every dog-friendly motel on the way. I love you."

"I love you back twice."

She felt better, clearer as she drove. "One more stop, Zorro, papers to sign. Then we're on our way."

She gave herself a full week for the drive—and the option of longer if she decided to take a detour. It occurred to her that at nearly twenty-eight, she'd never really seen the West.

She'd attended a writer's conference in Denver before she'd been published, done an author event in Oregon—Zoey's arrangements. But other than that, she'd never been west of Illinois. And she'd never driven through plains and mountains, through miles of farmland.

Rather than all the open making her jittery—and spiking the underlying fear—she felt free. She turned into rest stops and picnic areas. She avoided big cities but took time to explore smaller towns.

And bought souvenirs along the way with an eye toward silly Christmas presents or mementos she'd display in her new home.

She saw corn and wheat fields in Iowa, and more in Nebraska, cowboys in Wyoming, and dipped down into Utah to explore canyons.

And made notes there with a glimmer of an idea for a future book.

Nevada offered the desert and baking heat.

Every night she texted her family and included a picture of some highlight of that day's adventure. And slept those nights tired from the journey, and peacefully enough with Zorro curled up beside her bed.

"What do you think, Zorro?" She glanced in the rearview to where he sat with his nose out the window. "Are we having fun?"

He sang his woos and yowls, added a couple of yips.

"That's right. We're all about the fun."

As she crossed into Oregon, she knew she'd made the right choice. She felt lighter, looser, quieter of mind than she had in months.

When Zorro gave out a little whine, she pulled over. She let him out to do what he needed to do while she walked with him and admired the rolling hills, green with summer, the drama of the ringing mountains.

Vineyards climbed the gentle slopes, spread in their tidy rows over the flatland. Houses and farms dotted the green, and the river wound its way through.

"Nearly home now, Zorro," she murmured. "Nearly home."

She visualized locking a door behind her and the door becoming a wall. The wall receding into the distance. She looked ahead now to whatever stood before her.

"Okay, Zorro." She opened the back door so he'd jump in. "Last leg of this part of our journey."

Not far now, she thought. She'd considered driving a few more hours the day before, but hadn't seen the point in arriving in the dark and trying to orient herself, and her dog, after a full day on the road. This way, she'd arrive fairly fresh, unload her luggage and the boxes she'd packed in case the movers were delayed with the rest.

She'd get her bearings, let everyone know she'd arrived. She had a cooler with provisions she'd grabbed at a mini-mart if she couldn't face the short drive into town to stock her kitchen.

She had a list—she always had a list—of what needed doing and in order of priority. At the end of today's list was a long, hot shower. Maybe she wouldn't have a bed until tomorrow, but she'd have that shower in her excellent bathroom before making do with an air mattress for a night.

A guest room waited for her at Zoey's, of course, but she wanted—needed—to end this journey in her own.

With the bedroom door open and unlocked.

She'd gotten books on native trees, shrubs, flowers, grasses, and passed the time trying to identify some from memory as she drove. She felt fairly confident on the Pacific madrone—she had some on her property—due to the red-brown bark, and the Douglas fir because huge. She admired the small crab apple with its little yellow fruit.

All so different, she realized, from what was behind her.

Since her property was partially wooded, she'd get to know the trees. And since the realtor had hyped the fact the sellers had landscaped with native plants, she'd get to know them, too.

She had another book to help with that.

And the birds, as they'd left feeders.

Just how would the city girl, even with some suburban experience, manage in what seemed awfully rural now that she drove through it?

"We'll be fine. It's not just a new chapter. It's a brand-new book."

She looked forward to it, she told herself. Even looked forward to the work. Unpacking, putting her things in place, arranging furniture. Eventually buying more, as this place—no, her new place—was more than twice as big as what she'd moved away from.

It wasn't too big, was it? She felt those doubts creeping in, and imagined smashing them like bugs.

"No, it's not. It'll be nice to have more room. So shut up and think of that pretty view outside the office. Think how wonderful it'll be to write in that space, with that view, with that quiet."

Maybe too quiet? No cars driving by, no kids riding bikes, no neighbors mowing lawns or running snow blowers.

Just her, the dog, and a bunch of birds.

"Please!" She shook herself. "Stop, stop, stop. Town's ten minutes away, and Zoey's twenty. Writers need solitude. You want some of that. And goddamn it, it's too late to second-guess it all now."

And it's all beautiful, she thought. Different, but beautiful.

She hated feeling anxiety bubbling up, resented the need to dig down for the confidence that had once been right there, always there. She hadn't come this far, taking these big leaps, to lose her purpose now.

New book, she reminded herself, opening chapter.

Arden Comes Home.

She made the next turn, then the next, then taking a steadying breath, prepared to make the last onto the short, narrow drive that was hers.

The first thing she saw wasn't the house that looked like part of the woods that ranged beside it, or the wide windows that opened to trees, to valley, to the mountains beyond.

She saw Zoey.

Even as tears burned her eyes, she let out a squeal that had Zorro scrambling up from his back-seat nap.

While Zoey waved her arms in the air, Arden pulled up. She sprang out of the car, leaving Zorro to leap into the front and out the open driver's-side door.

"You're here. You're right here."

"Well, yeah." Zoey stopped waving her arms to throw them around Arden. "Welcome home! Oh, I can't believe you're here, really here. Not for a visit. Not for a few days. You're just really here."

The bubbling anxiety vanished. "I can't believe you are. Shouldn't you be at work?"

"I took today off. Boone and the girls can't wait to see you, but me first!"

"Where are they?"

"Preschool for Lexy, day care for Maddy. Welcome to you, too, Zorro. Sing it!"

When he did, Zoey pulled away to give him a rub. "Zorro, the magic singing dog. Having you around will put off Lexy's begging for a puppy. We're not there yet."

"You look wonderful."

"Back at you. You know, we made the right choice when I went short." Zoey patted her short, sleek, sophisticated pixie. "And you went back to long." She gave Arden's braid a little tug.

"How did you know when I'd get here? I nearly drove through last night."

"We've been tracking you the whole way. Remember, we all got that app."

"Right. Forgot. I need to text Aunt Jen."

"I did that. Let's grab some boxes or whatever and go in. I bet you can use a drink."

"Zoey, it's eleven in the morning."

"That's why the drink's mimosas, made—of course—with Valley Vineyards champagne."

At the back of the beefy SUV Arden had bought for the trip and her life in Oregon, Zoey shook her head.

"How did you manage to stay so organized on a weeklong, cross-country trip?"

"If I didn't keep it all organized, it would've been chaos at every stop."

"My life is chaos," Zoey said cheerfully, and grabbed the duffle Arden used for those stops. "And I love it."

"Check you with your gorgeous husband, two adorable kids, and high-powered career." Arden pulled out one of her suitcases and the box holding Zorro's bowls, treats, and toys.

"And check you, bestselling author—"

"For two weeks."

"Bestselling author with her adorable and faithful dog and seriously charming new house."

"It is charming, isn't it?" Arden paused to really take it in. "I mean, there are some things inside I'll want to change, eventually, but out here? Nothing. I love how it looks, sort of farmhouse, sort of woodsy, like it belongs here. I like how the walkway circles, and the portico around the oversized front door. The landscaping's pretty, welcoming. I've been studying how to keep it up."

"You have great views. Using that bump-out on the second floor for your office? Wow."

"It's not too big, is it? It's just me and Zorro."

"It's just right. Open up and let me in."

Arden put her key in the lock, turned it. "You're my very first guest. So yeah, mimosas sound good."

She opened the door into the spacious living area with its stone wood-burning fireplace and wide windows that let the summer sunlight stream in.

But rather than the empty space she'd expected, she found her furniture arranged.

"How did—"

A delighted Zoey waved her hands again.

"We overruled you. We got the realtor to open it up and had the movers come over the weekend. You were not coming home to an empty house, not on our watch. You can rearrange, move things, whatever. But it's all here."

"Zoey, I . . . I need to cry a little."

"All you want. It means everything to me, Arden, that you're here."

"Thank you, so much. You had to work like stevedores."

"The movers did most of it. I supervised. Boone got your Wi-Fi and all that dealt with. And the girls and I had fun unpacking stuff. Or Lexy and I did. Maddy mostly toddled around and got into everything. God, that girl is just like me."

"This is so . . . I worked up a chart where the furniture would go."

"Of course you did."

"This is really close."

"I know my best friend."

Arden drew her into a hug, swayed with it. "When I crossed into Oregon, I knew I'd made the right choice. Absolutely. Then, as I got closer, I started worrying. The house was too big, too remote, too quiet."

"And now?"

"What you said. It's just right. It really is just right."

In the kitchen, where Arden ran her fingers over her light gray counters, Zoey popped champagne.

"You have lots of good storage—and we stocked your pantry, your fridge."

And put her favorite cobalt bowl filled with lemons on the counter.

"Seriously? God, what have I done without you for four years?"

"Pined, of course," Zoey said with a smile that sparkled like the wine. "Selfishly, I want you settled in and happy so you never think about moving away. You'll like this kitchen. You've got this massive island, the wine fridge, the ice maker, microwave drawer. All these rustic cabinets. The glass fronts? You'll keep them looking like a showroom. That'll annoy me some. And Boone's already lusting after your fancy French range in that classy blue."

"I'll never be worthy of it."

Zoey handed Arden a flute, took her own. "Here's to us, together again."

"I missed the hell out of you. Now I don't have to. And Travis, April, and the kids are a day trip away, so I don't have to miss them as much. Your mom and dad? Two years tops."

"I'm counting on that."

After filling Zorro's water bowl, she did as Zoey asked and started a tour.

"They had this room set up as a home office—and the room I'm taking for mine as a playroom for their kids. I'm going to make this a library. Which I probably mentioned, as I see boxes marked 'Books' in here."

"You might have mentioned it a couple dozen times."

"I'll need bookcases, and I'm thinking one of those cute little electric fireplaces, big gushy leather chairs."

"Gushy leather's a must."

"I think the table I have works in the dining room. The way it's open to the kitchen, it's not a formal space, but I'm going to look for a buffet or server or hunt table. Something. But not new."

"Antique store and flea market in Riverbend, and more of both a little farther on. April haunts the flea markets when they're here. Then, like a crafty witch, turns trash into treasure."

"She's got that knack. Since I don't, I'll find something not new, but not in need of that knack. Look! Birds at the feeders. I think there's a downy woodpecker."

"Lexy worried about the birds so we drove over every week and filled the feeders. Supplies in your garden shed."

"I have a garden shed," Arden murmured. "And the most thoughtful cousin in the history of cousins."

She found they'd set out her guest towels, fancy soaps in the powder room, arranged her guest room furniture in the main-level guest room.

Upstairs, they'd laid out her bedroom furniture, and Zoey's touch—added fresh flowers in a turned wooden vase.

"You haven't left anything for me to do."

"Oh, there's plenty. You've got an excellent walk-in closet."

"It pales before yours."

"True, but mine's magnificent. You might want to contact the company I used. They could make yours nearly magnificent, and more efficient, which matters to you."

"It does. I love that I have one of those cute electric fireplaces in here, and the bathroom! So much space, the big-ass shower with a rain head."

"Being nearly six feet tall, you'll appreciate that big-ass shower. Nice quiet colors, too, wood accents, very spa-like. You deserve it."

"Whether I do or not, I'm going to wallow in it."

She'd need to furnish the other bedrooms, but no hurry there.

Her office made her heart swell.

"This is like a dream. I can see the valley, the vineyards, the mountains."

Zoey pointed west. "Expect glorious sunsets."

"I know I should turn my desk around so my back's to that view, but I won't. The owners—previous owners because mine now—installed the cabinets, that bench for the kids, but I can use them. The wall color's fine, that pale, dreamy green, but I think I'll have the white cabinets painted. Slate gray, forest green, something like that. Moodier. And I love the wood ceiling, the pitched wood ceiling.

"And I know it's picky, but I don't like the doorknobs. I want something more rustic throughout."

"It's not picky when it's your house."

"My house." On a hoot, Arden grabbed Zoey again. Zorro wagged and nosed between them, singing.

"The basement. I nearly forgot I have a basement."

"Excuse me, lower-level walkout."

"Whatever, it'll need to be finished one of these days. It works for storage and my gym."

"Equipment's down there. Boone said it's set for a flat-screen if and when you want one. Oh, login and password, in your desk. You can change them to whatever you want, but he wanted you to be able to get on without any problem."

"My cousin married a genius."

"I did." With a smug smile, Zoey patted her hair. "Because I have exceptional taste. Now, do you want a break or are you ready to dive in?"

"I say dive, but let's top off these drinks and I'll take Zorro out, let him get acclimated."

Arden talked more in the next three hours than she normally did in three weeks. They had so much to say. As always Zoey proved herself a dynamo.

Since Zoey decreed you couldn't feel all the way home until suitcases were empty and put away, they started with the closet.

"You need more clothes."

"I really don't."

Hands on hips, Zoey circled the much more than half-empty closet. "To be worthy of this closet, you need more clothes. You have some nice things for when you do events or go to New York, or on a date."

She paused there, gave Arden a look.

"Not in a while."

"Michael seemed nice."

"He was nice. He is nice. We just didn't work."

"But you had sex with him."

"Twice. It was nice."

"Okay, the last *nice* crossed Michael off. Though we wish him well."

"We really do."

"To rewind, you have some good things, just not enough. We'll go shopping."

"Zoey—"

"Understands you live and work primarily in sweats or jeans, which who wouldn't if they could? But more is needed here. You also need a good, stylish trench or raincoat. You're in the PNW now, baby, and the winters in this valley are chilly, rainy, and foggy. So some good water-resistant boots, a trench, a rain jacket with a hood."

"All right, that's reasonable."

With her fashionable eye trained, Zoey pulled out a dress.

"And you need to replace this little black dress. I remember this from before I left Ohio."

"It's classic."

Before Arden could make a grab for it, Zoey whipped it away.

"It's dated. You know what works on you, you always have. We'll go shopping and you'll find what works on you."

"I forgot how bossy you are."

"No, you didn't. We'll have fun. Now, you don't plan on having three guest rooms, do you?"

"No. One up, the one down for now. I thought I might use one up here for a kind of den, with a TV, comfy sofa—which I need to buy. But I need to think about it.

"And it suddenly strikes me this is a lot to clean."

"I'm really happy with my cleaning service. I'll text you the name and number."

"It's just me. I don't really need a service." Or someone she didn't know, really know, in her house.

"Arden." Head angled, Zoey stuck a hand on her hip. "How many hours a day do you work?"

"It depends."

"Do you put in a workweek, possibly more?"

"Yes."

"And you make a living. Give somebody a job so they can do the same." She patted Arden's arm. "Let's unpack another box. We should hang some of your art."

"I'll need to unpack my tool kit."

"We'll do that. You'll show me where you want things, I'll hang them. Between us, who's the handy one here?"

Arden hunched her shoulders. "You are."

"There, there. Remember, Travis is worse than you are. I got all Dad's skill."

"I know who to call when I need something fixed."

"You do. You know," she said as they walked out, "the longer I'm here, the more the house feels like you."

"You really think so?"

"I really think so. The style. It's simple but not plain, not ordinary. All the quiet, muted colors—peaceful, soothing. The wood—it's warm, mellow. I wasn't sure about the location before, to be honest."

"No?"

"You've spent your whole life in a city or a neighborhood. This is neither," Zoey said as they went downstairs. "But it feels like you, and you." She gave Zorro a pat on the head. "It's sort of a writer's retreat, and still minutes from a town with shops, restaurants, a really pretty park. You've got the river, the mountains, the vineyards."

"And you."

"And me, which goes without saying is number one on the list of advantages. You're probably going to want more art than you have. There's a really terrific little gallery in town you should check out."

"Then I will."

By the time Zoey got ready to leave, Arden had art on the walls. Yes, she needed more, but she intended to be selective. She had family photos and mementoes arranged on the built-ins flanking the fireplace. Her mother's iron candlesticks on the mantel along with her father's old mantel clock.

She'd organized her makeup, skin care, hair products, and all the rest in her bathroom in the meticulous way that made Zoey sigh.

"I should have you organize mine."

"Anytime."

"You'd just tell me I don't need eight mascaras. Are you sure you don't want to come for dinner?"

"I appreciate it, but I'm going to take a long, hot shower in my fancy bathroom, get into pj's, feed Zorro, fix a sandwich, then my dog and I are going to kick back, bask awhile, read awhile, then sleep in our own beds in our new house."

"Sunday."

"Sunday, I'll be there."

Zoey hugged, held on. "I'm so happy. Text if you need or want anything."

"I've got it all, but I will. Thank you. I love you."

"You're welcome. I love you."

She stood in the doorway, waving Zoey off. Then stood, took stock.

Alone now, she thought. In the quiet, with the valley spread out like a painting.

"But I don't feel that way. I don't feel alone. I feel good."

She closed the door, turned. "This is our place, Zorro. Our house. And we're going to live our best lives right here."

Chapter Nine

Arden considered it another Day One.

She'd slept, long and deep, and if she woke before the sun, she considered it a bonus. She noted Zorro not only had his current favorite stuffed llama companion, but his secondary—a unicorn—as well as his squeaky ball, his nonsqueaky ball, his tug rope, and his big play bone surrounding his bed.

All his comforts, she got that. After all, she had him, and she had Burnie. She went down to make her morning latte in her big, bright kitchen, tossed a jacket over her pajamas before walking out with the dog.

"We both need to get used to where we are now. It still doesn't seem real."

But she could smell the lilies, the big, elegant clumps of them near the back patio, and see the feathery white plumes of something she needed to look up rising above fernlike foliage near the trees. She had ferns, too, and hostas. Some pretty pink cups on tall stems. Bleeding hearts—she knew those.

She'd explore, identify the flowers and shrubs that made up what was now hers. And hope she was up to maintaining it.

She liked that it didn't look meticulously planned—which, she admitted, she'd have done. Instead, it all looked natural.

As she sipped her coffee, and Zorro explored, she watched the first light bloom over the eastern range.

It filled her, that dawning. The beauty and the promise of it. She lived here now, in a place where she could see for miles, could watch the sun rise in one direction, set in another. Where she could hear birds start to chatter as they got busy.

It reminded her to check the bird feeders.

She had a cagelike deal for suet cakes, three different feeders for seeds, a hummingbird feeder, and a stone candlestick birdbath.

"Plenty to eat, for now. We'll check every day."

Finished with his morning duties, his careful exploring, Zorro leaned on her leg. He looked up at her with his soulful golden-brown eyes full of love.

"I don't think there's a sweeter dog or a better boy in the universe. We're going to come out and play later, but it's time for me to get busy now."

She fed the dog—mudroom perfect for that—made herself a protein smoothie. What had been set up as a coffee station now served well as a coffee/smoothie bar.

Then she indulged herself and walked through the house.

Bookcases, and plenty of them, she thought as she paused at what would be her library.

She walked out to stand in her living room. In a couple of months, she'd build a fire—once she looked up how to build a fire—and cozy up on the sofa with a glass of wine.

Upstairs, she studied one empty bedroom, then the other. She'd find the right bed for one, the right sofa for the other.

She had plenty of time.

"And I'm wasting it when I could and should be working."

She'd make her list first, she decided. Then write until noon. Eat something, then dress, and with that list, she'd head to town to check out the antique shop, the flea market. If she found what she wanted, she'd bring it home or arrange for delivery. And maybe find a hardware store or something along those lines.

She really wanted to change out the doorknobs. No doubt she could find a huge variety online, but she'd worked at an independent bookstore.

She believed in shopping local as much as possible.

She sat, let herself drink in the view as sunlight spread over the valley.

Then she opened the file on her current story, and let herself fall into it.

She'd worked in those dog-friendly motel rooms, but with her brain and body tired from the day's drive, had only managed short stints.

It felt good, really good, to write when she felt fresh and eager. When it didn't flow, she poked, she prodded until it moved along.

She liked her main character—a smart-mouthed, take-no-bullshit woman with a soft spot for strays, and a three-legged orange tabby named Triangle.

It was the first time she'd attempted to build a central character as a cop, and so far, she found it fun. Challenging, but fun. Detective Lil—not Lily, not Lillian—Trace of the Portland PD.

Arden figured since she'd decided to live in Oregon, she might as well use it as a canvas.

Now Lil, and her cranky, twenty-years-on-the-job partner, investigated a double murder.

Deep into it, she didn't surface until Zorro poked his nose on her arm.

"What?"

He gave her his long, liquid stare, and when she checked the time, she saw she'd gone nearly a half hour beyond noon.

"Okay. Be a good boy. Give me five minutes." She held up a hand, five fingers, as she'd used in training. "Let me finish this thought."

He sat, patient, and when she saved and shut down, sprang up to bounce and turn in circles.

She grabbed a Pepsi on the way out, drank as they both wandered and walked. She could skip the shopping, go back to work. But . . .

Priorities, she thought. She had a house to furnish.

She dressed—jeans, a T-shirt. She really didn't need more clothes, but since she'd be out with people, she added makeup, brushed her hair, braided it.

Definitely presentable.

She grabbed a light jacket.

"Let's go for a ride."

As he always did, Zorro raced off singing, raced back with his leash in his mouth.

"Who's the best boy ever?"

He sat, and eyes gleaming with a grin, lifted both front paws.

"That's right. You are."

She'd already looked up the addresses, so she plugged those into her GPS. This would serve not only as a shopping expedition, but as another way to orient herself to the area.

Before she could pull out, she got a text from Zoey.

Just checking how it's going.

Going great. Up early, basked, worked, basked. Now on my way to the flea market, antique store, maybe the hardware store.

In all those places drop April's name, tell them she's your cousin. Her name has weight.

Will do. And will let you know if I score.

She liked the drive, and since Zorro had his head out the window, ears flapping, he did as well. Traveling on back roads, with everything green and gold, kept her relaxed. She passed a tidy little farm—horses grazing—a vineyard, then a bend in the river where she spotted people paddling canoes, kayaks.

Maybe the city girl—former—could try that.

Maybe.

She followed the river now, the Willamette, as it wound its way toward Riverbend. Guided by the GPS, she turned before the bridge that would take her to the heart of town, and took the road that skirted the near edge.

Her mouth dropped open in surprise when she saw the flea market.

The big barn of a building had long offshoots on both sides. From the size of it, Arden calculated you could spend a solid week inside before seeing everything.

Maybe longer.

And she imagined April likely shed tears of joy whenever she came here.

"But I have a mission."

She parked, turned to Zorro. "You have your travel water bowl, your llama. I grabbed some shade here, but I'll leave the windows cracked a couple inches anyway. Be a good boy."

To keep him happy, she gave him a beef stick before she got out, locked the car.

When she walked in, the sheer scope of *things* slapped at her ingrained need for order. At the same time, there was something happy about it all. She imagined April excited by the hunt.

She couldn't deny a touch of that herself, but she had specifics to hunt for.

If only she had a map.

Rather than wander aimlessly, she tracked down someone who worked at the flea market.

"I wonder if you could help me. You might know my cousin, April Rogan."

"April! I sure do. I thought I met her cousin already."

"Probably Zoey. I'm another, and I've just moved to the area."

"How about that?" The genial-looking man of about sixty smiled at her. "Welcome to the Pacific Northwest."

"Thank you. I'm a little lost in here. It's so big. I'm hoping to find a bed—an iron head- and footboard, bed frame. Queen size. For a guest room."

"I bet Shirl has something for you. She'd be all the way in the back. You go straight down there." He gestured. "Then to your left. If she doesn't have something to suit you, try Melvin. You'd go all the way to the right from Shirl, and about halfway up the side."

"Thanks so much."

"Good luck!"

She started through. Voices echoed; a baby started to cry. A man's voice said, clearly: *Jeez, Annie, make up your mind sometime this century.*

Arden checked her anxiety level, and found it dead low. She'd not only handle this, she'd enjoy it.

Still, distractions lurked everywhere. She saw a display of green glass—bowls, pitchers, plates, cups—all under a black light.

It all glowed, like dishware from another planet. Fascinating.

She saw a three-tiered table with fluted edges and wondered how it would look in her living room. She saw displays of dolls, of figurines, of dishes.

She spotted a gooseneck floor lamp with a crackle globe she knew she wanted. Bed first, she ordered herself, but noted the position of the booth before continuing.

She noted the position of a few others before reaching her destination.

And saw the bed. Or rather, the head- and footboard leaning against the wall.

A sturdy woman with a shock of coin-bright blond hair and huge red-framed glasses gave Arden a practiced smile.

"Help you find something?"

"Yes. I'm looking for a bed. Frame, head- and footboard."

"We got a few. This one here? We just put it out this morning. Sturdy. Steel pipe, powder-coated bronze."

Deep, rich bronze, curved ends, slim bars, and the interesting detail of the circle centered up on head and foot.

Simple, she thought, but not boring.

"King size, too. Tall girl like you'd sleep well in a king bed."

"King size."

She'd have to get new bedding, but she had room. She'd never had the luxury of a king bed, and with her height . . .

She realized she didn't want it for the guest room. She wanted it for her own.

"I'm Shirl."

"Arden. I was looking for something like this for a guest room, but . . ." She ran her hand over a rung.

New mattress, new bedding, new pillows.

"You wouldn't happen to know where I could find a new king-sized mattress and box springs?"

Shirl's smile spread. "I sure do. Local, are you?"

"I am now. I just moved in yesterday."

"Welcome. I can make you a deal." After tapping a finger on her chin, Shirl named a price.

"How much to deliver it? About fifteen miles. And set it up?"

"Stairs?"

"Yes, second floor. And to move my current bed to the guest room—same floor."

"Seventy-five. First, I've got something over here you might want to see. Going to need nightstands, aren't you?"

Among the clutter, she had two with iron legs and drawer pulls the same deep bronze as the bed. The dark wood of the top and the generous drawer appealed, as did the open shelf below.

A perfect spot for a couple of to-be-reads.

Arden opened and closed the drawers.

"Damn it, Shirl," she said, and made Shirl laugh. "How much for the works?"

She bought the works, and the gooseneck lamp, the table—piecrust, the seller called it. Then she and Zorro drove through town, out the other side, where she tested and bought a mattress and box springs, stopped again to buy two sets of new sheets, king-sized pillows, a simple cream-colored duvet, and shams.

She let Zorro out to walk and pee, and shot him a look in the rearview when they got back in the car.

"This is exhausting. But I'm going to finish. Antique shop's right on the main street downtown. Um, Spruce Street. Then the hardware's on the way out again. I know exactly the doorknobs I want now, inspired by my new bed."

She found the antique store charming, and much easier to navigate than the flea market. Add a whole lot quieter than any of her other stops.

She didn't expect her luck to hold, and when it did, decided this was a magic day.

The owner-operator, a woman in her thirties with a shiny brown ponytail and bright blue eyes, showed her the winner.

"My husband refinished this."

"It's beautiful."

The right size for the room, with simple lines, good storage—if she ever needed it.

"It's what they call a flame grain. I think it really adds interest. It's from the early twentieth century, has dovetailed drawers."

"I'm afraid it's perfect."

"Really? I'm glad to hear it. Did you notice the china cabinet right over here?"

"Oh, well, I . . ."

She noticed it now.

"It's from the same period, but it's not a set. Still, they really complement each other."

She didn't need a china cabinet. She didn't have china, or things to display in it. But . . .

"How much for both, and will you deliver?"

Once more she got back in the car, sighed.

"Hardware store, and watch me. I'll end up buying a chainsaw."

She made her way to Riley's Hardware, grateful she drove in the direction of home.

When she parked, she checked Zorro's travel water.

"I swear, last stop. I know exactly what I want. They either have them, can get them, or don't and can't. I'll be quick. Promise."

She went in, found a bright, clean shop. And one more than twice the size she'd expected. Organized, too, but what did she know about hardware? She saw a clerk helping someone in a paint section, another with a customer in the lighting section.

She would not look at lights. Doorknobs only.

An older man—a tall one, easily six-three—checked out another customer.

Since she knew what she wanted, she headed toward doorknobs.

A number displayed themselves on a section of wood to represent a door. Good idea, she mused as she worked her way through from the ornate to the bland and everything in between.

Her luck held, as she found exactly what she wanted—then realized she'd need to change out the exterior locksets, too.

No problem.

The older man walked over. He had a lanky build, cat-green eyes, and silver hair where several streaks of black still lingered.

"Afternoon. Can I help you today?"

"Yes, you can. This one, in the oil-rubbed bronze, and the same finish in that one, with dead bolt."

He grinned at her. "That was easy."

"It's all so organized it makes it easy."

"I appreciate that. I'm Joe Riley."

"Oh, this is your store? It's the easiest I've been in today, and I've been in too many today."

"Rehabbing, are you?"

"No, I just don't like my doorknobs. I moved in yesterday."

"Is that right? From?"

"Ohio."

"Funny. I thought you looked familiar, but I guess not."

"My first time in here. I'll eventually be back for paint, but I'm holding off. I think twenty-one interior doorknobs and three exterior fill today."

"Twenty-one? I'm going to check my inventory, but I wouldn't have that number in stock."

"I'm not in a hurry, as long as you can get them."

As they walked toward the counter, a dog walked around it. A long-eared, glossy brown hound, he stepped right over to give Arden a sniff.

"You have a dog." She instantly leaned down to pet.

"That's Elvis."

"Because he ain't nothing but a hound dog."

Joe let out an easy laugh. "Got it in one. He's a friendly one, but he really seems to like you. That grumbling sound he's making? That's his I-like-this-one grumble."

"I like him, too. He probably smells my dog. He's out in the car."

"Well, go get him!"

"I . . . really?"

"Would he have a problem with Elvis or the rest of us?"

"No. Zorro likes everybody, on two or four legs."

"Got a black dog, do you?"

"Black Lab. If you're sure, I'll bring him in while you check about the knobs. He's been mostly stuck in the car all afternoon."

"Cut him loose awhile."

She went out, put the leash on Zorro. "I've got a dog-friendly store, and you can make a friend. Don't embarrass me."

He looked shocked she'd think he would.

His tail wagged as she walked him in, then his whole body wagged.

"That's a handsome boy," Joe said from behind the counter. He wore readers now over those green eyes. "Nothing like a good dog, is there?"

"No, there's not."

The two dogs sniffed each other everywhere, bumped bodies.

One grumbled; the other sang.

"Carries a tune, does he?"

"His happy sound. You should hear him when I put music on."

"No, nothing like a good dog. I didn't ask, privacy or pass-through on the interior knobs?"

She only had to hear *privacy*. "Privacy locks from the inside?"

"Correct."

"All of them privacy."

His eyebrows quirked, but he just nodded. "I can send you home with three of those, and the exterior today. Need to order the rest. Should have them by Tuesday."

"That sounds good to me. Oh, these lamps."

They stood on the far end of the counter.

"Beauties, aren't they? Mixed wood, hand-turned bases. My grandson made them."

"Made them?"

"He took my knack with wood and tripled it. Likes to make things in his free time. I saw he was making one of these, talked him into making a set. We've got a small lighting section."

"Yes, I saw. They're for sale?"

"As soon as I get them tagged and put up."

"How about I say sold, and take them with me?"

Joe's eyebrow lifted again. "Don't you want the price?"

"I do, and I hope you're a fair man, because I really want them. No, I need them. I bought a new bed today—well, new to me—and nightstands, and these lamps need to be on those nightstands."

He studied her, nodded. "They're priced at two-fifty each, but we're going to make it four hundred for the set."

"Let me repeat. Sold. Thank you. I'm Arden," she added as she offered her hand.

"It's nice to . . . Wait a minute. That's it!" He snapped his fingers on both hands. "I knew you looked familiar. Arden Bowie. I read your books."

Pleasure had to fight its way through surprise. "Seriously?"

"I knew that face. I've seen it on the back of your books. You're prettier in person."

"Now I'm flattered all over the place."

"You tell a damn good story. Wait until I tell Gideon I met a real author. That's my grandson. It's his afternoon in the woodshop."

"Mr. Riley—"

"Joe."

"Joe, you've made my day, potentially my year."

She drove home buoyed. Not only had she crossed several items off her list—added things that weren't on it—but a complete stranger had recognized her because he read her books.

And liked them!

"How's that for a first day, Zorro? And you know what? I'm going to put my dresser in the guest room—not now, but when I find what really suits my new bed, and those lamps."

Maybe find an antique mirror to go over it. She should've looked while in the antique store.

No, no, her mind had been too crowded. Plus, she'd shopped more in one four-hour stretch than she had in any given six-month period.

Take a break, settle in a bit more, and don't get carried away.

When she pulled up to the house, she found that feeling again. The absolute pleasure. And wasn't she adding to that, selecting pieces specifically for this place, this time of her life?

"Give me time to haul all this inside, put it out, or stow it. Then, my very good boy, you can run around the back as long as you like. While I have a nice glass of wine on the back deck."

While Arden sat on the deck, enjoying birdsong and wine, Dustin sat in his room.

He'd come to appreciate the shithole of a room. There, at least, he didn't have to play the game, didn't have to answer questions, come up with sympathetic remarks for the losers in his talk therapy sessions.

He'd had a full day, too. Slop for breakfast, his work detail—frigging laundry—his session with the asshole shrink, slop for lunch, a visit from dear old Mom, the group-talk bullshit, the hour of outside time (hard-earned), slop for dinner. Common-area time, twice daily.

He hated that, having to tolerate the assholes locked up with him, pretend to be friendly, play stupid games.

Now, in for the night, but before lights-out, he could relax.

He'd been sure, so sure, he'd score early release. He'd taken all the steps, earned the label he knew some of the idiots who ran the place termed a model prisoner.

Or patient, if they knew someone could hear.

But the deal was stone. Five years, not a day less.

He liked sitting in his room, lying on his cot, planning what he'd do to make the lawyer, the judge, all of them pay for stealing five years of his life.

He was thirty now, for God's sake. He'd spent his thirtieth birthday locked up in a loony bin with a bunch of losers, crazies, and assholes.

And what had his mother done? She'd brought him cupcakes. Fucking cupcakes.

They'd taken the last years of his twenties, and he could never get them back. He vowed his thirties would be his decade.

He'd take whatever he wanted, however he wanted. He'd punish everyone who'd stolen from him.

His father had taught him not to get mad, but to get even.

The son of a bitch hadn't visited him, not even once in nearly five years, but he'd always had solid advice.

Getting mad meant making mistakes. He understood that now.

So he'd control his temper. Jesus, he'd had enough practice the last four years. He'd control himself, and he'd get even.

He imagined a big target, all those rings with the bull's-eye, and one by one, put an image of those who needed to pay over it.

One by one, he obliterated them. He listened to their screams, to their pleas. It actually calmed him to see it, feel it, hear it. The nightly ritual not only soothed him, it reminded him he remained in control.

They couldn't see inside his head. They only saw what he let them see.

Then last, always the last step in the nightly ritual, he put Arden's image over the target. She, the most important, the target of his affection. She, the woman he'd chosen to love, honor, obey, and serve him. Until death.

He'd need to punish her, for her own good. For a time, once they got to the cabin, he'd need to keep her locked up. Let her know how it felt to be locked up.

He imagined he'd need to keep her on a leash, or in shackles after that. Until she learned her lesson. Until he was sure she'd learned her place.

He'd take care of her, of course. Provide her with a home, with food, with clothes.

Then it would be just the way it had been in the dream he'd had the first night in this shithole.

He'd provide, she'd be grateful.

And they'd be happy.

Since he knew the time was coming, he picked up his book. He wasn't allowed any of Arden's, so he chose books set in various areas of the country to help him select where they'd live.

He opened it at random, just before the guard glanced in the little window in the door.

"Lights out," he called.

Dustin smiled, nodded, set the book aside.

He lay down on his bunk. And when the lights went out, thought that when he had Arden, when he needed to lock her up, he'd keep the room dark.

So she'd know just how it felt.

Chapter Ten

While Arden worked out, she studied the unfinished walls and imagined. The glass doors of the walkout brought in good natural light and that was a plus.

But she'd rather have French doors than the current sliders. Replacement could go on the consideration list.

Either way, she could easily make this entire level into an attractive, livable, multifunctional space.

Storage, yes, home gym, absolutely. Update the very basic bathroom, definitely. The rest could turn into a secondary living space. Add a gas fireplace, a whopping big-screen TV, cozy, comfortable furniture.

An antique bar!

But when would she ever use it?

If she turned it into a family room, where was the family?

Though she wanted it, from where she stood now, she didn't see marriage and kids in her future. She wouldn't cross them off the Maybe Someday list, but she couldn't visualize them.

She liked men, but had never met one who'd pulled at her heart and mind and libido. Without that pull on all three, why make promises to another person?

Just dating had so many complications. Then sex added still more.

She liked sex. One of the reasons she'd slept with Michael, a very nice man, had been to prove to herself after a long abstinence that she could enjoy healthy sex.

And she had.

But she was fine with abstinence, and could certainly take care of her own needs when necessary.

Maybe she had a yearning for children, but she could and would be content to be the doting aunt, the fun aunt. Not everyone was wired for marriage and kids.

And how, she wondered, had thoughts of how to finish her basement turned into an internal debate on her single status?

Enough of that.

She spent the rest of the morning doing what she liked best: writing.

At Zorro's bark, she looked up. Though she had the windows open, she barely heard the truck pull in. But she saw the logo on the side, did a quick chair dance.

"Oh boy, oh boy!"

She didn't mind losing track of time when it meant new bed delivery.

Shirl's husband and son carried the headboard, footboard, and bed frame upstairs, while she went down to get them some drinks.

By the time she got back, they'd hauled her mattress and box springs into the guest room. They started on the bed frame and headboard as Zorro looked on.

"You've got a good solid bed here," Bob commented.

"Yes, but I'm about to have a better one."

She wanted to hover, but made herself give them room as they carted and carried.

"Nice house." Luke—she gauged him at roughly twenty—glanced around as he carried a nightstand up the steps. "Just you?"

"No." Arden laid a hand on Zorro's head, and left it at that.

Should she tip them? She'd never bought a flea market bed before, and didn't know the protocol.

She decided to err on the side of generosity, and got no argument when she did.

Even as she let them out, a van pulled in.

"Looks like the rest of the bed's here." Bob nodded.

So once again, Arden had the thrill of watching a couple of guys muscle her mattress and box springs up the stairs, and put them in place.

Once they left, she made up the guest room first, then put her new, freshly laundered sheets on the new bed, fluffed out the duvet, added the pillows, immediately deciding she'd look for accent pillows and a cozy throw.

She placed Burnie, then went to get the lamps she'd stored in her closet. Added a candle—Lavender Mist—from April's craft shop.

Hands clasped, she studied the result.

"Oh, good choice. Right choice. I love it! I'm seriously in love with it."

So saying, she dived onto the bed.

"So much room! I could have sections. One side for reading, the other side for laptop streaming, and the middle."

She spread out like a starfish while Zorro put his head on the side of the bed and watched her.

"I'm happy here," she murmured. "It hasn't been a week, but I don't feel out of place. I feel in place."

She sat up, hugged herself. Then frowned at the doorknob on her closet. "Absolutely wrong, especially with this new look."

She got her tool kit, the knobs Joe Riley had had in stock, and set to work.

Zorro sat beside her, watching, and occasionally muttering in his throat as if offering advice.

Twenty minutes later, she admitted failure.

"I could probably look up how to do it on YouTube, but Zoey can figure it out."

Instead, she went back to her office to do what she did best.

By Sunday, she had her new/old sideboard and so-far-empty china cabinet in place. And bearing gifts, she set out for Zoey's.

On the way, she gave Zorro a refresher.

"You haven't seen the girls since Christmas. You need to be on your best behavior."

She translated his look as: *Please. As if I wouldn't be.*

Still relying on her GPS, she drove deeper into the valley, skirting the river, and into the leafy neighborhood with its big homes, manicured lawns, tidy playground where her cousin made her home.

The house had a massive garage and multiple decks that perfectly suited Zoey, Boone, and their family. As did that leafy neighborhood with bikes, tricycles, playhouses in backyards.

Arden pulled around the circular drive with its island of flowers and shrubs.

By the time she gathered up the gifts, started to herd her dog, the door opened.

Boone, handsome as ever, stepped out. He had the just-turned-three Lexy riding on his back. The girl had her father's coloring, his same wide grin.

And to Arden's melting heart, her maternal grandmother's eyes. Jen's eyes.

Arden's father's eyes.

Lexy squealed and bounced. "Hi, hi, hi!"

"Hi, hi, hi, back!"

"Doggie!"

When she wiggled, Boone slid her down. "Be gentle."

"Doggie," Lexy said again, and Zorro wagged right into the hug.

"I want a hug, too."

"Let me give you a hand. You came loaded."

"I did." Arden handed him both big bags, then scooped up the girl. "Do you remember me?"

"Aunt Arden. Has doggie."

"That's right." Technically first-cousin-once-removed Arden, but they'd gone with the simple and easy.

"My turn." Boone set down the bags to wrap arms around both Arden and Lexy.

"Looking good," he told her. "Settling in?"

"Settled. And thanks for the internet, and all the rest."

"No problem. We're crazy happy you're here. Come on back. Zoey's in the kitchen."

"I thought you were top chef around here."

"I am, but she decided to bake."

"Uh-oh."

"Actually, I think she's got this."

They walked through the foyer, the living room, past home offices. On the other side of the house, Arden knew, they had a first-floor guest suite where grandparents generally stayed on visits.

The finished basement, definitely a family room, had another guest suite. Often hers. But she wouldn't need it now.

Everything opened then to the chef's kitchen with its acres of white cabinets, the huge island with its black-grained white waterfall countertop. A dining room ranged on one side, a family lounge on the other. Since the day was fine, they had the accordion doors open to the patio and the grounds beyond with its playhouse, swing set, pretty garden.

Zoey stood at the counter, arranging a variety of berries on a two-layer cake thickly filled and topped with whipped cream. Maddy, at sixteen months, sat in a high chair, banging with a spoon and hooting.

Considering it music, Zorro added his song and had the toddler adding giggles.

Maddy had inherited her father's dark, springy hair, his eyes, but the rest of that adorable heart-shaped face was all Zoey.

She grinned at Arden, then waved her spoon in the air before banging it.

"I'm going to free Maddy in a second and get me some kisses. But first I have to say wow."

With a satisfied nod, Zoey placed another berry. "I know, right? I impress myself. Sure, it's a box cake, and the rest is mostly whipped cream and berries, but it doesn't fail."

Zoey angled her head. "And look at you. You did your hair."

Arden fluffed at the long, loose waves. "I also impress myself. Now, come to Aunt Arden, you little cutie."

And if holding that delicious bundle brought on a yearning, she could deal with it.

"How about some wine?" Boone asked her.

"Yes, please. And." She set Maddy on her hip, looked at Lexy. "How about some presents?"

"Presents!"

"Yours is in that bag there."

Diving to it, Lexy yanked out tissue paper, then squealed.

"Horsie!"

"I bought her from a cowgirl in Wyoming. Give her a big squeeze."

As a doting aunt, she knew Lexy had a zoo of stuffed animals, and favored pink. When the girl squeezed the horse, it let out a long, loud *Neigh.*

Zorro immediately backed away.

"Of course," Zoey muttered, and rolled her eyes at Arden. "What do you say, Lexy?"

"Thank you! Love horsie." And made it neigh again.

When Maddy tried to reach down for the horse, Arden shifted her. "You've got something else."

Arden set another bag on the counter. "What could be in here? Let's find out."

She helped the toddler pull out tissue paper, discouraged her from eating it by taking out a colorful box. "Let's open this up."

Once she had, she set the equally colorful cube on the floor with Maddy, crouched down.

"Do you like music? I listened to music for thousands of miles. Now you can make it."

Taking the girl's hand, Arden pressed a blue button with an icon of a guitar. The cube let out a riff that had Zorro retreating again, and Maddy laughing.

"More!"

"One of her favorite words."

Arden showed her how to press another. A drum beat enthusiastically.

"You did this on purpose. Noisy toys."

"Absolutely." Arden tossed back her hair as she smiled up at Zoey. "It's my duty as a doting aunt. I didn't forget Mom and Dad."

Boone opened a stand holding a diamond-shaped slice of orange calcite.

"For your collection."

"This is a beautiful piece, Arden."

"I stumbled on a little rock shop in Idaho."

"And this." Zoey held up a streaming suncatcher of glass stars. "Is gorgeous."

"Nevada desert. Who knew? I had to stop myself from doing all my Christmas shopping in July, but I did a chunk of it."

"Thank you." Zoey hugged her. "But don't think you're getting out of shopping with me. Next Saturday. We're going to work on making your wardrobe worthy of that closet. No argument," she added. "You've already shopped without me for a bed and dining room furniture."

"And I love all of it."

"I'll see for myself when I pick you up on Saturday." Zoey glanced down to where Maddy made music and Lexy squeezed her pink horse. "And you owe me."

They ended dinner with cake—which didn't disappoint—and a family video call. Travis and April sat on their deck, views of the Pacific at their back, with Jonah, the oldest, on his father's lap, and Trent, busy at almost two, on and off his mother's.

"That ocean view." Jen pressed a hand to her heart. "I'll never get used to it. And Zoey, your garden's beautiful."

"I'm still surprised how much working in it relaxes me."

"We need a family chat from your place, Arden," Doug told her.

"That's a promise. I may not be able to whip up a meal like Boone, but I can manage."

"And you're all having a gorgeous day. It's pouring rain here."

Travis pointed at the screen. "Come west, young man and woman."

Smiling, Jen took Doug's hand. "Eighteen months."

"Really?" Zoey pressed her hands to her cheeks. "Really, really?"

"We worked it out," Doug said. "Eighteen months is pushing it, but doable."

"May I point out, again, the view of the mighty Pacific." April flowed her arm back.

"Hey, hey!" Zoey narrowed her eyes. "Oregon has that, too. And your choice of mountain ranges. Add wine."

"We don't know which state, but"—Jen held up a finger—"we're aiming for something between all of you."

"Zoey and Boone already have Arden," Travis pointed out.

"Don't put me in the middle."

"The middle-ish is what we're hoping for. We'll figure it out." Jen leaned her head on Doug's shoulder.

Arden put finding the right location on her list.

She made more lists, and one to start on the next week.

She wanted that throw, those pretty pillows for the bed. And even with the larger bed, the room could use a chair or bench or something.

And if she had a china cabinet, she needed to find some interesting things to put in it. Not all at once. That way lay madness.

She didn't think she could brave the flea market again so soon. But she could handle downtown.

She opened a bank account, tried a couple of gift shops. She found a dragon carved in carnelian. Though she knew Boone would love it, she loved it, too.

It would go in her china cabinet.

She fell in love with a wooden bowl, saw it on her sideboard. Then learned she'd picked up another piece of Joe Riley's grandson's work.

In the gallery Zoey'd recommended, she fell for a painting by a local artist. All the dreamy greens of the thick forest, the quiet tones of the stream, the subtle light and shadows would be another calming touch for her bedroom.

She loaded the car and promised herself she'd take a month off from buying things she wanted but didn't need.

She did, however, need her doorknobs, so she put Zorro on the leash and walked to the hardware store.

Joe stood behind the counter again and sent her a smile.

"Afternoon. I was about to give Elvis a treat." When he said the word, Zorro plopped down to sit. "Somebody's got somebody trained."

"I'm not sure which of us, but he'd love one."

Joe passed them out. "Show Zorro where you have your snack."

Elvis led the way behind the long counter.

"I've got your doorknobs in the back. You've got a load of them. Where are you parked?"

"Oh, just a half block down. I can carry them. I'm stronger than I look."

"That may be, but Gideon'll take them down for you. Have you got someone to switch them out for you?"

"No. Yes. Maybe. I tried and failed, but my cousin's pretty handy. I can ask her."

"Good customer service has kept me in business for forty-seven years. My grandson—here he comes."

"Pop, I've got . . ." He broke off when he saw Arden. "Sorry."

Arden's first thought was it shouldn't be legal for a human being to be that good-looking. He had his grandfather's height—maybe an inch more—and lanky build. From the black streaks in Joe's hair, she imagined the older man had once had the same thick black mane, though the younger's waved a bit.

He had the same cat-green eyes, sharper features, with cheekbones that looked like they could slice an apple.

She and her teenage friends would have deemed him smoking.

"Gideon, this is Arden Bowie. The writer I told you about."

"Right. Doorknobs."

"Yes. I . . . just bought one of your bowls."

When he frowned a little, Joe chuckled.

"Vickie over at Valley Gifts nagged him into putting a couple of his pieces in there."

"It's beautiful."

"Thanks. I'll get your hardware."

"You do that, Gideon, and go on over and install them for her."

"Oh, I couldn't ask you to—"

"Save your breath," Gideon advised. "He looks easygoing. It's a mirage. I need an address."

Joe reeled it off before Arden could try another protest.

"Meet you there," he said, and walked into the back.

"He's good with his hands," Joe said. "Puts time in the store because he thinks I need the help. Was a cop down in LA. A detective."

"Oh."

"Well, things happened," he said simply, vaguely. "And when my wife passed near to two years back, I guess I did need the help."

"I'm sorry. It's so hard to lose someone we love."

Joe's eyes softened, shifted to hers. "You say that like you know it."

"I do."

"He'll like changing out doorknobs more than checking stock or mixing up paint. You're doing me a favor."

"That's sneaky."

He grinned. "Sneaky works. But it's true enough. You come visit anytime, and not just when you need hardware. Elvis likes the company."

"You can count on it."

She walked Zorro back to the car.

Now she'd have Mr. Smoking Hot installing doorknobs all over her house. Upside? Doorknobs.

She couldn't really find a downside. She couldn't imagine a grandson of Joe Riley's as less than trustworthy. Add former police detective who'd come to help his grandfather when he needed it.

True, she'd felt a flutter in her belly and a tingle through her body she hadn't felt in a very long time. But she considered that a good thing.

She might spend her life as the doting aunt, but she could still appreciate a seriously attractive man.

He beat her to the house, so she got out of the car quickly.

He drove a big, burly pickup. He looked like a man who could drive a big, burly pickup. Or a sleek, curve-hugging sports car. Or an eat-my-dust motorcycle.

"Sorry. I know Joe put you on the spot."

"Not the first time."

Zorro leaped out of the car and bounded over to the new human.

And Arden saw that sharp-featured face could soften with a smile.

"Hey there. You're a handsome bastard, aren't you?"

In agreement, and as if to return the compliment, Zorro leaned against Gideon's legs, looked up at him with desperate love.

He gave the dog a fast, full-body rub that had Zorro crooning in his throat, then singing full out.

"Listen to you."

"He sings when he's happy. Well, especially happy, because he's always happy."

"I hear that. Got a name?"

"He does. He's Zorro."

"Sure he is."

"I'll let you in. You can start anywhere. I just have a few things to get out of the car."

"One of the exterior locksets on the front door?"

"Yeah, and the other on the side, the mudroom, and the third off the kitchen to the back deck."

When she unlocked the front door, Zorro bounded in.

"Anywhere there's a standard brass knob, it gets switched out."

Zorro bounded back with his tug rope. Shaking his head, he danced in front of Gideon.

"We'll get to that." But he gave the rope a couple of tugs. "I'll get my tools, start at the front."

He went to his pickup, Arden to her SUV, and Zorro paced back and forth between them.

Gideon glanced over, saw the load in her cargo area.

"A few things?"

"Well. I just moved in last week, and my house was smaller than this one, so . . ."

"Right. I'll give you a hand."

Together they carted in boxes, bags, the wrapped painting. And the leather pig she intended for the library.

"You bought a pig."

"Footstool. For the library. When I make the library. Ah, can I get you something? Coffee? Pepsi?"

"Maybe later." With that, he went out for his tools.

Arden hooked the bag holding her new pillows and throw over her shoulder, and managed to carry that and the painting upstairs.

By the time she took a painting down, put the new one in its place, arranged the pillows, the throw, studied, fussed, approved, then set the other painting in the guest room for future hanging, she found he'd replaced the front door lockset and had started on the coat closet.

"It's better, isn't it? That finish and style."

"Yeah."

"Okay, good. You get to the lower level through the kitchen. It's unfinished down there, but it has a few doors. Just shout out if you need anything."

"Got it."

When she walked off, and the dog trailed behind her, Gideon considered the fact that he was installing a privacy lock on a closet.

He knew his pop, and Joe would've explained about pass-throughs. So why, he wondered, did anybody want privacy knobs on closets?

Not his business, he reminded himself, but he was curious. Puzzles, questions without easy answers, secrets, they always pulled at him.

He'd been a cop for nearly ten years, so training and instinct pushed him to look under the surface, read signs, read people.

Take the closet. One winter coat, two insulated vests, one dressier coat—maybe cashmere—hung on one side. Two hoodies, a leather jacket, given her height would hit her mid-thigh, a lightweight jacket hung on the other side.

Nothing flashy.

Winter boots—two pair—hikers, obviously new, stored in clear boxes. As were a few scarves, winter caps, and gloves.

Maybe she hadn't had time to get messy, but considering the closet and what he could see of the rest of the house, she struck him as a woman who liked order, leaned toward the practical.

She didn't lack style—she was right about the damn doorknobs—but she kept it low-key.

As he worked, moving on to a bedroom—what he pegged as a guest room suite—he passed the time analyzing her.

Guest room because why buy a two-and-a-half-story house, then live on one floor? And it didn't feel lived-in. Welcoming enough, he supposed, but not used.

No, there'd be another main suite upstairs, and that would be hers.

When he changed out the closet knobs—empty closet but for spare pillows and a neatly folded blanket—he nodded in satisfaction.

Guest room. He liked figuring out the hows and whys.

And Christ, he missed being a cop when figuring out the hows and whys mattered, made a difference. Almost two years now, and he still missed it.

He didn't think about it every day, couldn't let himself, but he still missed it.

Instead of doing what he believed mattered, he'd spend a couple hours—probably more—changing out doorknobs.

That's how his life ran now, and no point bitching about it.

So he put it aside as he worked his way through the main level.

Obviously, the room with stacks of boxes clearly marked BOOKS—add the leather pig—she intended for that library.

Needed a deeper paint color, bookcases, furniture, and, to seal the deal, a fireplace.

As he worked his way through, he decided he liked the house. Great layout, excellent views. And he couldn't fault her taste.

Maybe it struck him as odd to see his bowl on her dining room sideboard—but it always struck him as odd to see something he'd made in someone else's space. And he couldn't figure out why she had an orange glass dragon as the only piece in the cabinet.

But the furniture, the space, and the use of it got top marks.

The dog came back to him as he finished the exterior mudroom door. And this time dropped a ball beside him.

"Can't play now, pal." But he gave Zorro's head a rub.

When he walked back into the kitchen from the mudroom, Arden came in from the other direction.

"Sorry. If he's bothering you—"

"He isn't."

"It's a lot of doorknobs." She smiled at him. "Do you want a break? A cold drink, coffee?"

"I wouldn't mind coffee. Black coffee, if that won't insult your fancy machine."

"It lives to serve. And you get to be the first black coffee it's served in this house." She took a white mug out of her perfectly organized cabinet.

"This is taking up a lot of your day. I could make you a sandwich."

Amused, he studied her while the machine ground beans. "What kind of sandwich?"

"Oh, well, I've got deli turkey, ham, salami. Swiss, pepper jack, and provolone cheese, arugula, sprouts, radicchio."

Fully entertained, he slid a hand into his pocket. "No peanut butter and jelly?"

"I've got the jelly. Not a fan of peanut butter."

"Maybe next time. What do you want to do with the old knobs?"

"I hadn't thought about it." Her bottom lip poked out a little. "I shouldn't just toss them. Recycle? Maybe someone could use them?"

"I can take them back. Pop will know someone or someones. What do you want for them?"

"Oh, nothing. Really. I'm happy not to have to figure it out."

"Okay. I'm going to head downstairs. Your boy wants to play ball."

"Yeah. I'm going to take him out."

BOOKS

PART TWO

Healing

What wound did ever heal but by degrees?

—William Shakespeare

Chapter Eleven

When he got downstairs, Gideon realized he shouldn't have been surprised by her gym equipment. Top-of-the-line weight bench, elliptical, the rack of dumbbells, the kettlebells, medicine balls.

Tall, slim, long-limbed, but he'd noted those long arms had tone.

The space needed sections, and a fireplace. And a big-ass flat-screen. The bathroom, unlike the rest of the house? Stuck at builder grade.

But she had plenty of light, and a nice lead out to a patio.

He could see her there with the dog. Throwing the ball with those long, toned arms. And the dog racing after it, rounding back to drop it at her feet.

He watched while she pointed, and the dog ran out. She winged it—good arm—high and long. The big Lab followed the ball—an outfielder ready to make the out.

He leaped, snagged it in midair. And the side retires, he thought as Arden applauded.

She—or someone—had trained the dog well. He figured she had. He recognized a bond when he saw one.

He had a soft spot for a good dog. The demands of the job and the small house, smaller yard, in LA hadn't allowed for one.

She'd switched to a Frisbee as he started back up to the third floor.

Upstairs, he took care of an empty room, door, closet, the hall bath. Then came to her office and wondered how anyone got work done facing that view. Another good space, but the stark white of the built-in cabinets jarred with her setup.

He'd have gone dark and moody, but it wasn't his house.

Her desk didn't offer much of a clue as to what she worked on, and he admitted to curiosity on that.

A good desk, good high-backed swivel chair, the computer, a big chunk of some sort of stone with waves of blues and greens, a touch of purple.

A spiral notebook—closed—a file folder, also closed. A blank notepad, a green pottery cup holding pens and pencils.

Between his mother and father, he'd grown up in houses with staff. Cooks, housekeepers, groundskeepers.

As far as he'd seen, they had nothing on Arden Bowie as far as keeping a home clean, tidy, and organized.

He did another bedroom—still in progress by the lack of a dresser, the painting leaning against the wall.

When he walked into the primary bedroom, he nodded.

Yes, her space. The interesting bed—simple but not staid. The obligatory heaps of pillows.

He could hear his grandfather.

Jesus, Colleen, what's the point of all these damn fussy pillows?

They're soft and pretty, Joe. A bedroom needs the soft and pretty.

You're soft and pretty enough for me!

Nearly two years now, Gideon thought, she'd been gone nearly two years. And every night, his grandfather took all those pillows off the bed. And every morning, he put them back on again, just as she had.

That was love. Deep, enduring, real.

He got that odd sensation when he saw his lamps. He didn't make things to sell things. He made them because he could, because he liked working with wood. He liked the process, the feel, the challenge.

But he couldn't deny they really worked with the bed, the nightstands.

He figured the dresser belonged in the in-progress guest room, but that was her choice.

The tall, gooseneck lamp in the corner added, he supposed, a touch of Bohemian. And it worked.

Needed a chair. Two would be better, with the lamp between and just behind.

Though he'd seen the outerwear in the coat closet downstairs, the walk-in surprised him. He'd expected big. He hadn't expected her clothes to not fill even a quarter of it.

He'd never known a woman unable to fill a closet, regardless of size.

He'd investigated a murder where the victim's wife had a closet nearly as big dedicated to shoes and bags alone.

Give her time, he decided.

When he finished the last knob, he went down, loaded up his tools, loaded up the boxes of old knobs, then went back in to tell her he was finished.

Finally.

He found her in the kitchen, at the island, doing something on a tablet while the dog lay comatose at her feet.

She rose.

"I got your keys, front, side, and back, and the tool to unlock the interiors. You know how those work?"

"Sure. The little thing you stick in the tiny hole and wiggle."

"Yeah, close enough." He set them on the counter. "You missed some knobs."

"I . . . Damn it, I counted three times."

"Linen closet pulls, lower bath, built-in pulls, your office. If you want consistency, and it feels like you do."

"Oh. Whew! I'm leaving the downstairs until I decide how I want to finish it, and I want to have the office built-ins painted. That white's just too bright. I'll figure out the knobs when I figure out the paint.

"Do you know somebody for painting, who knows what they're doing, and won't take weeks to do that job?"

"Not me."

She smiled at him; he watched her lips curve.

"Understood."

"Yeah, actually. My grandfather will send you the contact."

"Great. That's next on my list. I've been ignoring that blinding white, but it's all kinds of wrong. Right for a playroom, but wrong for my space.

"I really appreciate all this. I know it took a big chunk out of your day." She reached in her pocket, pulled out folded bills.

He said, "No."

She looked a little pained, a little uneasy. Then her eyes—a deep true blue—held steady on his.

"I have Oreos."

"What kind?"

"Double Stuf."

"I'll take them."

"They're fresh," she said as she walked around the island to open the fridge. "I've only had two." She handed him the package. "Thank you."

"No problem."

She walked him out, and he heard the lock snap when she closed the door behind him.

He thought he had a good handle on her now, though no doubt, more lurked under the surface.

Take the photos—a number of framed photos throughout the house. Most with the same group, or individuals from that group. Some with other women. A few of a couple—tall man with reddish hair, a pretty blond woman with those deep blue eyes.

He'd pegged them as her parents even before he'd seen another of them with the gangly redheaded teenager Arden had been.

But not a single photo of her with a man who wasn't part of that group. Which told him no serious relationship at this time.

Which didn't matter. She wasn't his type.

He liked her house, he liked her dog, and he supposed on such short acquaintance he liked her well enough.

He checked the time, saw that his grandfather would close up shop within a half hour. No point in driving back, so he'd head home, put something together for dinner.

Since they were right there, he pulled out a cookie while he considered. Whatever he tossed together wouldn't include radicchio and sprouts.

Maybe fry up some potatoes, toss some burgers on the grill. And because the spirit of Colleen Cullen Riley would haunt them both otherwise, he'd add some sort of vegetable.

He and his grandfather tended to trade off cooking detail, or they'd grab something in town, maybe bring home takeout. They shared cleaning and laundry duties, but that didn't amount to much, as they had Janey come in every other week to do the serious stuff.

Though he'd initially come to Riverbend because Pop had needed him, and his career in LA was over, he'd found contentment.

He missed the work, no question, but he didn't miss LA. Not anymore.

He turned toward home and the little farmhouse where he'd often spent a week or two, sometimes longer in the summer, as a boy. He'd liked feeding the chickens—still did—and didn't mind working the vegetable garden.

As far as actual farming, that had been all of it.

His great-grandfather had had the working farm, but had sold most of the land long before Gideon was born.

Now vineyards, other houses, a horse farm surrounded the house and the two acres remaining. And that suited them all.

Joe Riley hadn't wanted to farm. He'd liked building things, working with wood, and had converted the barn that remained into a workshop, again before Gideon was born.

But Joe, a born shop owner, craved his own. He liked people, liked helping them figure out or find what they wanted. He needed the interactions, the conversations, not the solitude.

Gideon pulled up to the house on the gentle hill with its working blue shutters against walls of butter yellow.

A little sunshine, his grandmother had claimed, through rainy winters.

He skirted the house to deal with the chickens first, found himself, as always, amused by the chicken palace he and his grandfather had built for the six spoiled hens.

On the ground level, they squawked in greeting when they saw him. A ramp led them up to the actual house—with a window and a tin roof.

When he'd seen to them, he walked by the—much smaller now—vegetable garden, up the couple of steps to the deck he'd helped build the summer before college, then in the back to the kitchen.

And poured himself a glass of local red.

His grandmother had pushed to have the kitchen updated about five years before. It looked like her, Gideon thought now. Warm with her favored yellow walls, the cherry cabinets Janey kept gleaming, the big farm sink and sturdy old kitchen table she wouldn't part with.

So neither would Pop.

No stainless steel appliances for Gram. She'd wanted that retro blue, and got them.

He scrubbed and prepped the potatoes, then got out his gram's old cast-iron skillet before stepping out to start the grill.

He made the patties—she'd taught him how, just as Pop had taught him how to work with wood.

He didn't start cooking until he heard his grandfather's truck. Joe would never turn a customer away, even if they lingered past closing. Or if they knocked after he put up the Closed sign.

Joe came in with Elvis, who immediately walked over to sniff at his empty food bowl.

"Good thing I didn't bring home a pizza."

"That sounds like tomorrow's dinner to me."

"You got it. All right, Elvis, I got you covered. How'd it go at Arden's place?"

"All in. I've got her old knobs in the truck. She said to pass them along to whoever needed any."

"That's good of her, and I'll see to that." After filling the dog's bowl, he picked up the wine Gideon had poured for him. "So, what's her story?"

"She's a woman who wanted new doorknobs."

"Gideon, everybody's got a story. You've been all through her house with that detective's mind of yours. That detective's mind you've had since before you could walk.

"You know her story."

Gideon stepped out to put burgers on the grill, then back to add potatoes to the hot oil. "You know, Pop, since you've got her books on your shelf, you could ask Mr. Google."

"That's messing with privacy. And half the time, more, I figure the internet's full of shit. You've got an opinion."

"She's neater than your aunt Martha, more organized than the CIA. Tight with her family—going by photos around the place. Her dog loves her, is well-trained but not regimented, and she loves him back."

"I could see that part myself."

"Seems to me she knows what she likes, and she's taking time to get it, a little bit at a time. She's got a high-end coffee machine and stocks radicchio and sprouts. She offered to make me a sandwich."

"That's a kindness. If you leave out the sprouts."

Gideon laughed, stirred potatoes. "She tried to give me a cash tip, and when I said no, she gave me a package of Oreos."

"I like that girl." Joe slipped out, flipped the burgers. "Keep going," he said through the open door.

"If you go by the furniture, she's got good taste. Nothing fussy, fancy, just good and solid. She has some serious gym equipment, wants one of the main-level rooms for a library. She could use it, as she has a bunch of boxes marked 'Books.'"

"Makes sense, given she writes them."

Gideon stuck a bowl of peas in the microwave.

"She has more on the shelf of her nightstand. Let me ask you something."

"Ask away."

"If Gram had a closet as big as your bedroom, what would she do with it?"

"Fill it up."

"Right? She hasn't. You have more clothes than she does."

"I've lived longer."

As Joe brought the burgers in, Gideon transferred potatoes to a dish lined with paper towels.

"I'd say her story is, she's a nice, dog-loving, organized woman with good taste, doesn't mind the quiet, has close ties with family, no boyfriend—nothing in the closet for that, no photos. Probably spends a lot of time at her desk—second dog bed in her office. One who probably eats healthy—smoothie maker, sprouts—but isn't afraid of Oreos. Oh, and she must like dragons."

"Dragons?"

"A stuffed one with the mountain of pillows on her bed, a glass one in a china cabinet. That's it, so far anyway, in the cabinet. So a fanciful streak in there somewhere."

"Now, see?" Joe pulled out two plates while Gideon took out the peas. "You've told me about an interesting woman, one with some layers."

"Maybe. One thing I haven't figured out."

They sat, Joe scooped fried potatoes onto his plate. And because—Gideon knew—he felt Colleen watching, took it easy with the salt.

"What's that?"

"Why would she want to be able to lock closet doors, the pantry doors, all the doors from the inside?"

Frowning, Joe added pickle chips to his burger. "I wondered about that. It seems to me, somebody who wants that thinks they might need a place to hide."

"Yeah, but from what?"

"You've got that detective's mind, Giddyup, you can find out."

Gideon just shrugged. "Not my business."

The longer Arden lived in the house, the more sure she was that she'd made the right decision.

She felt productive in the office, relaxed in the bedroom. She loved watching Zorro romp around the yard while she tried her cautious and inexperienced hand at gardening.

And wasn't that the primary goal? To be relaxed, productive, and happy in her home?

Safe, yes, important, but without the rest it just led, as she knew too well, to stagnation.

She went shopping with Zoey because her cousin wouldn't take no. She replaced the old black dress, added a few more things to her closet. Not enough, according to Zoey, but her cousin accepted it as a decent start.

Mostly, she'd just had fun.

She gave it another full week, then went back to town because she considered it more important—and more enjoyable—to outfit the house rather than herself.

She found her dresser—just rustic enough, with its dark wood and iron pulls. And the wood-framed oval mirror she'd hang horizontally hit the mark.

She found a chair—curved back, wood accents, dark-blue-and-cream pattern—and matched it with a nice little table.

And considered her bedroom all but done.

She'd nearly turned for home when she decided to hit the hardware store. Office next, she determined, and that meant paint.

This time she found Gideon at the counter while Joe helped another customer.

Elvis came over to greet her and Zorro while Gideon nodded.

"Hi. I'm going to plunge into paint."

"Sounds messy."

"I expect it will be. You can make up those little cans for sampling, right?"

"Sure. Plenty of choices on the tabs over there. Do you have something in mind?" he asked as he came around the counter.

"Probably dark green, but maybe a more middle green, or dark blue for contrast, or . . . Simple this is not, really."

She studied the intimidating tabs with their varied colors.

"Like this maybe." She pulled one out, tapped the darkest. "Or this one—a little gray in it. Or shit, this deep blue. Or no, this one here, this green has a kind of navy undertone, I think."

She took a breath, huffed it out. "I've been thinking about this since I bought the house. I should have a better handle. Three choices. That's it. I'm limiting it to three. More only leads to chaos and confusion."

"Okay."

"Not the blue. Forget the blue. I know that's wrong. This one's close to what's on the walls, so . . . no. These two, and I'm going to pick one more."

"I'll get the two mixed while you work on the third."

"Thanks."

She pondered, compared, second-guessed. Then chose another as Joe came over.

"Nice to see you again."

"You always have what I need."

"We aim to please."

"Bull's-eye so far. It's time to paint the office cabinetry, and since it is, I also need a dozen cabinet pulls, same finish as the doorknobs. I have the size."

"Then let's go fix you up."

She chose her pulls—much easier than paint. Gideon had her three samples waiting while the dogs took a nap together.

"Got the square footage of the cabinets?"

"I do. Joe said to give it to Tessa Miller—the painter—and she'd pick up what I needed."

"Got a paintbrush for the samples?"

"No. I guess I'll need one. No, three, so I can try each one fresh."

"I'll get those for you."

"Thanks."

Test them first, she decided as she waited, decide, contact painter. In that order.

When he brought over the three brushes, she took out her credit card. "Wait until I start on the library. I'll be even more of a pain in the ass."

"You're not." He flicked a glance over. "Yet. Some of the customers Pop gets are. I know the difference."

"I think it's going to be this one for the cabinets. But this one might really work for the library walls."

"Could."

She smiled. "I don't mind other opinions because I can always ignore them. Give it a shot."

"First one's too dark for the library, the third one's too . . . I guess it's bright."

"So, at this stage, our opinions match." She tapped her card on the machine. "Thanks. Let's go, Zorro."

"Come back and see us," Joe called out.

"You can count on it."

Though another customer came in, Joe walked over to Gideon.

"Did you read her book, the one I handed you the other day?"

"Not yet."

"When you do, you'll see she's not just a pretty woman with good taste in dogs and doorknobs but a smart, clever one."

Gideon knew Joe Riley and Colleen Cullen had fallen for each other when they'd still been teenagers. And that had held strong for over a half century.

Just as he knew his pop hoped Gideon would find the same.

"Maybe, but I'm not in the market. And if I were, she's not my type."

"First is your choice, but I think you're wrong about the second."

When she got home, Arden took the sample paint right up, laid down a shopping bag to protect the floor. She shook, then opened the cans and brushed each color on the cabinets.

"In this light, it's that dark green, but we'll go down, clean the brushes in the mudroom, then come up for a fresh impression. Another impression tonight, in lamplight, another in the morning, and so on."

Satisfied, she took everything down to the mudroom. When she set the brushes aside to dry, Zorro let out a bark and made a run for the front door.

She still got that clutch whenever someone she hadn't expected knocked on her door. Since it had been over four years now, she accepted she always would.

But she followed the dog and peeked outside.

A man, slim in jeans and a red polo, richly blond hair swept up and shining in the sunlight, stood with a covered dish in one hand and a little fluffy blond dog on a leash attached to a pink rhinestone collar.

He looked harmless, but so had Dustin Dubecki. Still, Dustin hadn't had a covered dish or a cute little dog. And she hadn't had Zorro.

She took a steadying breath and opened the door.

"Hi!" When he smiled, the dimples in his cheeks woke up. "I'm Jamie Stuart from right around the bend, and this is the goddess of our home, Isis. We come bearing brownies. Nick, my husband, decreed I had to wait a couple of weeks before coming over, give you time to settle in. We walked down a little while ago, but you weren't home. Then I saw your car come back, so. Here we are.

"I didn't want to leave them at the door because then you couldn't ask me in, and I really want to see what you're doing with the place. I won't stay over ten minutes. I'll set my phone alarm. I can be a chatterbox."

She had to laugh. "You don't say."

He smiled winningly. "They're excellent brownies. I followed Nick's recipe. He's a baker, professional. If you haven't stopped into Sugar, Spice, and Coffee, you're missing out."

"I haven't, but I will. I don't think I'm missing out, since I'm getting those brownies. Come in."

"Thank God, because I'm dying to . . . Oh, I love your living room furniture! Calm colors, lovely lines. I adore your big, beautiful dog."

"He's Zorro."

"The fox! Brave and true." He handed Arden the dish so he could give Zorro some love. "Oh, a singing dog."

"He is that."

"You're adorable," he told Zorro, and kissed his muzzle. "You're welcome to bring Zorro when you come to our next Sunday brunch. We're very dog friendly."

"So am I. Isis is so cute."

"Our sweet Yorkie-poo."

She lived nearly ten miles from town, Arden thought. Wouldn't it be good to know her closest neighbor?

Especially when he had a cute dog.

"I suppose you want me to share these brownies."

"I did make them with my own two hands. From this sight line I can see the kitchen. The Simpsons did a good job on the updates there. We only moved in three years ago. They were lovely neighbors. When they told us you'd bought it, and you're a writer, I got one of your books. *Rebound*. Intense! Nick's reading it now, and I'm halfway through *Whispers*. I'd have finished, but a boy has to sleep."

Okay, since she found him charming, she thought, she'd get to know him, at least a little.

"In that case, you should come back to the kitchen."

"Love to. I already like you. You'll like me, too. I'm irresistible. Oh, I adore your dining room style! Vintage. I'm all about vintage. It so completely works. And I see you have one of the God of Hot and Sexy's bowls."

"You know Gideon?"

"Not really. I may be a happily married man, but I'd be dead if my heart didn't . . ." Eyes rolling, he banged his hand against his chest. "When I see that gorgeous creature. Do you know him?"

"Not really. But he did install my doorknobs."

"Girl." The dimples just twinkled. "I hope that's a euphemism."

"No, sadly. Would you like coffee?"

"I'd love it. Your machine! Lattes?"

"My specialty. Is it all right to give Isis a—I can't say the *t* word without great expectations."

"Neither can we. She would graciously accept." Jamie took a stool at the island. "Tell me you're loving the house, the area, our adorable Riverbend."

"So far, yes to all."

"I'm so glad. And clearly you're already making the house your own."

"Little by little. The empty room—they had a home office. I'm going to make it a library."

"Perfect. A wonderful spot to curl up with a book on a rainy winter's night."

Enjoying him, she served him a brownie and his latte. "So do you work with Nick at the bakery?"

"Good lord, no. My man is up every day before dawn, and that's not for me. I don't really bake, though I do make an excellent omelet. Which you'll see for yourself at Sunday brunch. We have them once a month."

"Ah, you're a kept man."

He sighed as she took the stool beside him. "I used to dream of being a kept man. By a movie star, or a sheik. Nick's love and excellent business sense allow me to pursue my passion. I paint."

"Fine art?"

"I hope so."

"That's . . . wait. J-period-Stuart! I bought one of your paintings."

He gave her a friendly swat on the arm. "You did not."

"I did. A forest scene, moody, wonderful light and shadow. *Green Shadows*—that's it. I loved the book, but I bought it because I loved the painting."

He studied her as he sipped his latte. "I knew it was meant. We're going to be best friends."

"That slot's already taken by my cousin. Zoey and I've been besties since I was fourteen."

"I'll take the best-friend-not-also-related slot."

Studying him over the latte, Arden felt herself smile. "It happens to be open."

Chapter Twelve

The visit reminded Arden she liked having neighbors. Especially when they proved entertaining and interesting. Add in someone who'd made her laugh so much inside a half hour her sides ached, and you had a winner.

She decided she'd accept the Sunday brunch invitation and marked it on her calendar.

She took two days to decide on the paint, and opted for the deepest green—her first instinct. And yes, the other would work for the library, and be gorgeous against dark wood bookcases.

She contacted the painter, and three days later, set up a temporary office in the dining room.

Tessa Miller arrived on the dot of eight.

A petite blonde, curvy and compact, she wore white painter's pants and a black tee. She had a small hawk tattoo on her right inner forearm and a trio of studs in each ear.

"Arden Bowie?"

"Yes."

She shot out a hand. "Tessa Miller. Hey, doggie."

"Zorro. He's very friendly."

"Easy to see that. Can you show me where you want me to set up?"

"Yeah, upstairs."

When they reached the office, Tessa looked around.

"So this is where you write books, huh?"

"It is."

"Joe said I should read one—he's a big reader. I figured I might try the audio, listen while I'm driving. I need music when I work. Earbuds, so it won't bother you."

She gestured to the built-ins. "That's where you want the Dark Forest Green?"

"Yes. Everything that's white gets painted."

"Yeah, yeah." Tessa nodded as she scanned. "That's going to work in here. I'll set up."

"I'll be in the dining room. I can work there. If you need anything, or want coffee, a cold drink, just let me know."

"Bring my own, but thanks."

Arden left her to it, and within an hour had forgotten the painter painted. She'd written her main characters, and herself, into a corner, and needed to find the way out.

In writing her way out of it, she took them all down a path she hadn't planned on. She checked her notes, added a few more, then continued because the new path caught her interest.

"Sorry."

The voice made her jump. And Tessa winced.

"Double sorry. You were into it."

"Oh boy, yeah. It's okay. Heart started up again."

"I wanted to tell you the first coat's done. I'm going to take a lunch break, then come back and do the second."

"I lost track. I can make you a sandwich."

"I—really?"

"Sure. I need to let Zorro out, and I'm still keeping an eye on him when I do. I've got turkey, ham, chicken, and roast beef from the deli, provolone, mozzarella, sharp cheddar, and Swiss. Arugula, sprouts, radicchio, Boston lettuce. Mustard—Dijon or spicy—mayo and aioli."

Tessa blinked tawny hazel eyes. "Wow, you must like sandwiches."

"They're my go-to."

"I wouldn't mind one. Any of those or any combination thereof works for me. I eat anything."

"Great. Whole wheat or rye?"

"Dealer's choice."

After setting Zorro free for his run, Arden laid out ingredients.

Tessa took a counter stool. "I figured you'd be snooty."

"Oh? Why?"

"You write books." Tessa lifted her shoulders, let them fall. "I don't mind snooty as long as it pays on time. But you're not."

"I'll still pay on time. Joe tells me you're the best painter in the area."

"He's not wrong, even though he's a softie." She watched Arden build the sandwich. "That sure beats my method of slapping a couple of slices of ham and American cheese out of the wrapper between two pieces of bread."

"My father taught me making good sandwiches is an art." She cut it neatly in two, slid it across the counter. "Want a drink with that?"

"Got milk?"

"I do."

"Aren't you having one? The sandwich."

"Actually, I'm saving mine for dinner later. I'm on a roll in there, and I think it'll ride straight through that. So I'm making a smoothie."

She poured Tessa a glass of milk.

"I like your tattoo."

"My hawk. It's my husband. Hawk Miller. I took his last name because mine was Kazimieras."

"That's a mouthful."

"Tell me. Blame my Latvian ancestors. And you get tired of spelling it for people all the damn time. This is a hell of a good sandwich."

"It's one of my things."

Arden traded the sandwich makings for smoothie ingredients.

"Before you go back upstairs, would you mind looking at a room down here? I'm not ready to start in there yet, but I think I have the right paint color. I could show you, see what you think."

"Sure." Tessa took another bite of sandwich. "Do you want honesty or validation on your choice?"

"Since I want to enjoy the room, and live with it for a really long time? Honesty."

"Check. You really drink that? With avocado in it?"

"Healthy fat. Without healthy fat in my diet, I fade into a scarecrow."

"Never been my problem. I always wanted to be tall though."

"I always wanted to be petite."

Tessa grinned. "Ain't that always the case?"

When they finished, Arden got the little paint can and a brush. Then led the way to the proposed library.

"Let's see it on the wall."

"I'll just get something to put on the floor."

"No need." Tessa took the can, the brush. She pulled an opener out of her pocket. Slapped some on the wall without spilling a drop.

"Good, rich color," she said. "What's this room?"

"A library, eventually. I want dark wood bookcases."

"Okay. I see that. You want to live with it awhile, and definitely choose the wood first. But cozy and moody with a touch of class? That's a good choice.

"Who's doing the cabinetry?"

"I don't know yet. Do you know someone?"

"Have Joe talk Gideon into it."

"Oh." Arden considered, thought of her lamps, her bowl. "Does he do cabinetry, too?"

"He knows his way around wood. Easy to see you're embracing the elevated rustic in your place. Yeah, he could do it. LAPD's loss is Riverbend's gain."

"I heard he used to be a police detective."

"Yeah. He did the right thing, ended up getting kicked in the balls. Anyway, Joe could talk him into it. I've gotta get back to it. Thanks for the sandwich."

"You're welcome."

Arden took the paint and brush back to the mudroom. She gave Zorro his afternoon treat and wondered just what the right thing had been. And how did a man like Gideon Riley get kicked in the balls?

She wanted to ask, really wanted to ask. But since she knew, too well, what it felt like to have people poke and pry into your life, especially the hard parts, she let it go.

Amazed at the change two coats of paint made, Arden settled into work with a vengeance. The novel's progress, the progress in making the house her home spiked her mood high enough she invited Zoey and her family to dinner.

Sandwiches were her go-to, but she made damn good spaghetti and meatballs. And she found cooking on her gorgeous stove a pleasure.

They'd celebrate her first month in Oregon.

Through Jamie, her new, non-related best friend, she learned Nick's bakery took special orders. She tried her luck with a loaf of Italian bread and a dozen cannoli.

After working till noon, she went down to make the meatballs. While they browned, she started the sauce. Though she didn't often cook other than the quick and easy, she enjoyed it quite a bit when she cooked to share.

And her stove? A dream.

She used her mother's recipe, and the scents rising up brought her mother right there.

"That's nice," she whispered. "It's nice to remember."

The Sundays, or rainy Saturdays, when her parents had time for more than the quick and easy. Her mom making meatballs, her dad baking bread.

They'd had such a nice rhythm. Not perfect, not fairy-tale shiny. There'd been hot looks, sharp words, or simmering silences now and again. But they'd always come back to that rhythm.

As an adult who'd seen relationships come and go, including a couple of her own, she admired what they'd made together.

Two people with demanding careers, her mother a pediatrician, her dad a lawyer. But they'd never stinted on home and family. On her.

They'd loved each other and loved her. That had been the center of everything.

Though she'd lived half her life without them now, she'd always have that center.

She added the meatballs to the sauce and set it on a low simmer. After setting the kitchen to rights, she turned to her snoozing dog.

"Let's go for a ride."

He jumped up, and crooning, ran to the mudroom, then came back with his leash.

"That's my boy."

People worked in the vineyards; horses grazed in fields. A woman with a big straw hat over gray hair past her shoulders weeded her front garden. Arden saw a heron—what she thought was a heron—sail over a curve of the river, then over the cattails beyond.

Her life now, Arden thought, absurdly delighted. Her life, a short drive to town for baked goods and watching a heron's flight.

Riverbend bustled. Ten minutes out, she lived in the quiet, and here people walked the sidewalks, breezed in and out of shops, sat for lunch under awnings.

"We've got it all, Zorro."

She had to hunt for parking, and when she found a slot, turned to Zorro.

"I won't be long. Be a good boy."

She walked the two blocks briskly, and since she had the dog in the car, and sauce simmering, resisted window-shopping on the way.

She turned into the bakery, and her senses rejoiced.

It looked like a candy box with its cheery chocolate browns, candy pinks, and snowball whites.

And smelled like cookies baked in heaven.

She wondered if she could come back in her next life as a baker just to spend hours engulfed in the glorious scents.

The staff wore candy-pink shirts and chocolate-brown pants and, despite the busy, plenty of smiles.

She waited her turn at the counter, where a young blonde, pretty as one of the cupcakes, rang orders.

"Hi. I'm here to pick up an order. Arden Bowie."

"Give us one sec."

During the one sec, Arden listened to the voices. She loved overheard conversations.

I'm eating this cupcake for lunch so I get happy and don't just go back to work and tell my boss to shove it.

The way things are going, I don't see how they last the summer. She's got one foot out the door already.

She looks just like Carrie did at that age. Look at those cheeks!

"Arden."

Pulling herself back, she looked at the man—white chef's coat over broad shoulders, brown hair bundled up under a low-crowned chef's hat. He had blazing blue eyes in a rawboned, cream-colored face.

His big, wide-palmed hand reached out to take hers.

"You're Nick."

"Hello, neighbor."

"I was thinking you should've named this place Heaven, because if heaven doesn't smell like this, I don't want to go."

He grinned. "Sometimes it's my heaven, sometimes it's my hell. Either way, I'm glad you came in. Jamie's decided you're the goddess of neighbors."

"He's wonderful."

"I think so. Italian bread and cannoli. Italian night?"

"I've got spaghetti and meatballs simmering."

"Sounds good. Robin will take care of you, and I'll see you a week from Sunday."

"Looking forward."

When she turned to take her slice of heaven home, she nearly bumped into Gideon.

"Hi. Sorry."

"It's fine."

Robin the cupcake blonde's smile increased in magnitude. "Hi, Gideon. Your coffee order's coming right up."

"Thanks."

He was right here, Arden thought, and she really didn't want to take Tessa's advice and use Joe to pressure him.

While she couldn't match Robin, Arden bumped up her smile.

"Have you got a minute?"

"I'm waiting for coffee, so . . ."

"Right. When Tessa and I were talking paint colors for my library, she—"

He held up a finger, then reached for his wallet.

"One large black coffee, one large coffee with caramel cream."

Robin all but sang it.

"I'll just walk out with you."

Arden waited while he paid, picked up the take-out bag.

"Enjoy," Robin told him.

"Always do."

"I take it they make good coffee," Arden said as they walked out.

"Best in town."

"Not surprising. I met Jamie the other day—Nick the baker's husband. Turns out they're my neighbors."

"You should be able to score some free samples."

"Already have. I don't want to keep you," she added as they stood on the sidewalk. "But Tessa mentioned you when I told her about the built-ins I wanted."

He had a way, she realized, of looking at you so those green eyes seemed to drill right through your forehead and into your brain.

"That's not something I do."

"Does that mean it's something you can't or won't do, or something you don't usually do? Let me preface this by saying I'm not looking for fancy, you know, carving and curlicues or complicated. Simple, straightforward bookcases leaning toward rustic. Leaning, not obsessively rustic."

"What would be obsessively rustic?"

"Well, you know, rough wood, which you'd never be able to clean without risking blood. Cows or horses in the corners. Just good, dark wood—and I don't know what that would be. And I'm not in a rush. I can wait."

"Six months?"

She didn't bat an eye. "Sure. I plan to live there forever, so six months is small change. I want good, solid, lasting, not quick. If it's something you can't or won't, or just don't want to, maybe you can recommend someone. It's just . . ."

He waited, and the way he waited made Arden think he must've been a smart cop.

"I know your work, at least in bowls and lamps, and I feel like I know you and Joe. I'd rather, when possible, have someone I know working in my house."

He waited a long beat.

"I'll take a look."

"Really? Thanks. Now?"

"No, not now. I can come by later. Four, no, more around four-thirty."

"Great. Thanks. Even if you decide against, I appreciate you taking a look. Do you remember where—Of course you remember. See you later."

He intimidated, Arden thought as she walked back to her car. Whether he tried to or not, he just did. That steady gaze, the ridiculously good looks, and that don't-speak-unless-you-have-something-to-say manner.

Despite that, she already knew she wouldn't be nervous with him in the house. And that mattered.

She gave Zorro a treat for the ride so the scent of bread and pastries didn't tempt him to be a bad boy. And realized she might have liked a coffee with caramel cream.

She'd have to try it at home.

And at home, she checked her sauce—doing well. She tried her hand at some flower arranging with choices from her garden.

Not half bad.

She decided to pretty herself up a bit for her first dinner guests. She chose new pants—not jeans, sweats, but actual pants she'd bought on her excursion with Zoey—and paired them with a top—not a tee or sweatshirt—Zoey had already matched with it.

Coincidentally, a kind of vanilla caramel color for the pants, and Zoey—never wrong about such things—hit it with the more structured shirt that headed toward copper.

She even put on a belt, and the brown leather sneakers her cousin had nagged her into buying.

"You've gotten this far, do the rest."

Earrings—why not her good gold hoops, the twisty ones? She bumped up her running-into-town makeup, then took her hair out of its braid so it waved around her shoulders.

She studied herself, nodded, and decided, like her flower arrangement, not half bad.

Downstairs, she set the dining room table, got out the high chair she'd bought so Zoey and Boone wouldn't have to haul one over whenever they visited.

As if he knew something was up, Zorro paced back and forth with her as she worked rather than settling down with a stuffed or chew toy.

"Yes, we're having company. Which is why I'm opening this lovely bottle of wine to breathe. I'm rewarding myself with a glass after I make the salad."

As she tossed it, Zorro set off the somebody's-here alarm.

"It can't be them. It's only quarter to five. Shit! The God of Hot and Sexy."

She covered the salad, stuck it in the fridge.

He should've just said no. He knew better. But he hadn't built bookcases since he'd made them for his house in LA, and left them behind, as he hadn't wanted to drag anything with him.

He'd sold his house furnished, packed up what clothes he wanted, donated the rest. He'd loaded up his new truck and headed north.

And that had been that.

Now he actually toyed with the idea of building bookcases again. For someone else.

He could've given Arden a recommendation for someone good and trustworthy, and should have. But there'd been something about her appeal that hit a soft spot.

So here he was, walking to her door when he could've been home or headed there.

He heard the dog barking as he approached the door. She opened it before he got there.

She looked . . . different with her hair loose. A lot of hair spilling all over. He knew enough about women to know she'd played around with her eyes, deepened the color of her lips.

He hoped she hadn't done it for him. Maybe she wasn't his type, but the woman had a look, and it struck a chord.

"Thanks for coming," she said as the dog wagged up to him, around him, leaned on him, sang to him. "I honestly didn't intend to start on the library for weeks, then I tried the paint in there. And, well."

"I'll take a look."

She smelled different, too. something fresh and subtly alluring. As he stepped in, another scent curled around his senses.

Cooking.

As she started back, he saw the pot on the stovetop, wine on the island.

Probably had a date for dinner, he decided. She'd been here weeks now, so she probably had a date.

"As I told Tessa, I welcome opinions on the paint." She gestured to the brushstrokes on the wall. "Because I can always ignore them."

"Works."

"I think so, too. So I want cabinetry that plays well with that. I thought the little fireplace on that wall, but—"

"Between the windows. You can ignore the opinion, but you'd be wrong."

"I'm not wrong because I also decided that. You'd arrange the chairs so you'd see the fire, and the outdoors. I actually sketched it out. I can't draw, but . . ."

She took a sheet of paper off a box, handed it to him.

He studied it. "No, you can't draw."

"True, but still, ouch."

"I get the drift. Floor to ceiling along the three walls, and under the window casing there and there."

He looked over, sized her up. "You're tall enough you could reach the top shelves."

"I am, but I'm thinking I might get a library ladder, because cool."

"A lot of bookshelves."

She spread her hands and pointed to the boxes. "I have a lot of books."

"I can see that."

"And I'm not done there yet. I'll mix in some family photos and things, but mostly books."

"Adjustable shelves?"

"Yes, please. Oh, and I want to outline the cabinets—well, outline the inside of the cabinets—with those lights. The tape lights? My uncle can do that at some point. Or my cousin Zoey. They're really handy. I'm not."

"I'll keep that in mind. Plywood or solid?"

"Solid, absolutely."

He gave her a look. "What's your budget?"

"I haven't decided."

He sighed. "You need a budget. How would you know if I gouge you?"

"Joe would scold you."

He shook his head, but his lips curved.

"Not cherry because I'm damned if I'm putting a dark stain on cherry. Maple's a choice. Oak's better. Oak with a dark but transparent stain."

"Transparent because?"

"The grain comes through. Leans rustic, plus more character."

"I'm after all that."

"The books are the showpiece, the cases the frame. But the frame matters."

"It does. What's my budget?"

If you looked close enough, you could see tiny amber flecks in her eyes, he noted. They shimmered some when she smiled.

"I need to measure."

"Oh, I did that. They're right on the drawing."

He just looked at her.

"And you want to measure yourself because how would you know if I measure correctly? I'll get out of your way while you do that. I'll be in the kitchen when you're done, or if you need anything. Do you want coffee?"

"No, I'm good."

When she left, he stood a moment. It would be a really nice room, character, atmosphere. As long as she didn't frill it up. He hadn't seen any indication she went for the frills.

He got out his measuring tape.

It took him nearly a half hour, and when he walked into the kitchen, she stood stirring something in the pot that made his stomach yearn while she held a glass of wine in her other hand.

She glanced over, jolted, and actually lost some color.

"Sorry."

"You're quiet." She cleared her throat. "You just startled me. Spaghetti and meatballs." The words tumbled out of her. "I'm having some of my family over for dinner."

The high chair in the dining room told him one of the guests wouldn't drink a glass of Chianti.

She drank some now, breathed out.

"Would you like a glass?"

"I'm driving."

"Right."

"Half a glass." He had a fondness for that label. And, he couldn't help it, he wanted to give her a minute to settle down.

When she got the glass, her hand shook, just a little, so he picked up the bottle and poured the half glass himself.

"I've got a rough estimate. Rough," he repeated. "For the oak. I'll work up a firm one, but this'll give you the range."

When he gave her a cost, her bottom lip poked out. Not a pout, he knew. She'd done the same when looking at paint samples.

Thinking. Considering.

"That's fair. I'm not as naive about this as you think. My uncle did two really lovely built-ins for their family room a few years ago, so I know what the materials cost. Add labor and the order of magnitude, that seems fair."

She'd settled, even relaxed again. He could see it in her smile.

"And obviously, I believe in paying the artist."

"Craftsman."

"It really is the same thing. I've never understood why they make it two divisions. But I—"

She broke off when the dog barked and raced.

"Hold that thought."

Before he could just say they'd talk details later, she was off and running.

Like a damn gazelle.

Chaos poured in. It came in the form of a man with a kid on his hip, and a woman with a toddler on hers. The kids squealed, bounced. The older one pushed and wiggled her way down to fall on the dog like a brave soldier on a grenade.

It seemed apt, as everyone hugged as if they'd been to war.

"Everything looks great," the man said. "And wow, something smells amazing."

Arden grabbed the toddler, who planted a sloppy kiss on her aunt's—he guessed—laughing mouth.

"It's her newest thing," the woman said. "I hope you're inoculated.

Day care's a miasma of germs. We need to give Boone the tour, plus I want to see . . ."

She trailed off as she spotted Gideon. And smiled. "Well, hello there."

"Come on back, come on back." Arden and the toddler led the way. "This is Gideon, who in a few months will see I have the library of my dreams. Gideon, this is my cousin Zoey, her husband, Boone, and their undeniably adorable daughters, Lexy and Maddy."

As if to prove how adorable, Maddy pitched herself forward. Good reflexes had Gideon catching her one-armed. At which time she planted the next sloppy kiss on him.

Zoey let out a peal of laughter. "Sorry, she has no boundaries."

"It's okay. Nice to meet you, too."

When Lexy deserted the dog long enough to try to climb up Gideon's leg, Boone snatched her up.

"I'll get out of your way."

"No, finish your wine," Arden insisted.

"So you're a carpenter."

Gideon glanced at Zoey as she relieved him of Maddy.

"Sometimes."

"Gideon's Joe Riley's grandson. Riley's Hardware."

"Sure, I thought I'd seen you before. I was in there several months ago," Boone told him. "If you can't find what you need at Riley's, Joe'll find it for you."

"Who's driving?"

Zoey held up a fist. Gideon watched them do rock, paper, scissors with Zoey's rock crushing her husband's scissors.

"Woo. More wine for me. So you grew up in Riverbend, Gideon?"

"No, LA mostly. Thanks for the wine."

"You're welcome to stay for dinner."

"Pop's expecting me. With takeout." Though now he actively craved spaghetti and meatballs.

"Just one thing, flipping back to the library. I'd really need to see a sample. You know, a piece of oak with the stain."

"You'd be a fool not to. I've got scrap oak and the stain. I'll drop it off. Nice meeting you all. Especially you." He gave Maddy's belly a light drill with his finger.

"I'll walk you out."

"I know the way."

Zoey waited until the door closed behind him. "All right, tell me how is it you have the most beautiful man ever born—sorry, Boone."

"I've got eyes, and my one sorrowful glass of wine."

"Building your library."

"Just the bookcases." Arden lifted her own wine. "Just lucky, I guess."

Chapter Thirteen

Gideon dropped off the stained wood samples in Arden's mailbox at the end of her driveway, along with the official estimate. He sent her a text to let her know they were there.

That way, he avoided conversation and the temptation to take her up on the coffee she'd probably offer.

Since he had the day free, he thought he'd start on the design he'd worked up for a salad bowl set deal. He didn't really get why people wanted or needed a specific bowl for salads, but they did.

And he had some nice olive wood.

He could turn a good, deep bowl, slightly V-shaped, some small ones, then the tossing tools.

It would keep him busy.

Too much time on his hands meant brooding. And brooding ended up annoying him.

Besides, he liked his life here more than he'd expected to. He missed being on the job, and accepted he always would.

He'd wanted to be a cop as long as he could remember.

But now he wasn't.

He knew being here helped his grandfather, but it helped him, too. He had a purpose here. Not so much at the store. They both knew pretty much anyone could do what he did there.

But he served as a companion, a housemate, a sounding board. Pop wasn't alone and mired in grief. He could and did help around the house, with the meals, the garden, the chickens.

House repairs, when needed? They usually did together.

All that left him plenty of time for his hobby. And there he had access to a workshop and tools he'd never have managed in LA.

He could make bowls, lamps, cutting boards, boxes, maybe a table, a bench. Whatever he wanted, whenever he wanted.

He didn't get tagged in the middle of the night to stand over a dead body, or investigate a home invasion. No high-speed chases or foot pursuits. No writing up reports or digging into case files.

Christ, he missed it.

His phone signaled a text when he pulled up at the house.

Arden. He hadn't expected a response so soon. That made her either an early riser or one of those people attached to their phone even in sleep.

> Quick work, thanks! And since your total is damn close to the rough estimate, clearly you're many levels superior to me at math. But most are. Definitely the oak. I'm mulling the stain, but leaning heavily toward door number one, the dark walnut stain that shows the grain. But yes to the estimate and the oak. And once again, I won't pester you about how long it takes.
> I appreciate this. Also want to add a thanks for taking it so well when my niece threw herself at you and kissed you on the mouth.
> I'll let you know re the stain in a day or two.

Gideon read it through, decided she'd managed to have a conversation anyway.

> **Oak's the right choice, so is the dark walnut stain. But let me know if you want to make the wrong choice on that. I'll let you know when I have something to install.**
> **The kid was fine. Women routinely throw themselves at me.**

He considered. Salad set or bookcases, then started to back out again. Might as well go get the oak. He stopped when she texted back.

> Understood. It's taken a heroic effort for me not to do the same.

He let out a laugh. Sarcasm. He liked it.

Then he drove off to get his supplies.

He'd made a joke. Unexpected, Arden thought. She wasn't sure her impulse to reply in kind had been the best idea. Which was why she generally resisted impulses.

But done now.

She studied the wood samples she'd leaned against the wall with the paint swipe. He was right about the stain, which meant she was right about the stain.

But she'd come back and study again in the afternoon light, and then in lamplight.

And next trip into town, she'd talk to Joe about the fireplace. She'd start hunting for her chairs. Big, gushy leather chairs. A couple of interesting tables, lamps. A moody piece of art—think Jamie—for over the fireplace.

All on the list.

"Six months," she told the room, "and you'll be mine. I'll take a book out of my beautiful bookcase, sit in my gushy leather chair in front of my adorable fire, and read by the light of my interesting lamp."

But now her list consisted of workout, shower, then writing.

Nine months, Dustin thought as he suffered through another group session. As long as it took a woman to squirt out a squalling kid.

He could handle it. He'd think about it as his own rebirth, and he'd handle it.

He'd walk out of this hellhole a new man. Smarter. More careful and controlled. They'd taken his leather bracelet long ago, but he no longer needed it.

He'd walk out a man in control, and with access to his goddamn money again.

And with his purpose clear.

The cabin. Somewhere out west, remote, secluded. He'd need to take care of that. Payback. How he'd enjoy working his way down the list of people who owed him five years of his life.

Arden. The prize at the end of all his suffering.

Waiting to see her again hurt, sometimes with a pain so deep and throbbing he wanted to pound his fists into someone's face. Anyone's face.

He'd done that once in the first weeks of the endless five years. The paunchy, rubber-lipped little asshole had deserved it. Snickering, always snickering.

But Dustin had paid for that few minutes of pleasure and release.

Isolation, medication, loss of privileges.

So he'd learned to save up the pain.

And she still came to him in dreams. The dreams soothed him, always soothed him, whether he punished her or pleasured her.

He often did both in dreams.

And when, finally, they united again, they'd have a lifetime.

They'd live for each other, need only each other.

He'd have to train her, of course, but he'd be patient as well as firm. And he'd enjoy it.

"You're smiling, Dustin."

Dustin forced himself to tune in to Gavin Norse, the idiot therapist who ran the group.

"Can you tell us what makes you happy today?"

"Hope." Dustin broadened his smile. "I have hope, and I wouldn't have it without all the help I've gotten here. In a few months, I'll be back in the world. I've been a little nervous about that, anxious, you know? But today I have hope."

"Easy for rich boys to have hope."

Randy Sovini, the fat little psycho who'd thought his grandmother was a demon, so he'd decapitated her. Dustin imagined beating in his skull with a bat as he put on a solemn look.

"It really isn't. You have to find hope. You have to look for it and find it. It's really easy to find despair or anger. I always found those. Hell, I didn't even have to look for them.

"I didn't think I was good at anything, so I'd give up. You know, fuck that, and expect more. Lots of more I didn't have to do anything to earn, you know? I always figured if I wanted something, I should just have it. I'm not going to live that way anymore."

Because I will have all I want. Everything and more.

"Mommy'll take care of you."

Dustin nodded earnestly. "Sure she would, Randy. I'll probably need to lean on her some at first. But I know I took advantage of her, and I treated her like shit. She still loved me. One of the things I have hope for? I'm a better son. I'm sure going to try to be."

Right up until I choke the life out of her.

"I feel good today because I looked for and I found hope. I'm going to hold on to it."

"Thank you for that, Dustin. Sam, can you tell us something you hope for?"

"I hope we don't get that fucking tuna fish salad for lunch."

That brought on some laughs. Dustin joined in as he thought: Asshole. Pathetic assholes. And wished he could set fire to the whole damn place as he walked out.

As scheduled, Arden stopped into the hardware store on her next trip to Riverbend.

She'd left Tessa painting the library, which told her she liked and trusted Tessa enough to leave the house with her in it.

She saw Joe with a customer, didn't see Gideon, but the clerk—she flipped through her mental files—Corey—came over.

"Hi. Hey, Zorro, hey, boy. Did you come to see Elvis?"

"He sure did. I'm here because I'm told you can get electric fireplaces."

"We can do that. I'll show you a catalog."

When the dogs got together, Corey, mid-twenties, little beard, and nut-brown eyes, pulled out a catalog.

"So many."

"You take your time. Just let me know if you have any questions."

When he went off to ring up a sale, Arden paged through.

She'd looked at them online—what she considered part of the process.

There was one style she kept coming back to, so she focused on those choices.

"Did Corey get you started?"

She looked up to smile at Joe. "He did. But . . . tell me what you think of this one."

Joe adjusted his glasses, pursed his lips. "It's a good brand or we wouldn't sell it. For your library?"

"That's the plan."

"My opinion? It's a good choice to go with the bookcases you've got Gideon building."

"You think? I think. I like the stone, the varied browns, and that the mantel's not fussy, just a slab. It's the right scale for between the windows.

"Is Gideon around? He'd have an opinion."

"Not today. He'd be in the shop, I imagine, building those bookcases of yours."

"Well, hooray for that. This one, Joe. I know the size works. I did the cardboard cutout thing on the wall for this size. It sits directly on the floor, and the width seems perfect."

"Plugs right into the wall, too. No hardwire. Easy install."

"Music to my ears."

"I'll get it ordered for you."

"While I'm at it, I need a grill for my deck, and I will go modern on that. Bells and whistles, the works. My aunt and uncle are coming from Ohio, and my cousin and his family from California for a few days. My house tour includes a cookout."

"I can help you with that. Your parents aren't visiting?"

"I lost them when I was fourteen."

She saw his face fall into both sorrow and sympathy. "Arden, honey, I'm so sorry."

"Me, too. They were great, and I didn't have nearly enough time to make sure they knew I thought they were."

He rubbed the back of her hand. "They knew."

At the end of the day, with Corey doing the closing, Joe walked back to his woodshop. He'd spent many an hour working away in there. Taught his son how to use and respect power tools, taught him about wood and how to use it.

It hadn't taken with Liam all that much, though he learned well enough. But his boy had other talents, other ambitions.

He'd taught Gideon the same on his summer visits, or school holidays when he'd come. And while that boy had had other ambitions, too, what Joe had taught, Gideon learned very well.

Joe heard the saw going, a happy sound to his ears, over the music Gideon tended to have banging out.

He stepped in, saw Gideon guiding wood along the blade.

And the completed unit, a stack of finished shelves, and another shelf in the clamps holding the facing on until the glue firmed up.

He waited—safety first—until Gideon raised the saw.

"Making progress."

Gideon hit the remote to turn down the music, pulled off his safety goggles. "Yeah. I wanted to do the shelves for the first one, see some in there. But figured I'd start on the next while the last shelf glued up."

"Arden was in the store today. Ordered an electric fireplace. Floor unit, stone surround. It'll look good with these cases."

"She knows what she wants." Gideon pulled two Cokes out of the shop fridge.

"You know my weaknesses," Joe said as he took the bottle. "Ordered a grill, too. Fancier than what we've got in stock. Got family coming in for a visit. They'll be staying at the other cousin's place—the one you met—but Arden's having them all over for a cookout."

"The ones I met seemed nice enough."

"The way she talked, I think she's close with all of them. Did you know she lost both her parents when she was just fourteen?"

Gideon lowered the bottle. "No, I didn't. What happened?"

"I didn't press on that wound. Didn't seem the place to, with customers in the shop. My sense is this aunt and uncle likely took her in, raised her from there."

"Had to be rough."

"Losing someone you love always is, but a young girl, losing her parents?" Joe shook his head. "Hurts my heart. I think the aunt and uncle must be good people. You can see she loves them. When she ordered the grill, and she went whole hog there, she laughed and said her uncle was going to drool over it. It was the way she said it. You could see the love."

"Rough as it was, not everyone's as lucky in the aftermath."

"No, they're not. You'd know that, have seen that, from your work in LA. Miss it still, don't you?"

"I'm happy here, Pop. That's the truth."

"I know it. And having you around makes me happy."

He moved over to the finished cabinet, ran his fingers over the wood. "This is fine work, Giddyup. Fine, good work. You know you could make a living at this."

"Then it wouldn't be a hobby."

Joe slanted over a look. "She's paying you for the work."

"People get paid for hobby work. Reg makes his living teaching, but he sells his photography."

"He's good at both. We should have him and Della over, do some grilling ourselves before we run out of summer. You two hit it off the first summer you met, couldn't have been more than six. And you picked it right up where you left off every time you came to visit after that."

"I'll text him."

"Do that. Meanwhile, you've got this sanded down and ready for stain. We move it over there, away from the saw and the dust, I can give you a hand with that."

Gideon took a slow drink. "What's your rate?"

Joe grinned. "Two lunches and a week's worth of coffee."

"You're hired."

Arden sat back from her keyboard, stared at her screen.

She'd made the right choice in sitting down at her desk on a Saturday afternoon instead of completing her list of household chores.

She'd made the right choice and finished the first draft.

And really thought she'd nailed the ending. It worked.

She hoped it worked.

Evening had settled over the valley while she wrote. She'd stopped only to feed Zorro, let him run while she made a sandwich for herself.

She'd eaten at her desk, but the time, the effort?

"So worth it."

Her fingers itched a little, but no, no, she would not start the second draft now. Her brain needed a rest. And so, she admitted, did her neck and shoulders.

She'd shut down, then go figure out what to wear to her first monthly Sunday brunch.

And after that?

She swiveled so Zorro's head came up.

"How about popcorn and a movie?"

He got up to do his downward dog stretch, yawned, then sang his agreement.

"Settled."

She'd wear a dress, she decided. If she couldn't wear a dress to Sunday brunch, where? The soft yellow one Zoey had talked her into. And, Arden admitted, her cousin hadn't had to push too hard on it.

She'd wear it with the little white sweater over it.

Heels? Why the hell not? The nude pumps worked. And she'd wear her mother's locket, her good twisty hoops.

"And done. See, if I had more clothes, this would've taken longer. Popcorn time!"

Since she wanted to share with Zorro, she settled on the living room couch with her popcorn, a well-earned glass of wine, and the flat-screen she'd brought with her from Ohio.

She decided on an action-adventure because she liked the cast. Though Zorro lost interest and curled up to doze, it kept hers to the end.

Since she wasn't ready to call it a night, she opted for a second glass of wine and a double feature.

She chose a highly rated drama. Long before the credits, she, like Zorro, dozed off.

The banging on the door woke her. Groggy, annoyed, she pulled herself out of bed. In sleep pants and T-shirt, feet bare, she stumbled her way to the door by the glow of streetlights coming through the living room window.

"Just a minute! God, hold on."

Half asleep, she fumbled with the lock, then opened the door.

"I brought you flowers!"

Fear hit an instant before he did. The blow struck her face, and she tasted blood as she fell.

Stars, she thought, stars circling again.

He scattered the flowers over her as she tried to push herself away along the floor.

This time she screamed. She screamed so her ears rang with it, but no one came to help.

"You shouldn't have fucked with me, Arden."

He dragged her up by her hair, struck her again, then let her drop so her head struck the floor and brought more stars spinning.

"You need to learn a lesson, and I'm going to teach you."

He fell on her, dragged off her shirt. As she fought, as she screamed, his hand closed over her throat.

She could only see his eyes, eyes filled with mad fury, as her lungs wept for air, as her throat burned.

She woke choking. As she struggled to breathe, her vision started to go gray. Sliding, she thought. Sliding away.

Barking, whining, Zorro laid his paws on the sofa. He lapped at her hand, her face.

Her arms came around him, held on, held close until she could breathe again. Because he trembled, she stroked, soothing both of them.

"I scared you, I know I scared you. But I'm okay. I'm okay. You're with me, so I'm okay."

She lay back down, stroking his head, waiting for her heartbeat to slow.

"What brought that on?"

She hadn't had a dream like that in months. Longer. Even when nerves had kept her too often confined to the house, she hadn't had dreams like that.

Overtired, she decided. Worked too long. Add the wine, popcorn, drama flick, whatever. But she was all right now.

If it happened again, she'd contact Dr. Wren for a refresher. She knew better than to let something like that go.

For now, she'd assume it was a one-off.

"We're going up to bed, my very good boy, my good, brave boy. But you should go out again first, and I could really use the air."

It helped, that cool air, the night quiet. She heard an owl call through that quiet, and found the sound calming. A few lights sprinkled across the valley, but it slept under a shimmer of stars. And from here, she thought it slept peacefully.

When Zorro rounded back to her, they went in. She locked the door, then took a minute to assess herself.

No, she had no need, no urge to wedge a chair under the knob. She carried her bowl, her glass into the kitchen, put them in the dishwasher.

She knew she'd locked the mudroom, but didn't think it obsessive to check.

They went upstairs, she changed into her sleepwear, then went in to brush her teeth, do her nightly skin care.

Normal, normal, she thought, though Zorro sat in the doorway and watched her.

"I scared you. I scared me, too, but everything's all right now."

She studied the woman in the mirror. Not pale, not haunted around the eyes.

That part of her life? Done. She didn't live in that apartment anymore. She didn't even live in the same state, the same freaking time zone.

And he was locked up for months yet. He didn't know where she lived now—and that information wasn't in her bio.

She wasn't just safe here, she felt safe.

"Bedtime," she told Zorro.

He circled his bed, chose his nighttime companion.

She took off the shams, the decorative pillows, but kept Burnie.

She turned off the light, stretched out in bed with an arm around the dragon. And assessed again.

No anxious need to lock the bedroom door or close and lock the window she left open an inch or so for the air.

"Just a bad dream," she murmured. "People have them."

She closed her eyes, listened to Zorro's steady breathing, the breeze tickling the leaves, the call of the owl.

When sleep held off, she did her relaxation breathing and visualized.

She saw herself in her finished library, the dog sleeping in front of the fireplace where the flames danced. She sat in that big, gushy chair with a book while snow fell soft and silent outside.

Maybe it didn't snow much or often where she lived now, but she could imagine it.

So her world? At peace. Her home? Safe.

Imagining it all, she slept.

Chapter Fourteen

She woke in the morning, calm and clear, and early enough to address some of the domestic chores she'd neglected the day before.

As she worked, she reconsidered the idea of a cleaning service. And dismissed it, again. It was just her, and she—by nature—kept a clean and organized house.

But above all that, she couldn't talk herself into feeling comfortable having a stranger in her house. Not yet, just not yet.

Plus, she told herself as she headed to shower, all done now.

She took her time with her makeup, worked her hair into a fishtail braid—no small feat. When she put on the dress, checked the mirror, she decided the time and effort were worth it.

She'd meet people. That prospect didn't bring on anxiety. She could leave anytime she wanted or needed. But by God, she'd make a damn good first impression.

She put on the earrings, the locket, the little white sweater and nude heels. And considered herself dressed for a Sunday brunch.

"Overdressed? Shit. Stop it. Too late now anyway."

To cap it off, she turned to Zorro.

"Forgive me for this."

She hooked the red bow tie around his collar.

"You look dashing." And a little perplexed.

Downstairs she pulled the champagne out of the fridge and nestled it in the pretty cloth bag she'd bought for it. After hooking on Zorro's leash, she kissed his nose.

"You'll meet people, too, so best good boy behavior."

She walked him out into the warm, puffy-cloud day. Even in the heels she could manage the short distance.

She'd seen the house on her drives to and from town, and admired it.

A paved path bisected the charming front garden and led the way to a house with a stone base rising to golden cedar shakes. Its wide windows sparkled in the sunlight.

She walked to the bold red door, pressed the bell. And heard the chimes play "Für Elise." She still had a smile on her face when Jamie opened it.

Since he wore a silvery blue vest over a pink shirt, she decided she hadn't overdressed.

"Look at you! A ray of sunshine." Taking her shoulders, he kissed both her cheeks. "And you, young dapper gentleman." After greeting Zorro, he took Arden's hand. "Come in, come into our humble home."

She saw nothing humble about the high-ceilinged foyer with its modern take on a crystal chandelier, the curvy antique benches, the table holding a vase of pink lilies and white roses.

"It's beautiful, but I expected no less. Thanks for having me."

She offered the champagne.

"And she brings us bubbly! I take credit for having a classy neighbor."

He led her past the curve of a staircase to an enormous kitchen with the biggest island she'd ever seen, a dining room with a table already set like something out of a magazine, and a generous lounge.

And people, at least a dozen people, along with a few dogs.

"Nick, my love, the lady needs a mimosa. Everyone! This is the magnificent Arden and her handsome escort, Zorro. I'm going to introduce you, darling, but don't worry about remembering names this first round."

A good thing, Arden thought, as he reeled them off, including dogs. Zorro already made himself at home, sniffing dogs, shoes, everything.

She knew Tessa, though she might not have recognized the painter at first glance in the swinging floral dress and her sunny hair loose and nearly to her shoulders.

She met Tessa's Hawk with his quick grin and curly brown hair, and learned he served as a sergeant in the Riverbend police department.

While she tried to file names with faces—Marcus, Leo, Bonita, Rosa, Will—the doorbell rang again.

Jamie went to answer while Nick brought her a mimosa.

"Thank you. This is amazing. Your kitchen is just spectacular."

"Made to order. That and Jamie's studio were priorities. And we decided if we loved and stayed together after that, we'd make it through anything."

"Cissy, Dom, this is Arden, our new and treasured neighbor, and her handsome Zorro. You know everyone else. Now it's time for all good dogs to go out and play. Come on, boys and girls. Arden, come with me so you can be sure your boy is safe and happy."

He led her out to a paved patio. Beyond it, a fenced area—white picket—held what she could only call a dog playground.

It boasted a tunnel with the head of a dachshund, a low seesaw, a two-sided ramp, padded mats to lounge on, hoops, benches, a watering station.

She thought of it as a kind of doggie condominium.

"Wow."

"Ridiculous, isn't it?"

Yes, but also—"Sweet and charming."

"Isis loves her playdates. There's a nice little dog park in town, but this is right here. All right to leave Zorro?"

He was already running around with a poodle with a bow in her hair.

"I'd say he's found a slice of doggie heaven."

"Then let's go back in. It's nearly time for the feast."

He didn't exaggerate.

She didn't know what crème brûlée French toast was, exactly, but she wanted some. And mini cinnamon rolls, omelets, a fancy quiche, herby hash browns served in triangles, bacon, scones with lemon curd, and more.

The table sat twenty, and every seat was filled. The guests covered the bases with gay, straight, married, single, Black, White, Brown, young and old and in between.

Conversation flowed easily, and so did the champagne.

She ate, talked, laughed, and remembered she enjoyed socializing from time to time, even outside of family and the familiar.

While they drank cappuccino, and some actually had room for blueberry crumb cake and whipped cream, Jamie drew Arden from the table.

"You haven't had the house tour."

"Oh, I'd love one. And a chance to walk off some of that food. Honestly, Jamie, it's all amazing. Like something out of a movie."

"Could there be a better compliment?"

"You actually do all this every month?"

"We do, and enjoy every minute. So many of our friends lead busy lives. This is a chance to get together for part of one day, and not lose the connection."

He took her down, and she wasn't surprised to find the lower level beautifully finished, including an antique bar she now coveted, then back upstairs to the second floor.

When she stood at the open French doors of the main bedroom, she sighed.

"Now I want one of these for my own. French doors, a balcony."

"You'll never regret it. Nick, Isis, and I often sit out here, watch the sunset, or come out to linger in the moonlight."

"Other than Zorro, I don't have anyone to watch or linger with."

"You will."

Maybe. Someday.

"Not on the list yet."

"You told me about your lists. Put your dream man on there."

"I'd have to come up with dream man qualifications first. You and Nick really have made a beautiful home. Every detail's just perfect."

"We are fussy."

"You're discerning men with excellent taste. Nick told me the kitchen and your studio were the big ones. Can I see your studio?"

"Next and final stop."

He led her to another set of steps.

"The attic," he told her. "Every artist needs a garret."

At the top, he opened a door.

They'd left the beams exposed, and between them the sun poured through the skylights. One section of a wall had exposed stone, and they'd added a fireplace and a cozy seating area. A napping couch, two leather chairs, a planked wood table.

Paintings hung along the walls; others leaned against it.

Beyond that lived the artist's world. A bench table with a stool held organizers for brushes, palette knives, and other tools she couldn't name. Shelves held paints, some in tubs, some in tubes, brush cleaners, stacks of canvases.

In the center of it all stood an easel, and the unfinished painting on it of a single tree, flaming red, on a rocky hillside.

"This is some garret, Jamie."

"A dream of mine, a long-held dream of mine, come to life."

"It's a really good dream. And that?" She gestured toward the canvas. "It's going to be wonderful. The solitary tree, but brilliant in that solitude."

"You get me," he murmured.

"I've seen your paintings throughout the house."

"Nick loves me."

"I'm sure he does, but that's not the only reason for it. I bought the one in my bedroom before I met you, so that wasn't love of the artist."

She turned to him. "Do you take commissions?"

"Sweets, I have to earn my keep, so absolutely. And if it's for you, no question."

"I want something for my library, over the fireplace I ordered. I don't know what it should be, but your work, well, works."

"I'd be thrilled to do a painting for you. Why don't Nick and I walk down later and take a look? Tessa told us your library—the color—makes her think of an old manor house in England, so I'm dying to see it."

"Yes, please."

When she walked home with Zorro, she felt comfortably tired from champagne, food, and company.

"We had a hell of a good time, didn't we?"

If dogs could smile, he did.

Arden went to work on the second draft. With the family visit coming soon, she had to lock that out of her mind through the day.

In the evening she worked on her cookout menu. Not burgers and dogs, not this time. Steak and salmon. She had no idea how to grill salmon, but that's what the internet was for. It could also prove useful for finding the best sides to go with both.

For dessert? Nick would provide.

She had to make time to buy a picnic table, some deck and patio furniture. She decided not to resist the strings of party lights, which required the purchase of a ladder.

As she set up the ladder, she congratulated herself on time management. Her second draft hummed along, she had a picnic table on her deck, the cute outdoor chairs, the Adirondacks and umbrella table on the patio.

Now all she needed was the grill, and the ability to hang party lights.

She'd consulted the internet there, too, and if she failed, she'd text the much handier Zoey.

She'd studied the process, bought everything needed. She took a long breath, then climbed the ladder to measure and mark where the cup hooks needed to go.

Satisfied, she got the hooks to screw them in. Which, she discovered, wasn't nearly as easy as it looked in the demo.

She'd managed three, through persistence and swearing, when Zorro barked and nearly jolted her off the ladder.

Then she heard an answering deep bay of a bark. She'd heard it a couple times now. Elvis.

Her grill!

She got off the ladder, down from the deck, and ran around the house.

Zorro was already showing Elvis the front yard. She saw Joe, Gideon, and someone else climb out of the truck.

"Got your grill," Joe called out. "She's a beauty. Took a while to put her together."

"*A while*'s minimalizing it. This is Reg," Gideon added, and he set a ramp on the tailgate of the truck he'd backed in.

"Slave labor. Hi. It is a beautiful grill, and terrifies me."

The man wore a fielder's cap that said RIVERBEND HIGH over a mass of light brown hair. He was about her height with cheerful blue eyes and a scatter of freckles over a boyish face.

"Thanks for helping. Oh, it's really big, and really shiny. And—is that my bookcase?"

She'd have scrambled up the ramp if Gideon hadn't blocked the way.

"One. I want to get it in place, make sure it works, doesn't need any adjustments. One," he repeated.

Since she hadn't expected any, one equaled a huge bonus to her day.

"You've got that padded thing over it so I can't really see. I want to—"

"Grill first. And it ain't no lightweight."

"I can help." Before he could object, she flexed both arms. "I can help."

"Yeah, she can." Reg grinned at her. "Those biceps are better than mine."

It wasn't a lightweight, but the four of them got it down the ramp, carried it around the house. Paused to adjust and maneuver it up the deck steps.

"Here, right here. Whew!" Arden rolled her shoulders. "My uncle might cry when he sees this."

"Got every bell and whistle there is." Joe gave it a nod and a pat.

"Do you know how to work that thing?" Reg wondered.

"I read the manual online. I'll read it again tonight. Thank you so much. Let me get you all a cold drink. I made iced tea, it's pretty good."

"Wouldn't mind that." Joe looked at the ladder, the light strings on the picnic table. "Hanging lights? Nice touch."

"I hope so."

"Why don't I take care of that for you? Giddyup and Reg can bring in that bookcase. Then we'd take that cold drink."

"Oh, I don't want you to have to—"

"He likes it," Gideon said simply. "Come on, Reg. This one goes in the front door."

"I'll open it for you."

She hurried in, jogged to the front door. Ordered herself to only squeal and bounce in her head.

Don't bang it, don't nick it, she thought as they angled it through where Gideon led the way to the library.

When they stood it up, she purred, then reached out to touch.

Gideon brushed her hand aside. "Go away."

"What? I want to—"

"You're thinking too loud. Go get the iced tea or whatever. We need a couple minutes."

She didn't like it, but calculated she'd see it in place quicker if she let him have his way.

She took a glass out to Joe.

"He kicked me out."

"He'll do that." Joe looked down from the ladder. "You're going to be happy with it, and the rest when they're done."

"I already am."

She went back in and straight to the library.

She put a hand to her mouth, then to her heart. Happy didn't come close. The dark, grainy wood against the deep green walls, so rich and warm. The clean lines kept it all simple and right.

She understood why he'd wanted to see it in place himself, as it was a corner unit.

"It's gorgeous, Gideon. Can it stay? Can I put books in it?"

"Yeah, it stays, and that's what you want in it, so go ahead."

"The small cabinets at the bottom really work, add a little something."

"And since you want those lights, they'll hide the plug. Anyway, that's one."

"Come back, have some tea."

"You've got a really nice house," Reg commented as they walked back to the kitchen.

"Thanks. The longer I'm here, the more I love it."

"From back east, right?"

"Brooklyn originally, then Ohio. Now here, and the Pacific Northwest really suits me. Part of that's being lucky enough to walk into Riley's Hardware one day and finding Joe."

"He's the best."

"I'm going to go out and give the best a hand."

Reg nodded at Gideon. "I'll play the usual unnecessary backup."

"I'll add cookies to the iced tea."

Gideon paused at the door. "Oreos?"

"Not this time. A gift assortment from my neighbor, Nick the baker."

"The SS and C guy?" Reg asked. "His cookies make all other cookies weep with envy."

"I'll bring them out."

By the time she did, along with the rest of the pitcher of tea, they'd nearly finished. Gideon stood on the ladder now, screwing in the light bulbs.

"Fast work, and hung just like I wanted."

"You had it all measured out," Joe said, and helped himself to a cookie. "They'll add a touch when you sit out here in the evenings."

"I really appreciate it. I know it would've taken me three, maybe four times as long. I'll think of you when I sit out here tonight."

"What's the first thing you're going to grill on that monster?" Reg asked her.

"I'll probably test it out tonight, maybe grill some chicken. Because the main event is when my family comes. Porterhouse steaks and wild salmon fillets, add the grill basket I got for roasted vegetables, spiced shrimp cooking on the side burner, and it's going to get a workout."

Studying her, Reg munched on a cookie. "What's the criteria to be part of your family, and are there any openings?"

"I think you earned honorary status today."

"Careful." Gideon screwed in another bulb. "There's not much to him, but he eats like a horse."

"I have that power. The Rileys always set an extra plate for me when I was around, then I got lucky and married a smart, beautiful, tolerant woman who likes to cook."

"She married down," Gideon said as Joe rolled his eyes.

"So true. But she loves the way I . . ." He looked at Arden, wiggled his eyebrows. "Entertain her."

Joe let out a laugh. "All right, boys. There's a lady present."

"It's okay, Joe. Ladies like being entertained."

Gideon shot her an amused look as he finished the last bulb. With the cord neatly secured to the corner of the house, he pushed the plug in the outdoor socket.

The lights snapped on, and Arden applauded.

"That should do it. Where do you want the ladder?"

"It goes in the shed. I'll take care of it."

Ignoring that, he folded it and took it down himself.

"You've all made my day. Grill, lights, bookcase. I wish I had burgers and beer to offer instead of iced tea and cookies."

"These do fine. You've got a nice place here, Arden. Pretty garden, birds at the feeders, nice trees."

"I really love it."

"Mind if I walk through on the way out? I'd like to see the house, and that bookcase in place."

"Of course, come in."

She led the way with the dogs trailing behind, and Gideon after them.

"Pretty kitchen. It's got the feel of being used and well tended to."

"A girl's gotta eat. I've got a lower level, but that's unfinished."

"Got plans?"

"Not yet. I haven't decided exactly what I want. Just can't see it yet. Once I do, I can move right along, but until? There's a lot of debate and consideration."

"My Colleen would've loved that dining room, those pieces. Of course, she'd've had that china cabinet filled right up."

"That's still in the debate and consideration stage."

When they reached the library, Joe put his fists on his hips and nodded.

"I can see the fireplace you picked right there. Good choice, very good choice. When those bookcases are in, you're going to have a hell of a room here. I bet you'll fill them up fast enough."

"No debate or consideration required, or not much. Just have to decide which genre to start with, then it's alpha by author."

"Genre, alphabetized?"

She glanced over her shoulder at Gideon. "It's a library. And when I want a book, I'll know where to find it."

"I had a feeling you were a woman who likes to keep things in their place." Joe winked at her. "We'll let you get to that. Gideon, you're likely to get more help from me now that I see where those bookcases are going."

"No raising your rates."

"Negotiations are always open."

He surprised and pleased Arden by bending down to kiss her cheek. "The house looks good on you."

Reg climbed in the back seat of the truck. He glanced back as Arden stood waving them off with Zorro at her side.

"I like her."

"Who don't you like?" Gideon tossed back.

"Hitler. Caligula. The Zodiac Killer. I'm not fond of Billy Adams, who bullied the crap out of me in middle school. His family moved to Seattle, I think, so I didn't have to deal with him in high school. Maybe he reformed. But I don't forget. Anyway, I like her. She's just your type, Gid."

"No, she's not."

"Sure she is. Maybe not in looks, as you usually go for the curvy little brunettes, but all the rest? Smart, self-sufficient, funny, good taste, likes dogs.

"You should ask her out."

"I don't know why he hasn't," Joe put in.

"Because I'm not interested."

"If I were forty years younger, I'd ask her out. Make that thirty. Maybe she likes an older, wiser man."

"You should do that, Pop."

Joe gave his grandson a wide smile, arched his eyebrows. "Just maybe I will."

The woman under discussion spent the next two hours filling her single bookcase. It took time, as now and again she had to open a book, read a passage. Or two.

Then she had to just sit on the floor and admire how they looked.

She hooked an arm around Zorro when he sat beside her.

"It really feels like home now. It's not all the way home until there are books—lots of books—on the shelves."

With a sigh, she tipped her head to the dog's. "We're all the way home, Zorro. Home. Safe. Happy."

And happier yet when she prepared for her family cookout.

She'd seen everyone at dinner at Zoey's. It had been so good to see them again.

But tonight, she'd have them in her house. Her home.

She had appetizers—purchased, she wasn't Gordon Ramsay—wine, beer, soft drinks, lemonade, and juice boxes. She had the outdoor table set—fancy, because Jamie insisted on coming down to help.

And would come with Nick for dessert, as he refused her invite to the cookout part.

Desserts—thanks to Nick. Mini cream puffs, cupcakes, and the magnificence of an angel food cake and berry trifle.

The salmon fillets marinated in the fridge, the steaks waited, and she'd prepped the vegetables for the basket.

"We're ready," she told Zorro.

And a good thing, as he raced to the front door.

They piled out of two vehicles, her aunt, uncle, Travis, April, Zoey, Boone, and four excited kids.

"I love it!" Jen called out. "We've seen pictures, but I love it more now. What a handsome house, Arden."

"I'm so glad you're here!"

There were hugs, good, hard hugs, though they'd seen each other the night before.

"Come inside, take the tour. Or drinks first."

"Tour first," Jen insisted. "I'm dying to see it all."

"Seems solid." Doug took a long, careful look as they walked to the door. "No issues with it?"

"Not a one. At least not yet."

She grabbed a kid at random, Travis's youngest, Trent. Two and raring to go.

She took them through, starting with the second floor. Listened to the voices filling her house, and realized she'd missed that.

No question she needed the quiet, but she needed them, too.

As often as she could get them.

"You've done so much, and it's all so you," Jen marveled as they started down again. "And in barely two months."

"It's been an adventure. I'm having fun with it."

"You've got good bones here, Arden." Doug studied as he went. "A lifetime home if you want it."

"I do, and I feel firmly planted. Plus, I've been doing some research for a location for the two stragglers."

"Pacific views," Travis reminded them.

"City or town living," Doug said. "Or close. Convenience, some walkability."

"Riverbend's got all that." Zoey flashed her brother a big smile.

"As long as we're within driving distance of all four of our grandbabies." Jen snuggled Maddy, who rewarded her grandmother with a sloppy kiss.

"Well . . ." Now April smiled. Smugly. "What if Travis and I added one more to our side of that scale?"

"Really?" Jen lit up like a candle. "You're having another?"

"Lucky number three."

"Wait a minute, wait a minute." Zoey held up her hands. "First, yay. Congratulations. But us, too." She pointed at her belly, then held up three fingers.

More hugs, some high fives.

"How far along are you?" Zoey asked.

"Six weeks."

"Me, too! Just confirmed today."

"That's where you were!"

"That's where I was, Mom. Now?" One hand on her belly, Zoey sent her sister-in-law a glinting look. "It's a race!"

On a laugh, April nodded. "Challenge accepted."

"We should pause the tour for a celebratory drink," Arden decided. "You two are stuck with lemonade."

When they finally walked out onto the deck, Arden waited for Doug's reaction.

He stared at the grill, held his hands out like a supplicant before an altar. "Oh, you magnificent bastard. Daddy's here!"

"You're steaks, I'm salmon and shrimp."

But he busied himself going over every inch of the grill. "You have a smoker box," he said reverently.

"We'll try it out next time. I believe this adds weight to the scale."

"Doesn't seem quite fair," Travis muttered.

"I've earmarked a couple of locations pretty close to equidistant. Because I love April and the kids, and you come with that package."

"You've got one of those tunnel crawls in the yard." April laid a hand on Arden's arm. "And a seesaw. That's so sweet."

"Inspired by my neighbors—you'll meet them over dessert. Zorro loves it, but I thought the kids would, too."

"Set them free," Travis said.

Boone topped off his glass of wine. "I'll take first watch." He glanced back as he started down to the yard, carrying Maddy as the rest of the kids raced out. "And that grill? It's downright scary."

"I am not afraid." Rubbing her hands together, Arden grinned at her uncle. "Shall we begin?"

Chapter Fifteen

In the end, the party decreed the family now boasted two grill masters.

"This?" Hand on his belly, Doug pushed back from his plate. "This is how you eat like kings." He held out a fist for Arden to bump.

"Teamwork," she said.

"Add the bounty of the PNW. Which . . ." Zoey shook her head at her daughters. "A couple of princesses enjoyed a lot."

"Yeah." Rising, Boone lifted Lexy. "I've got this one."

"Smart, seeing as Maddy has salmon in her hair." Zoey drew the younger out of the high chair. "We'll go clean them up a little."

"We're right behind you. You know," April added as she boosted her youngest onto her hip, "I could probably needlepoint a minivan that got decent mileage, but I've never conquered the surf and turf medley."

"But your manicotti's gold."

April smiled at Travis. "Excellent response. We'll be back in five with nonsticky hands and faces."

"Expect stickier ones after dessert," Arden warned.

"Since we definitely need a break before that, while they clean up kids, we'll help you clean up dinner." Jen rose. "And you can fill us in on those locations. Coming here has made it clear this needs to be home."

Nodding, Doug began stacking plates. "We'd talked about downsizing, but we need a place big enough so we can reinstate monthly family dinners."

"And with six grandchildren before we even get started? A space we can designate as a playroom. Plus, three bedrooms. Overnights, maybe long weekends with those grandkids."

"I need a good-sized deck or patio," Doug added. "Because when we get out here, I'm having one of those grills."

"So . . ." As squeals, loud complaints, a shriek of toddler laughter bounced through the house, Arden loaded the dishwasher. "*Downsizing* is a relative term."

"So's family." Jen leaned in, kissed her cheek.

As they cleared the dinner mess, kids ran through the kitchen with Zorro, tongue hanging out, racing with them. Travis, taking his turn at watch, herded all outside again.

Arden watched them go. "I need a swing set."

"You sweetie." Now Jen hugged her shoulders.

"It's going on the list."

Arden enjoyed every moment of the noise and interaction, even when Maddy took a tumble that ended in wails and gushing tears.

When Jamie and Nick, along with Isis, joined them, it only added to the fun. Her neighbors and her family clicked. She watched Nick play with monster trucks, Jamie help build a block fort. Over and around the kids, conversations ranged from baking to art, movies and books, remodeling—and there, her neighbors and Doug bonded like glue.

They talked under the party lights while Maddy slept on her father's shoulder and Trent's head drooped on his mother's.

Later, as she settled in bed, Arden thought she had so much of what she wanted. Family, friends, work that sustained and satisfied.

And a home she loved, felt proud of.

Most of all, a home she felt safe in.

She'd known the time would fly by, but when her aunt and uncle went back to Ohio, she comforted herself by remembering the holidays would come. This year, now added to the rotation, she'd host Christmas dinner.

Time for a new list. Or three lists, she thought. Gifts, decorations, menu.

But for now, as summer waned, her focus returned to the book. Day after day, she immersed herself in the work, and with the work she felt little hitches and snarls from the first draft smooth out in the second.

Another two weeks, maybe three, she decided, then she'd let it sit and soak for a few days before she went back to it to shine and polish it all up.

By her calculations, she'd finish with plenty of time to plan and prepare for the holidays.

Then she found the leak under her bathroom sink.

"Well, shit, and I was about to celebrate a good day's work by bringing in some flowers, some ball tossing, and some wine on the back deck."

She mopped it up. After emptying the tub she used to hold cleaning supplies, she used it to catch the drips.

Crouched, she studied the slow, steady drip. Then she looked up how to turn the water off on the pipe.

Her uncle had shown her long ago, but not on this particular sink or this particular pipe.

"It probably just needs tightening. I have a wrench." She studied the pipe as Zorro nosed under her arm. "I think I can do this."

She went down to the mudroom for the toolbox Doug had given her for her eighteenth birthday, as he'd given one to Travis, one to Zoey.

She knew what a pipe wrench looked like, so chose that.

Hesitated.

She could make it worse.

She could call Zoey, or just look up local plumbers. Maybe Jamie and Nick knew one, or Joe absolutely would.

But really, it probably just needed tightening.

She started back out, then Zorro left her side to run barking to the front door.

With a hand pressed to her jumping heart, she told herself it was probably Jamie. If so, at least she'd have a consultant.

But when she looked out to check, she saw Gideon.

Pipe wrench in hand, she stood a moment, closed her eyes.

She didn't have to be interested in a man to wish he hadn't shown up at her door after she'd worked all day, and in some of her oldest sweatpants, had her hair yanked back in a tail, and wore not even a trace of makeup.

"Oh well."

She opened the door.

He studied her. "Should I consider that a weapon or a tool?"

"What? Oh, a tool. I've got a leak upstairs, which just had to wait until my uncle left—well, a week ago, but still. He can fix anything that can be fixed, but he's not here."

"What kind of leak?"

"The kind that drips water under the sink on all your under-the-sink things."

Still watching her, he petted the wagging Zorro. "You need to turn the water off under the sink."

"I did that. I looked it up to make sure I knew how, but I did that."

"I'll take a look. Which sink?"

"In the main bathroom upstairs, the left side. You fix leaky pipes?"

"Not usually. Hand over the wrench."

She hated to be that woman, that woman who'd rather have a man handle some tool-requiring task than do it herself. Then justified it because she'd have happily handed the wrench to Zoey.

He angled his head. "Do you have a problem with me taking a look at your leaky pipe?"

"No. No, I do not." She gave him the wrench. "I think I could probably do it," she said as she led the way up. "But the fixtures in there are higher-end than I've ever had. And before, I'd have called my uncle anyway. At one eight hundred Doug Fix This."

"Why have a pipe wrench if you don't use it when you need it?"

"Uncle Doug gave me the toolbox, loaded, for my eighteenth birthday. Family tradition. And I did use it once back in my apartment, but it only slowed down the leak because it needed a new gasket or sticky stuff."

"Uh-huh."

"That one," she said, and pointed.

"I can see that."

He also saw she'd lined her cleaning supplies—likely taken out of the organizer now under the leaking pipe—on the counter like soldiers in parade formation.

He crouched down, took a look at the pipe. Then he went under the sink, headfirst, face up.

"Are you going to stand there and watch?"

"No. I'm going to get down here and watch." She hunkered down while the dog sniffed Gideon's boots. "I can't call my uncle, obviously, and my handy cousin has a full-time job and two kids. So I'm going to watch what you do in case it happens again.

"Unless I need to call a plumber."

"Not this time. It looks like you've got a loose slip nut. I'm going to check the gasket first. If it's good, it just needs tightening."

"See, that's what I thought! That's what I was going to do. Except for checking the gasket first."

"Ever tightened a slip nut?"

"Not in a while, and only after the third date."

He paused, shifted enough to look back at her.

She knew amusement when she saw it in the gorgeous green eyes.

"If you overtighten, you could strip them. Gasket's fine."

"How do you know? I might have to know sometime."

"No cracks or wear. You see that, you want to replace them."

"From Riley's."

"Sure. You need to tighten the slip nut, counterclockwise. Hand-tight, not Iron Man tight. Start with the one up here—closest to the drain."

She listened as he explained, as he checked the next slip nut. Her uncle explained this way, she realized. Patiently step by step.

"Should be good." He turned the water back on, then eased out. "Try it."

She turned the faucet on, then crouched down beside him.

"It was sort of seeping and slow dripping. Now it's not."

She turned her head, smiled at him. "Thanks. In my zeal to repair, I probably would have turned those things as hard as I could. I know better now."

She had skin like glass, he thought, and those tiny shimmering flecks in her eyes. And right now, she smelled like something exotic that bloomed in moonlight.

Catching himself, he shifted back an inch.

"I'll take a look at the other sink, since I'm down here anyway."

"Oh, let me get the stuff down there out of the way."

Another organizer thing, he noted, looked like hair stuff and so on. The woman had a lot of hair. And it smelled damn good, so whatever she stockpiled under the sink, worth the price.

"These are good."

"Excellent. Hopefully, I won't have to reach for the pipe wrench again anytime soon, but if I do, I know the process."

She replaced the hair stuff, then loaded the other thing with cleaning products, slid those under the first sink.

"You stopped by at just the right time."

"I brought a couple of bookcases."

"You—well, Jesus, Gideon, bury the lede."

"You had a wrench in your hand."

"I wasn't expecting bookcases. Just you? No other muscle today?"

"The other muscles are busy. I've got a dolly. You've got muscle. You can help get them off the truck."

"Yes, I do, and yes, I can."

As September evenings ran cool, she grabbed a jacket on the way out.

She needed the muscle to help him maneuver the bookcase down the ramp, then up the three steps to her front door. He wheeled it into the library, and together they set it in place.

"Twice as wonderful."

In the first, he noted, she'd started with Jane Austen, ended with Arthur Miller. While he hadn't read either, he'd passed the time with several between.

"And one more today. I didn't realize you'd bring them one or two at a time. It's great for me."

"The shop's good size, but it's a hell of a lot of bookcases. Easier to move a couple out when they're done. Pop's doing some of the staining, so it's moving along."

"He does good work, too. Does he have a date tonight?" she asked as they started out for the second case.

"Sort of. He's meeting some friends for dinner, then he has a library meeting. He's on the library board."

"I'm surprised the women in town don't move on him. Handsome, smart, sweet, handy."

"He has women friends, but my grandmother was it for him."

She held her breath until the second bookcase reached the dolly.

"The lucky ones find their it. And dating's overrated anyway."

"Is it?"

One hand to steady the bookcase, she walked along beside the dolly.

"Yes. Overrated and mostly just a pain in the ass, full of frustration, anxiety, unreal expectations. It's just fraught."

"Okay." He didn't intend to ask, he really didn't. But. "Why?"

"What am I going to wear? What does this outfit say?"

"Right, I stress over that for hours."

She laughed, shrugged. "Easy for you to say. What am I going to talk about? Am I talking too much? Why does he talk so much? Am I going to be bored, engaged, interested? Will this lead to sex, and will that be any good? Should I wear my might-have-sex underwear, or is that pitifully obvious if there is sex?"

"What color is it?"

"Depends on the outfit chosen for the date. Is it little-black-dress date, jeans and shirt, fancier cocktail wear, outdoorsy activity?"

A little breathless from the effort, she helped him place the bookcase.

"How many dates is this?" she continued as she ran a hand over the bookcase. "Did the first date end, if this is not date one, on a firm yet friendly handshake?"

"If it did, that date was a bust."

"Probably. Or a light, casual kiss, or a long, lingering one?"

"Sex isn't on the menu for date one, I take it."

"That's not a hard no, but a pretty solid give-it-some-more-time. It's all fraught and a lot of trouble. If sex is the end goal, just have sex and forget all the dancing around it."

"That's an interesting take."

"Just my observations and experience. Look how these make this room. The fireplace is delayed, but Joe said next week for certain. I don't care what the weather is, I'm lighting it. And sitting in one of the chairs that'll be here in a day or two."

"Have fun with that."

"Oh, believe me, I will." She turned to him. "Do you have a date?"

"No."

"All right then, I'm going to fix you a sandwich."

"Why?"

"Because you fixed my leaky pipe and brought me two more bookcases. And you said Joe's having dinner with friends. I'm going to make myself a sandwich, so I'll make two. You can take it with you if you'd rather, or I've got wine, beer, and soft drinks."

He'd figured to make a sandwich himself when he got home. Why not let her do it?

"I wouldn't mind a beer."

"Great. Come on, Zorro. Dinnertime."

He sang and danced in place, then bulleted toward the kitchen.

She gave Gideon a beer—not in a bottle, which would've been fine, but poured into a pilsner glass. Then she fed the dog before pouring herself a glass of wine.

"What's your preference? I have—"

"Whatever."

She tilted her head. "Is that *whatever* as in *I'm a gambling man*, or knee-jerk polite?"

"I don't have a knee-jerk polite. I'll gamble."

As she laid out a host of ingredients, he wandered the kitchen.

Her stove, aesthetically beautiful, also looked like something requiring a pilot's license.

"Do you actually cook in here on a routine basis, or on that grill?"

"Yes, I do. But I had tonight designated for sandwich. I'm a third-generation sandwich artist."

"Artist."

"Color, texture, the melding of flavors. My grandfather taught my dad, my dad taught me."

He watched her work. "A lot of trouble for two pieces of bread."

She shot a finger at him. "You'll eat those words, Riley, along with this sandwich."

"Maybe. Joe mentioned you'd lost your parents when you were a kid. I'm sorry. It had to be rough."

"It was. It would've been a hell of a lot rougher without my aunt and uncle. I didn't really know them before. They lived in Columbus, we lived in Brooklyn, so we only saw each other a couple times a year. But they were right there for me, and I didn't make it easy on them. On anyone."

"Death flattens us, then pisses us off."

Exactly, she thought. Exactly.

"I'll say. They had a monthly date night. They were heading back home. Sixteen-wheeler, black ice, driver lost control. My dad died instantly, they said. My mom on the way to the hospital. I'm at home already brooding because I didn't have a boyfriend."

She flicked up a glance as she built the sandwiches.

"At fourteen, I still thought dating was desirable. I was writing in my journal about how crappy life was because . . . I can't remember his name now. Whatever boy I had a crush on at that moment didn't think twice about me. Maybe not once. Then the cops and the social worker came to the door, and the life I thought was crappy was over."

She looked at him. "You probably had to knock on a door when you were a cop."

"Yeah."

"Do you miss it? I don't mean notifications, that had to be hard on your end, too. But Los Angeles, being a cop."

"Not LA. I like it here, always did."

"Then being a cop?"

He jerked his shoulders. "That was then, this is now."

Clearly, he didn't want to talk about that, Arden thought, so switched it up.

"When did you move to LA?"

"I didn't. I grew up there. Mostly."

"Oh, I didn't realize that. Are your parents still there?"

"Mostly. They split when I was about six. Is this date conversation?"

She looked up with a laugh. "I consider it sandwich-making-and-eating conversation. And since I do, any sibs?"

"Half brother from him, half sister from her. From their second marriages. Sort-of steps—two sisters and a brother—from their third tries."

"Three marriages each? So they're optimists."

"You could look at it that way, or as the definition of insanity. Third try didn't stick either. Now they've circled back. They're living together. Mostly."

"Really? That's kind of nice. What's mostly?"

"They both travel for work."

She cut each sandwich in two, then went for chips from the pantry. "What do they do?"

"They're in the movie business."

"Well, that's interesting. Want another beer?"

"No, I'm good."

"So what do they do in the movie business?" She set his plate in front of him, then sat with her own.

"He's a director."

"Your dad directs movies? I like movies. Zorro and I often have movie and popcorn night. Maybe I've seen one of his."

"Maybe." He took a bite of the hefty sandwich. He had to admit, the mix and meld of flavors and textures hit solid on tasty. And packed a punch.

"Got some heat on it."

"I figured you could handle it."

If this happened to be a date, she thought, she sure couldn't claim he talked too much.

"How about a tiny bit more information? Like your father's name."

"Riley. Liam Riley."

"Okay, that name's familiar. Give me a minute. I haven't haunted the movie blogs since my crush on Tom Holland."

"When was that?"

"If I'm honest, it's ongoing. I would certainly make him a sandwich if he knocked on my door. But . . . Oh, oh! *Beaten Path*! Is that right? Is that one of his?"

"Yeah."

"I love that movie. If I'm scoping streaming options, and I hit it: Bang. I'm there. Action from the jump, sexual tension, great dialogue. And there's another, more recent . . . Shit, I'll get it. *The Unseen*. That's it. Scared the crap out of me. I watched it twice."

"Why?"

"Because it's really good, and I wanted to see what I missed, how I missed it."

She gestured with a chip, then ate it.

"The clues are all there, but it's all so layered. You need that solid script, and actors who can make you believe it's real, but you have to have someone with the vision and the skill to pull it all together.

"Does your mom direct, too?"

"No. She's one of the people trying to make you believe it's real."

"She's an actor? How about a hint, like her name?"

"Scarlett Dash."

Arden punched him in the shoulder. "No! Seriously? She's wonderful. I've seen plenty of her movies. And I binged *Solomon's Creek* a few months ago. She has such presence. Plus, she's just gorgeous. I figured you got your looks from Joe, but you've got some of her in there. Wait!" She held up a finger. "Your father directed *Solomon's Creek*. Is that how they got back together? Oh, I mean, jeez. That's so romantic."

"Now it's my turn for a *seriously*."

"Yes, seriously. A little weird for you, I guess."

"*Weird*'s the word."

"Well, I'm rooting for those crazy kids. Now I'm going to have to watch *Solomon's Creek* again. No pull to join the family business?"

"That's a solid no."

"You've got the looks for it. Since you own a mirror, I'm not telling you what you don't know. But no pull, no deal. I wanted to write pretty much always. Whenever I tried anything else, it felt flat. I don't think you can be good at something if it doesn't pull at you.

"So the Hollywood son opts to go on the job in LA, then relocates to the Willamette Valley and makes my bookcases. Woodworking must pull."

"I like it."

"You're good at it, again nothing you don't already know. I was good at retail. I worked in a bookstore part-time for years, and really enjoyed it. But it wasn't the big pull."

He could play the game.

"So the writer and former part-time bookseller relocates from Columbus to Riverbend and changes all the doorknobs."

"She did. And she really likes it. The area, and the doorknobs. I wasn't sure how I'd adjust from east to west, and city to more country, but I like where I landed."

"Miss anything?"

"My aunt and uncle, but they're planning to move out here in about a year and a half. And they'll be back for Christmas. Some friends, but we keep in touch. The house? It's probably the first thing I've ever just jumped into. I'm not impulsive. But I liked it, and I liked where it was. It felt quiet and safe. I needed a change, and I got it."

"Columbus didn't feel quiet and safe?"

Something there, he thought, when she took a moment to answer.

"I've never lived anyplace where I could keep windows open at night and hear an owl hoot. Or look out one of those windows and see for miles. See mountains. So, I like where I landed. Looks like we both hit the mark on that."

"I knew what I was getting, since I spent time up here—summer weeks, holidays now and then."

"Still a big change from Los Angeles. Will you take over the hardware store if and when Joe retires?"

Shrugging, he tipped back his beer.

"No pull, huh?"

"Sometimes you do what you're supposed to do instead of what you're meant to do. You make a hell of a sandwich, Legs."

She lifted an eyebrow. "Yes, I do. I can offer you half a Dove bar for dessert, as I only have one left."

"Tempting, but I'm good. And I need to get going."

Rising, he studied her long enough to make her easy smile turn quizzical.

"Do I have chili paste on my face?"

"No. It's an interesting face. You've got a mirror so I'm not telling you anything you don't know."

That got a laugh out of her.

"I'm deciding whether to skip the firm-yet-friendly handshake."

He liked impulse—in its time and place—so went with it.

He lifted her out of the chair and an inch or so off the floor. Before he kissed her, he read the surprise in her eyes, and something else.

The something else had him keeping the kiss—even though she packed a little heat herself—more casual and easy than the impulse wanted.

Her hands landed on his shoulders, and her fingers dug in, but he broke the kiss and set her back on the stool.

"Thanks for the sandwich."

"You're welcome."

"See you around." He gave the dog a quick rub, then walked out through the mudroom.

He'd been a cop long enough to recognize a victim. Someone had hurt her, he thought as he got in his truck. Maybe a boyfriend, maybe a stranger, but someone had put that look in her eyes.

Not his business, he reminded himself. And still he was sorry for it. Sorry it had happened, sorry he'd put that look back even for a moment.

And he wondered who, how, and why.

Chapter Sixteen

Autumn brought the color and it brought the rain. She watched both sweep across the valley from her office window as progress on her book streamed along.

Because it streamed, she realized she'd begun to lose some of her focus on the work back in Columbus. She'd let anxiety break through her discipline.

Not let, she reminded herself. It simply had. And she'd taken the steps, the right steps for her, to regain control.

Since Zoey had pushed her to buy rain gear, she braved the wet to go out to cut drenched flowers from the garden, to drive into town or to dinner at Zoey's.

She rewarded herself in the evenings by sitting in one of her new butterscotch leather chairs with a book in front of her new library fireplace.

Zorro, after some initial wariness, accepted her footstool pig. But he tended to give it a wide berth and napped in front of the fire, usually with his llama.

Since Jamie refused to let her see what he was painting for her, she couldn't visualize it. But contented herself knowing it would be exactly right.

As October loomed, she planned and prepped her first dinner party, with Zoey and Boone—no kids, at their request—Jamie and Nick, and considered her timing perfect. With her second draft completed ahead of schedule, she'd let it sit a day or two before going over it all again.

She fussed with her house until every surface gleamed. Once the table was set, she took a careful study of the space. And happily, thought her dining room had come a long way.

She'd fussed with herself, too, choosing the dark green dress from her still mostly empty closet, leaving her hair down, and adding a few thin braids to frame her face.

She had the Brie baked, the wine breathing, and the ham resting when Zoey and Boone came to the door.

"God, an adult evening!" Zoey hugged hard. "Thank you!"

"We love our girls, but." Grinning, Boone moved in for his hug. "We've been so busy we haven't had solo time outside of work in weeks."

"I know we're early, but we couldn't wait."

"Happy to provide. Let's get your jackets. It's actually not raining."

"Hallelujah. But," Boone warned, "expect the wet by dessert. Speaking of food, something smells amazing."

She took Boone's jacket to hang. "I sure hope so. Let's go have some wine and start adulting. Sparkling cranberry juice for you, Zoey, and the surprise inside."

"My fave pregnancy drink." Zoey hooked an arm around Arden's waist. "Boone, wait until you see the library. It's not finished, but it's wonderful even so."

"I'll say." He didn't just pause at the doorway but walked in. "That's a great-looking fireplace, but these bookcases are really something."

"I love them. I decided to add the photos and things along with books in every other one. I've already got a box of what goes in the next when it gets here. I thought about buying a library ladder, but I'm going to see if I can talk Gideon into making one."

"He does good work."

"He really does."

They went back to the kitchen, where Zorro sat and watched Arden pour the wine and Zoey's drink.

"And look at your dining room." Hands on hips, Zoey scanned the room. "Did Martha Stewart drop by for a consult on tablescapes?"

"The internet provides visuals. Nick and Jamie set such a gorgeous table for their monthly brunch, I felt I had to meet their standards."

"I'd say right on target." Boone sipped some wine. "I definitely feel like an adult."

"And baked Brie? Yum." Zoey started to help herself when Zorro raced back to the front door.

"Looks like Nick and Jamie couldn't wait either. We'll get this party started."

Arden went to the door. And found Gideon, Joe, Elvis, and a bookcase.

"Oh boy! Number four."

"And five," Gideon told her.

"Looks like we hit when you've got company. We'll get them in, and get out of your way."

"Joe, you're never in the way. Come in, come in. Gideon, you met Zoey and Boone. Joe, these are my cousins Zoey Rogan and Boone Yeoh."

"Nice to meet you. I just got my first look at these in place," Boone added. "Need a hand with that one?"

"We've got it balanced, thanks."

As they wheeled it in, Zoey eased toward the library door. "We were just talking about how beautiful these are."

"My boy knows his stuff. That fireplace looks just right, Arden, and would you look at those chairs? Somebody else knows her stuff."

"It's turning out just the way I imagined it. My neighbor, he's a local artist, is doing a painting for over the mantel. He won't let me see it yet. Oh, there's number four where it belongs. And number five finishes that wall. A whole wall of bookcases." Arden hunched up her shoulders in delight. "And more to go!"

"Tell me about it. Let's go get it, Pop."

"Yes, please. Have you eaten?"

"We're grabbing something on the way home."

"No, you're not. You're staying."

"That's a sweet girl." Joe patted her shoulder. "But we're not going to horn in on your dinner."

"You're not. I'd love for you to stay. I made plenty. As long as you like glazed ham."

Joe sighed. "Hit a weak spot."

"Then it's settled. I'm setting two more places."

While she did, Boone poured more wine. Arden took the glasses to the library as they installed the next cabinet.

"It fits so perfectly."

"That's the idea." Gideon glanced at the wine. "My truck, I'll drive and stick to one. You enjoy," he said to Joe.

"And I will. Thank you, Arden. It's been a while since I had a ham dinner."

"Come back and relax."

In the great room, Elvis sniffed his way around everything.

"It's the hound in him," Joe said. "Elvis, you settle down. We're guests."

"Our final two—the neighbors—have the cutest little dog. They'll bring Isis. You may know them, Joe. Nick's the owner/operator of Sugar, Spice, and Coffee."

"I sure do. So it's Jamie who's doing your painting. I met him at one of the gallery's art shows. I like his work."

"Me, too."

"We're admiring yours," Zoey said to Gideon. "I'd love to know more about bowl turning. I'm not saying I could build custom cabinets like those, but at least I know the process. I don't know anything about turning wooden bowls or those wonderful lamps Arden has. You must have a lathe."

"Pop does."

"I haven't used it much the last few years, but I'm pleased to say I taught Gideon how to work with one, even though he's one-upped me there."

Zorro raced to the door again. Elvis cocked his head, then followed more leisurely.

"That'll be Jamie and Nick."

When Arden opened the door, she found Nick carrying Isis, a hammer, and a wall hook, and Jamie holding a painting, unframed, with its back to her.

"Mine," she said, and reached out.

"Uh-uh-uh. No touching, no peeking. I'm hanging it unframed. If you want it framed, you need to wait a couple months. But we decided you deserved to see it hanging in place."

"I really do."

Nick set Isis down, where she wagged at Zorro, then walked to Elvis. When he lowered his long face, she exchanged sniffs, then licked him.

"Flirt," Jamie said. "Hello, everyone!"

"You've met Zoey and Boone, and I think you've met Joe. This is Gideon."

"I'm an admirer of your work." Nick held out a hand to Gideon.

"As we are of yours," Joe said. "Both of yours."

"We'll see what you think of my latest masterpiece. Got a stepladder, my darling?"

"Yes, out in the shed. Just let me—"

"Well, you must know your way around a hammer." As he smoothed a hand over his hair, Jamie gave Gideon a flirty look. "And I bet you wouldn't need the ladder."

"Probably not. I'll give you a hand."

"Nick, you keep Arden in the kitchen. And have a glass of wine ready for me. I'll need to celebrate success or bemoan my failure."

"I can wait five minutes. How long does it take to hang a painting?"

"Have you met Jamie?" Nick pulled a measuring tape and a small level out of his pocket, handed them to Gideon. "Something smells wonderful."

She had a houseful of people, Arden thought. Of friends. Add in two more bookcases and a painting.

The evening hit number one with a bullet.

"Let's get you that wine. Dinner's ready once my painting's hung. Everything's in the warming oven, and the ham's waiting for my hopeful carving skills."

Joe tapped a finger on his chest. "As the eldest, by far, and an experienced hand, I'll take that task on."

"I'll gratefully pass the carving knife to Joe."

She heard Jamie let out what could definitely be termed a giggle, and Gideon's quick laugh.

"Somebody else is a flirt." With a grin for Arden, Nick took his wine. "How's your family?" he asked Zoey.

"Very well, thanks. My parents will be coming out for Christmas, staying through New Year's. My brother and his family will drive up from Crescent City Christmas Day."

"This is taking longer than it should. You just smack a nail in the wall."

Nick slid a look toward Arden. "Again, have you met Jamie?"

"Add Gideon there," Joe put in. "Measure, measure, level, level."

"Well, give me a hint. Landscape, figure study, still life?"

"And end up sleeping in the guest room tonight? I'll just say that if Jamie hadn't promised it to you, we'd be hanging that in our house."

She waited, mostly pleased that the conversation flowed and her baked Brie with raspberry sauce seemed to be a hit.

Arms spread, Jamie stepped out of the library. "The big reveal. Be kind."

She didn't waste time.

The minute she stood beside him in the doorway, she pressed both hands to her mouth. Then turned to wrap around the artist.

"Thank you. Oh, Jamie, thank you."

"You barely looked at it."

"I'll look more in a second. It's the valley in moonlight. It's my view in moonlight."

"I sketched out sunrise, but—"

"No, moonlight. For this room, it's moonlight." She drew back, framed his face with her hands, and kissed him. "Thank you. Now move aside!"

She turned, stepped closer, and realized she couldn't have imagined it even if she'd known what he planned to paint.

Those gentle hills, the vineyards, the farms and homes, the mystery and majesty of the circling mountains, all washed in moonlight. A single cloud, thin, wispy, floated over the dreamy full moon that sailed in a diamond-studded sky.

"It's so right, Jamie. Moody, romantic, peaceful. The light, the shadows, the stillness. You've only to look at it to know everyone's safe and at rest."

"Not only so right for the room," Zoey said. "Arden, it's so you. You get her, Jamie."

"It was love at first sight for me. Thank God she didn't turn out to be a bitch."

"I grew out of that. It's an energy drain."

"She wasn't much good at it anyway," Zoey told him. "So you take commissions?"

"For the right person."

"I'm marketing director for Valley Vineyards, and there's talk about doing a fresh new label for our twentieth year." Zoey hooked an arm through Jamie's. "We should talk."

"Talk over dinner. Boone, would you get the dogs a you-know-what? Joe, if you're ready to carve the ham?"

"When it comes to ham, I'm always ready."

"I hope mine makes the grade."

While Joe carved, Arden pulled out sides. The rainbow carrots she'd roasted, the rustic mashed potatoes—a new one for her, so fingers crossed there—the green beans, and finally the biscuits.

"We're doing family style, so please, dig right in." She went back for the ham platter.

"I snuck a piece—the benefit of carving. The grade's an A plus."

He carried the platter in for her. "You're all in for a treat. When Gideon and I packed up those cabinets, we weren't expecting to be invited to a feast. We appreciate your hospitality, Arden."

"As do we all." Nick lifted his glass in a toast. "Everything looks delicious."

"Let's find out." She passed the potatoes to Gideon.

She felt a glow because the food was good—whew—and the company excellent.

"Arden, Boone wants the recipe for these potatoes. Rustic," Zoey added before Boone could speak. "That says manly to me, so you'd be in charge of them at our house. Arden's almost always been good at biscuits. Almost."

"It was one time!"

"One time, the first time. But she persisted."

"I figured baking powder, baking soda, what's the difference? And found out."

"You know your way around more than sandwiches."

She smiled as Gideon went for seconds. "I do. I don't do a lot of cooking. It's just me, but when I do, I like it."

"It's the focus." Boone bit into a second biscuit. "Arden's got laser focus on the task at hand."

"Except IT stuff. I moved here so I could call on Boone for that.

Then there's Zoey for household repairs. Though Gideon did change out my doorknobs and tighten my slip nuts."

Jamie burst out laughing. "Girl!"

"Truth. I have Jamie for art, Nick for sugar and spice, and Joe, who helps me find just what I want. I'm so happy you could all be here for my first dinner party."

"If I get much happier, Gideon's going to have to roll me into the truck."

"Eat up," Gideon suggested. "I can wheel you out on the dolly."

"In that case, maybe just a sliver more ham. A family favorite," Joe added. "My wife would make it whenever Liam—my son, Gideon's father—would come to visit. We did have to make accommodations that time, remember, Gideon? Which was the vegetarian, Dorcas or Julia?"

"Vegan, Julia, the third one."

"That's right. Colleen made up some fancy pasta dish, and it was just fine. But we went back to ham next time, as that was Julia's first and last visit. She didn't like we had chickens."

"You have chickens?"

Joe smiled at Nick as he ate. "We do. Our girls live in a hen palace Gideon and I built."

"Now you've done it," Jamie told him. "Nick's making noises about getting chickens. Fresh eggs for baking. I don't know if—"

Eyes wide, he broke off.

"Liam Riley? Your son? Not the director!"

Joe beamed. "That's my boy."

"Now *you've* done it," Nick said.

"Well, God! I absolutely adore *Beaten Path*. I can't count how many times I've seen it."

"I know, right?" Arden lifted her wine to sip. "I can come across it when it's half over, and I'll still watch to the end."

"And *Slip Knot*. It terrifies me, but I can't look away."

"Did he direct that? I love that movie."

"One of ours, too," Boone put in. "Our second date. The scene where who you thought was the good guy's revealed as the bad guy, and he's got the rope and the knife. He's walking up the steps in the creaky old house where the heroine's hiding. Zoey watched it with her eyes closed."

"I still do."

"Wait a minute." Jamie actually did jazz hands. "That means Scarlett Dash is your mother! She's glorious. A goddess, an icon. I adore her. She has such . . . presence."

"She's got plenty of that," Gideon agreed.

"I read they're back together. So romantic. Lovers reunited. Oh, tell me you like her," he begged Joe. "Tell me she's wonderful. Lie if you must, but don't shatter me."

"No need to lie. I love her. Always have. She kept in touch with Colleen and me after the divorce. More, if Liam couldn't bring Gideon for a visit—if he was on location or tied up—she would. She'd bring Ethan, Liam's other son, too, and Grace, her daughter. We stayed family.

"They were young the first time around. And just starting their climb. When it didn't work, they didn't go at each other. I'm hoping it sticks this time."

Following Boone's prediction, the rain started as a shower over dessert, then poured.

"October in the PNW," Zoey said. "It's good for the vines, and hell on my hair. I hate to break up the party, but we've got a babysitter to cut loose."

"And I need to get these old bones home."

Arden arched her brows. "I don't see any old bones."

"Trust me, I feel them. This was a wonderful meal, Arden, and an unexpected treat, from the first sip of wine to the last bite of apple cobbler."

"Couldn't have said it better. We need to scoop up Isis, Jamie, and make the dash home."

"We'll drop you off," Gideon told him. "You're right on the way."

"We'd appreciate it. This weather's hell on my hair, too. Now, remember, Arden," Jamie said as he rose to hug her. "Zoey and I are dragging you out for a shopping spree."

"Neither of you will let me forget."

"It pains me that my lovely friend considers shopping for herself a chore rather than a delight." He turned to kiss Zoey. "I'll text you."

Arden watched them all drive off in the rain, locked the door. In the glow of success, she walked back to clear dessert, blow out candles, wash the wineglasses.

Then she went up to change into sweats for comfort, pulled her hair into a tail.

She couldn't think of a better way to spend a few hours on a rainy night than shelving books in her library.

On the rainswept drive, Joe, relaxed and well fed, stretched out his long legs.

"She's a damn good cook."

"Who?"

"You can't fool me. And she's got a good, sharp brain in her head, and a kind heart. Pretty, too, and not in a dolled-up sort of way."

"Are you going to ask her out?"

On a snort of laughter, Joe shook his finger. "Maybe I would, but you've got an eye on her."

"Just one eye?"

"You've got both in that direction. I may not have your grandmother's sense about these things, but I see what I see, know what I know."

"She's interesting."

Joe puffed out a breath. "What're you going to do about it?"

"Haven't decided."

"These days." Joe sighed it, and got a grin from Gideon. "Young people don't just jump in the pool, swim around some. No, they've got to analyze the water first, get the exact temperature and depth, the pH before they stick a toe in."

"Maybe I stuck a toe in."

"Well then. Jump."

"She might not want to take a swim. Me either."

Joe shook his head, sat a moment in silence.

"Let me ask you something. Would you bring her around if I were making chicken potpie?"

"I don't know. Maybe. Probably. You make really good potpie."

"In all these years, you never once brought a girl home to meet me or your grandmother. I think Arden's one you would."

Gideon slanted Joe a look. "Are you making potpie?"

"Bring her home and I will."

When Gideon pulled up to the house, Joe started to get out of the truck. But Gideon sat, tapping his fingers on the wheel.

"Problem?"

I don't know, Gideon thought again. Maybe. Probably.

"I think I'll drive back over there, give her a hand shelving books."

Joe let out a cackle. "Is that what they're calling it these days? Get going then. Come on, Elvis, let's get into the warm and dry. I'll see you tomorrow, Giddyup."

Gideon waited, watching Joe and the dog walk through the rain, then into the house. Waited until he saw lights go on.

Unnecessary, he thought, but he felt better leaving knowing they were in the warm and dry.

In the library, Arden set out some of what she thought of as interesting things. Deciding what and where required more time than putting books on the shelves. After all, she wanted the right things in the right place.

So she sat on the floor and visualized. Changed her mind, tried again. She'd just picked the first interesting thing when the beam of headlights washed over the windows. And Zorro raced barking to the door.

For a moment she didn't move, couldn't move. Who would come after nine—nearly ten—on a rainy night? Almost everyone she knew in Riverbend had left only a half hour or so before.

Forgotten something. One of them forgot something, that's all.

And the door was locked, she had her phone, she had the dog.

She pushed herself to her feet, walked toward the wagging dog and the firm knock on her door.

Then her mind went to worst case. An accident. One of them had had an accident on the way home, and the police . . .

She ran the rest of the way to the door, snapped off the locks. When she yanked the door open, she saw Gideon.

"Joe? Is he hurt? Should I—"

"No. Hey, no, he's fine." Because they trembled, he put his hands on her shoulders. "He's fine. I dropped him off at home."

"He's okay? Everyone's okay?"

When she closed her eyes, he debated between pulling her in or letting her go. He let her go.

"Sorry. I'm sorry. I should've texted first."

"It's all right." She ran her hands over her face, back into her hair. "Why does the mind always flip to the bad? Come in. Did you forget something?"

"No. I had an impulse to come back and give you a hand shelving books."

"Oh." Her heart, on its way to settling, took another spin. "Why do you think I'm shelving books?"

"Tell me you're not, I'll call you a liar."

"I save all my lies for writing fiction. You drove back here to help me in the library?"

"Why not? I built the bookcases."

"Yes, you did, and yes, I'm just getting started on filling up the ones you brought tonight. I guess we'd better hang up your jacket."

"That'd be a start."

She took it from him, hung it while he gave Zorro the attention the dog desperately asked for.

"I'm just deciding what I'm putting where." She turned to lead him back.

"I thought it was alpha order, by genre."

"For the books, yeah. I'm mixing in some pieces every other cabinet."

"Every other." Of course she was. "Systematic."

"Yes, but I don't want it to look regimented. The books are different, and that's organized."

"I didn't say anything."

"You thought it. Top shelf, first on this wall. You're taller so you can put it up there. In the center."

He took the dragon, wings spread as it sat on a large green egg. As much, he thought, defending as nesting.

"You've got a thing for dragons."

"I've got a thing for dragons. That's it. Perfect. I'm putting mysteries, suspense, thrillers in this section, and it won't look regimented when I'm done."

"That part doesn't." He gestured to the three she'd filled. "Regimented's when you buy books by the yard so they all look the same and you never plan to read them anyway."

"That's right. And that's not a library, it's . . ."

"A status display."

"That's right!" she repeated. "The next two shelves are all books. Hardcovers. Then a shelf for things, the next for a combination of books and things, and the bottom shelf for paperbacks."

He started at the top; she started at the bottom.

"Why aren't your books in here?"

"I've already read them."

"Like you haven't read most if not all of these? Something wrong with your work?"

"No."

"You've got copies, go get them."

Crouched at his feet, she looked up.

"You wrote books. This is a library. You put books in libraries. And, apparently, dragons."

She stood up. "You're right. My books, my library. I'll be right back."

He went back to shelving, leaving room. When she came back, he took them, slid them into place.

"I'm next to Lawrence Block. Isn't that a kick in the ass?"

Gideon tapped *When the Sacred Ginmill Closes*. "Hell of a story."

"It really is. I nearly shelved it in Classics."

He tapped one of hers, her newest. "This was pretty good."

"You read it?" It still came as a jolt.

"Pop wasn't going to give me any peace until I did. I liked it."

"Thanks."

She looked at him, and he saw her bottom lip poke out a little, as it did when she thought something through.

"Okay. I want to tell you, right off, I'm not very good at this."

"Shelving books. More like scary good at it."

"You didn't come back just to help me in the library."

"That would be up to you."

"That's right, and I'm not going to pretend like I haven't thought about it, about you. Or that I didn't know how this could go if I asked you in. I asked you in anyway, so I'm letting you know I'm not particularly good at sex."

Interesting, he thought, yet again. The woman was so damn interesting.

"So I should lower my expectations?"

"It wouldn't hurt. And you should also know if this turns into a one-off, I won't hold it against you."

He waited a beat. "Thanks."

"I still want my bookcases, and the library ladder I'm going to talk you into building."

"Okay. Is that it?"

"I guess so."

"If this turns into a one-off, I won't hold it against you either. You'll get your bookcases. We can discuss the ladder."

"Fair."

"Let's try this again first."

He kissed her much as he had the first time, in what she felt was barely controlled need. And like the first time, it made her yearn for more. All those flutters and aches reminded her she could yearn and feel and want.

"Arden." He pulled the tie from her hair, wove his fingers through it as it fell down her back. "Let me take you to bed."

Chapter Seventeen

She wasn't nervous, but needy. Needy to be held, to be touched, to give part of herself, if only for a night, to someone she wanted. Someone she trusted.

As they started up the stairs, she understood the giving meant more to her than to him. He didn't know, couldn't know, how this basic human need conflicted with her ugly memories and her fears.

It wasn't nerves that had her pausing, turning to him, as they neared the top of the steps, but the need to push the fears away.

"Sorry, could we just . . ." She locked herself around him, poured those needs into the kiss.

She threw him off. He'd expected she'd want slow and easy, and he'd intended to take his time, to give her time. He'd follow her lead.

Instead, she started a blaze when he'd prepared to strike a single match and let it all kindle.

So following her lead, he let instinct take over. He had her pressed against the wall, his hands rushing over her, the long torso, the narrow hips, the small, firm breasts. Though she trembled, she tugged at his shirt, released some buttons, popped off another before she dragged it away.

Then her hands ran over him, fingers digging in as they circled and stumbled toward her bedroom.

In the light of one lamp, with the rain pounding, he backed her against the door, managed to work off his shoes while her moans and gasps were muffled against his mouth.

Then he hiked her up, off her feet, so he could feast on those breasts, on the skin that smelled of secrets and seductions.

Inch by inch he lowered her until their mouths met again. Holding her suspended, he circled to the bed with her arms and those long legs chained around him, and her heart hammering against his.

And her mouth met his again and again like a woman starving.

He fell onto the bed with her, rolled once, twice.

Their eyes met, and in hers he saw all those secrets, all those needs before she dragged his mouth back to hers.

Oh, to feel like this. Just to feel and feel. Those big, strong hands on her body, the ripple of muscle as he moved over her. Hard-palmed hands, taut muscle.

With that strength, with that muscle, she knew he could take what he wanted. But how could he take more than she gave when she was willing to give all in this moment?

Everything in her ached and trembled, but not from fear. From the thrill. And the blissful shock of freedom.

She could take, be taken, and feel nothing but a wild, whippy pleasure.

Her heart pounded like the rain; her breath caught and released on sighs and gasps that spoke of the deep, dark joy of simple lust.

His body, a wonder to her, hard, hot, and, at the moment, hers. As she explored those angles, those planes and ridges, she let herself bask in that wonder.

She had someone who wanted her enough, needed her enough to give himself.

When he worked his way down her body, hands, lips, tongue, something in her coiled like a spring. Layer after layer of sensation floated down until the weight seemed too much, the pressure too strong, the heat too intense.

She started to push away, to tell him to stop. Stop. Wait.

Then it burst free, and as she gripped the iron bars of the bed, she cried out not in protest but in stunning, breath-stealing release.

She shuddered under him even as she went soft as melted wax. The combination had the fire she'd lit threatening to consume him.

When he brought his mouth back to hers, the sound of helpless pleasure she made frayed the last thread keeping him tethered.

"Arden. Look at me."

She opened those fascinating eyes, heavy now, dazed now. Her hair, gold fire, glowed in the lamplight.

To torment them both, he slid into her, slowly, then deep, he held. As the ache in him became a throb, and the throb edged toward pain, he waited.

Those gold flecks against the blue glimmered as she rose to him.

Now a blur of passions unleased, quickened breath and urgent speed as they both took all. The sound of rain vanished; the world beyond them simply went away.

She saw him, saw him as she rushed to the edge. Then let go.

She lay naked, but didn't feel exposed. She felt weak and wrecked, and wonderful.

When her mind began to come out of the fog, she had to remind herself this once, just this once, might be enough for him.

She'd accept that, and, in fact, be grateful because he'd helped her open a door she hadn't let herself walk through in far too long.

"Pretty damn clever of you, Legs."

"Huh?"

He still lay over her, so his lips moved against her throat.

"Telling me you weren't good at sex and I should lower my expectations so you could blow right through them."

"I . . ." Ridiculous to feel flattered, she thought, but she did anyway. "It's probably pent-up energy, since it's been a while."

He lifted his head, looked down at her. "See, now I'm compelled to test that theory."

Rolling, he reversed their positions.

"You know your dog kept an eye on things, or me."

She shifted enough to look around. Zorro curled on his bed, but he didn't sleep.

"Bedtime," she said. The dog rose, circled three times, then settled down with his stuffed llama.

"He's not used to this kind of activity."

"How long have you had him?"

"About two years now."

"That would be a while. Something wrong with the men in Columbus?"

"I've been busy." She tossed her hair back.

And made his mouth water.

"The slower pace here in the valley should free up some of your time."

"It could."

She lowered her head to his shoulder, closed her eyes when he stroked a hand down her hair.

"You seem to keep pretty busy yourself."

"I manage to make time for what matters."

"Could you tell me one thing?"

"Maybe."

Her lips curved. She liked that about him, liked he didn't give the unqualified yes to something he might want to back out of.

"If we both make time for this, is it just this or something else? No wrong answer."

"I don't know the answer yet, but I plan to find out."

"Okay." She let out a sigh because while there wasn't a wrong answer, he'd hit the right one. "Why?"

"That's two things."

"It was a two-part thing."

"You're an interesting woman. And no, you don't get to ask how, or why I think so. It just is. Plus, I like your taste in books and doorknobs. Unless you've got a problem with it, I'm going to stay tonight. I've got a theory to test."

Her lips curved again as she lifted her head. "I don't have a problem with it."

In the morning, she wouldn't have called it a problem, but it was strange to find herself sharing a bed. She lay a moment, feeling the warmth and shape of him, and took stock.

Yes, it pleased her to have spent the night with a man she liked and enjoyed. It certainly pleased her to have slept deep and dreamless after having sex with him, twice in the bed, once in the shower.

The thought of spending more time with him added more pleasure.

When she heard Zorro start to stir, she slipped out of bed. She put on her flannel pants and sweatshirt. She'd gathered them up the night before, and to Gideon's obvious amusement, had laid them—along with his clothes—neatly on the bedroom chair.

She couldn't help herself.

She took the dog down, let him out before making her morning coffee. And as usual, outlined her day in her head.

Feed the dog, have breakfast, get in a workout, check emails, texts, glance at headlines. She'd planned to give the book another day to sit, but she really wanted to get back to it.

As the rain continued, Zorro made quick work of his duties. She'd already resigned herself to adding the chore of wiping off wet or muddy paws a few times a day.

While her now-dry dog enjoyed his breakfast, she stepped back into the kitchen to make hers.

She jumped nearly six inches when she saw Gideon.

"Jumpy in the morning?"

She held out both hands as she caught her breath. "Did you used to be a cop or a cat burglar?"

"I was a cop who caught cat burglars. So you're an early riser."

"Yes. Sorry. I can offer you a breakfast smoothie, which I'm about to make, toast—whole wheat or rye—an English muffin, oatmeal—instant—or cold cereal."

"Coffee. I'll figure the rest out from there."

She made his coffee, then began to get her ingredients for the smoothie. "I've got plenty for two of these."

"No. That's a frozen banana."

"Better for texture."

He watched her work for a moment. "You're putting seeds in there."

"Chia seeds, and yes, I am." To the rest, she added her protein powder. "It's still raining. A lot."

"Shocker. It's purple," he said after she sent her machine whirling.

"Blueberries will do that."

When she finished, she smiled, sipped. "Yum."

"You can't possibly mean that."

"But I do. Want a sip?"

"Oh, hell, no. I'll get something at home, where we eat normal things like eggs and drink actual coffee. Just what started you down this path of chia seeds and frozen bananas?"

"Going through middle school being known as Toothpick, Spaghetti Legs, and/or No-Ass Bowie."

"Kids are mean bastards."

"They sure can be. So, calories, protein, resistance training. I need them all, as I have the metabolism of a hummingbird."

"You look pretty good."

He said it so casually, she laughed. "Well, thanks."

"I'm heading out to get my calories with something that didn't go through a blender." He set his empty cup beside the sink. "I've got a thing with Pop tonight, but the day after, I could spare you making a sandwich or blending up a potential Chia Pet and bring takeout."

She sipped her smoothie and smiled. "That would be fine."

"Any preference?"

"Not really."

"How do you feel about pizza?"

"I feel very fondly about pizza as long as there aren't mushrooms or anchovies anywhere on its surface."

"I can work with that."

He took her smoothie, set it on the counter, then hooked an arm around her waist. When he kissed her, it didn't land anywhere close to casual.

"Thanks for setting out a spare toothbrush. I'll see you tomorrow."

When he left, Zorro followed him to the door, earned a goodbye rub. When the dog came back, Arden sipped her breakfast.

"I think I might possibly have the beginning of a potential relationship."

Gideon got home just as Joe started cooking breakfast.

"I take it you and Arden shelved a lot of books last night."

"My grandfather's a hell of a smart-ass."

"Proud of it. She feed you?"

Gideon got himself another cup of coffee. "She does smoothies. This one was purple. She puts seeds in it."

"Well, looks like you'll just have to settle for bacon and eggs."

"Thank God."

"Are you going to see her again?"

"I'm going to pick up a pizza and go over in a couple days."

"I'm glad to hear it. I like that girl, Gideon."

"It turns out I do, too."

They had a companionable breakfast, with the dog dozing under the table and the rain falling as if it had a score to settle. Joe sat back with coffee while Gideon dealt with the dishes.

"Weatherman says this'll keep up until midday tomorrow."

Gideon nodded. "I'll bring in some more firewood."

"That'll be good. Is Arden set there? She's got a wood-burning."

"I don't know. I'll check. Look, Pop, I jumped in, but I'm just treading water right now. She's got something in there. It makes her skittish when she doesn't want to be."

"You could ask her."

He couldn't claim not his business, not honestly, now. But.

"We'll see if and when she trusts me enough to tell me."

"All right then." Joe rose. "I'll see you later this afternoon when you come in."

"I can take the morning if you want to stay home awhile."

"Nah, you go on, work on those bookcases. I've got some paperwork to see to before we open."

"I'm going to turn a bowl first. It's been nagging at me."

"Then Elvis and I'll see you later."

Alone, Gideon set the kitchen to rights. He went up for a quick shower, and who could blame a man for remembering the one he'd taken late at night when he'd had company in the steam and the spray?

But he had things to do, so set that memory aside and went out through the wet to the shop.

Lights, the morning's music. He'd already selected the wood, made his cardboard template. He put on his safety goggles, his thick leather gloves, chose his band saw blade, made his adjustments.

With his template circle in place, he turned on the saw, brought it up to speed. Sure and cautious, he fed the left edge of the wood blank and followed the edge of the cardboard.

He kept his eye on the awl he used to hold the template in place, rotated the wood until he had that perfect circle.

With his music and the rain banging, he chose the faceplate for the lathe.

At the lathe, he unlocked the headstock as his grandfather had taught him long ago. *Rotate the headstock*, he heard Pop tell him, *not the wood*, and as he used the handwheel, he felt the threads turning smooth.

While he worked, with the sound of rain, music, machine, with the scent of sawdust, his mind focused on the steps, on the wood, on the shape he wanted to create.

Any outside worries, concerns, questions just slipped away with the feel of the wood.

He measured the blank, marked it, then drilled holes in the center for the faceplate.

Time passed, and he relaxed into it. He cleared away some of the bark area, creating the flat area he needed before attaching the faceplate, checked, approved.

He'd always thought of it as him and the lathe working together, rather than simply man and machine.

He spent an hour, then two. Stopped long enough to decide between coffee and a cold drink. He went with a Coke and, drinking it, studied his progress.

If he didn't screw up from here, he thought it would turn into a damn fine-looking bowl. Good-sized salad bowl. He'd make the smaller ones another time.

He began to shape the bottom of the bowl, creating another flat area, tailstock end wide enough for the four-jaw chuck and the tendon shoulder.

It took patience, but he always found that here. As the tendon changed shape, he had to stop, true it, tighten the jaws when necessary.

Step by step, minute by minute, tool by tool until it came time to start removing the wood up to the tendon line.

He'd had more than one bowl go flying at this point in his pursuit of this craft.

He checked the time, calculated he had enough.

With the lathe turning, he used the spindle gouge to mark the bowl's center. After stopping the lathe, he used foam padding to protect the wood surface, then started the lathe again, slow speed. And saw, satisfied, it turned true.

He had enough time to sand the interior, then clean up, and grab something to eat before he headed into town.

When he finally stepped out of the shop, he saw Tom Franklin, Riverbend's chief of police, crossing the yard.

"Hi there, Gideon."

"Chief. Do I have to go bail Pop out?"

Tom, a genial sort who could turn hard-ass on a dime if and when called for, chuckled.

Though closer to his father's age than his grandfather's, Gideon knew Tom and Joe had been friends for decades.

"Good thing you're around to keep him out of trouble. I just came from the store. Joe said you'd probably be back in the shop."

"Yeah, working on something. I've got some time before I have to head in, keep my eye on the man. Want coffee?"

"Wouldn't mind a dry spot and a cup, thanks."

Tom, stocky, keen-eyed, a short bush of hair gone Brillo-pad gray, stepped into the kitchen and took off the dung-brown Stetson he'd worn for two decades.

"Had some half-wit tourist driving like it's a speedway on a sunny day in May. Ended up in a ditch. He's fine, and so's the nitwit with him. But his Porsche's never going to be the same."

"Some people lose half their driving IQs at the first drop of rain."

"That's God's truth."

Since Tom often frequented the kitchen, Gideon knew the chief took his coffee as strong and black as he did. He handed Tom a mug.

"Thanks. I'm going to sit a minute if you don't mind. I won't keep you long."

"It's okay. I've got some time." Gideon took his own seat at the kitchen table.

"Well, you might've heard I had a little health incident a couple weeks back."

"I did, but Joe said you came out fine. You look fine."

"That's what I say. Gave me aspirin, got me on blood thinners." Now he rolled his eyes. "Treatment plan with health foods, exercise. Want me to lose ten pounds, and I guess it wouldn't hurt. As far as heart attacks go, it didn't amount to much. They even call what I had a mini, for fuck's sake. Mini."

Shaking his head, he drank coffee.

"But that hasn't stopped Sherry from worrying herself into a frenzy, and nagging me to do yoga."

"Yoga?" Gideon grinned at the image. "Namaste."

Tom answered Gideon's grin. "She signed me up for it at the gym, and with a personal trainer. And she bought some heart-healthy cookbook."

"The woman loves you, Tom."

"She must to tolerate my ways for thirty-seven years. And I love her back and then some. It's got the kids worrying, too. TJ came down from Seattle, Greg's joined the gym as my—get this—accountability partner, and Angie buys me this tracker watch."

He tapped the watch on his wrist. "Steps, calories, sleep, and my fucking heart rate, BP, and who the fuck can figure half of it out anyway?"

"Looks like your kids love you, too."

"I'm grateful for it. Grateful to have a wife and grown-ass kids, grandkids who love me. The thing is, besides the damn yoga, eating better, and all that, I'm supposed to cut back on stress. Hard to do with the family worried. Hard when half-wit tourists end up in ditches. Drunks trade punches until somebody's in the ER, series of break-ins, somebody beats his wife for the third time, or she grabs a gun and shoots him."

Tom shrugged. "Six thousand, eight hundred, and forty-six souls in Riverbend last count. I've got twelve good officers and a hell of an operations manager, but I'm in charge."

"Are you thinking of retiring, Tom?"

"Not thinking, that part's done. I'm doing it." Tom puffed out his cheeks, blew the air out audibly. "I've been chief for twenty-four years, and on Riverbend's force for ten more. That's a long time to protect and serve, longer than you've been alive. And I need to give this to Sherry, to my family."

"You're a good cop. Always have been."

"I am, and I have been, and it's time for someone else to step in, step up. I'm asking you to do that, Gideon."

The man had laid it all out, Gideon realized, and still he hadn't seen it coming.

"Me? Jesus, Tom. You've got Hawk or—"

"I talked to Hawk, and we both knew going into that talk this isn't for him. He's a damn good sergeant, but he doesn't want chief and he's not wired for it either. None of them are. Kim comes closest. You know Kim Chung?"

"A little, yeah."

"Well, she's a damn good cop, but she needs another ten years under her belt before she'd make a good chief. And I don't want handing it over to an outsider."

"I'm an outsider."

Now Tom scowled, and a trace of the hard-ass came with it. "Fuck you are. You're a Riley. You were ten years a cop in LA, a detective, Major Crimes."

"And you know how that ended up."

"I do." Those sharp eyes looked hard into Gideon's. "You did what was right. You stood up for what the badge is meant to stand for. You got the shaft, but you stood up. I had one condition when I said I'd retire. I needed to turn this responsibility and this privilege over to someone I respected, and trusted. A good, honest, no-bullshit cop who could lead and shoulder what needs to be shouldered.

"That's you. I talked to the mayor, the town council."

Gideon wasn't easily stunned, but that one got him.

"Hold on, Tom."

"No, you do that a minute." Tom slapped a finger on the table. "Hold on, and hear me out. I talked to them because I wasn't going to come to you with this if they started quacking and huffing at the idea. They didn't, so if you decide to meet with them, they won't give you any trouble. The job's yours if you want it. You'll have to do the meeting, but they're not idiots. At least not half the time."

Tom nodded when Gideon said nothing.

"Take some time to think about it. I didn't say anything to Joe, but I figure he's got a pretty good idea why I wanted to talk to you. If you want to run this around with him, that's fine and good. I'm taking four weeks to tie everything up, so think it over."

Tom rose, stepped over to lay a hand on Gideon's shoulder. "Riverbend would be lucky to have you, but if you decide against, no hard feelings. Think it through, let me know."

"I will."

"I gotta get going." Tom picked up his Stetson, put it on. "Thanks for the coffee."

Alone, Gideon stared into his coffee. Just like that, he thought, his life could change again.

If he let it.

He didn't say anything about his conversation with Tom when he got to the store, even when he caught his grandfather's questioning look.

He did the job he'd moved to Riverbend to do. Worked the register, waited on customers, answered questions, mixed paint.

At six, he helped Joe close the store.

"We're coming in the same time tomorrow. I'll leave my truck," Joe said, "ride with you."

They went out in the rain, drove the half mile to Around the Bend, where they had their monthly steak dinner.

They sat in the same booth, had the same server, ordered the same meal—New York strip, medium rare, loaded baked potato, roasted brussels sprouts, and one glass of local cabernet each.

Gideon always found the routine a comfort.

"Ready to talk about it?" Joe asked him.

"I guess I am."

"I take it Tom's decided to retire."

"Yeah."

"You're taking the job."

It didn't come as a question, but a statement, so Gideon shook his head.

"I don't know. I haven't had time to think it through."

"Thanks, Hailey." Joe gave their server a smile when she brought them the wine and warm sourdough bread.

After a quick and easy conversation, Joe turned back to Gideon.

"Let me take something out of that thinking. I love you, Giddyup, and when my time comes, I'd turn the store over to you if that's what you wanted. You don't, but you'd take it, run it, because you'd think it's what I want. It's not, not for you. You're no shopkeeper," he added. "You do fine because you're not lazy and if you do something, you don't do it half-assed. You could make a decent living woodworking. Money's never going to be a problem for you, but you're a man who wants and needs to make his own, and you don't want to make it through your craft."

"Hobby."

"Call it what you like. Gideon Joseph Riley, you're a cop. It's what you want, and always have."

Gideon just frowned into his wine. "I turned in my badge for a reason."

"A couple of them," Joe agreed. "You stood up against dirty cops, exposed them for what they were. They're the ones who didn't deserve that badge. You paid a price for it, and it could've been your life, but you did what was right. You might've kept going, despite them, if we hadn't lost your grandmother. If you hadn't come to make sure I got through."

"No, I was done, Pop." That fact, however painful, was fact. "I was done with it."

"Maybe so, and there's no blame or shame there. You turned in that badge, and you never once dishonored it. I can't look at you and find a reason you wouldn't pick up this one."

Joe sipped some wine. "If you need a little more incentive to do what we both know you want, what we both know you're meant to do? You're fired."

Gideon let out a laugh. "Come on, Pop."

"I'm serious. Don't you use me to stop you from doing what you want. I won't let you. Who the hell knows why things happen? People say there's always a reason, and maybe that's true. But the fact is, what happened in LA happened, what happened to my Colleen happened. What's happening now is happening now. When it's offered, laid right out? Take what you want, Gideon, what you need."

Everything in him lifted, and what he'd closed off opened again.

"I guess I will, since I'm out of a job. I love you, Pop."

"You're a bright spot in my life, Giddyup. You make me proud."

Chapter Eighteen

They had take-out pizza, streamed a movie they both enjoyed, and had sex. The next time Gideon came over, Arden cooked. Then he brought Chinese.

At the end of two weeks, he hauled in another two bookcases. On another rainy night, with the dog curled by the fire, he helped her shelve books and interesting things.

He studied the photo of Arden and her cousin. "Spring break?"

"Good guess."

The picture Dustin had stolen, Arden thought. Seeing it helped her remember the happiness the picture preserved, and how one person could destroy it.

"Neither one of you've changed much."

"Oh, I don't know about that." She sat cross-legged on the floor, loading the bottom two shelves. "Two years after that was taken, she met Boone. That was it for her. Him, too. Now she's a wife, mother of two with another on the way, and a marketing exec in Oregon.

"Me? I dreamed of being a writer, imagined living in New York while secretly writing a novel between work and classes. And was seriously stuck on a lit major named John Jay Haverstam."

He looked down at her. "Did you just make that name up?"

"I did not. He wore horn-rimmed glasses and a man bun, intended to write the Great American Novel and live in seclusion in Maine—I think it was Maine—while he wrote another Great American Novel.

"He was my first."

"Your first what?"

"Serious boyfriend and sexual experience."

Curious, Gideon studied the photo again. His cop's eyes pegged her at nineteen or twenty.

"How old were you in this picture?"

"I'd just turned twenty." She looked up at him. "I got a slow start, as most boys weren't very interested in a bookish, flat-chested girl who hit six feet if she put on kitten heels. Apparently, I'm making up for that now."

"Happy to help. Did he? Write the Great American Novel?"

"Not yet. He did send me a note of congratulations when my second book came out. Though carefully crafted to mark my success in the arena of popular fiction, which I know he considers one narrow and slippery step above graphic novels—"

"I like graphic novels."

"Me, too, as you'll see when we get to that section of the library. But John Jay Haverstam sees them as an insult to literature, the bastard son of publishing."

She slid another paperback into the bottom shelf.

"So while he congratulated me, I tasted his bitterness in every word, a flavor I found delicious, as when I got back from that spring break, which was about six months into our relationship, he told me that the relationship had run its course for him. I no longer inspired him, and he needed fresh stimulation for his art."

"So, he was a dick."

"Absolutely." She said it with the brightest of smiles. "A dick who's teaching high school English—an honorable and essential profession, which I'm sure he hates—in New Jersey. I'm a published writer who gets to do what I love every day, living in a beautiful spot in Oregon with my faithful dog. And I'm having regular sex with a guy who looks like you."

"Because you developed better taste in men."

"No question. I'd feel sorry for him, except for the careless and callous way he dumped me, because I'm doing what I always wanted to do, and he's not."

"Having sex with me? Oh, you meant writing," he said when she laughed.

"I did. It's a tremendous gift to be able to do what you love, what you want and wanted. It makes me want to be good at it, do it right."

He went quiet so the only sound came from the rain and Zorro's quiet snoring.

"I'm not working at the hardware anymore. Last day today."

"Oh, I didn't know that. Are you going to concentrate on your woodworking?"

"No, it's a hobby. It's not . . . Chief Franklin's retiring."

"Chief Franklin?"

He shot her a look between annoyance and frustration.

"Chief of police, Arden. You should know who's in charge of the local cops. He's retiring. I'm taking the job."

"Oh. Well, that's . . . That's big news."

"I met with the town council a few days ago. It's official now, so I'll start going in, get a sense of how it works here, the officers under me, the administrative stuff."

"This is good, right?" She pushed up to stand. "It's good big news. It's something you want."

"All I ever wanted was to be a cop." He stuck his hands in his pockets. "Since I'm going back to that in a place with under ten thousand people, you might hear why I stopped being one. I don't go back into it, no reason to. But taking this job, it might come up."

"All right. Do you want to sit down?"

"No."

If he went through it all again, he needed to move, not sit.

"I made detective, and I put in for Major Crimes. That's what I aimed for, that's what I got. It didn't take me long to figure out my partner was a bad cop. Taking bribes, doing shakedowns. There were three more of them on the job in on it that I knew of—know of. I needed evidence, and I got it. When I got it, I turned them in."

"What else could you do?"

"Look the other way."

He wandered the room as he went through it.

He hated going through it.

"You couldn't look the other way," she spoke quietly. "Maybe some could, but you couldn't."

"Some of the people they shook down, planted evidence against, were bad guys. These were three men and one woman with careers and families, who went through doors and risked their lives and took plenty of those bad guys off the street. I could've looked the other way. I didn't. I didn't because I couldn't."

It hurts him, she thought. It still hurts him. God knew she understood how old wounds could throb and ache.

"You crossed the blue line."

"That's right. There were plenty who supported that, and some who didn't. Four wrong cops were off the force, faced charges. Cases they'd worked on had to be reopened, and the department had to deal with the fallout, public fallout. I made that choice, and I'm not sorry for it."

He shrugged. "I took some blowback, and I'd expected it. The looks, the talk, flat tires, a dead rat on my doorstep, that sort of thing."

"That's wrong, Gideon. Just wrong."

"Right, wrong, it happened. I handled it for the best part of a year. Then I took a transfer, handled that. It followed me anyway. I got another partner, good guy, solid cop. We worked well together. We were investigating a drug ring, gang members."

It still stuck in his throat, still ground glass in his gut.

"To wind it up, we got pinned down in a firefight, and I called for backup, shots fired. The car that responded took its fucking time. They knew it was me, and took their time. Time enough my partner took a hit."

"Oh God, Gideon."

"He's bleeding, half conscious. I call in the officer down, I'm pissed, scared shitless he'll bleed out. Backup got there fast, easy since they were sitting in their car around the goddamn corner. Another car got there right ahead of them. They'd hit the sirens when they got the call for backup, but they'd been farther away than the other. We resolved the situation, got Pete to the hospital. He made it, and he's back on the job."

"What happened to the ones who failed to respond?"

"I don't know. I stopped caring. One of them came up to me at the hospital, when we didn't know if Pete would make it. He said: 'It should've been you. It should've been you, and if he dies, it's on you.'"

She still spoke quietly when she said, "Motherfucker."

That surprised a half laugh out of him.

"It took three of them to pull me off him. I turned in my badge the next day. I was done. I didn't know what I'd do, just that I was done. A couple weeks later, my grandmother died. Pop was lost. I was lost. So, we worked through it together."

Done, Gideon thought. He'd gotten through it one more time. Hopefully the last time.

"I don't look back there, Arden. It's over, and I'm okay with that. I never expected to pick up a badge again, but, well, Pop fired me."

Even as her eyes stung with tears, she laughed. "Of course he did. He's such a good man. So are you."

"Doing what I had to do doesn't make me a good man."

"I disagree. I've been with, as you aptly put it, a dick. I've been with a—I guess I'll say a fun lover with a lazy streak, and with a very nice man who wasn't any more right for me than me for him. I know a good man when I'm looking at him.

"I'm sorry for what happened, and the way it happened. But it brought you here, and it seems like here's where you're supposed to be. Chief Riley."

"Ha. That'll take some getting used to."

"You could try a Jesse Stone and insist everyone call you by your first name."

"I've noted your collection of Robert B. Parker novels. But I think I might get off being called chief."

"In that case, I'll try to remember to call you that once in a while in bed."

He came to her, drew her in. It had been easier to tell her than he'd imagined. Just as it was easier to keep coming back to her, to see himself continue to come back to her.

"We could go up, try that out now."

She tipped her face up to his. "Good idea, Chief," she said, and kissed him.

Later, she lay warm beside him, listening to the rain. She wondered if she should tell him what had happened to her. He'd understand, the man she knew him to be would understand. The cop she imagined him to be would have heard and seen worse.

Part of her, most of her, simply wanted to forget it had ever happened, to keep riding on this slow and easy road of being with him, learning about him, enjoying him.

Why bring Dustin Dubecki into something both comfortable and exciting? And already a little scary because she was falling in love.

Maybe she'd already landed.

Couldn't she just hold on to what was now for as long as it lasted?

He'd be out in a handful of months, out in the world she inhabited. But not here. And surely after five years she'd no longer be his obsession, the target of his delusions. To say it all out loud would bring everything flooding back again.

Did she tell Gideon, be as honest with him as he'd been with her? Or did she keep that door shut and locked until what lurked behind it simply didn't matter any longer?

Maybe the best choice was to do nothing for now, to see if what she and Gideon had begun together proved real, real enough to last.

As she closed her eyes, she found his hand, and linked her fingers with his.

Though he couldn't explain it, Dustin felt the weight of the last few months ahead more heavily than the four years behind him. He lay in bed after lights-out every night, not relieved another day was behind him, but in despair of the days yet to come.

All the same, so much the same, when his life, his freedom, his needs and wants lay outside the walls. He imagined they waited for him, she waited for him, just as he waited for them and her.

Every night, he went over exactly what he would do when he walked beyond those walls. He'd let his mother buy him his first real meal. After that, she'd need to buy him some decent clothes. He'd used the gym every day once he'd earned that privilege, so he'd kept in shape despite the crap food. He'd built more muscle.

Of course, he'd need a car, something that could handle the remote mountain roads around the cabin he imagined.

He'd need a fully loaded laptop, cell phone.

He'd need to gain access to her money as well as his because he'd want cash. Plenty of cash. He'd use it to buy the cabin once he'd found it. Somewhere people minded their own business, and a man could live off the grid.

Building it himself would take too much time, but he'd have plenty of time to make improvements. He'd need to put money, a lot of money, in an offshore account—or two—definitely needed a gun. And he'd need a fresh new ID for that.

He'd figure it all out.

Then he'd kill his mother.

He'd hunt down the lawyer, the judge, give them what they had coming. The cops? He'd take them out if he could; otherwise, he might have to let them live awhile. He could come back for them when they thought themselves safe.

Probably smarter.

Besides, he'd need to get Arden. As much as he wanted revenge, he wanted her more. If she resisted, he'd just have to remind her who was in charge.

In any case, she needed to pay a price for not telling the truth of how she'd led him on, how she'd wanted exactly what he'd given her.

He'd take care of that, then together, they'd drive west.

Those miles, those days remained a blur in his mind, but he could see them, always see them, in the cabin, in the mountains. Arden in the kitchen making dinner, him sitting by the fire enjoying the drink she'd fixed for him.

That image helped him carry the weight of those last months and survive the tedium of the days.

When his mother came to visit, he—as always—put a shiny smile on his face to cover the roiling hate. He'd gotten so good at it, sometimes he fooled himself into thinking he felt glad to see her.

Then she hugged him, and all the rage and disgust poured back.

"Dustin." She gripped his hands, drew him down to sit with her. "I have some hard news. About your father."

"He still hasn't come to see me. Not even once. He doesn't call or write either, ever. Doesn't he know how much that hurts me? You're the only one, Mom. The only one who cares about me. Can't you tell him I've learned to be the man he tried to teach me to be?"

With some effort, he worked up a single tear and let it slide down his cheek.

"I know I've been a disappointment. I'm going to make it up to you, I swear. And to him if I can."

"I'm proud of you, of the work you've done to get well. You needed help, and you accepted it. I'm sorry your father hasn't . . ."

Trailing off, she took Dustin's hands again. "Dustin, your father's very ill."

"What? Like the flu?"

"No." Her hands gripped his harder. "It's cancer."

"That's bad." The breath backed up in his lungs. "That's bad, but they have treatments. They can take it out, and he can do chemo, and—"

"Dustin, baby. By the time he went in for tests, by the time they found it, it was stage four. I didn't know until recently when he contacted me. They did all they could, but it had already spread. It's terminal, and he's decided to end the treatments and stay home for . . . He only has two or three months left."

He could have killed her for that alone.

"That's not true! Why are you saying that? Dad's strong. He's the strongest man I know. He wouldn't give up."

He didn't have to force the tears now. As they flooded his face, he yanked his hands free. "Why are you telling me horrible lies? Why are you such a bitch?"

"Dustin."

As one of the aides moved toward them, Theresa shook her head. "No, please. I'm fine. We're fine."

She took a breath. "Dustin, I wish they were lies. For your sake, I wish they were. I know how much you love Paul. It's not giving up, my darling. Please listen to me. It's acceptance. It's a very real need to spend what time he has left at home."

"The doctors could be wrong. He needs better doctors. You need to get him better doctors."

She wasn't Paul Dubecki's wife, and hadn't been for a very long time. But she pushed aside the part of her that worried her son, still, refused to accept that.

"Sweetheart, I went to see him. He wanted to speak to me in person, so I went to see him last week. They're not wrong, sweetheart. I'm sorry. I'm so sorry. He's fought it for nearly a year, and that fight took its toll. He is strong. Mitzi told me they'd given him six months, and he fought for nearly a year."

"Mitzi." Dustin sneered out the name of his father's second wife. "What the fuck does she know?"

"She's gone through this with him. Whatever you think of her, Dustin, she's gone through this hell with him."

He'd kill her, too. He should've thought of it before. Kill that whore bitch and the little brat she'd pumped out to try to take his place.

"For all we know she poisoned him so she'd end up a rich-as-fuck widow."

When she heard what she thought of as the old Dustin, Theresa pulled back.

"Stop that now. Stop it. I know you're shocked and upset, but don't talk that way. Your father has terminal pancreatic cancer, he's fought as long as he could fight. He only has a little time. I hate this for you, Dustin. I'd spare you if I could. But he's dying, and he wants to see you."

The war raged inside him between the boy who'd worshipped his father and the one who'd hated and feared him.

"He never came. Over four years, he never came."

"I know. And he knows, and regrets. Dustin." She pulled tissues out of her pocket, handed them to him. "He's not physically capable of coming to you now. His dying wish is to see you, speak with you, spend some of the time he has left with his son.

"I'm doing everything I can, and so is your father, to secure you compassionate release."

"What do you mean?"

"You still have several months left on your sentence."

"I *know* that!" His hands balled into fists. "You think I don't know that?"

"The doctors are clear Paul won't live that long. He wants to see his only son before he dies, and, as I said, he can't come to you. We could arrange a visitation, but we're both hoping to have the rest of your time commuted.

"You've accepted help, responded to treatment. It's only a few months for you, but a lifetime for your father. We're petitioning the courts, and your medical team has agreed you're ready to leave. There may be stipulations, but we're very hopeful we'll get a positive ruling in a week or two."

Calculation dried his tears, but he continued to wipe at his face.

This changed everything.

"I have to see him, Mom. I have to tell him I'm sorry. I have to say goodbye."

"I know." She shifted, enfolded him in her arms. "I'm going to do everything I can to make that happen."

Of course she would. And so would he.

He wept in his therapy session, and read aloud the letter he'd written. Not with his father in mind, but his own freedom.

"I wrote this because I'm not sure I'll have the chance to say this to my dad.

"'Dear Dad, there's so much I want to say. Before anything else, I want to say I'm sorry. I'm sorry for the pain, the grief, the embarrassment I caused you. I'm sorry I spent so long angry about what I thought I didn't have, and didn't appreciate enough all I did. I didn't appreciate you enough.

"'You showed me what it is to be a man, but I chose, for too long, to remain a selfish boy. You taught me right from wrong, tried to instill in me a sense of duty and responsibility, and I looked away, sought the easier ways until, through my actions—a childish rebellion, I see now, against the good and true standards you set—I caused you to turn away from me.'"

Holding up one hand, he looked down as if choking back sobs until he could continue again.

He'd practiced.

"'For this, for a long, long time, I blamed everyone but myself.

"'I've learned, Dad. I've listened, I've atoned. My forever regret is not having the time to show you. To hold your hand as you once held mine. To be the son I should have been all along. To make you proud of who I can be.

"'I don't want to say goodbye. Instead, I'll say please forgive me for the harm I caused. And please watch me from heaven so you'll see I've finally become a man you can respect.

"I love you, Dad. Dustin.'"

He dried his eyes, prepared to talk through what he'd read.

He considered it a fine piece of fiction.

Just under three weeks later, Detective Brill sat in the courtroom. She'd report to Venmar, currently laid up with the flu, once they had a ruling.

But she had a sick, angry feeling what that ruling would be.

He looked harmless, she thought, sitting there, hands folded, head respectfully bowed, in his smart suit. He'd had his hair cut in a boyish style.

His mother sat behind him, perfectly dressed, perfectly coiffed. Brill had never quite decided if the woman was callous or simply credulous.

Did she actually not see the monster she'd birthed, or did she just not care?

Brill saw it. She saw through the average-to-ordinary looks, the good lines of the designer suit, the bullshit haircut. Not cynicism, she reassured herself.

She saw it.

He rose when the judge entered the courtroom, sat again, listening attentively as the judge spoke of the psychiatric evaluations and reports, the petition itself.

"Please stand, Mr. Dubecki. The woman you harmed isn't in this courtroom today. I'd like to know what you'd say to her if she were."

"Your Honor, I can't ask her to forgive me because what I did was unforgivable. The harm I caused Arden Bowie, physically, emotionally, I . . ."

He trailed off, looked down a moment as if composing himself.

"I hurt her, and I wouldn't ask her to excuse what I did because I was ill. Why should she? I guess, if I had the chance, I'd say I hope she's been able to put the harm I caused behind her. That she's happy and, um, fulfilled. She doesn't need to know I'm sorry, Your Honor. Being sorry doesn't make up for what I did. But if it would help her in any way, I'm very sorry.

"And, Your Honor? I'm grateful for having my mental illness addressed and treated."

"Do you believe your treatment is complete?"

"No, sir. I believe it will never be complete. But I believe, absolutely, that I can and will continue that treatment through counseling and therapy."

Practiced that, didn't you? Brill thought. Just the right amounts of humility and conviction.

Son of a bitch.

It didn't surprise her when the ruling went in his favor, or when the judge ordered weekly counseling through the remainder of his sentence.

She watched him embrace his mother.

When his eyes, appropriately damp, met Brill's, the monster inside smiled.

That didn't surprise her either.

She walked out, contacted her partner as she left the courthouse. In her car, she waited. The cold, gloomy day smelled of snow coming. The solid gray sky looked poised to open for it.

Christmas madness had already shoved leftover Thanksgiving turkey aside. She'd have to do some shopping before much longer.

The kids? No problem. They'd have lists. Her husband? He'd just shrug, smile, say he didn't need a thing.

Big help he was.

Then her parents, her sister, her brother-in-law, two nieces, and a nephew. Jesus, her in-laws—but she'd lean on her husband, and hard, on all of those.

And he'd be the one hauling out the tree on December 1, as excited as the kids.

She let her mind wander until she saw Dustin come out.

He shook his lawyer's hand enthusiastically, then added a quick guy-hug. With his mother, he walked out to a dark gray Mercedes. Brill already had the make, model, plate number.

She gave them some room, then followed. They didn't drive to the two-bedroom house his mother had purchased—and either being careless or credulous had put in their joint names. Nor did they take the route to Upper Arlington and the Victorian mansion where his father lay dying.

Instead, the sedan parked at a local grill.

So a celebratory lunch, Brill thought.

She drove by, turned, and headed back to the station. She'd swing by the house where Dustin would live on her way home later.

Now, she needed to get back to her desk. She had to make the call she'd hoped she wouldn't have to make for another five months.

Chapter Nineteen

Arden sat at her desk, looking out at the valley where the fog billowed like smoke over the hills and fields.

But she didn't see the gray-soaked green, the mountains peaked with white beyond it.

She saw Dustin Dubecki's face as he choked her.

He'd choked her, beaten her, violated her. And they'd let him go.

Five months early. Five months where she could have, and damn it, should have continued to feel safe. Five months more to continue to build the life she wanted.

"He doesn't know where I live," she reminded herself.

Only a handful of people did.

Though her legs felt weak, she pushed to her feet so she could walk to the window.

The courts, the shrinks, they all deemed him ready for release. Early release—compassionate release—because his father was dying.

Detective Brill didn't think he was ready. She hadn't said it, but Arden had heard it clearly.

But he didn't know where she lived. More, he'd have no reason to come after her again, not after all this time.

He'd find another target, develop another obsession. And that made her sick. He'd hurt someone else, and that someone else might not have neighbors to save her.

"He's thousands of miles away, and he has to report to a therapist every week. Nothing's changed for me." She laid a hand on Zorro's head as he stood beside her, leaned against her in the way of comfort. "Nothing's really changed."

But she glanced around at her office door. Yes, she felt an urge to lock it, but she could control it. Would control it.

She wouldn't be a prisoner in her own home, not ever again.

But she had to prove it.

"Okay. Okay. The hell with researching a new book. Let's go outside."

Zorro immediately dashed to the office door. She followed more slowly, but she followed.

She'd go out, throw the ball for her dog.

Then she'd come back in, build a fire in the living room. She could turn on some music, make a soup or a stew for dinner.

Gideon was coming, if his duties as chief didn't keep him away.

She really hoped they didn't.

Gideon stood over the body in the tub of the upstairs hall bath of the three-bedroom Colonial. The room with its peach-colored walls smelled of blood and death and strawberries.

Lori Wheeler's long blond hair floated on the surface of the water along with a thin skim of bloody bubbles.

The razor she'd used to slit her wrist lay on the tile floor next to the bottle of bubble bath.

She'd been sixteen.

Hawk Miller stepped in behind him.

"The coroner's team's on the way, Chief. Kim's talking to the parents and the brother."

"What do we know, Sergeant?"

"She got home from school, right about three-fifteen, said she had homework, went to her room. The mom was finishing up some work in the home office, and the kid—the younger brother—came in complaining that Lori had been locked in the bathroom for an hour."

Hawk looked at the girl with pity.

"Mom figures he's exaggerating, but went to check because Lori's been upset the last couple days."

"Because?"

"Rough patch. The boy she'd been seeing dumped her, she tried out for the spring musical, didn't get the part. Had a fight with her best friend, tanked a big test."

Hawk lifted his shoulders. "High school hell shit. Mom got worried enough when Lori didn't answer that she got the key, unlocked the door, and found her. She rushed in, tried to pull the girl out of the tub, knocked over the razor and bubble bath bottle. The kid—the brother—called nine-one-one."

Gideon nodded. "Did she leave a note?"

"In her room. It just says: 'I don't want to be here anymore. What's the point?'"

Gideon could've answered that if she'd asked him. The point was to get through it, because high school hell didn't last forever. Nothing did but death.

"See if you can find a diary, a journal, get her cell phone. I'll talk to the family."

They'd never be the same, Gideon thought when he left the nice Colonial with the Chevy Suburban in the drive. This day would stand as an indelible mark between Before and After.

It wasn't his first teen suicide, but it was his first as chief, and that weighed just a little heavier.

"I'll write it up, Chief."

Deputy Kim Chung hit five-two and looked like some little girl's pampered doll. He'd watched her spar with Hawk, and take him to the mat.

The only one holding back had been Kim.

She had deep, dark eyes that now held the combination of frustration and sorrow that sat like lead in Gideon's gut.

"The boy who dumped her? My sister used to babysit for him and his little brother. That's another family who'll sail in the dark for a while."

"Holiday dance at the high school in a couple weeks. She had the poster on the board in her room, the new dress in her closet. Sixteen," he murmured. "Everything hurts more."

Back at the station, he contacted the school principal. They'd need to arrange for counseling.

He dealt with some paperwork. Cops always had paperwork, but head cop? he thought. Jesus, it never ended.

Since the station house coffee when he took over made pine tar seem palatable, he'd brought in machines for his office and the break room.

That single simple act had cleared any lingering wariness about the new guy. He drank a cup now standing at his window, looking beyond the parking lot to the mountains.

Hawk rapped on his doorjamb.

"I'm caught up. Brig's got a bad tooth, so I've got Moreno covering his morning shift so he can get into the dentist. Patterson and Yang caught a vehicular, no injuries."

Gideon drank some coffee. "Why didn't you take this job, Hawk?"

"I'd rather stand here and tell you all this than stand in there and have somebody tell me. And I'd sure as hell rather not deal with the media that'll come calling for a statement on Lori Wheeler.

"You're a good boss, Gideon."

"It's early days yet."

"I know one when I see one. We had that unattended death this morning. I can go by, get the coroner's report on that and the suicide."

"I'll do it. That's why I'm chief." He checked the time. "I'll head there now, get the reports filed, then call it a day."

"I was hoping you'd say that."

He took his own truck, and did his duty. Ben Granger, age ninety-six, had sat down to watch the morning shows after his breakfast of oatmeal with raisins, then had just dozed off into the long sleep.

A long sleep, Gideon thought, after a long life. Lori Wheeler had the opposite, a violent, self-inflicted end to a short one.

He texted Arden to see if she wanted him to get takeout.

Not tonight. I made tortilla soup.

You can do that?

I guess you'll find out.

Heading your way now.

Not home. He was careful not to call it home. Spending three, occasionally four nights a week in someone's house didn't make it home.

Even if he had a few things in the closet, in the bathroom. For convenience.

He had to admit he felt comfortable there, and that worried him some. He liked being with her, listening to her, even talking to her.

He liked her dog, her house, and her carefully thought-out plans for it.

She remained interesting. And she'd yet to complain when work kept him away, or called him out at night.

He'd nearly finished her bookcases. Who'd have thought he'd get a kick out of shelving books—alphabetically and by type? Her taste and scope in the reading world went well beyond his.

He liked that, too.

And she, clearly, had a love affair going on with his grandfather. That alone made her someone he valued.

Had it been a big step for him to take her over for Pop's chicken pot-pie? Yeah, but he'd found it an easy one.

The population of Riverbend was down by two today, he thought as he pulled up to her house. In the homes of people he'd sworn to protect and serve, grief would live awhile.

In a young girl's home, longer than a while.

But here, in this house, he'd end his day with soup and a woman who appealed to him more, he had to admit, than he'd prepared for.

He heard the dog bark as he approached the door. She hadn't offered a key, and he hadn't asked for one.

She opened the door with a smile, but he saw it.

Something off, something wrong.

He greeted the dog, who sang his happy song, then kissed Arden when she leaned in.

"Not a drop of rain today, but plenty of fog. And it still feels raw enough for soup."

"Rain's coming tonight, and tomorrow's a wet one."

Since she liked things in their place, he hung up his jacket, put his weapon on the shelf next to her tub of scarves.

He didn't wear a Stetson. He kept a ball cap in his truck, another in his official vehicle to grab if rain warranted.

"It smells good."

"That's what I thought. I'm about to have a glass of wine. Or there's beer if you want. How's the crime fight going in Riverbend?"

"We're holding our own."

"What, no gunfights, no locked-door murders?"

A locked-door suicide, but he wouldn't bring it up.

"Maybe tomorrow."

He went for a beer, watched her pour wine. He didn't intend to ask. People, even people you were involved with, had a right to privacy.

So he didn't intend to ask, but he did.

"What happened today?"

"Oh, I'm researching a new book." Wine in one hand, she turned away, picked up a spoon, and stirred the soup. "I'm sort of all over the place right now. I still need to find the next nugget."

"Arden. What happened today? Something's wrong. It's all over you."

With her back still to him, she put down the spoon. "I don't know where to start. I wanted to leave it behind. I knew I couldn't, but I thought I had more time."

Something clutched in his gut. "Are you sick?" Hands on her shoulders, he turned her.

"No, nothing like that. I'm making it bigger than it needs to be. It happened, it's over. I'm here."

"What happened?"

"I got a call today from a police detective from back in Columbus. Detective Brill. She was one of the responders when I was attacked."

He'd known it, seen it, and still it jolted. "Attacked? When? How?"

"That's not where I should start. The beginning's where I should start. I know that."

"Why don't we sit down? You've got a nice fire going in the other room. Let's go sit down, then you can start wherever you want."

"You're used to this. You're used to hearing stories like this."

"Not from you. Start where you want," he repeated as he led her back into the living room. "Take your time."

"I didn't want to bring it with me. It seems so pointless. And I know how stupid it sounds, but I felt like if I didn't talk about it, tell anyone, it stayed back where it happened. Stayed back, and had nothing to do with here."

She'd been raped, he was nearly sure of it. He knew the look, the tone. So he just waited.

The dog, sensing distress, brought over his stuffed llama, put it in her lap.

"He came to my first book signing—nearly five years ago. Harmless-looking guy, about my age, who said he was trying to write a book. He wanted to talk to me about it, over coffee or a drink. I had plans with friends, but I wouldn't have anyway."

She took him through the stalking she hadn't recognized as stalking. The break-in, and what went missing.

She remembered details, and that didn't surprise him. Some victims couldn't or wouldn't, but she had a knack for the details.

"I was so annoyed when he came to my door, my apartment. Sometimes when I'd think back, I visualize not opening the door and telling him to fuck right off. I know it wouldn't make any difference if I'd done exactly that. He'd have found another time and place."

She took a moment, turned the wineglass in her hands, but didn't drink.

"He was different when he came in with his goddamn flowers. Acting like we were involved, like I'd led him on, like he had a right, how he'd take care of me. He was going to buy us a house in the mountains somewhere, somewhere quiet, and he'd provide for me. He said other things that made me realize he'd imagined this whole relationship, and I'd done nothing to encourage him there. And the way he talked about women knowing their place infuriated me.

"I was so pissed off, and I wasn't going to take that bullshit. He changed again, and just for an instant, just a heartbeat, I saw it. When he hit me, my face just exploded, and my head slammed into the door. I saw stars, literally, and I think I went out for a few seconds because he was on me, all over me. Pulling my shirt off. I started to scream, but he squeezed . . ."

She brought a hand to her throat. "Choking me, no breath, no air. Hitting me again and again. And then his hands . . . he rammed his fingers in me, and I couldn't stop him. He stuck his tongue in my mouth, and I bit it, and raked my hands down his face, and the blood . . ."

When her breath started to hitch, the dog at her feet whined, pressed his head against her knee.

"Take a breath. A slow one. Then take another."

When she had, when she laid a hand on Zorro's head, she went on. "I couldn't scream, even when he let go of my throat. Nothing came out but, I don't know, croaks.

"He started dragging me by the hair to the bedroom. He knew where it was, said things about the bedroom so I knew he'd been the one to break in. He—he—slammed my head on the floor, more stars. Going to teach me a lesson. Going to give me what I asked for. He'd finish raping me, then he'd kill me. I knew it, but I couldn't stop him."

Closing her eyes, she took a slow sip of wine. "My neighbors, the ones I told you about, heard the thumping and the crashing, and John came up, pounded on the door, shouted for me. Dustin ran out, shoved by John. John would've gone after him, but he saw me on the floor, half naked, bleeding, half conscious. Instead, he stayed with me, shouted for Monica to come up.

"I told you she's a physician assistant."

"Yeah, you did."

"She stayed with me, while the police came, in the ambulance, in the hospital until my family came, and even then, she and John stayed. I had a concussion, a couple of black eyes, cuts and bruises. The throat was the worst."

She breathed again. "Anyway, everything he'd told me was a lie. His parents were divorced, not dead. And wealthy on top of it. Some serious money. He wasn't writing a book or working part-time. They found my things in his apartment, and a kind of shrine. My picture, my books. In one of them he'd copied my handwriting to write a salutation. 'To Dustin, the only man I've ever loved or ever will love. Yours always and forever, Arden.'"

He waited, then asked, "Was he found competent for trial?"

"They made a deal. He admitted everything he did, but he didn't understand it was wrong. Irresistible impulse, they called it. Five years, five, in a secure institution, mandatory treatment and all that. He wouldn't be allowed to try to contact me in any way."

"He's getting out soon?"

"Sooner. Now. His father's dying. He's got weeks, maybe a month or two at best. He's been a model patient. Detective Brill's not buying it. She's careful what she says to me, but I can tell. She's promised to watch him, and I know she will. But."

She shifted, looked at him directly. "After I got out of the hospital, I stayed in. I could barely talk, my face was all bruised up. I told myself that was why. But it wasn't enough to lock the door. I'd put a chair under it. Then I started locking the bedroom door at night, putting a chair under it. My office door when I worked. I could write, and I think that kept me from losing my mind."

"Did you get counseling?"

"After a while, yes. I didn't want it, didn't want to talk about it, but I knew I couldn't live like that. It helped, it helped a lot. I ended up buying a house. I didn't want to stay in the apartment, not when I could feel myself wanting to make those excuses again. I really liked working at the bookstore, and I'd started back, but I'd quit because I just couldn't deal with it. Buying the house, then getting Zorro, it was good for me.

"Until it wasn't," she said with a sigh. "I missed Zoey, so much, but she's not the only reason I moved here. I needed the distance from what had happened. I needed to be someplace he didn't know about. When he got out, I wouldn't be there. No chance of seeing him on the street, in the grocery store. I wanted to feel safe, and I have. I do. Now he's out, and I can't quite convince myself I'm still safe. It's not rational, but—"

"Why isn't it?"

"It's been nearly five years, and he's halfway across the country."

"Five years, five minutes, doesn't change what he did to you. He violated your home and your person. Rational doesn't mean shit, Arden. You're entitled to feel how you feel."

"You sound like Dr. Wren," she murmured.

"Then listen. You took care of yourself right down the line. You fought back. You bit him, you scratched him, and the woman I'm looking at would've kept fighting as long as she could. You felt safer behind a locked door, you locked the door. You got counseling, and you moved out of the place it happened. You got a dog—very smart move—and when you needed more, you moved here."

He touched her then, carefully, just a hand over hers.

"Today you find out the son of a bitch is out. Not having a reaction to that's what I'd call irrational. And you made goddamn soup."

"I needed to keep busy."

He touched her again, a hand to her cheek. And watched her eyes well. "You don't give up. I thought pretty much right off you were an interesting woman, and it didn't take long to see you were a smart one, capable. I'm telling you as someone who's spent a lot of time thinking about you over the last few months, and as a cop, you're also a lot stronger than you're feeling right now."

"That's good, because I don't feel strong right now."

"What's your impression of Brill?"

"That she's a good cop, a good person. Her partner, too. Um, Detective Venmar. I think they did all they could. And they—one or the other—would check in on me now and then. They didn't just forget. It mattered to me they didn't just forget."

"You've got good cops keeping an eye out back east. And you've got one doing the same here. Lean into that some."

"I didn't want to tell you." The tears spilled now. "I hate feeling like a victim, hate acting like one. But I knew I had to tell you in case I start locking doors again."

"You need to lock them, lock them. Just let me in. And not a victim, Arden. A survivor."

She pressed against him, held on. "Thanks. I just want to stay here a minute, with you. Just a minute. Then we'll go have soup."

In that minute, just that minute, he admitted what he'd worked hard to deny.

He'd fallen in love.

Considering the time difference, Gideon set his mental alarm for five a.m. Arden rose early habitually, but not that damn early. When he woke, he slipped out of bed to dress in the dark.

Since the dog followed him downstairs, he let Zorro out, made coffee. With it, he sat at the island and used his phone to do a run on Dustin Dubecki. White male, age thirty, five-ten, a hundred and fifty.

Once he'd familiarized himself with some background, he brought up a couple of photos. He intended to print one out when he got to the station, post it for his officers.

Since the dog waited patiently at the door, Gideon let him in, fed him, then over a second cup of coffee read through some news reports of the attack.

They played up the local author, debut author angle, and highlighted Dubecki as the son and heir of Paul Dubecki and Theresa Lester. The senior Dubecki had inherited his father's thriving lumber and building supplies enterprise, expanded it, bought up some farmland, built a resort, and had gotten in on the ground floor with the home improvement shows on cable.

The mother came with her own bundle. Theresa Harvey Dubecki Lester sprang from Harvey Developers.

Dustin Dubecki was born rich, privileged, advantaged, Gideon thought, and twisted. Nature or nurture, a combination of both, he didn't know. He didn't care. Keeping him away from Arden was all that mattered.

He checked the time again, took a chance Detective Brill had the eight-to-four shift, and called.

"Detective Brill."

"Detective, this is Gideon Riley. I'm chief of police in Riverbend, Oregon."

"Riverbend, Oregon. Would this be in regards to Arden Bowie?"

"That's right. I'm aware of the details of the assault, so far as she can tell me, and aware Dubecki was released yesterday. I'm also aware she trusts you and your partner. She also trusts me. You'll want to check my bona fides, and once you're satisfied, I'd like to see the case file."

"I can look into that."

"I'd appreciate it. How about an opinion?"

"On what?"

"On the odds Dubecki's mentally healthy, rehabilitated, has his violent and obsessive tendencies under control, and will live out a productive, law-abiding life?"

Her answer came without a beat of hesitation. "I'd give that zero to none."

"Funny. Me, too. I'm going to give you the number at the station. You've got my cell number. I'll be in house in a couple hours."

"All right, Chief. I'll get back to you."

Since he was up, awake, he went downstairs and used her gym space for half an hour. He figured she'd come down before much longer, so opted for breakfast first, then he'd shower and dress, head into work. No, he'd have time to stop by Pop's first.

Gideon made a decent omelet if you didn't want it pretty.

After studying the contents of her fridge—the woman had a thing for yogurt he'd never understand—he decided cheese and some of her deli ham would do the job.

He had the first one done when he heard her coming seconds after the dog got up to greet her with a good morning song.

"Breakfast? You woke up early and hungry."

"Omelets, more or less. You can actually have something solid for breakfast. This one's done. Eat." He pushed the plate at her.

"Thanks. Just let me feed Zorro and get some coffee."

"I fed him, and it's not coffee."

She made it anyway, then sat as he finished up the second omelet. "You were right about the rain. I wasn't sure how I'd feel about rainy winters, little to no snow. But so far, I don't mind it."

"Easy to say when your work commute is up a set of inside stairs."

She smiled, took a bite. "It is, isn't it? This is good, Chief. Nice to wake up to."

She sat there at the pristine counter with its bowl of fruit, her hair spilling down her back, over her shoulders like a glow of sunlight on a rainy day.

He thought she was nice to wake up to.

He sat, brushed a hand over that glow. "I talked with Detective Brill."

Her fork paused in midair.

"She'll check me out, and when she's satisfied, she'll send me the case file."

"All right."

Because she didn't sound sure of that, he gave her more.

"Arden, I want you to know I'm looking out for you. It's not insulting or patronizing, it's my job. I'm good at my job."

"I'm not insulted."

"Good, because it's not just my job. It's you."

When she looked at him, he saw the trust. "Do you think he'll come here?"

"Just because the odds are slim doesn't mean we don't prepare. You want to feel safe. I want you to feel safe. So I'm telling you I'll do everything I can to keep you safe. I want to post his picture at the station, brief my officers."

She put down her fork. He watched, waited as she thought that through.

"In my head, I know, no question, no wiggle room, that I didn't do anything to cause what happened, what he did. I'm not to blame for any of it. It infuriates me that sometimes I feel ashamed and embarrassed. It's like knee-jerk."

She picked up her fork again. "Might be time for a little shot of Dr. Wren—my therapist."

"Never a bad idea."

"What you did—talking to Detective Brill—what you want to do, it's your job, and it's for me. No, not insulting or patronizing. I'm glad you did it, glad you're doing it."

"Good. I want to tell Pop. I don't keep things from him, but I will if that's what you need."

She let out a sigh, then stiffened her spine.

He swore he could see her do it.

"I don't mind. It's more having to say it all again that's hard. I know he's your family, but he feels like mine, too."

"Also good. Listen, I can come back tonight."

"You're hauling out the Christmas decorations with Joe tonight. Which reminds me I have to unpack mine."

"I can help him with that my next day off. Or you could come over, give us a hand with it."

She could go over, and she'd enjoy it. But.

"I need to prove to myself I'm okay here, alone. That I can spend the night alone in my own house."

"All right, but if you're not."

"I know how to find you."

Later, alone, she stood at her office window looking out at the rain. She was okay, better in fact. She knew what to do, what she had to do. Take back whatever power she'd given Dustin Dubecki over her the day before. Reclaim it.

So she would.

And like Gideon, she had work to do.

Chapter Twenty

Despite the fresh four-hundred-thread-count sheets, the down-filled pillows and duvet, sleep hadn't come easy. But when it finally got there, Dustin slept deep, and he slept long.

He didn't wake until nearly noon, and felt very pleased.

Fuck all the guards and rules and doctors and grinding routines.

He could do whatever the hell he wanted, whenever the hell he wanted. And no one, no one would ever lock him inside a room again.

Even if he had to do whatever in the crap shoebox of a house he had to pretend to be grateful for. First chance, he'd sell it, turn that into cash.

Maybe he'd stow some in the shell company he wanted to set up, but he'd need to follow through on making some good new identification and all that.

He'd already started to research how on the loaded laptop his mother had bought him. He started looking at mountain property, too. Maybe the Rockies or the Cascades. He'd taken a look at Maine, dismissed it. Dismissed the east altogether.

Something pulled him west—the idea in his head of the wide and the wild. He wanted those big-ass, mean-looking mountains where men—real men—wore guns on their hips and had long guns in their pickups.

Maybe he'd grow a beard and get some shit-kicker boots.

He had the start of a new wardrobe, the suit he'd worn to the stupid courtroom, some jeans, dress pants, sweater, shirts. Jesus, the woman had teared up over him trying on new jeans.

She was, and always had been, an idiot. An idiot, and a pathetic excuse for a woman, wife, mother.

But for now? Useful.

According to the "rules" he had until the first week of January to start looking for a job. And seven days before he had to go to his first post-release therapy session.

He hoped to be on his way west, with Arden, by then. But he needed to decide just where, and find the right place for them to settle down together.

Wherever, whatever, it would be better than this dinky little house in the suburbs.

His starter home, his mother called it, for his fresh start.

She made him sick.

Now he had to get up, go out there, and play the good and grateful son. Good practice, he supposed, as he'd have to do the same—and add repentant—when they went to see his father.

So he got up, used the poor excuse for an en suite to shower. At least he could use all the hot water he wanted, had good soap, decent Egyptian cotton towels.

He dressed in new trousers, the navy cashmere sweater, the Cucinelli dress boots. The new haircut made him look like some ass-kissing choirboy, but like his mother, he considered it useful for now.

Studying himself, he decided he looked stylish with a lean toward conservative.

His father would approve.

When he went out, the open concept let him see the eat-in kitchen, the stingy-to-his-eye coffee station, and his mother sitting by the living room fire with a book.

Music played quietly.

She'd furnished the place for him, and he couldn't fault her there. She knew how to dress rooms, so no need to stage the place when he put it on the market.

He expected she'd dressed for the husband she hadn't deserved. The waist-nipping purple vest over the crisp white shirt, the dark gray pants with the faintest sheen. The diamond studs accenting the diamond hoops with a single dangling pearl to complement the heirloom pearl necklace she favored reminded him to take her jewelry after he killed her.

That asshole Lester had given her a hell of a wedding set.

She rose when she saw him. "Good morning! I was just thinking I should wake you so you could have a good breakfast before we drive to your father's."

"I'm sorry I slept so late." He gave her the puppy dog eyes she always fell for. "It was hard to get to sleep. Honestly, part of me kept thinking I was dreaming, and if I went to sleep, I'd wake up. Crazy, right?"

"I think it's a lot to adjust to, and I'm glad you got some good rest. Now, why don't you sit down? I'll make you breakfast, get you some coffee."

"Aw, gee. You don't have to wait on me, Mom."

"While I'm here, that's what I'll do. How about an omelet, with feta and prosciutto?"

"That sounds amazing."

She could actually cook. Somewhere along the way she'd taken lessons from a French chef. For fun, she'd said.

He remembered his father had accused her of having an affair with said chef, so she'd stopped taking the lessons.

Guilty as charged, in Dustin's mind.

"I spoke to your stepfather earlier. We're getting some snow back home."

Cleveland. He'd never live down spending part of his life in Cleveland.

"He sends you his best."

She chattered away as she went to the kitchen, put on an apron.

"We're hoping you'll come home for Christmas. Wyatt has to leave for a business trip in a few days, and has to be in London until right before Christmas. I thought I'd stay, help you settle in, then we'd drive home for the holidays."

Talk about sick? The idea of spending Christmas in Cleveland with her and the fuckface she'd married made it hard to hold back the puke.

"I don't know if I should be that far away from Dad."

"I understand, honey, but I'd hate for you to spend Christmas alone. We could come back quickly enough if . . . if you're needed. Something to think about," she added as she brought him coffee.

"I will. I'm just so worried about him."

"I know. So am I."

Lying, cheating bitch, he thought as he sent her a wistful smile.

"I guess I need to get a car. To get to therapy, to start the job hunt."

"Why don't we look into that tomorrow? We need to get your finances in order, too. Get you started on the right track."

"I'm ready for that. Choo choo," he said, and made her laugh.

She could've gotten him a place in Upper Arlington closer to his father. An urban condo with all the amenities, a big, updated house that suited his station in life, something with one of the long front lawns that said the Important live here.

Of course, nothing she'd have bought him would've compared to his father's house on its four manicured acres.

The gated, picture-perfect Victorian said Important with every inch of its ten thousand square feet. She'd taken him away from all this, the elegance of the creamy brick turrets, the towering ceilings, graceful staircases. The seven bedrooms, five with en suites that earned the term.

Until she'd married the asshole, at least they'd had a home close by where he'd spent every other weekend at his father's, and two weeks during the summer break.

But she'd wanted a more modest home, something more *manageable.* And that meant nearly half the size, no pool or tennis court.

She'd never understood the symbolism.

Then she'd married the asshole, and they'd moved to Cleveland. His father let him go, just like that. Her fault, Dustin thought.

So, sure, he'd had a pool there—indoors—but it hadn't been the same.

She'd robbed him of his home.

And his father married the gold-digging bitch who'd tied him up by pumping out a bratty girl kid.

They'd end up with more than half his inheritance, unless he found a way around it.

The brat rode horses, so hadn't they built a small stable, a riding ring? Maybe he could help her have an accident, break her neck in a fall.

He'd think about it.

"You're so quiet, Dustin."

"I guess I'm trying to prepare myself."

She sent him a worried look, put a hand out to rub his arm.

"I hope you can, and I guess I should help you. Your father's lost a lot of weight. His hair . . . it's coming back, but he lost it during the chemo. They've set up his room for his medical needs so he's in a hospital bed, and there are machines, monitors. He'll tire easily."

"He'll know me though, right? He'll know me."

"Yes, yes, of course. He asked for you. Dustin, I know he needs to make things right with you, and for you. I hope you can let him."

"Yes. I want things to be right."

Theresa pulled up at the gate, waited for security to pass her through.

All of Dustin's yearning, all his anger, all his envy rose up as he looked through those gates at the house.

It had been his, and would never be his again. Fuck the house, his father, his mother, all of them.

He'd burn it down.

He'd get exactly what he wanted and deserved because he'd take it.

His mother reached for his hand as she drove through the open gates. He had to fight the urge to use that hand to pound into her face.

"You take as much time with him as you need. He may sleep for a short time, but if you want to stay, it's no problem. You can just text me when you're ready to leave."

"Aren't you going in?"

"He wants to see you, darling, not me. He wants to see his son. I'll do some shopping, see if I can get you some Christmas decorations."

"Okay. I can do this."

"I know you can."

Even as he got out of the car, the butler—a new one, not the one he remembered—opened the grand front door.

"Mr. Dubecki, I'm George. Please let me take your coat."

As he did, Mitzi came down the stairs.

Blond, curvy, and nearly twenty-five years younger than his father, she held out both hands to him.

"Dustin. I'm so glad you're here. I'll take him up, George, thank you. His aide's with him; she's a godsend."

She kept a hand in his as they walked through the entrance hall that smelled of the roses and lilies—all white—on the center table.

"He's having a good day. I think because he knows you're coming."

"I—I should've brought something."

The curved railing gleamed their way up the stairs.

"I promise, all he wants is to see you. He's weak, so he may need to take breaks. Please be patient with him."

"Why wouldn't I?" He snapped it out before he could stop himself. "He's my father."

"Sorry." Her voice cooled, but she continued to lead him down the wide hall to the double doors of the main suite.

He might need her, too, Dustin remembered. For now.

"No, I'm sorry. I'm nervous, and I don't want to break down in front of him."

"Don't worry." She gave his hand a squeeze. "I've broken down countless times."

She went through into the sitting room, called softly. "Susan?"

The woman in pale blue nurse's scrubs, cargo pants, tennis shoes stepped over. Her dark hair, streaked with gray, curled around a narrow face.

"It's Dustin. His son."

"He'll be pleased." She spoke in low tones, then gave Dustin an appraising look. "He's been looking forward to seeing you. It's important not to upset or agitate him."

"I won't do that."

"If he needs something, you can press the button on the side of the bed to call for me. He may drift off. You can sit with him when he does, or call for me. An hour's all he'll handle, and that's optimistic."

"I understand."

"We'll give you some privacy." Again Mitzi squeezed his hand. "Please don't leave without saying goodbye."

"I won't."

They went out, eased the doors shut behind them.

He stepped up until he could see the bed, the monitors, the tubes. A table held a pitcher of water, a plastic cup with a straw.

There were flowers on the tables, on the dresser, but they couldn't cover the scent of sickness.

The smell of dying.

When he approached the bed, he thought it had to be some sort of ugly joke. This old man, this bald, sunken remnant of a man, the skeletal face pale, slightly yellow, wasn't his father.

Even the hands that lay against the white sheets looked old, useless, worn out.

He imagined they'd brought some sick homeless man off the street, put him here to play that ugly joke.

His hands balled into fists, then his fingers opened as he saw himself closing them around the imposter's throat.

Then that husk of a man opened his eyes.

Paul Dubecki lived in those eyes. Hard, fierce, cold as winter.

Shock bubbled up in Dustin's throat. "Dad."

A bony hand reached for his. Though it sickened him, years of respect and fear had Dustin taking it.

"Dustin." The voice, weak and hollow, still had the memory of a bite. "Put down the rail. Sit close."

Tears threatened as he obeyed.

"Men don't cry when faced with hardship. They meet it with strength."

"No, sir."

"I won't spend my last days with regrets. I want to make peace."

"I know I've been a disappointment to you. I—"

"You have been, I won't bother with lies in the time I have left. But I wasn't as good a father as I should have been. I've done better with the girl. I expected more from you. Too much. I was too hard in some ways, too lenient in others."

"You provided for me. You gave me everything I have."

Paul shook his head, gestured to the cup. Dustin held it while he sipped, then waved it away.

"I should've made you earn more, and been less harsh when you failed. My only son."

He paused, eyes closed again.

"I blamed your mother, and rightfully, but I had a responsibility. I blamed you, but you were ill. It took becoming physically ill for me to understand you were mentally ill. I should have come to you when you were institutionalized."

That grated, oh, that grated. There's nothing wrong with me, Dustin thought. Not a goddamn thing.

Since he had to say something, he settled for a truth. "I wanted you to come."

"Too proud, too angry. I regret that."

"It's in the past now."

Paul sighed. "So much is. You're well now."

"I'm going to make you proud. I'm going to make a life you'd respect."

"Not important now. Make one you respect. I'm offering you forgiveness, Dustin, and asking for it from you. I made mistakes, and now have little time to correct them."

There was a boy inside him, a young boy who wanted, who needed.

"You could get better, get well. You could get well and strong again. I'll help you."

In the wasted face, those eyes glittered hard.

"Don't waste time on fantasies. Leave that for the women, for the weak and foolish. You're my son. I withheld affection, attention, and replaced it with money far too often. There are provisions for you in my will—"

"Don't talk about that. Dad, I—"

"It needs to be said. There are provisions. For you, for my daughter, for others. The bulk of my estate will pass to my wife."

Dustin felt his blood run cold, then hot. So hot.

"I want you to make the life you can respect. I wish you to be happy in that life, and to know you're a man. You're my only son. I want to give you something in love. If there's one thing I have that matters to you, that means something to you. One thing I could give you in remembrance and affection, what would it be?"

Paul managed a smile. "You can take some time to think what that may be, but I don't believe you can take long."

Dustin rose, had to turn away, walk away. He stood by the French doors leading to the terrace that overlooked the grounds. The acre of woods, the little stable, the gardens that would be lush in season.

All this should be his. All of it.

He'd suffered under this man's dominance and disapproval all his life, and for that he'd get a provision, and one thing?

Maybe he should end the old man's suffering. A hand over the mouth, fingers pinching the nose. It wouldn't take long, not long at all. And the last thing his father would see?

His only son.

He turned back, ready to end it, and saw the photo.

The Retreat, they called it. The house in the mountains of Washington State. All wood and glass. Rustic but stately. Remote.

He had a flash of his father splitting wood, another of him sitting by the fire where that wood burned, sipping a drink while his mother cooked dinner.

They'd had staff, yes, he remembered, but only day staff. So his mother had cooked; his father had split and stacked wood for the fire.

They'd been happy there, a family there.

Of course, he thought now, how could he have forgotten? Then again, some part of him never had. That's where he wanted to make his life. A cabin in the mountains.

This house, these mountains. As he dreamed of them, and Arden.

He took the photo—ignored the fact it showed his father with Mitzi and the brat, and took it with him to the bed.

"I still dream of this place sometimes, Dad. I loved it whenever we went there. I have such good memories of us being there. If I could have anything, it's this, because of those memories. You could take whatever else is in the will away. This is all I want. We went fishing in the river, and hiking on the trails. I could do that again, and remember you."

"The Retreat. I feel unburdened there." Those fierce and sunken eyes met Dustin's. "You were only a baby when it was built. I have memories, too. If this is what you want, it's yours. I'll arrange it."

"I'll take care of it. Make a good life there. I promise you."

"I'm so tired. I need to rest."

"I can sit with you while you sleep."

"There's pain coming back. Send the aide in. She knows what to do. I feel unburdened now. I need to rest."

"Yes, sir. Thank you."

He meant it. Now he had the perfect place, the right place, to make his life with Arden.

When alone, Arden didn't lock the inside doors, and considered it a win. In fact, she felt lighter, more in control again. She'd taken a hit with Dustin's early release, but she'd handled it. And telling Gideon had tipped the scales.

Time, she decided, to get serious about Christmas.

She shopped, once for a few insane hours with Zoey and Jamie, then more sanely on her own.

She unpacked the decorations she'd brought with her, bought more. On a rare bright Saturday, she dragged out her ladder and prepared to string her new outdoor lights while Zoey and the girls watched.

"The way you're doing that, you might have it finished by Twelfth Night."

"Know-it-all."

"Yes, I do. Jeez, get down, you're making me twitchy. You watch the girls, and I'll string the lights."

"Ha. How easily she falls into my trap." Happily, Arden came down, then scooped up Maddy before the toddler could sample the taste of a rock.

She frowned up at her cousin. "I was doing it that way."

"No, you weren't. You're good at a lot of things, pal, but for things like this when I'm not around, you should wait for Gideon."

"He's taken the weekend shift, and the sun's out. I couldn't waste a sunny day."

"Makes you lucky I'm here. You could also have tapped Jamie and Nick. I saw their house after our shopping trip. I'm surprised I can't see those lights from my house."

"It is pretty awesome." Jiggling Maddy, she watched Lexy throw the ball for Zorro. The fact it rarely sailed more than two feet didn't dim the dog's enthusiasm.

In half the time it would have taken her—might as well admit it—Zoey worked her way to the finish.

"Here comes Jamie and Isis, as promised," Arden told her.

Zorro deserted Lexy to greet them, and offered the ball to his girlfriend. She accepted.

Jamie slapped his hands on either side of his face. "Pregnant ladies don't belong on ladders."

"I was practically born on a ladder."

"Bring that precious cargo down. I'll finish that."

"And done." She stepped down, patted her belly. "Boy or girl, this one will know how to string Christmas lights."

"You must have more. Festive!" Jamie insisted.

"I do, but I thought—"

He cut Arden off with a wave of a finger. "We outline your portico and front windows. That's bare minimum. If you don't have enough, we have more you can borrow."

"Okay then." Zoey put her hands on her hips. "Let's get to it."

As they worked, with Arden primarily designated to chase after the girls and dogs, Jamie and Zoey fell into a rhythm.

"You're good at this," she told him.

"Years of practice. I adore Christmas. Arden's smoking hot is busy protecting Riverbend, mine is finishing an absolutely spectacular six-tiered wedding cake—lemon velvet with pastry cream filling. But as delicious—I had samples—as the cake itself, the design! Cascading sugar flowers in the bride's colors of rose and silver, tiny, edible pearls scattered over each tier. A work of art. But I digress. Where is your baby daddy on this bright Saturday?"

"Stuck at work. The cake? The Anson-Carmandy wedding tonight?"

"That's the one."

"It's huge. It's at our vineyard. Two hundred and seventy guests—not including a wedding party of twelve, add bride and groom."

She stepped back to admire their work. "Fist bump, partner. We're good." Then she turned to call out to Arden. "Food! We must have food. Then naps." She gestured to each girl. "While naps are happening, we'll do the inside."

By midafternoon her new tree stood framed in the living room window. Jamie, with his artist's eye, took over the mantel, draping it in greenery, red berries, glittery gold ribbon.

He arranged candlesticks with gold tapers.

"Perfection," he declared. "We just need your stockings to complete, then I'll do the library. Where are they?"

"I don't have stockings. Aunt Jen has mine. I mean the one she always hung."

"Which she's bringing, along with hers and Dad's, Travis's, April's, their kids' when they come, since Boone and I are doing Christmas Eve."

One hand fisted on a narrow hip, Jamie waved a finger in the air. "This mantel isn't complete without stockings for Arden and Gideon."

"Oh, I don't think Gideon expects—"

"Eh!" The single sound cut her off. "Mandatory. We'll take care of it. And although I still say you need a tree in your office, I am well pleased."

"Everything looks wonderful. You guys are the best. To reward you, I'm making a festive holiday mocktail—I tried it out, it's good. For those of us without precious cargo, I say Bellini."

They had drinks, and she made snacks for the girls when they woke from their nap.

"I've got to get these kids home. Thursday night, Arden. I'll let you know when Mom and Dad get there. And I'll see you and Nick here, Jamie, for Christmas dinner."

"We wouldn't miss. We're so touched you'd include us."

"Face it, handsome. You're family now."

Zoey gave him a kiss on the cheek, hugged Arden.

"I just love that girl," Jamie said after Zoey bundled all her precious cargo into the car.

"Me, too. And she's right. You're family now."

"You're going to water me up, girl. I need to leave soon myself. I promised Nick a quiet dinner and a lazy evening after the day I know he's putting in. But I wouldn't mind a send-off Bellini."

"Have a seat by the fire, enjoy your excellent work, and I'll make us both one."

Family, she thought as she mixed the drinks.

She brought in the drinks, clinked glasses.

A kind man, a sweet one, and one who'd already enriched her life.

"You and Nick have made my moving here, living here, being here so much more than it might've been."

"Are you trying to water me up again?"

"I'm afraid I might, but I want to tell you something because good friends and family don't, or shouldn't, hold things back. It's something that happened to me, it'll be five years ago this spring. But like Gideon said when I finally told him, five years, five minutes, it still happened."

"Something bad." Eyes drenched, not in tears but sympathy, Jamie curled his fingers around hers.

"Something bad."

She told him, in broad strokes rather than details. He held her hand throughout.

"My darling girl." Eyes wet with those tears now, he put his arms around her, held fast. "I'm sorry, so sorry. I know how terrified you must've been, and how hard it is to put it behind you. Violence. I'll never understand why some get off causing someone pain. I'm glad you told me."

"I never talked about it except with my therapist. I thought that was the way to put it behind me. But it's always there. When I told Gideon . . . I don't know. It helped."

"You haven't talked about it with someone who'd been assaulted, someone who knows what it's like?"

"No. Dr. Wren suggested groups, but I just didn't want to go there."

"Now you have me."

"Oh, Jamie. You were attacked?"

"Years ago. First, let me say I was lucky. I didn't formally come out to my family because, well, they always knew, and they accepted, loved me. Which was different for Nick—but that's another story. I was in my last year of art school, and on spring break I went down to Fort Lauderdale."

He patted her hand, then picked up his drink. "I admit, without shame, I was a bit of a slut in those days. I was in a bar—a gay bar, obviously—and nicely buzzed, left with someone. We walked awhile, the surf, the breeze, the starlight. And then? He beat the living shit out of me."

"God, Jamie."

"I tried to fight back, tried to run, but neither worked. I realized afterward he'd targeted me for just this, to pound me with his fists and ugly slurs. I think he meant to kill me, to prove he wasn't gay—which, trust me, he was.

"The pain, the fear—you know."

"Yes."

"A group of girls saw it. They'd been partying, but they saw it, and they ran—not away, but toward us—screaming. I swear to you, I can still hear them, and it's like music. They called the police, and they ran him off and, I have no doubt in my mind, saved my life. Shelley, Becca, Soledad, and Hannah. Bastard fractured my cheekbone, detached my left retina, broke four ribs, bruised my balls, baby, but I didn't die."

"Did they catch him? The police?"

He shook his head, and she knew he'd relived it again. As she did.

"No, they never did, and for a long time I had nightmares he'd come after me again. Therapy helped, my family helped, my art helped. But something stayed broken inside me. The rest healed, but he'd broken something inside me, and I lived with that."

He simply looked at her a moment until she nodded. "Yes, you live with the break."

"I lived, I painted. I laughed and I ate and did all the things, but I lived with that. Until I met Nick."

He let out a sigh, and smiled again.

"I don't care how schmaltzy it sounds because it's truth. Love healed me. It happened, and nothing changes that. But I survived it, then I healed. So I know, and anytime you need to talk to someone who does, I'm here."

"You keep in touch with them, don't you? The girls who stopped to help you."

"Damn right. I went to Hannah's wedding—she has an adorable set of twin boys now. And when the great goddess gave me Nick, we went to Soledad's wedding together. All four came to ours. As fate would have it, Becca met my beloved brother Matthew at our wedding. After some fits and starts, they moved in together a couple years ago. They're taking the plunge into matrimony in June."

"You're kidding! That's amazing."

His dimples sparkled. "The great goddess works in strange and wonderful ways."

She tipped her head to his shoulder. "I'm so glad she gave you to me."

"Ditto."

BOOKS

PART THREE

Strength

Promise me you'll always remember:
You're braver than you believe,
and stronger than you seem,
and smarter than you think.

—A. A. Milne

Chapter Twenty-One

Dustin kept busy, researching on his laptop, carefully funneling money into numbered accounts.

He had learned a thing or two from his father, after all.

He worked around what he thought of as his mother's hovering. He visited his father every day, driving himself now in his new BMW sedan.

He'd trade that in on a muscular truck or monster SUV once he headed west. But the stylish sedan suited for now.

He made certain to express his gratitude—adding a few tears—when his father transferred the house in Washington State to his name. Something about probate, estate taxes, he didn't care.

The Retreat belonged to him.

Information he didn't share with his mother.

Since he had the car, he drove to Short North. He needed to keep an eye on Arden's apartment. The minute he parked the car, he had to fight the urge to just go in, bring her out—drag her if need be—and head to their new home.

He knew better. He had work to do first. Completing the work on his new identity, and using that to buy a gun. He could use that on the lawyer—no forgiveness there just because of the early release. He'd make it look like a robbery, a mugging.

The judge? He needed to work that out. An accident seemed best.

The two cops? Trickier. He might wait on that. Come back in a year or two. His mother? He'd have to wait until his father died.

Then, that done? Arden.

But the urge kept calling to him.

He pulled his ski cap over his head, low enough to cover his hair, most of his forehead. He added sunglasses.

She might be working. He'd just take a quick look in the bookstore. A quick, careful look.

His parka added bulk, and the scarf hid a little more of his face.

He only wanted a look. Just a look. He'd lived too long without one.

Jittery with excitement, he walked in. He saw they'd painted the walls a pale green, changed the order of the stacks.

It irritated him.

He saw customers browsing the books, the sidelines, but he didn't see Arden.

A woman came up to him, bouncy brown hair, ready smile.

"Good afternoon. I'm Cassie. Can I help you find something?"

"Just browsing. I haven't been in for years—I moved to Connecticut. I'm back visiting family for the holidays. I remembered this bookstore, the variety, the terrific customer service."

"Thank you, and welcome back."

"You know, I particularly remember a tall woman, wonderful hair. Like rose gold. She was so helpful."

"You must mean Arden. I'm afraid she's not with us anymore. She moved out of state. Did you know she's an author?"

He tried to process moving away. Out of state. Not there.

His smile came as more of a grimace. "No!"

"Arden Bowie. She writes thrillers. We have all her books."

"I'll have to get one."

He bought all four, paid cash. Outside, he put them in the trunk. Seething, he got behind the wheel. He'd need to keep them hidden where his hovering bitch of a mother wouldn't find them.

He'd smuggle them in to read, one at a time.

The selfish whore had written three books while he'd been locked away. She'd played around with her hobby while he'd lived in hell.

He'd fully intended to allow her to continue her hobby until their first child came along.

She could forget that now.

The bookstore bitch hadn't known or wouldn't say where she'd gone. And the bio on the book flap didn't include that.

She'd changed her hair, let it grow long. Without his permission.

He'd cut it off if he wanted, but he liked it long. Long was better. But he might whack it off to teach her a lesson.

He'd find her, wherever she'd gone. There were ways to find anyone, especially when you were meant to.

He was meant to, he thought as he pulled away from the curb.

She belonged to him. He'd remind her.

When he got home, Theresa immediately rushed to him. "Dustin, thank God you're all right. I've been so worried."

"Why? Jesus, I'm a grown man."

"Yes, but I been trying to reach you for over two hours! You didn't answer your phone, calls, texts."

"I guess I forgot to turn it back on. You know I turn it off when I'm with Dad, and before that I had therapy."

"Yes, but Mitzi said you'd left well over two hours ago."

His eyes went cold. His right hand fisted. "Why are you checking up on me?"

"I wasn't. I wanted to ask if you'd stop and pick up some milk. We're nearly out. Then you didn't answer. It started to sleet, and I was worried."

"I didn't answer because my phone was off." In his mind he saw his hands around her neck. Something inside him shouted:

Do it. Just do it. Do it now.

"We had that sleet. The roads are slick. I couldn't help but worry when you'd left your father's so long ago."

"I needed some time. I went to the park, walked around for a while. He looked really bad today, and he slept most of the time. His breathing sounded . . ."

He turned away, dragged off his ski hat as if overcome.

"I expected each breath to be his last. You need to get off my back."

"I'm sorry."

You're going to be, he thought. But when he started to turn to her, when he started to answer the shout inside him, her phone rang.

"Oh, it's Mitzi. Let me tell her you're all right. Mitzi, he's—Oh, oh no. I'm so sorry. Do you want us to come? Is there anything we can do? Yes, of course. Of course. I know you did, so did he. We're here for you, and for Willow, whatever you need. Whatever we can do. Goodbye."

She lowered the phone, looked at Dustin with damp eyes. He knew before she said it—he wasn't an idiot. But he kept his face blank.

"Dustin, darling, I'm sorry. Your father's passed."

She put her arms around him, held him close. "I know this is hard, so hard, but I hope you take comfort in knowing his pain is over, and you had this time with him."

"I knew." He actually choked up, so it made the sobs come. "I knew in my heart this would be the last time I saw him, the last time we spoke. He's gone. My dad's gone."

And with that death, his mother could live. Temporarily.

Gideon had read the case file. He could and did maintain his objectivity when reading the words, the notes, the reports. But couldn't, just couldn't when he looked at the crime scene photos.

Blood, her blood on the apartment door, on the floor, the overturned table, the shattered lamp. He couldn't look with an objective eye at the photos of Arden's bruised and battered face. The haunted look in her blackened, swollen eyes.

And not when he viewed the feed from her nanny cam.

Once he had, he'd closed the door to his office until the leading edge of his rage had passed.

She said Dubecki would have killed her, and she was right. He knew prosecutors made deals that didn't go down easy with law enforcement, but this deal?

Bullshit. Bullshit, and all kinds of wrong. The man who'd struck her down, who'd torn her shirt off when she'd been unconscious, who'd choked her, beaten her was a predator. A violent, dangerous, delusional predator.

But rage wouldn't help her, so he took time to let it burn off.

He had some conversations with both Columbus detectives. And when done, he felt he knew Dustin Dubecki as well as possible.

An obsessive, narcissistic, violently misogynistic and delusional sociopath.

Like his Ohio counterparts, he didn't believe Arden had been the first woman he'd targeted.

He gave himself an hour a day to dig deeper, and felt that time paid off when he spoke to the president of the college where Dubecki had flunked out in his second year.

"Yes, I remember Mr. Dubecki very well. His mother made a large donation. I spoke with her personally a few times. Simply? Mr. Dubecki didn't appear to find it necessary to do the work, and in fact plagiarized an essay in the last semester of his sophomore year. Despite the donation and his mother's advocacy, we have a very strict policy on plagiarism. He was expelled."

"Other than academically, did he cause any problems on campus? Were there any complaints from female instructors, students?"

"He was difficult, often missed classes, and yes, some of his instructors cited him for behavioral issues. Arguing, insulting. There was a female student who lodged a complaint. She felt he was harassing her, stalking her."

"I'd like to speak with her."

"Chief Riley, I wouldn't feel comfortable giving you her information."

Which meant, Gideon thought, he had it or could get it. "Could you contact her, give her my name and number?"

"I read about his assault on the woman in Columbus a few years ago. Does this have to do with that?"

"It may."

"I'll see what I can do."

For Gideon, his position as chief of police meant more than riding a desk and organizing officers. Like his predecessor, he wanted the people he served to know him. So he took patrols, handled calls, and as much as possible, kept an open door policy for his officers and the residents of Riverbend.

As it neared the end of his shift, he took a call with Kim on a residential break-in.

The homeowner, Livvy Forrester, finished her classes as an instructor at the fitness center, picked up her kids—ten and eight—from after-school care, and had come home to find a pane of glass broken out from the mudroom door.

She'd ordered her boys back to the car, called the police. Then, armed with a hammer from the tool kit in her trunk, walked in to find the Kindle she'd left on the kitchen counter gone, presents she'd wrapped and put under the tree with the wrapping torn—and some missing.

"I kept looking around," she told Gideon. "They got my husband's laptop, the Xbox, about two hundred in cash, my grandmother's pearls. They're not real, but they mean something to me. The toboggan."

"Toboggan."

"For the boys, for Christmas. We had it up in our closet. We're going for a week right after Christmas to a ski resort, Mount Hood."

For the first time Gideon saw her eyes well, her lips tremble as grief edged through anger.

"The kids are really looking forward to sledding and snowball fights, and . . . Oh shit."

"Why don't we sit down?"

"Can't, just can't. We had gifts upstairs, most of them wrapped. We're meeting my family at the resort. They got some of that, too."

She looked away, a woman who carried her forty years on a fit, leanly muscled body.

"I haven't called my husband. He'll be home soon anyway. Bastards, taking a kid's sled."

"Officer, why don't you go talk to the neighbor on this side, find out if they saw anything."

"I doubt it," Livvy said when Kim left. "They both work, the two kids are in high school. I sent my boys to my other neighbor—they're friends with those kids. She's across the street and home most days. But this is her errand-running day. She didn't see anything, anyone."

She scrubbed her hands over her face. "I want a drink. Weeknight before five be damned, I'm having a goddamn drink. Do you want a drink?"

"No, thanks. What time did you, your husband, the kids leave this morning?"

He took her through it, and after she'd poured herself a jumbo glass of wine, convinced her to sit.

As he worked on the list of stolen items, Kim came back.

"Jeff Pritchette, age sixteen. He's home sick today. He states that between puke sessions, he saw a white Ford Transit cargo van, maybe a

2015, in the driveway. He's into cars," Kim added with a smile. "He didn't think anything of it, figured you were having something repaired, since he saw two men in work clothes. He was feeling really sick, didn't pay much attention, but he thinks they were white guys."

"Do you know anyone with a white cargo van, Ms. Forrester?"

"I—I'm not sure what a cargo van is, but, God, Keith Masterville has an old white van. I just can't imagine—he's done our handyman work since before my youngest was born. Just last week, he was here replacing the faucets in the hall bath."

"We'll talk to him."

When they did, they learned Keith Masterville, age sixty-eight, had whatever Jeff Pritchette had. Both he and his wife swore he hadn't left the house all day.

From the pale, sweaty look of him, Gideon believed it.

"Does anyone else have access to your van?"

"Not as such." Masterville rubbed a hand over his little gray beard. "I've been trying to work with my grandson, give him some work, teach him the trade. I let him drive it, but I'm with him when he does."

"Keith, Josh came by twice today." Rose Masterville looked at Gideon. "It's not like him to visit, much less twice in one day, but I thought it was sweet of him to check on his grandpa that way."

"He wouldn't—"

"Keith." She squeezed a hand over his. "Livvy and Ross are good people, and those boys of theirs? They shouldn't have their Christmas spoiled this way. Josh has had some trouble, with alcohol, drugs. He's taken money out of my purse, and other things. And the one he hangs with? Steve—ah—Steve Hogan? We won't even let that one in the house."

"God, Rose." Keith held up a hand, lurched to his feet. "I gotta—"

He made a dash, slammed a door behind him. The miserable sound of retching came through it.

"If Josh did this, it'll break his heart. Our daughter's, too. Keith loves that boy. He's tried so hard to set him straight. Josh could've taken the keys, Chief Riley. They hang on a peg in the kitchen. I wouldn't have noticed."

"Where would we find Josh?"

She sighed, closed her eyes, then gave them an address.

"Our girl works so hard, Chief Riley. She tries so hard. Josh's father left her, Josh, and our granddaughter when Josh was ten and Steffi eight. Steffi, she's good as gold, but Josh? It seems he looks for the easy way, then tosses it all aside."

They found Josh, and Steve, both of them happily stoned while they played on the stolen Xbox.

The toboggan leaned against one dingy wall, with various stolen items scattered around it.

Once they were in lockup, the Forresters informed, the stolen items recovered and logged, Gideon sent Kim home.

He sat at his desk, an hour past what should've been the end of his day, and wrote it up.

He'd just reached for his jacket, thinking cold beer, hot meal, when his phone rang.

"Chief Riley."

"Chief Riley, this is Felicia Cohen. Dean Harwell contacted me. You wanted to speak to me about Dustin Dubecki."

"Yes, I appreciate you taking the time to speak to me."

"No problem. It's been a few years, but I remember him."

"You filed a complaint."

"Yeah. He stopped being just an annoyance, and scared me. Now I find out he assaulted some woman, and my first thought was that could've been me."

"Can you tell me about it?"

"We had a class together, second semester, sophomore year. He sort of glommed on to me. I wasn't interested. For one, I was seeing someone. For another, he just struck me as creepy. Add he thought he was better than anyone else. When he asked me out, I told him I was seeing someone. He said something about how I should upgrade. Hold on a second.

"Dev? I'm talking to that police chief. The baby needs changing. Sorry," she said into the phone.

"That's fine."

"Let's see. I was in a political science club. He joined it. He had no interest, that was obvious, but he joined it. He bugged me about studying with him, or having coffee, a drink to talk about some class project. No and no, time after time.

"My boyfriend's car got keyed. I didn't put it together then, but after, I figured it had to be Dubecki. Asshole. Shit, that's a buck in the jar. Two bucks because I said the *S* word, too. We've got a toddler, so we're both trying hard not to swear."

"How's that going for you?"

"Over a hundred in the jar this month. We're banking it for our kids. Anyway, he seemed to lay off awhile—at least, I didn't get the hard sell. But he'd just show up. If I used the library to study, I'd see him come in, sit there, and pretend to study. His grades were in the tank, you know? Say I went to a chick flick with some girlfriends, he'd show up. I'd be shopping, look around, and he'd be in the store, that sort of thing. Seriously creepy."

As she paused, Gideon heard that amazing toddler belly laugh.

"I ignored it too long. Spring break a bunch of us went to Cancún, and I swear I saw him. Everybody said I had Dubecki Delusion, but I swear I saw him. But during finals week was when it went beyond creepy.

"I had really good grades and wanted to keep it that way. I used the library to study for my astronomy exam. Why I thought astronomy would be fun and easy, who knows? It was fun, but not easy, and my weak spot. I really wanted to ace it, so I used the library because my dorm mate had had a bad breakup, and I knew she'd be in there crying and raging, and I needed to study."

He heard her blow out a breath.

"He was waiting when I came out. It's late, really nobody around. He played it all casual, as if he'd just been walking, spotted me. He said he'd walk me back to the dorm. How a gorgeous redhead like me wouldn't be safe alone."

Redhead. Gideon noted it down, circled it.

"I said I was fine, but he kept walking with me, and saying how he'd given me plenty of time to admit we belonged together. Now that the term was over, we should go away together. He'd take me to Paris, and on and on even when I told him to fu . . . fork off.

"He grabbed my arm, and I lost it, shouted at him, called him a perv and other things that would cost me several jar dollars. His eyes changed. I know that sounds weird, but they did, and his fingers dug into my arm. I shoved at him, and he put a hand to my throat.

"And that's when campus security drove up. I kicked him, then I ran to the security car. He fled. Security drove me to the dorm, and I made the complaint the next morning. I never saw him again. He got booted for plagiarism, and I never went anywhere those last few days of the term alone."

She let out another breath. "Wow. I haven't thought of any of that for a long time, but I sure remember it. I think I got lucky. I think he'd have hurt me. Instead, I came back junior year, then senior year, graduated, with highest honors, by the way. I got a job I love, lived with, then married my guy, and we've got two great kids. I look back at that night now, and realize I got lucky. He's a sick, dangerous man, Chief Riley."

He agreed completely. He spent more time at his desk, wrote up the interview, then sent copies to the detectives in Columbus.

She had the fire going when she opened the door to him.

The first thing Gideon noticed after the scent of something that stirred the hunger he'd ignored was a pair of stockings, as white as the snow on the mountains, little bells hanging off the sides of the Christmas-red cuffs.

One bore her name on the cuff, one his.

"Aren't we a little old for Santa?"

"Not according to everyone else. Jamie tapped April. She made them."

Fascinated, he gave them a closer look. "Like with her hands?"

"Apparently. If you don't want—"

"Who said I didn't? I guess you expect Santa to stuff something in yours."

"I would not object." When she lifted a hand to his cheek, his heart opened as if she'd put a key in a lock. "You put in a long one."

"Yeah. I guess I'm late for whatever smells so damn good. Besides you. You always smell so damn good. And you're sneaky about it."

"Sneaky?"

"You change it up, so who knows what to expect? Summer garden, autumn forest, sexy siren, fresh and breezy."

"Perfume samples. A small, harmless addiction. Which I'll continue, since you actually notice."

"I would not object."

Lifting her off her feet, he let his hunger take a different form as he kissed her. The low sound she made in her throat, the way she wrapped her arms, then her legs around him, turned the hunger insatiable.

He carried her to the sofa, tumbled onto it with her.

He'd yet to take off his coat.

She'd imagined pouring them both wine to go with the meatballs in red sauce she had simmering. Sipping it while the pasta boiled, while they talked about his day, hers.

She'd had such a good one, toying with the opening of a new book. Then the stockings arrived, with their Christmas tree hangers. She'd gotten such ridiculous joy in putting them up. So she took a picture, sent it to April along with her giddy thanks.

The happiness inspired the spaghetti and meatballs, then he'd been late, much later than usual. And she'd worried some.

She thought anyone involved with a cop worried some.

Now he was here, his mouth hot on hers, his hands all over her body as if he couldn't taste or touch enough.

Happiness exploded into need.

She shoved at his coat so he reared up long enough to shrug it off, toss it aside.

Where neither of them saw the dog circle it, then curl down on top of it with his increasingly raggedy llama.

"You need to take this . . ." She struggled with his shirt, then managed to pull it over his head. "Off."

He did the same with her sweater.

Her hands ran down, hit his weapon.

Breathless, she rained kisses over his face. "You're still armed, Chief."

"I've got it. I've got it."

The holstered gun thumped onto the table.

"Don't wait. Don't wait."

"Can't."

How could he wait when everything in him pulsed with need for her? When he felt that same desperation from her as well?

He dragged her pants down her narrow hips, and buried himself in her.

Then, in the glow of the fire, in the twinkle of Christmas lights, with a thin, icy rain just starting to sizzle against the windows, she matched him stroke for urgent stroke.

He felt her rise, peak, break, but couldn't stop. Wherever this mad need had come from, he had to feed it.

As she went lax under him, he gripped her hands, fixed his mouth on hers to swallow her moans.

When release came, it slashed through him, left him weak and dazed so he collapsed on her, struggling to find his breath and his sanity.

They lay silent and still until she glided a hand down his back.

"I'm going to save this particular perfume sample for special occasions."

"Maybe warn me first."

"Not a chance."

He managed a weak laugh, then pushed up enough to look down at her. "I'm more than half crazy about you, Legs." He shook his head when he saw surprise flicker in her eyes. "You're a smart woman—part of the half crazy about. You knew that already."

"It means more to hear it, especially when I'm more than half crazy about you."

"I guess that makes us even." He lowered his forehead to hers. "I'm good with it. I didn't expect to be."

"What did you expect?"

"Can't say, because I don't know. Maybe I figured I'd finish your bookcases and we'd move on."

"You only have four more to build."

"Plus a library ladder." He lifted his head again, watched her. "Then there's that basement to finish off. That's going to take a while."

"I'd need someone handy to help with that."

"Yeah, you would."

"I have other things on my list that require someone handy. In exchange I'll have an unlimited supply of perfume samples, and occasionally make spaghetti and meatballs."

"Is that what that is? I'm starving."

"Then we should eat. I haven't fed Zorro yet either." She glanced over, laughed. "He's taking a nap on your coat."

Gideon looked around, shrugged. "Good thing he didn't try out my gun."

Before long, the evening matched what she'd imagined. With wine and conversation as the pasta boiled.

"It's always fun to start a new book. The possibilities are so open. Then . . ."

"Work."

"A lot of work. Fun, too, but work. I really love working here. It's so quiet, so serene. Since you worked late, I'm guessing your day wasn't so quiet and serene."

"Residential break-in toward the end of the day. They took handy, portable electronics, some cash, tore open Christmas presents, took what looked good to them, rifled through the upstairs, got a fake string of pearls, a man's watch, and a toboggan."

"A . . . toboggan?"

He told her about it while she dealt with the pasta and he put together a salad with what he thought of as her fancy lettuce.

"Both of them stoned," he finished while they ate together. "Playing on the Xbox they'd stolen, drinking beer, smoking weed, and eating Doritos and Reese's Pieces."

"Honestly? That sounds like a disgusting combination."

"They seemed to enjoy it, at least until we got there. They tried claiming they'd bought all the stuff, from some guy. And gee, they didn't know how the prescription meds—sitting right out in plain sight and not prescribed to either of them—got there. Oddly, all of the meds came from clients Masterville worked for, and had taken his dumbass grandson on the jobs."

"Good work, Chief."

"Good luck, and a couple of dumbasses."

"I feel sorry for the grandparents, the mother. It sounds like they tried, did everything they could."

It made him think of Dubecki and his rich, indulgent mother.

"Some people don't much care. See it, want it, take it. Somebody gets hurt by it? Screw them. Now they'll both likely spend the next decade learning the hard way.

"This is really good, Arden. I can cook next time."

"Can you?"

"You've got that big, fancy grill out there. I can handle it." He wound some pasta on his fork. "Something else came up today. I know you well enough to understand you'd want to hear it."

She braced herself. "Is it about Dubecki?"

"First, I'm going to tell you his father died. The funeral's in a few days. Next, I'm going to tell you I located a woman he went to college with."

"How did you . . . That's what you do," she said, and picked up her wine. "Did he hurt her?"

"No, but she believes, and I agree, he would have."

She couldn't quite define how she felt as he told her the story. Somehow relieved, in part, she hadn't been the only. Grateful someone else hadn't been hurt as she'd been. Horrified he'd followed the same sort of pattern before.

"Arden, she's a redhead."

"A . . . oh." As her hand reached instinctively for her hair, she eased out a breath. "Oh. So he could have a sick thing for red hair."

"Maybe. Two can be a coincidence. I don't like them, but they happen."

"Where did he go after he got kicked out of college?"

"He came into a chunk of his trust fund, took off to Europe. Harder to track, since it's been a while. It looks like he spent about six months over there. Then he came back, worked for his stepfather. That didn't pan out. His mother's family has a foundation, so they gave him a job there."

"And that didn't work out."

"No. He traveled some more, loafed around would be my take, then he moved back to Columbus. And saw you."

"You think there have been others besides me and the one in college."

"Maybe she was the first, maybe not. But I don't think he went years between targets. I don't think he's capable of it."

"Neither do I. You'll look for others."

"I'll do what I can."

Reaching out, she touched his hand. "I know it's what you do, and add being more than half crazy about me, but thank you. For looking, and for telling me."

"I may be edging toward three-quarters crazy about you. You make really good spaghetti."

Because he put her at ease, made her feel safe, she rolled more of her own.

Chapter Twenty-Two

The day of his father's funeral, Dustin stood stoic, head bowed. Though he let his eyes glisten.

Dear old dead Dad had wanted the full deal. Two days and evenings of viewings where his bored-brainless son had to stand, sit, converse, offer his arm to the now-widowed gold-digging bitch. And pretend to give two shits about the female spawn who watched him, too often with cool, unblinking eyes.

He thought of various ways to kill the little brat. He'd considered burning down the house with the bitch and the brat in it. But decided there might be a way to get rid of them, then he'd get the house after all.

He'd give it a couple of years, then come back and take care of that.

Between his duties, he acquired, for a tidy fee, identification, driver's license, passport, social security, with background, credit cards—with credit and tax filing history. Costly, yeah, but better, by far, he had to admit, than he could've done.

Paying someone burned a little, but he wanted to get moving.

The day before the funeral, using the new ID, he bought a Glock. A 9mm, standard size pistol.

He filled out all the paperwork, shrugged when, as he'd gone in near to closing, he'd have to wait until the next day for the background check.

Then he drove to a sporting goods store, bought a shotgun and shells, a hunting knife and sheath, Timberland boots, and an insulated vest with pockets handy for ammo.

He considered it an excellent start. He'd pick up more—a rifle, more ammo, and whatever else he'd need for his life in the mountains—on his way west.

Though his father hadn't been one for churchgoing, he'd decreed a funeral service. A shit ton of people attended, including the governor, a state senator. Some did readings. Mitzi had asked him to do one, but he'd declined. He'd told her he wouldn't be able to talk without crying.

Some opera singer sang. Twice. An old guy gave a eulogy that droned on and on.

Still, the casket with its blanket of red and white roses took center stage.

Then a graveside service, complete with freaking bagpipes and more speeches. After all that? After hours of all that? The "bereavement gathering" at the mansion with fancy catered food and drink.

He thought it would never end. Dead to his mind meant dead. He didn't believe in heaven or hell. Only life and death. So you got all you could get, took what you wanted while alive, because dead? It's over, pal.

When they finally got back to the house, he could see the fatigue on his mother's face and decided to help her out with that.

"I'm going to fix you some tea."

"You don't have to fuss. I'm fine."

"This was rough on you, Mom. Mitzi really leaned on you. You helped organize the funeral, all of it."

"She's grieving. She loved your father."

"Sure, but you need to let me take care of you now. You'll drink some tea, then lie down."

"I am tired. It's already so late. Tea would be nice, it'll smooth out the edges. Then I'm just going to bed. I feel like I could sleep a week. You should rest, too, Dustin. We'll be traveling to Cleveland in just a few days."

"That's right."

"We could go tomorrow, but I feel we should stay another day or two in case Mitzi and Willow need us. And Wyatt won't be home from London until next Wednesday anyway."

"No problem."

When she sat in her funeral black, closed her eyes, he added a couple of sleeping pills to the tea. He knew one put her out, so two would keep her out while he took care of some business.

"I know I've said it before, but I'm so glad you reconciled with your father before he passed."

"So am I."

He gave her the tea, then loosened his tie. And waited.

When her eyes drooped, he rose, took her hand.

"Come on, you need to rest."

"I can barely keep my eyes open. I guess it all just hit me."

He helped her to her bedroom, where she sat, slipped off her shoes.

"Take a nap."

He lifted her legs, and before he'd tossed a throw over her, she'd gone out.

"Stay that way."

He went into his room, changed his black suit for black jeans and a sweater, his dress shoes for the new work boots.

While he didn't yet have the Glock—no time to pick it up—he had the knife.

The cold, clear day had gone into a cold, cloudy night. It made him feel lucky. With temperatures in the teens, clouds blanketing moon and stars, few people would be out and about.

He didn't know where Arden had gone—yet—but he knew where her aunt and uncle lived.

So he'd pay them a visit. He'd wait until the lights went off, then break in.

He imagined slitting the uncle's throat. Take out the biggest threat, and with that done, the aunt would tell him what he wanted to know.

Before he slit hers.

After that, he had decisions to make. He'd weighed the pros and cons of his options over and over.

He'd pick up the gun the next day, and he could use it to kill the asshole lawyer. Or, what seemed smarter, he'd pick up the gun, then be on his way to wherever Arden had gone.

He'd save the lawyer, the judge, the cops for later. Add the brat and her mother. Kill them, burn down the mansion.

He'd never live in Ohio again. The Retreat, his, and his sanctuary. Nothing and no one could touch him there.

If he couldn't have the house where his father had lived, had died, why should anybody?

He imagined the thrill of paying back all those people who'd screwed up his life, then reminded himself spreading out the kills spread out the thrill.

He drove carefully, keeping to the speed limit. He liked the way the Mercedes handled, so he'd take his mother's car. She couldn't drive, since she'd be dead.

He'd driven by the Rogan house before, to check it out. It sat in the quiet neighborhood with the Christmas tree in the window, the lights twinkling outside. The driveway lay clear of snow, as did the walkway.

He drove by, gave it twenty minutes while he stopped in a market for road snacks for the next day's journey. As he started by again, impatience had him considering just going up, knocking on the door.

Force his way in, kill the man . . .

As he considered, the tree lights, the outdoor lights went off.

Other than the lights flanking the front door, the house lay in darkness.

He circled the block, pulled right into the drive. You drove a rich man's car, he thought, nobody called the cops.

He'd already decided the front was too exposed. He went around the side with its handy privacy fence, studied the back.

He'd need the element of surprise. He knew the man was about twice his age, but he looked strong.

Crouching, he studied a basement window. A skinny one, but he could get through it. Pry it out with the knife, no sound of breaking glass.

And no chance some nosy neighbor spotted a broken window. He wanted a solid head start.

It was cold work and took longer than he liked. The frigid air snuck down under his scarf, and even with gloves his fingers felt numb. He'd nearly resigned himself to breaking the glass when it finally gave way.

He wiggled through, found some sort of worktable directly beneath. That gave him the height to pull the window back in place.

Sure, cold air would slip in, but the dead were already cold.

By the time someone checked on them, he'd be hundreds of miles away.

Inside, he switched on his flashlight. Storage room, he saw as he scanned. And gave them credit for organization. After easing open the door, he saw a family room, a set of stairs leading up.

It occurred to him then he should break the window after all, take some things, mess up the place.

He'd take care of that after. Then the idiot cops would look for murdering thieves.

He went up and directly into the kitchen/great room combo. Surfaces sparkled and gleamed under the beam of his flashlight. He switched it off—people might notice that beam bouncing around.

And he paused, listened, heard not a sound.

When his eyes adjusted, he crept through. Home office, powder room, living space, and the stairs leading up.

His heart thumped, the sound like thunder in his ears so he wondered the house didn't shake.

But nothing stirred as he walked slowly up the stairs. When one creaked underfoot, his thumping heart stopped.

And still nothing stirred.

He moved past an empty bedroom, a hall bath, a room that looked like they'd converted it for crafts or something equally useless, another empty bedroom.

He stared into the dark recesses of what had to be the main, imagined them sleeping. The man would never wake again.

But when he slipped in, he saw the bed neatly made, and empty.

"Motherfuckers!"

He barely stopped himself from stabbing and slicing the knife through the pillows.

All the trouble he'd gone through, and they weren't even here? Angry tears spurted into his eyes. Fucking unfair! He'd done all the work, and got nothing?

He could wait, just wait until they came home, then . . . But the car, they'd see the car.

He ran down. He'd move the car, and then . . .

He thought of the home office.

He went in, closed the curtains, turned on the light.

They'd have something. Her email, correspondence. She'd talked about her family in interviews, so he knew they were tight. They'd have something.

He'd get into the computer and find it. Find her.

He sat, caught his breath. Closed his eyes until he'd calmed again.

Because people left passwords in all-too-obvious places, he opened a drawer. In it he found an address book.

"Christ, who uses these anymore?"

He opened it to the *B*'s, and there he found her.

"Riverbend, Oregon."

He sat back, laughed until tears came. She'd gone west, just as he'd always planned. Somehow she'd known. Because they were connected, she'd known.

The wrong state, but close enough.

"I'm coming, Arden. Just a few things to clean up here, then I'm coming. We'll start the New Year together."

He added her name, address, phone number, and email to his phone. And light of heart, left the way he'd come in. He gave himself a mental high five. They'd never know he'd been in the house.

When he got back to the crap box where his mother slept, he popped a beer, chugged some. Then using the excellent luggage she'd bought him, he packed all his new clothes. She slept on while he took the travel case that held her jewelry, took the cash from her purse, and the few hundred more she'd kept in her underwear drawer.

He'd stop by an ATM in the morning, pull a couple more thousand out of her account just to tide him over.

Since he knew the passcode for her phone, he opened it, checked her texts. As expected, she'd texted her fuckwad of a second husband twice that day, and he'd responded.

He studied the style, the shorthand, then sat and wrote a text of his own.

> Long, terrible day, but it's over now. I just woke from a much-needed nap. I'm writing this, then going back to sleep. Sweetheart, I need a break. I'm taking Dustin to a spa for

> a few days. Mitzi leaned on us both hard, poor thing, and I really need some quiet and some pampering. So does Dustin—he's really been a rock through this. I'm going to turn off my phone and just be. I hope you understand. We'll drive home from there, and be rested, relaxed, and ready when we're all together on the 23rd. I miss you so much and love you even more.

"Yeah, that sounds like her." He added the heart emoji as she did to all her texts to the asshole.

He set the phone aside, then turned to study his mother. He'd wanted her awake and aware when he did this. But he was ready to get some sleep himself.

He walked to the bed, shoved her onto her back. She barely made a sound. So he straddled her, began slapping her, just firm taps at first, than sharper, harder.

He saw her eyes rolling behind the lids as she moaned a little. So he kept hitting her, palm of the hand, back of the hand, palm, back. A trickle of blood slid out of the side of her mouth.

Her eyes, heavy, glassy, opened. "Dustin."

"Yeah, that's right. It's the son you didn't care enough about to keep the family together." He closed his hands over her throat. "The son you had locked away for nearly five years."

She struggled, weakly, and the weak was a disappointment. But her bloody mouth tried to find air, and her feet drummed on the bed.

And that was satisfaction.

"You had this coming. Payback for every time I had to pretend you mattered."

He eased his grip so he could hear her draw one last painful breath. So he could hear her try to choke out his name.

Then he squeezed until the fear in her eyes went dull, until those eyes fixed. Until her convulsing body went limp.

"I never loved you, not even a little."

Looking down at her, he felt the same desperate excitement he'd felt when he'd strangled the girl he'd picked up hitchhiking in Nevada, who wouldn't put out even after he'd given her a ride.

He was so hot and hard it was nearly painful.

He took it to the shower, jerked off under the spray and steam. And felt renewed. He felt free.

He dressed, then took the jewelry off the body. The flash of her wedding set, the emerald ring on her right hand, the Cartier watch, the discreet diamond studs in her ears.

As he packed them, her phone signaled.

> Just getting up for the day and saw your text, baby. I know you've had a brutal time of it. I hate being away from you, not there to help you through it. Take the time you need. You know I wish you'd go on your own, but I understand why you feel you should take Dustin. I just don't want him to break your heart again. Tune out the world for a bit. I can't wait to see you again, hold you again, be there for you again. Until Christmas Eve Eve, my love. You're my everything.

"Fucker," Dustin said even as he composed a last text.

> **What would I do without you? Thank you for understanding. I only waited for your response before I turned off my phone. Travel safe, and come home to me.**

He added the heart, waited until Lester acknowledged the text with another stupid heart.

Dustin shut off the phone, tossed it aside.

After setting the alarm on his own phone, he went to his room to get a little sleep.

He, a man who'd accomplished the first steps of a mission, slept dreamlessly and well.

When the alarm woke him, he rose, made coffee, took a long, hot shower.

He glanced in his mother's room.

Yeah, still dead.

After he dressed, he boxed up what food and drink from the kitchen interested him. He loaded up the car, then let out a sound of anticipation when he got behind the wheel.

He'd hit that ATM, pick up his gun, then head west!

Yippee-ki-yay!

He lifted a middle finger to the house and the woman lying dead inside it. He found a station on the satellite radio that suited him before he drove away, singing along.

After a fun, casual meal at her cousin's house to welcome her aunt and uncle for their holiday trip, Arden drove home in the shimmering dark.

It had rained, of course, most of the day, but now the skies held clear and star filled.

Uncle Doug and Aunt Jen had extended their trip, and the next day would start scouting the areas she'd earmarked for their retirement.

They'd find their place, she knew it. And felt a rush of satisfaction that she'd have played a part in helping them.

As she drove up to her own home, she felt another wave of satisfaction.

"Look, Zorro, at our pretty lights, our pretty tree in the window. Let's go in, put on some sweet and silly Christmas movie, and wrap more presents."

She gave it two hours, took time to fashion elaborate bows. With more presents tucked under the tree, it felt like Christmas.

As she stood enjoying the lights on the tree, the simmering fire, the candles adding the scents of cranberry and pine, she thought she already had her Christmas wish.

A home she'd come to love where she felt safe and happy. A man she loved, and as he'd admitted to being more than half crazy about her, maybe a future there.

She could let herself want a future now. She wouldn't wish for it yet, but she could want it. A future with Gideon, someone she loved, someone who loved her. Children. A family like she'd had before that horrible night she'd lost her parents. A family like she'd been given after.

More stockings hanging from the mantel.

"We won't ask for it yet." Because he sat beside her, she put her hand on Zorro's head. "The New Year's not far off. Let's see what it brings."

She readied for bed, planning out her next week.

Work, bake Christmas cookies. Work, shop for her first-ever Christmas dinner in her own home.

And enjoy every moment.

When he woke in the morning, energized to begin, Dustin held his new Glock. He couldn't wait to use it. Though he felt it wiser to start his way west, he saw no reason some opportunity to do so wouldn't arise along the way.

But for his first stop, he headed to the airport, and long-term parking.

He switched plates with a Toyota SUV. He figured to put a few hundred miles between him and Columbus, then switch them out again.

He really wanted a big-ass, muscular truck for his new life with Arden, but that could wait. Maybe when he felt ready, he'd find a chop shop, sell the Mercedes on the cheap.

Money wouldn't be a problem.

Then he could buy a truck with his new ID.

And he should probably stop somewhere, find a firing range. He wanted to practice with the Glock because when he used it, he didn't want to miss.

At the end of her day, Gideon brought pizza.

"This is just perfect. I had such a good day, and now there's pizza. And how was yours? Your day."

"Not bad. Pretty quiet, actually. The biggest thing involved a couple of women fighting over a pink cashmere sweater—twenty percent off, and the last in a size medium."

"Twenty percent off cashmere's nothing to sneeze at. Pink's not my best color, but I might have tussled over a mossy green or lapis blue."

"Lapis blue's pretty specific."

"Which is why I might have tussled."

He angled his head. "You look good."

"I feel good." She poured wine, then sat with him at the island. "The new book's moving well, my editor's high on the one I turned in. Aunt Jen and Uncle Doug spent today touring the three locations I picked out for them. They're leaning toward Myrtle Creek, which is just what I imagined for them. And?"

She picked up a slice of pizza, bit in. "It's almost Christmas. I'm going to bake cookies. I could start on those tonight if you want to help decorate them."

"You don't want me to do that. As a kid, if I came here, I'd do that with my grandmother. My skills there, just sad. In LA, the cook would rope me into it, same results. Once, my mother and I did cookies."

"Movie star cookies."

"Hard as rocks and not nearly as pretty. We did laugh our asses off though."

"I'm sorry you won't see them for Christmas."

"They're traveling." He shrugged. "It's how it goes. We'll catch up after the New Year."

"Well, it's Christmas Eve at Zoey's, and Joe's coming. Then it's Christmas dinner here. And I'm going all out, so I need to bake those cookies."

She didn't just look good, he thought. She looked happy.

"Into it, aren't you?"

"With a vengeance. My apartment was an apartment, the house in Columbus a stopgap. This is home. Plus?" She smiled over another bite of pizza. "I have a boyfriend."

"Aren't we a little old for that term?"

"Gideon, a woman's never too old for that term. And because I have a boyfriend who makes beautiful things, I hope he's made me something."

Now he frowned over the pizza. "Like what?"

"If I said like what, it wouldn't be a surprise."

"I'm still making you bookcases."

"Uh-uh." A firm headshake. "Contracted, Chief Riley, doesn't count."

"Now she tells me."

"You'll think of something. And because I've given you a challenge, you can sit here, drink wine, or go watch some sporting event, read a book, whatever while I make cookies. These are like a test-drive. I'm doing the real thing on Christmas Eve."

He sat there, finished the wine, switched to coffee. And eventually she coaxed him into decorating a few.

He hadn't lied. His skill in that area barely reached abysmal.

She had to laugh. "How can you make and build beautiful things, then glomp icing and sprinkles on innocent cookies so a snowman looks like a terrified and tortured prisoner of the North?"

"I warned you." He picked up the glomped-on cookie, had a bite. "Tasty though."

And as with the disaster he and his mother had baked, he found the fun was in doing it together.

"You can take what's left into the station tomorrow."

"All of them?"

"Sure. Test-drive checked off."

Turning, she wrapped around him. "Thanks for indulging me."

"I got cookies out of it."

She'd looked and sounded too happy, he thought, to have spoiled that by telling her he'd found another woman Dubecki had harassed. Another redhead.

He wouldn't keep it from her. He'd tell her.

But not tonight.

Dustin decided to take a little more time at O'Hare's long-term parking than he had at his stop in Indianapolis. He thought of it as a double switcheroo. He put his plates on a Lexus, then put those on a Subaru, and took the Subaru's for the Mercedes.

He didn't mind the cold, even though the wind blew bitter and sharp. He did mind the couple who drove up in a Ford Escort so he had to pretend to load luggage in his trunk.

They took so long unloading theirs he considered using them for target practice.

Could be fun. He'd shoot them—bam-bam—then dump their bodies in their car. But they hauled their bags away with their voices carrying on the wind.

I can't wait to get out of this freaking cold!

Aruba, here we come!

He watched them go, thinking they'd never know he'd had the power over their lives. If he'd chosen, there wouldn't be sun and surf, but a deep freeze in a Ford.

It perked him up so he whistled into the wind as he made the last switch.

He decided he'd earned a night in a decent hotel, so sat in his car, heater running, and pulled up Booking.com on his phone.

He booked a room for the night, plugged the address into the GPS. A hot shower, he thought, room service, a movie, plan out tomorrow's route, and yeah, find a firing range along the way.

Maybe he'd do some shopping before he left Chicago. Pick up some clothes for Arden. Something sexy, just for him.

She'd wear what he chose, what he paid for, what he wanted her to wear.

He checked in, made some mouth noises to the bellman about driving to Iowa to spend the holidays with his family. And shrugged off the warning about a storm coming in.

He ordered a steak dinner, capped it off with a slice of chocolate cake while he watched an action movie.

He played with his gun awhile, miming shooting the good guys, and when he tired of it, set the gun on his nightstand and turned off the lights.

He slept the blameless sleep of the sociopath. And woke to thickly falling snow. Looking out his window, idly scratching his balls, he said, "Fuck it."

He'd book another night if he had to. And if he had to, he'd do some of that shopping.

Over his room service breakfast, he checked the weather along his plotted route. Something he admitted he should've done before.

Adjustments for bad weather forecasts added time, and that frustrated.

But better more time on the road than sliding off into a ditch or having some asshole slide into him.

He called the front desk to extend his stay.

He'd get there when he got there. Arden would wait for him.

Chapter Twenty-Three

On the evening of the twenty-second, Gideon installed the last two bookcases with some help from Reg.

"I gotta say." Reg took a long, slow scan of the room, the deep leather chairs, the cheerful fire, the dreamscape of the valley over it. All framed with those streamlined cases filled with books and trinkets.

"This room's amazing."

Arden stood, hands clasped under her chin. "My favorite of all the rooms in the universe of rooms. Exactly what I wanted, what I saw in my head."

"Your head sees very cool stuff."

"Right now it's seeing hot chocolate with marshmallows. How about it?"

"I'd be all over that, but I've got to get on. We're taking Della's grandparents out to dinner. Nice work, Gid."

"They turned out."

"They really did." Arden smiled at him. "It just needs that rolling ladder to make it all perfect."

"Yeah, yeah."

"Building a library ladder? The man likes a challenge. Anyway, the next few days are going to be crazy, so Merry Christmas."

Arden sent him off with cookies from her final test batch.

"Do you want that hot chocolate?"

"I'm going for a beer."

"Well, that'll work with the chili. It's the first time I've made chili. It's not bad. Maybe missing something, but it's not bad for a first attempt."

He went into the kitchen with her, sampled from the pot on the stove.

"Needs more heat."

He opened a cabinet, studied his choices. She watched as he added Tabasco, red pepper, black pepper, paprika. He got a beer from the fridge, dumped half into it.

"I never thought of beer in there."

He stirred it a minute, then tested it again.

"Okay. Try it out."

When she did, it kicked, but in the way chili should.

"Yeah, that's hitting the mark. Obviously not your first pot of chili."

While she fed the dog, Gideon set down what was left of his beer, and though she hadn't asked, poured her a generous glass of red.

"Why don't we sit down a minute?"

Arden looked at his face. "Uh-oh."

"It's better you know than not. We dug up another woman Dubecki assaulted."

"How bad?"

"She's fine. She wouldn't talk to me. She said it was all a mistake. She lives in Baltimore now, married, works in sales. I tracked down the responding officer and got the story."

She took a sip of wine. "Tell me."

"About eight years ago she lived in Cleveland, and she and Dubecki dated. At that time, they both worked for his stepfather's company. From her initial statement, and other witness statements at the time, he'd gotten too possessive, pushy."

"Physically?"

"Not according to her statement, at that time. He tracked her through her phone without her permission, demanded to know where she was twenty-four seven, started pressuring her to quit her job. She would move in with him, take care of the apartment he had, and he'd take care of her."

"That sounds familiar."

"She finally had enough, broke it off.

"He didn't accept that, harassed her at work, at home. One night, he got into the house she rented, waited for her. He went at her when she came in, shoving her, slapping her. But she hadn't come home alone. Her sister was with her. She'd gotten a call just as they'd pulled up, so was still outside finishing that up. She walked in as Dubecki knocked the woman to the floor."

"He ran off."

"That's right. They called the cops, and in less than twenty-four, she recanted her statement, claimed it was a misunderstanding, and she'd just been angry.

"The cops knew it was bullshit, but she wouldn't budge. A few days later, she moved to Baltimore—where her sister and more of her family lives—with a job, a promotion, in another company where the owner happens to be a college friend of Dubecki's mother. She buys a new car, puts a down payment on a house."

"They paid her off."

"You'd have to look at the mother for that, but yeah. With her recanting, the sister sticking with her on it, charges dropped." He paused a moment. "She's a redhead. Her, the one from college, you. Two, maybe a coincidence. Three's a pattern, Arden."

"It's my hair?" Appalled, she lifted her hands to it. "It's really my goddamn hair?"

"No, it's him, and whatever twisted thing he has for redheads."

She had to get up, circle the kitchen as she searched for calm. "Three."

"That we know of."

"That we know of. And he's escalated one by one. It's, what, ten, eleven years since the woman in college. Eight years ago with the woman in Cleveland. Nearly five with me. He's been locked up since. But he's out now. He would've killed me, Gideon, I know it."

Even if he hadn't seen the recording, he knew it. "I believe you."

"He'll kill the next one. It may be a year, two years, three, but—"

"No, it won't. It won't take him that long. It's all pent up, Legs. Those years inside where he couldn't be what he wanted to be, do what he wanted to do."

She knew he was right, and it made her sick inside.

"There's a woman out there, living her life, and he'll fix on her, target her because she's the right age, in the right place, because of the color of her hair."

"The Columbus LEOs are doing the best they can."

"I'm not blaming them. I honestly don't know who to blame."

"Plenty of blame to spread around. He's been given too many chances. And the system that should have stopped him failed. Sometimes it does. He's a sick, spoiled psychopath who belongs in prison.

"He'll cross a line, Arden. He'll cross one his mother and her money won't be able to erase for him. Until he does, we'll watch him. The pattern is he moves on. He doesn't get what he wants from the woman he targets, he pays a price—and with you, a big one, finally. Then he moves on."

"You're telling me that following pattern, he won't look for me."

He wanted to. He wished he could.

"I can't tell you that. I'm only telling you it's more likely he moves on to someone else. But—"

"I'm the one who he'd see as responsible for making him pay a price, when, as far as we know, he never really paid one before me."

"We'll know if he leaves the area."

"Barely anyone knows where I am. I needed that boundary."

She took a breath, sat again. "It's better to know. But in my head, Gideon, I see a woman, not her face, I can't see her face. Just her hair. She's getting dressed for work, she's doing some shopping, or on a date, maybe out with some girlfriends.

"And he's watching her. I may be safe here, but she's not."

She reached for his hand. "And if he hurts her, or worse, I'm not sure I know how to deal it."

"Tell the story."

"What?"

"Tell the story, your story, what you know of his, theirs. Write it down. It's what you do."

"It's . . ."

"Think about it. You're going to be busy for a few days, so just think about it."

"I could . . . Yes, I can think about it. I wanted to put it—him—away, but it doesn't stay away. So I can think about controlling it all that way."

"Good. I'm hungry. Let's have some chili, because you're going to want to fill up those last bookcases."

She found her smile. "I really am."

"Then I'm going to want sex."

This time she laughed. "I believe I can agree to that."

Two days before Christmas, after a long flight from London, Wyatt Lester sat in the back of the limo, heading home. His trip had been complex, demanding, and exhausting, but ultimately successful. He looked forward, more than he could say, to being home, to sleeping in his own bed. With his wife.

He tried, again, to reach Theresa.

He didn't begrudge Theresa her few days of quiet—and worked on not begrudging Dustin benefitting from the same.

But he'd expected her phone to be on by now, for her to be home when he arrived. The best he managed was another voicemail, where he carefully schooled his voice to block the annoyance.

He didn't want any friction between them as part of his homecoming.

"Hello, sweetheart. We're finally back in the same time zone, the same state, the same city. I'm leaving the airport now, and should be home in thirty or forty minutes. I've missed you! I hope you enjoyed your quiet time, but I want to hear your voice, see your face. If you get this before I get home, call me. Don't text, call so I can hear your voice. See you soon, my love."

He didn't mention her son, just couldn't go that far. He understood her need there, and he'd supported her. Still, he'd made it clear this was the last time. He meant it, and knew she understood that. They'd talked it through.

She believed Dustin had conquered his demons. Wyatt had his doubts—serious and difficult doubts—but he loved his wife enough to take this last and final step.

He'd share his Christmas with her son, even share his homecoming. But in the New Year, the man—and he was a grown man, not a child—was on his own, back in Columbus. He'd need to get a job and start being productive.

He won't, Lester thought. He'd fail, make excuses, blame anyone else, but Theresa knew the days of bailing him out of trouble were done.

And if he hurt another woman?

"Jesus." Closing his eyes, Wyatt rubbed a hand on the headache his wife's son routinely caused.

Who would be to blame? Dustin, absolutely, but he and Theresa shared some of that blame. Paul, his father, no question some of the blame fell at his neglectful, mean-spirited feet.

Put it aside, he ordered himself. He'd do his best to give his wife the Christmas she so much wanted. One where they, at least, held the illusion of a family.

Dustin had lost his father, and that dealt a hard blow to anyone. So he could hold that illusion for a few days.

And after the first of the year, Dustin would go back to Columbus, find work, find his feet at last. Or he wouldn't.

Either way Wyatt Lester would take his wife to Nevis for two blissful weeks.

They needed it, he thought. Needed time to be a couple.

When he finally arrived home, the driver carried his luggage in where one of the house staff took it up to unpack.

It felt like Christmas—the big tree so beautifully decorated, the fire snapping, the mantel decked in greenery and white candles. White roses with red berries adorned the table in the entrance hall.

They'd host no holiday party this year. With his business trip, Paul's death, Dustin's release, they'd had no time or energy for it. But they'd decked the house in Christmas, and it lifted his spirits.

"It looks wonderful, Adele. Has Mrs. Lester arrived yet?"

"No, sir." The housekeeper took Wyatt's coat. "We haven't heard from her."

"I see. I'm sure she'll be here soon."

But as the day wore on to evening, she didn't come. He had a bite to eat, a brief nap. Then annoyance gave way to worry.

He called the spa she used most often and found she'd never booked a stay. Worry edged toward anxiety.

He had one of the staff try several other spas, and by nine that evening realized he had no idea where his wife could be.

Though he felt foolish, he contacted the Columbus police.

He paced. He made himself a whiskey and soda, and paced some more. He contacted her friends, one by one. And waited.

At eleven-twenty, the housekeeper knocked on his sitting room door.

"Mr. Lester, the police are here. They want to speak with you."

And with those words, Wyatt felt his entire world shatter under his feet.

In the early hours of Christmas Eve while Dustin ate Fritos and watched *Bad Santa* in his motel room near Norfolk, Nebraska, Wyatt Lester identified his wife's body.

On the two-hour drive from Cleveland, he'd tried his best to convince himself there'd been a mistake. But he'd known. He'd known.

Yet knowing didn't reach the shock, the horror, the grief, the fury of seeing.

Bruises marred her face, and beneath them that lovely face was colorless. Not white like the sheet that covered her body, but without color. Without life.

"He did this. He killed her. She loved him. She did everything she could to help him, to support him, and he killed her. Her own son."

"We're sorry for your loss, Mr. Lester," Detective Venmar began. "And we know this is a very difficult time—"

"You know?" He rounded on Venmar. "You know nothing!"

"Then help us know." Brill spoke quietly. "Help us find him."

He went with them—what else could he do? He sat with them in a room at the police station, agreed to allow the interview to be recorded.

"Dustin's father . . . Paul was a hard man, a demanding man, a casually cruel man. Though he was abusive, Theresa stayed in the marriage until Dustin was a teenager, as she felt she served as a buffer between him and Paul. Her duty as a mother. When she finally left Paul, Dustin blamed her, only her. She stayed too long, she should never have left, she broke their family, she didn't love him enough. Whatever stone he decided to fling at her at the time."

After rubbing his eyes, Wyatt stared straight ahead.

"He's very much like his father, only a hundred times worse. I met Theresa nearly two years after the divorce, and I loved her. This kind, generous, wounded woman. I tried to forge some kind of bond with her son, and for a time attributed his behavior, his rudeness, to his age. Teenage."

Pausing, Wyatt shook his head. "But I began to see what she couldn't. Dustin was simply made that way. And still, he was her son, so I tried. When Theresa and I married, Dustin called her a whore. I never forgave him for that. I buried it because she needed me to, but I don't forgive.

"Theresa felt she'd failed him. Nothing I could do or say changed that. She indulged him far too much. If we conflicted about anything, we conflicted there."

"Was he physically abusive to his mother?" Brill asked.

"No. I . . . Let me qualify. Not to my knowledge. That would have changed things. I would never have allowed it."

He took a moment, drank some of the terrible coffee they gave him. "In her first marriage, Paul required her to account for every minute of her day. She was expected to do as she was told, to submit, to be perfect—by his standards."

Letting out a sigh, he stared down at his hands. "Paul accused her of adultery if she so much as smiled at another man, while he had blatant affairs. In his world, men did as they liked, when and how they liked. Women were, well, to be plucked like fruit from a tree.

"Theresa and I had a partnership. And while I couldn't and didn't approve of her indulgence with Dustin, I didn't take a hard line. She'd had enough of that. I didn't take a hard line until he was arrested for assaulting the woman, the writer here in Columbus. The lawyer, of course, we would arrange for the lawyer. But no more. He wanted Theresa to go to the woman, to her family, plead his case, pay them off if necessary."

Venmar glanced at Brill before he spoke. "Did she attempt that?"

"No. Not only because we'd agreed no more, but because she was sickened by what he'd done, and desperate to get him the help she felt—knew—he needed. I agreed with her there. We were united on that."

He closed his eyes. "The last five years? A relief. Honestly a kind of freedom. She visited him regularly. I went myself twice."

"And how did that go?" Brill wondered.

"He apologized to me for all the trouble he'd caused. So sincerely."

Wyatt's face went to stone. "I didn't believe him, but I didn't want to believe him. I didn't forgive him, though for her sake I said I did."

"She helped arrange his early release," Brill pointed out.

"Yes. She'd bought the house. There were times she simply needed to stay overnight, or for a day or two, and it seemed the thing to do. A small house, a good neighborhood, somewhere when he got out, to start fresh. Then Paul got sick, terminal cancer. She forgave. Because that's who she is."

His eyes filled, but he forced the tears back. What he shed, he'd shed in private.

"I suppose death can bring regrets. Paul wanted to see his son before he died, wanted to spend time with him. To somehow make up for the cold, the cruel, the neglect. It was only a matter of months, and there would be conditions.

"She was so happy, so hopeful. I had to be in London, but we talked, texted every day. She was so happy Dustin and his father reconciled, that she had this time with her son. When Paul died, she gave his wife and young daughter all her support, and told me how proud she was that Dustin did the same. I thought . . ."

He had to pause, pull out all his strength to get through the next. "When she texted, after the funeral, that she needed quiet, needed to rest, I could only think what an emotional toll those days had taken. She'd take Dustin to the spa, they'd turn off the phones, the electronics. Just a few days away from the world. He'd lost the father he'd just made peace with. And on the twenty-third, I'd be home and so would she."

"This was by text?" Venmar asked. "You and your wife didn't actually speak? Could we see the texts?"

"Yes." He took out his phone, brought them up. "She didn't send it, did she?" The tears got through now; he couldn't stop them. "He did this, too. He knew I'd believe it, I'd want her to take the time she needed. Was she already dead?"

"It's possible. Mr. Lester," Brill continued. "We'll need to keep your phone for now."

"It doesn't matter. I would . . . I would like Theresa's wedding ring."

"She wasn't wearing it. She wasn't wearing any jewelry, nor was any found on scene."

For a moment, Wyatt only stared. Then the tears dried up, burned away in fury. And a disgust that outpaced even that.

"He took her wedding ring. He murdered her, then he robbed her. He's a monster. God, I always knew it. How could a woman so good give birth to a monster?"

If the detectives had thoughts on that, they didn't offer them.

"He took her car," Venmar told him. "Where would he go?"

"I have no idea. He has no friends, not even other monsters. Now he has no family. If you think he'd come to me, contact me, that I would help him in any way, I can assure you he wouldn't, and I'd see him in hell before I'd lend a hand.

"And that's where I want him. I want him in hell."

Gideon took the call at his desk. He listened, made notes, asked questions.

"He got a good jump on us," Brill told him. "TOD on the mother's the evening of the seventeenth, which corresponds with the last text Lester received from her phone."

"She didn't send it."

"Doubtful. He took everything of value, including her car."

Gideon noted down the make, model, year, color, plate.

"We think he switched plates. Venmar did some digging. We've got a report of stolen plates, replaced with the ones off the victim's from long-term parking at the airport in Columbus. That report came in last night—routine traffic stop."

"If he's smart enough to try that, he'll do it again if he stays on the road."

"Agreed. He didn't take her credit cards, and doesn't have any of his own, as far as we know. But he's got access to a shitpile of money. He's been funneling it out since his release. We're working on tracing it, but."

"Yeah. A smart guy would've used some of that for some new ID, and used that to get out of the country. I'd say he's smart enough for the first, but too dug in for the second."

"Right now, we've got nothing that points him toward Arden. And I add another *but.*"

"She thinks he's lost interest in her by now, and can't find her anyway. Here I add a third *but.*"

"I'd have contacted her, but felt it might go down easier coming from you."

"Nothing easy about it. Killing his mother wasn't impulse—just a matter of timing. He got what he needed from her, took the rest. This may or may not be his first kill, but he sure as hell won't stop there."

When he finished the call, he contacted the state police.

He got coffee before he sat again, did some mapping, some calculations.

Then he went out and broke the cheery Christmas Eve mood.

His operations manager wore a pair of antlers as she communicated with an officer on patrol. His sergeant bit off the head of a Santa-shaped cookie while he wrote a report. Two of his officers sat and argued over the ranking of Christmas movies.

Gideon walked over to the board, jabbed a finger on Dustin's photo.

"Dustin Dubecki is the prime suspect in the murder of his mother, Theresa Lester."

"Jesus fuck." Hawk swallowed cookie. "His mom?"

"Beaten and strangled, December seventeen, her body discovered last night. He fled in her vehicle. A dark gray 2025 Mercedes C-Class sedan. Note it down. Current stolen plate, Ohio plate, Charles, Union, Henry, five, three, eight, one. Updates on that if and when we get them."

"Do we believe he's headed here?" Kim asked.

"Unknown. We don't know if he's armed, but he's sure as hell dangerous. Staties are issuing a BOLO. The Ohio cops are working on making that nationwide."

He gave them what he had—not nearly enough. Then turned to his operations manager.

"Olivia, brief any officers on patrol or off duty."

"On that, Chief."

"It takes a solid thirty-seven hours to drive from Ohio to Riverbend, if he's coming here. The most direct route would've taken him through Chicago, and they got hit hard with a snowstorm that would've slowed him down or stopped him for at least a day, more likely two.

"Hawk, reach out to Chicago PD, see if there's any reports of stolen plates at long-term at O'Hare. Check Indianapolis airport, too. He could've stopped there. He may hit the airports in the bigger cities and switch the Ohio plates again. If you can push it, see if they'll send someone to look for the Ohio plate at the airports."

"I'll push it."

"He's going to run into more snow, if headed west, in Iowa, crossing Nebraska, Colorado, likely Utah. He needs to sleep, eat, piss. If he opts for back roads, it'll take him more time yet. I want everyone alert, starting now. If you spot him or the vehicle, call for backup."

"Chief." Olivia pulled off her antlers. "Ye and Harley responded to a domestic disturbance. Shots fired. Officer down. Harley's wounded, suspect inside the house holding his wife and two kids hostage."

"Gear up. Let's move. Kim, I need you to go keep an eye on Arden's place."

"Absolutely."

"She doesn't know the situation. I'll talk to her when I can."

In under two minutes, he sped, lights and siren, toward Green Valley Road. And he thought: What a fucking day.

At five, Arden carried cookies and more into her sister's house and greeted her insanely excited nieces.

"I was hoping to get here a little sooner, give you a hand." She peeled out of her coat. "But I hoped Gideon would make it to my place before I left."

"Where is he? He's coming, right?"

"Yes, but it's cop stuff so I don't know when."

She hauled up Lexy as the girl babbled about Santa, reindeer, presents.

Zoey shoved at her hair. "Good, that's good. He's coming. I really need to talk to you a minute. Joe called a little while ago, and—"

"Oh, he's coming, isn't he? I could've picked him up on my way. I didn't think of it. Yes, baby, I want to see all the presents, and I have one Christmas Eve present each for you and Maddy you can have tonight."

"I get a princess castle from Santa tomorrow!"

"Oh, wouldn't that be fun!"

"I've got her." Jen swooped in as Maddy tried to climb up Arden's leg. She settled the girl on her hip.

Zorro rushed wagging to the door.

"Lexy, hush for one minute. Arden . . ." Zoey trailed off at the knock. "Oh well. Brace yourself. Joe's bringing some surprise guests."

Jen threw a bolstering smile over her shoulder as she went to answer.

"Who?"

Zoey tried a smile of her own, but it came across a little fearful. "Gideon's parents."

"His—what?"

"Sorry, it all happened so fast, and I'm a little terrified."

They came bearing gifts.

Scarlett Dash looked like a movie star. In those first stunned seconds Arden realized the woman simply couldn't help it. She'd dressed casually, dark pants, a winter-white sweater, her butter-blond hair long and loose. And still she just radiated glamour.

Liam Riley, in jeans, a navy V-neck over a collared shirt, hit tall, dark, and handsome on the nose.

"Hello!" Scarlett's voice was warm cream over warm fudge. "Merry Christmas! You must be Jen, and this is . . . Maddy?"

"Yes, please come in. Doug! Come help Zoey's guests with their coats."

"Thank you so much for letting us invade your Christmas Eve. Zoey? We've heard so much about all of you! You have a beautiful home. We're so grateful you've opened it to us."

"You're more than welcome."

"I know we put you on the spot, but I just love surprises." Turning to Arden, she flashed a smile that would have melted a glacier. "Surprise! It's wonderful to meet you, Arden."

So saying, she enfolded Arden in a hug, a quietly exotic scent, and unexpected warmth. "Liam, come meet Arden."

"Working toward it. It's a pleasure to meet you. All of you. And apologies for the ambush. Dad told us Gideon's tied up at work, so it looks like we'll ambush him, too."

Boone stood, a little glazed-eyed but smiling. "Why don't I get everyone a drink?"

"Boone, thanks for having us. I'd love a drink."

"Santa's coming."

Scarlett beamed at Lexy. "I know! I can hardly wait." Without fanfare, she plucked the girl from a speechless Arden. "Maybe you could help me put some presents under the tree. I think there's one with your name on it."

"Boone, I'm Liam. Why don't I give you a hand with those drinks? It's one of my specialties."

Joe grinned at everyone, then lifted his shoulders. "I didn't know they were coming until they got here. Gideon won't know what hit him."

There, Arden thought, he had company.

"Sorry." Zoey gave Arden's hand a squeeze. "There wasn't time to warn you. Here, tonight's festive drink. Christmas champagne cocktail."

"It's pretty. Oh my God."

"Pomegranate. And yes, oh my God. Okay, Boone's on drinks. I need to set out some appetizers. So—"

Scarlett whisked back. "Oh, thank you, Boone," she said as he brought her the cocktail. "Doesn't this look lovely? Your girls are just adorable, Zoey. They sure love your mom and dad."

"We all do. We're really informal tonight. I'm going to set some food out—where the dogs won't be tempted."

"Elvis is obviously happy to have a friend. He's a handsome dog, Arden. Is he . . . singing?"

"Yes. He's happy."

"Who isn't on Christmas Eve? I wonder if I could have just a minute."

With that, she slid an arm around Arden's waist, guided her—a silk-draped bulldozer—toward the fireplace with its forest of stockings.

"A home tells you a lot about the people who live in it. This one's warm, welcoming, fun, and friendly."

Don't babble, Arden ordered herself. Please don't babble.

"Zoey, Boone, and the girls are exactly that."

"Gideon and Joe like them very much. I hope you're not upset Gideon's working late."

"He wouldn't be Gideon if he didn't do what needs doing."

"That's exactly right." Scarlett took a sip of her cocktail, and her eyes, a pure crystal blue, sparkled. "Well, this is as lovely as it looks. So." She beamed that smile again. "I can be pushy. I'm very good at being charming about it."

Across the room, Maddy let out a laugh that rolled and rolled and rolled, and had Scarlett glancing back with delight.

"But if I weren't pushy, I wouldn't be standing here talking to you. I understand Joe and Gideon have plans for Christmas dinner with you, your family, some friends at your home. Liam and I wouldn't dream of interfering there."

Oh yeah, Arden thought, that amused expression? Like mother, like son. Not just Scarlett Dash, but Gideon's mother.

"You don't have to push. I'd love you to come. We'd all love you to come."

"I knew I'd like you."

"Did you?"

"I did. When Joe first mentioned you—it takes careful and strategic pushing to get anything out of Gideon—I read your book. Your first. I enjoyed it. Then, with a little of that careful and strategic pushing, I knew you made Gideon happy."

She sipped again. "If there's one thing I love more than Liam, more than Joe—and I adore Joe."

"Who doesn't?"

"True. More than my work, and that's as much a part of me as my eyes. It's my children. I knew Gideon would be content here, in Riverbend, with Joe, but contentment isn't what a mother wants their children to settle for. So I knew I'd like you. And since I do, I hope Gideon brings you more than contentment."

"He makes me happy."

"He'll frustrate the hell out of you at times."

"No." Relaxed now, amused now, Arden drank. "Really?"

That earned a laugh. "He's like me there. His father? Despite being an exacting director, is easier. More like Joe in that he's never met a stranger. Gideon and Grace—his sister—tend to be more cautious. We want the lay of the land before we step onto it."

"*Cautious* isn't the word that sprang to mind when you came in."

"I already liked you, and by association your family. And I've kept you from them long enough. Just one piece of advice? Here's that pushy part of me again. Stand your ground when it matters to you. It may piss him off, but he'll respect it."

"I can't help otherwise. It may or may not be the way I was built, but it definitely was the way I was raised."

"Good. Now I'm going to go charm your aunt and uncle."

"They're big fans."

"Yeah? Well then, I have to plow that road."

Chapter Twenty-Four

Gideon downed a couple of Motrin, then handled the paperwork himself. His wounded officer would wear a sling for a time while he rode a desk, but he was home and safe for Christmas.

A woman and two kids under ten were shattered, but alive, also safe, and with family.

Dennis Ryder, however, wouldn't go home for Christmas for a very long time.

Why anyone would threaten to kill his family and himself rather than face divorce remained one of life's mysteries. It happened far too often.

In this case, after a long standoff, they'd managed to talk him down and out.

With duty done, he headed home. What he wanted? A long, hot shower, a very large drink, and a couple hours of quiet.

Since he was nearly two hours late already, the shower and quiet were off the table. He'd settle for the drink, shift his mood for company, noise.

Christmas Eve didn't stop because he'd had a rough one.

And when he could manage it, he'd screw up Arden's Christmas by telling her about Theresa Lester, and all the rest.

He wouldn't lie to her or soft-pedal. She deserved neither. So he wouldn't hold back, but he needed to tell her face-to-face, and not at a family party.

He pulled up at the Yeoh house, saw the lights shining, the tree in the window, his grandfather's truck, Arden's car.

And it helped with that shift of mood.

He got out of his truck, realized he could definitely use some food as well as that drink.

The door opened before he knocked, and there she stood, that amazing hair spilling over her shoulders like golden fire.

"Hi, um—"

He did what he needed, stepped in as she stepped back. He drew her to him, found her mouth with his, and just let the day, all the weight of it, float away.

"Gideon—"

"One more. It's been one of those."

When he released her, he ran a hand over her hair. "Merry Christmas."

"You bet. Ah, look who's here."

When she gestured, he saw his parents, standing together, both of them grinning as if he'd just won Olympic gold.

He said the only thing that came to mind. "Seriously?"

"Surprise." With a laugh, Scarlett ran to him and flung her arms around him. In his ear, she murmured, "I really like your girl."

Then she drew back, kissed him, hugged him again.

He held tight—he hadn't let himself dwell on how much he'd missed her—and glanced over her head at Joe.

"Don't look at me." Joe tossed up his hands. "I didn't know until they came in the door."

After exchanging bear hugs with his father, he looked at the two of them. "You said you weren't going to make it up until February, maybe March."

"We lied." Scarlett tipped her head toward Liam.

"She lied," he corrected. "She's better at it. I simply supported the lie. Is that what the chief of police wears around here?"

"It's what this one wears."

"Are you a bourbon man, Gideon?" Boone asked.

"I can be. I'm driving. As are other people in this house with drinks in their hands."

"Christmas Eve. One drink, followed by food and festivities." Boone handed him a lowball glass.

Gideon could only stare at it. "Bourbon isn't pink."

"It is when it's a Santa Smash."

Lexy danced at his feet. "Santa's bringing a princess castle."

"For me? How did he know I wanted one?"

"Silly." She giggled as he picked her up. "For me."

"Now that we're all here, a toast." Doug held up his glass. "To Santa, to family, and to surprises."

Gideon sampled the drink—not bad at all—and closed the door on the long, hard day.

He'd have to open that door again, but for a few hours he had the pleasure of watching his parents interact with Arden's family. He knew them, and their—he swore—innate skill for mingling with any group of any kind, of any size, in any place. But since he knew them, he saw they clearly enjoyed everything and everyone.

Not an act when his father sat with Maddy on his lap while she babbled and he made faces of astonishment, delight, shock, and concern.

Not an act when he saw his mother and Arden with their heads together—though that struck him as a little unsettling.

Joe finally managed a private word.

"How bad was it? I heard—I didn't say anything."

"Bad. If we'd had to go in—and it nearly went there—it would've been a lot worse. The wife's got some bruises, but he didn't touch the kids. Probably scarred them for life, but he didn't hurt them physically. He shot out the freaking window when the officers approached the house. Harley took one in the shoulder, through-and-through, so it could've been worse."

"You saved lives today. Remember that."

"They never went at each other." Gideon sipped the pink bourbon as he studied his parents. "Not once, at least never around me. They never gave me a reason to be afraid of them, not that way. Sure, the I'm-in-big-trouble-now way, but never that they'd hurt me, or each other. He'd have killed those kids, Pop. Because his wife didn't want him anymore, he'd have killed her and his own kids."

"But he didn't." Joe laid a hand on his shoulder. "You were there, and he didn't. This is what you wanted to do, were meant to do. And this is why."

If he'd had time, just a little more time, he'd have told his grandfather about Dubecki, but Doug came over asking if he could drop by and see Joe's workshop. So the conversation turned to tools and wood and projects.

The kids opened presents from his parents, with squeals of delight, and when, with much coaxing about Santa and the morning, they headed to bed, they took the stuffed panda and lemur—both pink like the bourbon—up with them.

More conversation—it always amazed Gideon when people just didn't run out—until Scarlett patted Liam's hand.

"This has been wonderful, just wonderful. And it's time for me to get my boyfriend home."

"She means that one." Liam shook a thumb toward Joe. "She'd throw me over for him if he'd have her."

"Without hesitation. I might even cook."

"Oh God, no. You can't do that to my dad. Scarlett's a brilliant actor, a crafty businesswoman, and a terrible cook."

"She is a terrible cook," Gideon confirmed.

"I am, but for Joe, I could learn. Meanwhile, I'm stuck with you, so up and out, Riley."

"You should go with them," Arden murmured. "Have Christmas morning with them."

He shook his head. He had to open that door again. "I'll see them for dinner."

So he followed her home and worked out the best way to tell her. The only way, in his mind, the straight way. Give her the facts, no sugarcoating, no easing away from the hard.

Then he hoped she could put it away. Be careful, be smart, but trust law enforcement to do its job.

The rain started as he pulled in the drive behind her, as if the sky opened to a thousand buckets.

Zorro raced straight for the mudroom door, shook himself as Arden hurried behind him, key out.

"It couldn't wait two minutes!" And laughing, she unlocked the door. Inside she pulled off her cap, her jacket as Zorro stopped at his water bowl to drink like a camel.

"I have to tell you, I couldn't even speak when your parents walked in with Joe. I'd just gotten there myself. Jesus, Gideon, your mother completely fills the room. All that sparkle. Warm, breathtaking sparkle."

"Yeah, she does that."

"And your dad? So like Joe, I'm not going to be nervous about having them for dinner. Hardly. Even though I've only made this rib roast once and that was two years ago. I got enough to serve fourteen, so that's good, especially since two of us are little girls, and another two are little boys. And I'm doing plenty of sides, so . . .

"Maybe some more than hardly nervous."

While she talked, he got out wine. He figured they could both use it once he told her.

"They're both pescatarians."

"What? They're—shit!"

"Kidding."

"Well, ha ha." She punched his arm.

"Sit down."

"Actually, I'm going to do the rub, prep the roast tonight."

"Sit," he repeated, and drew her down to a stool.

"I—I think that's a cop face. I think you're wearing your cop face."

"Dubecki killed his mother."

All the color drained from her cheeks. "Oh God. When? How? Is he in jail? Is he in custody now?"

"No, they didn't get him. The ME tags the time of death at between seven and midnight on December seventeenth."

"The seventeenth. You said you'd tell me if—"

"Hold on. They didn't find the body until last night. I wasn't notified until today. Then I had a hostage situation."

"But how . . . A hostage situation?"

"It's resolved, but it took time. And I wasn't going to dump this on you at a family party, so I'm telling you now."

Closing her eyes, she reminded herself to breathe, and to think.

"I'm sorry. I lose my head when it's Dubecki. His mother. She—she hired the lawyers. Both times. She helped get him early release. She did everything."

"For some, everything's not enough, or it's too much. He killed her the night of his father's funeral."

Sensing distress, Zorro leaned against her leg. She reached down, stroked his head as she drank some wine.

"He strangled her, didn't he?"

"That's right, and took her car, left the one she'd bought him. He used her phone to send her husband—on a business trip in London—a text. Going to a spa, going offline for a few days, need quiet, meet you at home on the twenty-third, and he bought it."

"He killed his mother, someone who tried to look out for him, take care of him. Detective Brill told me . . . I know she visited him every week, bought a house so she could sometimes see him more often. He'd just lost his father, and he killed his mother. He's not right, Gideon. Something in him is missing, or turned wrong, but he's not sane."

"Legally, he damn well is. He knew what he was doing, had to plan it, and he covered his tracks. Taking his mother's car. He put different lights—including the goddamn Christmas tree—on timers."

"So it looked like he was there, in the house."

"He went to long-term parking at the airport, switched the plates."

Her color had come back, he noted, but the haunted look in her eyes remained.

"Maybe he got on a plane."

"Not in Columbus. He's got money, and he's been funneling it out since his release, so he's likely got it stashed where he can access it. Odds are he's either got fake ID or he's working on that."

"So he could go anywhere." Her breath began to hitch. "He could come here. Somehow find out where I am, come here."

Gideon set her wine aside, gripped both her hands. "Look at me and breathe. I'm not going to tell you that's not possible. I'm going to tell you there are BOLOs out. I've put one out here to cover any possibility. He's smart, but he's twisted, and the twisted make mistakes.

"He killed his mother when he'd have been smarter to wait until she went back to Cleveland, then use that money to fly somewhere without extradition. Home free. He didn't. He couldn't. And she's not around anymore to try to fix him, try to pull him out of the muck."

"Maybe because she was. Someone has to be to blame, don't they?

The women he attacked, they led him on, they asked for it, they wanted it. His mother hires a lawyer, but he does nearly five years in an institution. She didn't make it all go away this time, so her fault."

"That's right."

"Mine, too, Gideon. I'm the reason he was locked up. So tell me straight, do you think he's coming here? If he's found out where I am. Or he's working on finding out so he can come finish what he started with me."

"Straight? I don't know. If he aims here, aims for you, it's stupid. He risks getting caught along the way because I promise you, they're looking for him. He has to know, if he's caught, it won't be shy of five years inside. It's forever."

She saw the logic, and it should have reassured. But it didn't.

"The part of him that's wrong doesn't believe he'll be caught. That part—I saw it when he choked me, when he hurt me—thinks he has the right, that he's above the rules, even taking his mother's car. And he thinks: Look how smart I am—the text, the switched plates. The fact is, he was smart enough, or lucky enough, to gain a week after killing his mother, to set it up so he would."

"It's more circumstance. Smart would be hanging out on the beach in Mozambique."

"Maybe, but it still worked for him. He could stop again, switch plates again. Which I can see you already thought of."

"That's right, and we're looking into it. He's a spoiled rich kid with a mommy complex who thinks because he has a dick women should do what he wants when he wants."

"And he likes to hurt people, women."

"That's right." No sugarcoating, Gideon thought, but a reminder. "Arden, what does he do when he's confronted with someone he sees as a threat?"

She breathed out. "Runs away."

"Also right. He's twisted, a violent sociopath, but he's also a coward.

"I'm going to move in here until he's back where he belongs."

"Wait a minute!" Galled to the core, she shoved up. "You think I need a man—someone with a dick—standing guard because I'm too weak, too helpless to take care of myself? You'll just . . ." She circled her arms in the air. "Move in like it's nothing, no big deal."

Gideon's eyes narrowed as he studied her. "Knock that off."

"'Knock that off'?" Her breath sucked in on a hiss. "Don't you tell me to knock that off."

"Just did. I'm moving in because it'll give both of us some peace of mind. I'm not standing guard. I've got work that means I have to leave the house when you don't. Weak and helpless, my ass."

Now he shoved up.

"He had you down once because he caught you off guard. You know who and what he is now. You moved across country, on your own, started a life here, on your own. That's fucking brave. He gets out like this and you're not nervous, you're stupid. You're not stupid. I'm moving in because we'll both sleep better at night."

"No, no, that's not what I want."

She wouldn't surrender to hysteria, though she felt some of it trying to bubble up. But she could be seriously angry.

"You don't just get to say here's how it is. I don't want you to move in so I sleep better at night. Goddamn it, when you move in, I want it to be because it's the next step we want to take. I'm entitled to that."

She snagged her wine, nearly sloshed it over the rim as she gestured with it before drinking.

"I want it to be because we want to be together. I want it to be because we're in love, and we'll take the step after that and then the next, because fuck peace of mind, I want marriage, I want kids. He's not going to screw up this part of my life, too. He's not."

She managed a shuddering breath, then drank again. "So you knock it off."

He realized he'd never seen her go seriously off before. Since the dog's reaction included trying to hide behind one of the counter stools, Gideon figured it didn't happen often.

And he found it fascinating.

He took his time, absorbing it, picked up his wine, sipped, set it down again while she seethed.

"Are you proposing?"

He watched fury turn to confusion. "What?"

"I mean, I don't see a ring. It's lame, might be insulting to propose when you didn't bother to get a ring."

The fury swung right back. "You think this is a joke?"

"No, serious question. Just because I have the dick doesn't mean I have to propose, but I have some standards."

For a moment, he wondered if she'd throw something, because she looked capable of it.

"Meanwhile, let me backtrack. I'm moving in because it'll give us both peace of mind—just shut up a minute, Legs."

"Oh. Oh! 'Shut up'?" With her shout, Zorro slunk into the dining room and under the table. "You don't tell me to shut up!"

"Just did. I'm moving in because we'll both sleep better at night. And I'm retracting the *until*. I want to be with you, Arden, seeing as I've been in love with you for a while now. That should cover it."

"Don't say that to placate me. Don't say that out of some need to protect me."

"That's bullshit, and you know it. What you're supposed to say is you're in love with me."

Tears blurred her eyes. "You know I am."

"Let me hear it."

"I'm in love with you."

He took her glass, set it down again. "I didn't know it, but I wanted it." Framing her face with his hands, he kissed her, and with a tenderness that had the tears spilling.

"Don't cry."

"Just a little. I've got so much going on inside me. The awful and the wonderful."

"Put the awful on hold. It's just you and me tonight."

"Working on it." She pressed her face to his shoulder. "I need to get something out of your stocking."

"Now?"

She drew back, then leaned in to kiss him again. She took his hand, pulled him into the living room. Obviously figuring the coast was now clear, Zorro followed.

After digging into his stocking, she took out a small, wrapped box with a little red bow.

"You don't wrap what goes in stockings."

"I couldn't decide if it went there or under the tree. Open it."

He pulled off the paper, opened the lid, saw the key. And just looked at her.

"It wasn't a 'move in with me' key. It was supposed to be a 'you shouldn't have to knock every time you come over' key."

"Still a big step for you."

"It was, but it looks like I skipped right over it to the next."

"You've got a list of steps in your head, don't you?"

"Maybe."

He took out his key ring, put it on. "Thanks."

"Zorro needs to go out. Then . . ."

"Prepping the roast."

"No, that'll wait until morning. We've got a little time before midnight, and I definitely plan to be in bed making love with you at midnight."

"It's a good plan."

"Good plans are my specialty. Now, the plan is, since I gave you one on Christmas Eve, you give me one. I want the one you made me."

"How do you know I made you anything?"

"Because I asked you to."

With a shrug, he picked up a present under the tree.

She stroked the paper, shook the box, angled her head.

"You could just open it."

"I like holding on to the suspense first. Before you open it, it could be anything. Like a set of Russian nesting dolls or a wooden statue of Boba Fett."

"Boba Fett?"

"It could be. A set of wooden candlesticks. A door knocker."

"Maybe it's a gargoyle."

The light in her eyes simply danced. "Maybe it is."

She sat, ripped off the wrapping.

"You tanked the guessing game."

"It's beautiful. A trinket box, and it's beautiful." She ran her fingers over the top and its carving of a dragon flying toward the sun. "You carved this?"

"You've got a thing for dragons or you wouldn't keep one on the bed. On a bookshelf, in the dining room."

"Zoey brought me the stuffed dragon for comfort when I was in the hospital. It worked, and started a trend." When she opened the box, music tinkled out. "Oh, a musical trinket box! It's playing . . . 'Here Comes the Sun.' It's perfect. I love it, and it's perfect."

Cradling it, she jumped up to kiss him.

"It's a big, fat, juicy bonus to be in love with someone who gets me. Thank you."

"For the box or the bonus?"

"Both. It's been a hell of a Christmas Eve." Since Zorro whined by the door, she walked over to let him out.

"Dubecki, parental surprise—I really like your parents—we fought our way into being in love and you moving in, and I'm holding the first thing you made especially for me."

She set the box on the table.

"I'm leaving it down here so I can show it off, but then it's going on my dresser. Or my desk. Desk. When I hit a rough spot or a wall, it'll cheer me up."

Zorro yipped once at the door.

"And you had a hostage situation," she said as he crossed over to let him back in. "I hope you'll tell me about it. I don't want you to feel you can't bring work home, or tell me about the hard parts."

There she was, he realized. The answer to questions he'd never thought to ask.

"If I'd had you in LA, everything would've happened the way it happened, because it had to. But I wouldn't have felt so isolated."

She held out a hand. "Why don't we finish that glass of wine, and you can tell me what happened today."

After he did, after she listened, he could put it away.

At midnight, with the rain drumming, with the wind whipping wet at the windows, they fulfilled the good plan.

Chapter Twenty-Five

Dustin spent Christmas snowbound. He'd managed to book a cabin in nowhere Colorado just below the Wyoming border. It wasn't much, but it had a big-ass fireplace, and plenty of wood.

He knew with the stupid weather and road conditions, he'd been lucky to get that far. Plus, it gave him practice building and maintaining a fire.

He had food because he'd stopped for it when he hadn't been able to ignore the weather or the forecasts any longer.

At his last stop, he'd seen his face on TV.

So they'd found the old whore's body, but he'd figured on it. Fuckface Lester got back from screwing around in London and got a big early Christmas surprise. He got a good laugh out of that one.

Still, seeing his face, hearing about a manhunt for him brought fear, too.

So he bought hair dye and wraparound sunglasses and decided he'd been smart to stop shaving.

He'd look hot in a beard anyway.

After the fear came a kind of pride. A manhunt. How cool was that? But he was the man, and he was the one doing the hunting.

They'd never find him. Sure, they had the car description, too, but his wasn't the only Mercedes sedan on the road, and his now bore Nebraska plates thanks to a late-night stop at a Walmart parking lot.

He'd spend a few days in the mountain cabin while they looked for him wherever. He'd dye his hair, and his beard—it was coming along. He'd practice with the gun, and the hunting rifle, with scope, he'd bought in Iowa.

He deserved a little R and R after all he'd been through.

He sat by the fire with its snarling bear head over the mantel, drinking a beer, munching on chips, and studying his mother's diamond ring.

Maybe he'd put it on eBay. Get an appraisal of the set, then put them up one at a time, so it didn't look like a set. He had the other pieces, the earrings, the watch, the emerald ring. The stuff she'd had in her travel case.

Sell a little here, a little there. Fresh cash couldn't hurt. Plus, if he gave Arden jewelry—she'd have to earn it—it wouldn't be from the bitch who'd busted up his family.

Eventually, he'd find some rube, sell the Mercedes on the cheap, and get himself a big, honking truck. Meanwhile . . .

He put the ring on the table, munched more chips.

He'd scrape up the Mercedes, maybe put a dent in it, like he'd been sideswiped.

He'd take it in, have it fixed and painted. Maybe a classy blue, or an in-your-face red. And the cops would chase their tails looking for the gray car.

He was so much smarter than the cops it was almost embarrassing.

He rose, walked to the window where the world outside spread white on black on white on a kind of steely blue. The snow had slowed, and what fell now fell thinly. But he remembered a near panic when he'd barely made it to the cabin.

Considering he'd expected to stay locked up in hell until spring, he was ahead of schedule. He could wait a few more days.

He didn't mind spending Christmas alone. Next one he'd spend with Arden. Meanwhile, he had a Hungry-Man turkey dinner to nuke up when he wanted it, plenty of beer and snacks.

Because, he told himself, he knew how to plan and prepare. Because he had brains and balls.

He decided he'd gear up, go out for some target practice.

As he put on his boots, he looked over at the picture of Arden he'd found on the internet, printed out, and framed.

He smiled, felt himself go satisfyingly hard when he picked it up, kissed it.

"Not much longer now, baby. After I teach you a lesson—or two—you're going to make me the happiest man on Earth."

He put on his parka, his hat, gloves. As he debated between the rifle, shotgun, or Glock, he reminded himself he needed to pick up some zip ties and duct tape. Handcuffs, too, because some lessons took time to learn.

He decided on the Glock, and smiling, aimed it at the photo. He went "Bang," then blew the photo a kiss before going out into the world of white.

On Christmas morning, Gideon made pancakes. That ranked as a surprise right up there with the sparkle of the diamond hoops he'd given her—which she wore now with her pajamas.

She'd leaned on Joe and gone with his advice on a woodworking tool. She had no real idea what it did, or why, but Gideon had.

And since he'd already put on the cashmere hoodie—the same color as his eyes—she knew she'd hit the mark.

"That was great. You're now officially in charge of pancakes. Now get out."

"Of the kitchen?"

"Of the house. Go spend a couple hours with Joe and your parents. They came all this way, Gideon, and they said they're going to video call with your brother and sister later this morning. You need to be there."

When he hesitated, she pushed.

"You know you do. And I have a lot to take care of. Come back after you've spent some Christmas with them and help me finish all that up.

"I have locks on the door, a dog, a phone. We both know you can't be here around the clock, so go, be a good son."

"I'll add the house to routine patrols."

"That's fine, Chief."

When he left, she put on a Christmas movie—something she thought of as smoochily romantic. She made the rub for the roast, prepped it, covered it, and put it in the fridge. Crossing her fingers first, she made the horseradish cream, then put that in to chill. The second sauce, a merlot au jus, came later.

Add honey-glazed carrots, scalloped potatoes, green beans almondine, the fennel salad with mandarin oranges—plus the bread and desserts Nick would bring—and she'd have a genuine Christmas feast.

She looked at Zorro, who watched her, wearing his shiny Christmas bow. He had his paws crossed over his newest pal, a stuffed sloth.

"All I have to do is pull it off."

Turning to the dining room table, she rubbed her hands together.

"You first."

When she finished, she stepped back, breathed out.

No, she hadn't been foolish buying the holiday dinnerware with its red rims, its pale gold Christmas trees, or the holly berry napkin rings, or taking the time to fancy-fold the napkins—the same pale gold as the trees.

Or the wineglasses with the red stems, the water glasses with the gold.

This? Tradition now, things she'd take out and use whenever she hosted a holiday meal. This? The start of a future, one she'd share with Gideon.

She dealt with the kitchen—and that was a mess—did a sweep through the house to make certain nothing else was.

After the holidays, she promised herself as she went in to dress, she'd give serious thought—combined with action—on finishing the lower level.

It struck her that she'd need to consult and decide there with Gideon.

That could be interesting.

She walked to the window. The rain had stopped, and while the sun played hide-and-seek with the clouds, light shimmered down on the valley. It tossed a glint here and there from the wind of the river.

How lucky, she thought, she'd come here, she'd found this place. Found home, found love, found a future.

Maybe fear had played a part in all that, but she'd leave fear behind now.

Because the dog stood beside her, she laid a hand on his head.

"Everything I want is right here, Zorro, and isn't that amazing?"

They'd find Dustin Dubecki and put him away. Right now, she realized, she believed that absolutely.

She wouldn't hide anymore, wouldn't check locks a second time. No more closing in, but an opening out.

"I'm going to see to that ring very soon."

Downstairs, she lit the fires, then bracing herself, put an apron over her Christmas-red dress.

"Here we go, Zorro."

By the time Gideon arrived, and used his new key, she had the roast in the oven, had begun peeling an impressive mountain of potatoes.

"I can see what I'm going to be doing."

"Grab a peeler. How was Christmas at Joe's?"

"It was good. I took a little heat for not bringing you." He looked in the dining room. "What? Did you take lessons?"

"Internet research. I have skills."

"Apparently. You look good, Legs. Nice dress, nice apron."

"Don't get used to the apron. Day after tomorrow, I'm back at work."

"So don't expect to come home to a hot meal every night."

Tossing back her braid, she smiled. "We'll negotiate. Cooking." She pointed to herself, then him. "Takeout."

"Fair."

When he picked up another peeler and a potato, she leaned against him. "We should add cooking together night or nights. This is nice."

"Unexpected. I sure as hell never expected you, or this." Turning his head, he kissed the top of her head. "Yeah, it's nice."

With the food in the ovens, and just as Arden finished fussing with some holiday crudités, Zorro began barking. When she went to the door, April, the boys, and Travis rolled in.

"They've got to pee," April said. "Me, too! Like now."

"Take the powder room. Jonah, upstairs with me. Travis, take Trent to the upstairs hall bath."

"Merry Christmas!" April called out as she made her dash.

Quiet Christmas Day time done, Gideon thought. He checked himself and found he didn't mind a bit.

That was fortunate, as the rest weren't far behind.

Still, he never slid easily into big social situations, so he designated himself as bartender. He made drinks, poured wine, and observed.

Jamie, in his reindeer sweater, fanboyed his mother, and made her laugh and sparkle. He saw his father in what seemed like an earnest conversation with Jonah about monster trucks. Doug and April played an endless game of Hungry Hungry Hippos with a couple of the kids. Jen had another on her hip as she talked to Nick and Travis.

Zoey and Arden disappeared briefly. When she showed up again, Zoey came up to him, kissed him.

"Ah, thanks?"

"I love my parents, my brother, his family, my husband, my kids. And this one in here." She patted her baby mound. "But Arden's my person. I think you might deserve her."

"Appreciate it."

"Now, because I'm disposed to love you, it's daisies over roses, popcorn over caviar, classic over trendy, and you hit home runs with the dragon box and the earrings. Good job."

"You brought her the purple dragon in the hospital."

"Yeah."

"Good job."

She lowered her voice to a murmur. "Will he come here?"

"I don't know. I can only tell you we're as on top of it as we can be."

Zoey nodded. "Well, I hope he's having a miserable Christmas. And we're not." She glanced toward the living room as Arden began passing out gifts. "And ours is about to get a lot noisier."

Kids squealed, remote-control cars zoomed, some musical toy banged out tune after tune.

Even when he'd been one, Gideon hadn't shared Christmas with so many kids. He found it fascinating, and entertaining when Jonah offered him the remote and a turn with his Grave Digger.

He found it more fascinating yet that Arden had gifts for his parents. A scarf in every shade of blue for his mother, and one in a variation of grays for his father.

When he managed a minute, he had to ask, "How'd you come up with the scarves?"

"Preplanning. I always have a couple of gifts put aside for emergencies."

"Of course you do."

"Arden, you've got something here from Santa."

"Oh boy. Uncle Doug always has a little something from Santa," she told Gideon.

She made her way over, evading the truck, the little dog who happily chased it.

She sat on Doug's knee as she unwrapped the small box.

"A . . . Skeletool." She took it out of the box. "It's so pretty! Pink and teal, and it has my name on it."

"Don't let the pretty fool you. Leatherman makes a good multi-tool, and this one's small and practical."

"Santa put a tiny pink flashlight on the carabiner."

"Because he knows I'm not ten minutes away. You've got needle-nose pliers, regular pliers, wire cutters, the knife. The carabiner, bottle opener, the bit driver."

"I have a bit driver."

"You never know," he said solemnly. "So keep it in your pocket."

"Santa's so wise and thoughtful." She snuggled into him, kissed his cheek.

"And he likes knowing good girls have tools handy."

"It's lovely, isn't it?" Scarlett moved over, put an arm around Gideon's waist. "Family. Not always conventional, God knows, but lovely. Your dad and I? This is a very happy Christmas for us. And look at Joe, down on the floor with that little boy, playing with action figures."

"He used to do that with me."

"One day, he'll do it with yours. Jesus, Gideon, you're going to end up making me a grandmother."

"And you and Dad will eat it up like ice cream."

"We absolutely will. You're making a good life here, Gideon. I really like the people you're making it with."

Her dinner hit all the marks, and that brought Arden both relief and pleasure.

"You might be stuck with Christmas dinner duty from now on," Zoey warned her.

"I'm up for it, as long as Nick and Jamie bring the dessert. No way I could conjure up anything as beautiful as that trifle or the glory of the bûche de Noël."

"I wanna eat the log," Jonah claimed. "Grandad can chop it up with a hatchet."

After cleanup, where Arden tried not to feel strange that a woman she'd admired on-screen and a man who'd directed some of her favorite movies pitched in, Nick served dessert.

"Best log I ever tasted," Joe declared, and laughed when Jonah made gnawing noises. "After all this, I'm going to have to join Gideon in his workouts."

"So say we all." As he did, Liam ate another spoonful of trifle. "I've had Christmas dinner at home, in strange places, remote locations, but I've never had one as happy and festive as this." He lifted his cup of cappuccino. "Much appreciation for the hospitality, and many compliments to the chefs."

"I peeled stuff," Gideon put in.

"Including the sous chef."

When the house found its quiet again, Arden sprawled in a chair.

"I'm full of food and happy and success. We did it."

"Not a lot of *we* in there."

"You peeled stuff," she reminded him. "Hauled out trash, played with half-crazed kids, herded dogs, and made sure everyone had their drink of choice. That's plenty of *we*."

He sprawled in a chair beside her. "What Zoey said? You taking this going forward? I think she's right."

"I have three hundred and sixty-three days to plan and prepare. That includes finishing the downstairs. You'd have ideas there."

"I could have."

"Starting with the people I'd need. Electricians, plumbers, carpenters. I've got Tessa for painting. And I know where to go if we want any built-ins." She smiled at him. "We'll talk about it when we recover from this Christmas."

"That could take a while."

"So, what are you doing New Year's Eve?"

"I'm on. People will drink, get rowdy and stupid. Sorry."

"No sorry, it comes with the job. I believe Zorro and I will enjoy a movie marathon with massive amounts of popcorn."

"That's a party."

"My kind of party. I loved this, but my social battery's happy to get a good recharge."

Since his read dead empty, he studied her. "We're going to do okay together, Legs."

She studied him in turn. "How about we change into clothes suitable for plopping down, and plop down to watch the best Christmas movie ever."

"That depends on what you see as the best Christmas movie ever."

"Please. *Die Hard.*"

"Yeah. We're going to do just fine together."

In the station the next day, Gideon had plenty to keep him busy. He had holiday incident reports—some people just couldn't get through Christmas without fighting or finding some way to cause trouble.

He had calls to take, others to make, a budget to reconcile.

With Harley on desk duty, he was an officer short, so took up the slack in patrol and calls.

He was riding back to the station after handling a fender bender when Brill contacted him.

"Detective, what's the word?"

"I've got a few of them. You've got the switched plates in Chicago—you gave us that one. I'm giving you one from Nebraska, near Wayne. The owner of the car can't say when or where. She didn't notice until the morning of Christmas Eve."

"Not airport parking this time. But no question he's heading west."

"No. But we learned this morning his father transferred some property to him before he died. The widow didn't think of it before. Actually, it was the kid, Willow, the daughter, who told us. The widow's in pretty bad shape. She's scared he'll come back for them so she's taking the kid to their place in the Caymans for a while."

"Where's the property?"

"Washington State. The kid says they call it The Retreat, and that Dubecki asked for it. Specifically. She states that the old man told Dubecki to ask for something he wanted, and this is what he asked for. It's up in the Olympic Mountains—a rich man's idea of a cabin at about ten thousand square feet."

"That's a lot of cabin."

"Yeah, and it's remote, private road. I'm going to text you the address. He could be just stupid enough to go there."

"Okay. Possible."

He thinks he has the right, Arden had said. Believes he's above the rules.

"We've alerted the locals out there. If he shows up, they'll bag him."

"It seems like he should've started heading north instead of due west from Iowa."

"The Midwest is getting hit hard with this storm system. He could be trying to avoid the worst of the snow, but we've got that in mind. How's Arden?"

"Tougher than she looks."

"Yeah, I got that. Let her know we're not letting up."

"I'll do that." He pulled into his slot at the station. "It matters to her that you haven't, and you're not."

"I'll say it right out loud. The son of a bitch should've gone to the state pen, and he should still be there."

"Can't argue. Things don't always work out right the first time around. His mother paid a hell of a price for it working out wrong. Arden won't."

"Hold that good thought. We get anything else, you'll hear about it."

"Same."

He sat in the car, studying the fog drifting around the mountains while he thought it through.

He'd asked for the house, so he'd wanted it for a reason. Gideon could see him heading there, thinking of it as some sort of hideout. Rich man's cabin at ten thousand square feet? It had all the amenities, and he'd want that.

But the isolation, the remote? Bound to bore him before too long.

Then again, they'd make sure, if that was his target, he didn't stay bored long.

Arden put together a file on the downstairs project, and by the time Gideon came in through the mudroom, had begun sorting through leftovers.

"Hi. Interested in a post-Christmas feast?"

"I had a slice of cold pizza for lunch."

"Then you are. Busy day, huh?"

"There are a lot of dumbasses in the world," he said as he gave Zorro a rub. "And a chunk of them live in Riverbend."

"The smart-asses are lucky to have you, Chief." She turned into a kiss. "I spent most of the day playing around with ideas for downstairs. I have a file."

"I bet you do."

"I'm on an alcohol purge for a few days and pushing water. Do you want a beer?"

"I'll join the purge."

"Water it is. There's enough of all this for both of us if we aren't greedy."

"We'll get to it. I have some new information."

"Oh. Dubecki."

He watched her react, adjust, settle. Yeah, tougher than she looked.

"And not that he's in custody or you'd look satisfied. Has he hurt someone else?"

"Not that we know of. He switched plates again in Nebraska."

She felt her insides shudder, but kept her hands busy with the meal. "So he's heading west."

"His father left him some fancy cabin up in Washington State, in the Olympic Mountains. He asked for it, specifically asked for it."

She stopped, looked at him. "A place in the mountains. Gideon, he talked about that. The night he attacked me, he said something about us living in the mountains, how he'd take care of me and I could write in the quiet."

"It's all part of his pathology, and now he's got the place."

"And he started traveling that way right after . . . His mother. His father died, he inherited, and he had no use for her after that. God, Gideon, he could grab some other woman and force her to go with him. Maybe he already has."

"We'll be checking missing person reports on his route. Arden, there's a good chance that's where he's going. Local law enforcement's been alerted. But I don't want you to think it's the only chance."

"I don't. I won't. But I'm not crawling into a hole. I'm not putting chairs under doors again. If he's put a target on my back, we're going to make sure he misses."

"Tougher than you look." Gideon ran a hand down her braid. "Brill said to tell you they won't let up."

"I know that. And neither will you." She turned to him, and felt her insides settle again when he held her.

"How about you feed the dog," she said, "and I'll feed us?"

"That's a deal."

Chapter Twenty-Six

Bored, antsy, and out of chips, Dustin mapped the next leg of his journey. He'd really have to push it to make it to Salt Lake City, and didn't see the point. So he'd aim for his night's stop in Wyoming.

Yeehaw!

Maybe he'd buy himself a cowboy hat.

He could pick out some cowgirl boots for Arden, save them for when she'd earned a treat.

He knew her size—eight narrow. He'd studied the shoes in her apartment closet because he'd thought ahead.

Like always.

He found his spot, made an online booking for the following night. Since it was late in the day and he had to pack up, he'd leave first thing in the morning. Stop somewhere for a good, hot breakfast, some road snacks.

He started to text the guy who rented the house, tell him he wouldn't need the extended stay after all. Another couple of days in this place, he'd die of boredom.

Before he could write the text, someone knocked on the door.

His first instinct was to get his gun. He shoved it into the back waistband of his jeans.

With a peek out the window, he saw a Jeep that looked as if it had put in a lot of hard miles. And a woman, young, pretty, in a white parka and a sparkling rainbow ski hat.

He opened the door.

"Oh, thank God! Hi!" The words just bubbled out. "I'm so lost! My GPS went out, and I forgot to charge my phone. Can you believe it? I know I made a wrong turn somewhere. If I could just use your phone, call my friends, and maybe get directions? We've got a place up here for the rest of winter break. Sorry, I'm Hailey, Hailey Parkinson."

He thought: Bullshit story. She'd heard there was a guy up here and wanted to check him out.

"Sure, come on in."

"Thanks. I'm such an idiot! I've been driving around and around. I was afraid I'd run out of gas, and that would just top it."

She had brown eyes, deep, dark eyes, and glittery red streaks in her dark brown hair.

"This is nice," she said as she looked around. "I've seen pictures of the place we booked. I hope it's this nice."

"Yeah, we like it. My wife should be back any minute now." He gestured to Arden's picture. "She went out snowshoeing. I'm a more read-by-the-fire guy."

"I'm with your wife. I love winter sports. Oh, she's pretty. She looks familiar. Wait! Is your wife . . . I can't remember the name. I got a book for Christmas, from my sister, the big reader. I haven't read it, but I swear that's the same picture on the back of it."

Staring into her eyes, Dustin smiled. "Her name's Arden."

"That's it! Isn't that weird? I got a book she wrote for Christmas and I end up here."

"Some things are meant."

He pulled the gun out, aimed it at her. "Take off your clothes."

"What?"

He saw shock come first, shock, confusion, then that delicious terror.

"Oh, Jesus, don't. No! Please, don't."

"That's okay." He balled his left hand into a fist, smashed it into her face. "I'll do it."

Yeah, some things are meant, he thought as she dropped.

She'd come to his door, alone, with that bullshit story and those glittery red streaks in her hair. He dragged off her cap, ran his fingers through it.

He'd told her he was married, but she'd still flirted with him. Even when she'd recognized Arden.

Just another slut.

When she moaned, struggled, he hit her again. He didn't want to fight to get her out of the parka and all the rest.

She'd asked for it. He deserved it after all the miles he'd put in, the boredom, the effort.

And bonus round, she had a nice set of tits.

When he filled his hands with them, her eyes, glassy now, flickered open.

She cried, she screamed, begged, pretending she didn't want what was coming.

It irritated the crap out of him, so he pulled the gun back out, rammed it under her chin. And watched those glassy eyes go wide with terror.

"Shut the fuck up, bitch. You're going to take it, you're going to like it, or this bullet goes straight to your brain."

"Please. Please don't hurt me. Please."

"Baby, I'm gonna rock your world. It's what you came for."

"No, no."

When he shoved himself into her, she turned her head away and wept.

He was a *man*. Taking what he wanted, what he deserved, what women tried to use to control.

"Look at me." Tossing the gun aside, he yanked her head around, closed his hands over her throat. "Stop that blubbering, and look at me."

She fought now, bucking under him, hands flailing. As the excitement built, he pumped faster, squeezed harder.

He swore, swore, he felt the life fly out of her as he came, like the two actions were melded. And he came with a roar of triumph.

His body shook; his hands clutched like vises.

Then he collapsed on her, winded, empty, and blissfully satisfied.

"Good, that was so fucking good. Good for you, too. Cutting off the oxygen increases the pleasure. You're welcome. Whew!"

Still breathless, he got up, studied her.

"I'm going to take a shower and figure out what to do about you. Looks like I'm heading out tonight after all."

Since he hadn't sent that text, he had the place for three more days.

Plenty of time before anybody found her. Since he felt energized and relaxed at the same time, he decided he could drive a hundred and fifty, maybe two hundred miles, depending on road conditions.

Fresh from the shower, he sat by the fire with barely a glance at the body lying a few feet away.

In the end, he packed up. He went through the things in her car, took the five hundred and sixty-two dollars in cash and a bag of pretzels. He debated over a couple of sweaters he thought would look good on Arden, took those, the white parka, the sparkly rainbow cap.

He left her lying on the floor, and drove away in the gathering night.

Happy to go back to work, Arden tried out the new daily routine. She shared a house now, full-time, so adjustments.

She let the dog out; he made coffee.

"It's a workout day for me."

"Me, too. Is that a problem?"

She lifted her shoulders. "Not for me."

They went up, changed. He let the dog in, put food and fresh water in the bowls while she filled two water bottles.

She wouldn't have said they worked out together. More, they used the same space, as his routine made hers feel like the equivalent of lying on the couch eating chips and dip.

When she was done, she went up, showered, dressed, and was still drying her hair when he came in. Yes, adjustments, she thought, as he stripped down and walked into the shower.

Downstairs, with the morning fog enveloping the house like gray curtains, he sliced a banana over cereal, and she made a smoothie.

"I'll bring something home for dinner."

"That'd be good. Surprise me. I'm going up to get started."

She walked over, kissed him. She liked it when he tugged her in so their lips lingered.

"Go fight crime, Chief."

"That's the plan."

As she went upstairs, she thought, with pleasure, the adjustments worked.

She finished her smoothie standing at her office window. She loved looking out at fog, the way it moved, shifted, tore, settled again. She liked how it haloed the mountains, blanketed the valley, and how mists rose up like faerie fingers from the river.

She thought she might get a kayak. Rent one first in case she hated it. But if she didn't, it could be fun to spend some time on a summer Sunday on the river she looked out on every day.

But for now, she'd enjoy the fog, and the rain that so often chased it.

She heard Zorro coming up the steps, watched Gideon's truck pull out, turn onto the road.

"This is our life now." She rubbed Zorro as he stood by her side. "I love our life. But that's enough daydreaming."

She sat at her desk, rolled her shoulders.

"And here we go."

It worked the next day, too, and though she knew part of it leaned on that first heady bliss of love, it just felt right. Having Gideon's clothes in the closet felt right, and his shaving gear in the bathroom.

While her hours generally ran fairly steady, his fluctuated, but it simply worked.

When he brought work home, he tended to use the dining room or kitchen counter, which said to her, home office downstairs.

She brought it up as he closed his laptop.

"Yeah, I could use it. Nothing the size of yours. I don't need that. Desk, shelves, decent lighting."

"I'm getting closer to seeing it. Fireplace, a whopping big-screen." So no TV den needed upstairs, and the bedroom would remain a bedroom.

Maybe, one day, a nursery.

"I want one of those things," she continued, "units, whatever, on the wall of the gym plumbed in where you can fill your water bottle. The bathroom . . ."

"Good size, but the smallest in the house. Maybe forget a tub, just a big walk-in shower."

"Exactly what I thought. So, good. I'm going in to look at tile samples, flooring, paint, all of that tomorrow, since you're on duty. I'll talk to Joe about the contractors."

"He won't steer you wrong. It's your house, Arden."

"I don't want you—"

"Hold on, let me finish." He rose, got a bottle of wine. "It's been a few days and, I'm officially off duty until eight a.m., so my alcohol purge is over. You?"

"I guess we're about to have a discussion, so yeah, I'll have one, too."

"It's your house," he repeated as he poured, "but I'm living here. I'm going to pull my weight, so we work that out. Food, utilities, and all the rest. That includes the work downstairs and wherever else you start itching to do."

"Gideon, I can afford it. When my parents died, there was the insurance, the house in Brooklyn, and the rest. Aunt Jen—Uncle Doug fixes things, she handles the money—she invested it for me. And I had a college fund, so there was that. I don't make a fortune from my work, but it pays the bills."

"Good to know. If my portfolio tanks and I lose my job, I can be your gigolo. Meanwhile."

Amused, he tugged her down to a stool and sat with her. "Do you know one of the excuses they used when they burned me on the force in LA? I wasn't a real cop because I had money. Serious money. The kind where you could sit on your ass on a yacht in the Med."

"Oh. I guess I didn't go there."

"So you didn't hook me for my money."

"It was the carpentry and the sex."

"Accepted. So, food, utilities, the general maintenance, that's on me. Improvements, additions, that kind of thing, fifty-fifty should work."

"What if I want to do something and you hate it?"

"I haven't so far." Idly, he tapped his glass to hers. "I like your style, Legs."

"Won't you need a workshop?"

"I've got Pop's, and using it gives me another reason to spend time over there, with him. If I ever need one here, I'll build one."

"And I pay half." She saw the hesitation, gave him a look.

He shrugged.

"Looks like we have a deal." She held out a hand.

She walked into the hardware store the next day with a long list.

"This is a bright start to my day." Joe came around the counter, drew her into a bear hug. "Is my boy behaving himself?"

"So far, so good."

"You keep your eye on him. Hey there, Zorro. Elvis wants to share a treat with you."

He went back behind the counter, produced two. The dogs stopped wagging and sniffing long enough to take them.

"Part of me feels like I took Gideon away from you, Joe."

"You put that part away. He stops by regularly, here, at the house. And we have our monthly steak dinner—you're not invited."

That made her smile. "So I've been told. Firmly. I love him like crazy, Joe."

He hugged her again. "That makes me a very happy man. I've seen the weight he pretended not to carry lift over these past months. You're the biggest part of that.

"Now, are you just here to visit, or are we going to do some business? I hear you're looking to finish that basement."

She pulled out her phone. "I have a list a mile long. Maybe two miles."

"Let's get to it."

She spent nearly two hours as customers came in, went out again. Joe brought her a Coke as she studied tile samples, catalogs, debated over paint colors.

"I'm seeing it," she murmured. "Yeah, I'm seeing it. Energizing for the gym. Get pumped! Relaxing but fun for the rest. Gideon decides on his office space."

"You call the names I gave you for estimates," Joe told her. "None of them'll hose you, or they'll answer to me. When you're ready, you let me know the materials you want."

It tumbled right into place, she thought as she ran the rest of her errands. She'd planned to find her vision for that space in six months to a year. And she had.

It didn't occur to Dustin until he'd reached Salt Lake City.

He'd made a mistake.

He'd booked that goddamn cabin in Colorado under his new ID. The ID that had cost him a lot of fucking money.

He should've hidden the body. No, he should've dumped the body in the car, driven it miles away, ditched it and her. Then hiked back to the cabin.

He could've done it.

Coulda, shoulda, woulda.

Now, when they found her, they'd track the credit cards and everything else.

The ID was compromised.

The stupid bitch had come to his cabin, flirted with him, had practically begged him to put it to her. But she'd recognized Arden, hadn't she? he asked himself as he pulled over to think.

Just think.

That's why he'd had to kill her. Not because he'd wanted to but because she'd given him no choice.

He couldn't use the ID, so he had to cancel the hotel in Salt Lake. Pay cash for another place.

No problem, no problem, he had the cash.

But now he had to pay for new ID, shift all the money around again. That cost more than money. It cost him time.

Screaming in frustration, he pounded his hand on the steering wheel.

The bitch with the sparkly red streaks screwed it all up for him. He wished he'd used the gun on her.

He had some time before they found her—probably. He'd contact the guy who did the ID, get that going. He'd cancel the room, get another room, the sort where they didn't ask for ID when you paid cash.

And yeah, get the car painted. Better to take the time to do that anyway.

He'd pay extra to have the ID expedited. Worth it. Plus, before long, he'd have Arden's money to add to the pile.

Women had no sense about money, and as the head of the household, he'd take control there.

Calmer, he breathed out, and got the ball rolling.

Arden had just started making a tortellini soup with Italian sausage when Gideon came in.

"Hey, you're early. I'm making soup—you'll like it. Not raining, but it's so chilly and damp out. And you just missed Woody the contractor. He had a job nearby so he came over to take a look. He's going to work up an estimate. He thinks he can start in a week or so."

Gideon reached over, turned off the heat under the sausage she was sautéing.

"What—" She only had to see his face to know. "It's bad."

"It's bad."

"He hurt someone. He's still coming this way, and he hurt someone. Tell me fast. Straight-out and fast."

Gideon put his hands on her shoulders. "He beat, raped, and murdered a woman, Hailey Parkinson, age twenty."

She sagged under his hands.

"You're sure it's him?"

"He rented a cabin, northern Colorado. The man who rented it to him ID'd his photo, the car. It's him. Keep breathing, Arden, and slow it down."

She hadn't realized she'd started to hyperventilate, and now worked to calm her breathing. She kept her eyes on his—it helped.

"When?"

"The victim was due several miles away, another rental with friends for winter break. She never showed, didn't answer the phone. Three days ago. He left her body in the cabin, her car outside. They didn't go to clean it, turn it until today when his booking ended."

"Twenty years old. Her parents, her family. Why was she there?"

"We don't know yet. They're figuring she got lost, and stopped at that cabin. I don't have all the details yet. It takes time."

Everything in her felt dark and tight.

"She doesn't have any more. He's done just harassing, assaulting. I knew that when he attacked me. Someone else will be in the wrong place, and he'll kill them. Her."

"Listen. As bad as it is, we've got something out of it. He booked the cabin and paid for it with a credit card under the name Jesse Flint. We can track that ID and card back all the way to Columbus, and forward to Colorado. We can track it, Arden. He used it again in Wyoming. A hotel, gas, food, a goddamn Stetson.

"He made a big mistake, and we can track him."

"You'll track him. He'll use the card again, and you'll know. I just need a minute."

She got water, drank slowly.

"There's something else you don't want to tell me, or wish you didn't have to."

"He used that ID to buy a gun, a Glock nine millimeter in Columbus. He picked it up the morning after he killed his mother. The ID's good enough to pass through the background check."

"He has a gun. Is that how he killed the woman in Colorado?"

"No."

Her eyes filled. "Did she have red hair?"

"No, but she'd put red streaks in it, for the holidays. Arden, he'd have killed her regardless. The minute she got to him, she was dead. The search for him? It's going to intensify now. You need to know that, too."

She drank the rest of the water, set the glass aside.

"I'm not going to fall apart. It doesn't do any good, and neither does crying. You came home early to tell me, and to be here if I fell apart. But I'm not going to.

"I'm going to make soup."

"Don't worry about that. I'll toss something together later."

"I'm going to make soup," she repeated. "Because I need to keep doing. He's using new ID and you have it. You're going to track him, and stop him, and lock him away where he can't hurt anyone else."

"That's right."

"I believe you'll do that." She swiped at her eyes. "You and Brill and Venmar and all the rest. So I'm going to make soup, and if I knew how, I'd bake bread with the yeast I bought thinking I'd look it up and try it."

"I can bake bread."

Shock blinked through the tears. "You can bake bread?"

"My grandmother. It's been a while, but yeah, I can do it."

"Okay. Okay. I'll make soup, you make bread. But first, you need to hold on to me a few minutes. I'm not going to fall apart, but you could just hold on to me."

When he did, she let out a long, shaky breath.

When she closed her eyes, she saw Dustin's face. So she opened them again and looked out the window, where the rain that had threatened all day began to fall.

She kept doing, and it got easier as one day passed into the next. Her work on the book kept her busy and out of her own worries for hours a day. At night, if those worries plagued her, she had Gideon to turn to.

She nudged away Zoey's push for her to come there, spend New

Year's Eve, and did the same with Jamie's for her to join him and Nick at a friend's party.

Not brooding, she assured herself. Just content to spend the last night of what had been a good year, a year of change and progress, and best of all love, in her quiet house with her very good dog.

After working through the afternoon, she took a walk with Zorro. She didn't mind the light drizzle, not when she could see across the valley or gaze out to mist-soaked mountains.

"This would probably be snow back in Ohio," she told Zorro. "I guess I didn't mind that either, really. Life's different when your commute to work is up a set of stairs in your own house."

It helped to remind herself how lucky she was. Yes, the book had stalled on her a little, but she'd figure it out. And stalling or rolling, she'd sit in her wonderful office every day and write.

Soon, her lower level would fill with workers and the sounds of progress. She'd watch her vision become reality. By the time it did . . .

"It'll practically be spring."

As they headed back, she told herself it wasn't foolish to block out the hard part. Yes, she'd taken a walk on a quiet road, had wandered down a path in the woods a bit, but she'd had her phone in her pocket and her dog by her side.

She believed the odds stayed low that Dubecki clung to his obsession with her, that he'd found where she'd moved and crossed the country for, what, retribution?

But those odds weren't zero so she'd stay alert, she'd stay cautious.

She'd taken back what he'd stolen from her. Confidence and the freedom that brought, the relief of feeling safe in her own home, the simple pleasure of a walk in the woods.

She couldn't and wouldn't give them up again.

And as Gideon had suggested, she would write it out. When she was ready.

Back in the house, she gave Zorro a treat, then added a log to the living room fire.

"Maybe I should've gotten you a party hat. You'd wear it, too. But then I'd wonder about both of us. Here's what we're going to do."

Zorro made his happy noises as she crouched down to rub him head to tail.

"I'm going to go up and deal with some office stuff. I know, I know, we humans always have something. But then, it's into pj's. I'm going to make you dinner, and make myself a delicious New Year's Eve sandwich. We're going to plop down, snuggle up, and watch movies."

Since he seemed on board, Arden got to her feet. Her heart lurched when he barked, then raced to the door. Jamming her hand in her pocket, she closed it over her phone. Under the buzzing in her ears, she heard the knock.

And when she looked out the window, saw Jamie.

"You see, you see," she muttered to herself. "You waste time and energy being afraid of a knock on the door."

She opened it to Jamie carrying Isis in one arm and a picnic basket on the other.

"Happy New Year's Eve! I waited until I could be close to positive you'd finished writing for the day."

"I have. Don't you have a party to get ready for?"

"Not for hours yet. We'd never get there before nine. And we wanted to spend a little more time this year with you and Zorro."

"At a picnic?"

"An indulgence picnic. In here I have a thermos of hot chocolate, a container of whipped cream—both made by my own delicate hands. There are petit fours, lighter-than-air macaroons, mini cream puffs, mini cupcakes made by Nick's baking-god hands. Some lovely dog nibbles as well."

"That sounds . . . amazing."

"Of course. You have a fire going, so perfect."

He set the basket on the coffee table, opened it. And handed Arden a tiara. "De rigueur for our final indulgence of the year."

"You brought party hats."

"Naturally."

He fixed a tiny and shiny pink hat on Isis, a blue one on Zorro, then put a glittery gold crown on his own head.

Touched, amused, Arden watched him spread a blanket in front of the fire. He took out a container, gave each of the dogs a treat.

"Now sit and be good, and there'll be more coming. But first." From the thermos, he poured hot chocolate into oversized cups. "Considering the occasion, there's a little peppermint schnapps in here." He added whipped cream, then sprinkled crushed peppermint over it all.

"Well, this is gorgeous."

"Sit, my queen."

She sat on the blanket, waited for him to do the same.

"To ending the year with a friend."

Smiling, he touched his cup to hers. "And to a glorious New Year to come."

She sipped. Warm, comforting, with a surprising and welcome zip. "Wow, this is just more amazing."

"I'm hoping the schnapps weakens your resolve so you go up, get your party on, and come with me and Nick tonight."

"Zorro and I have important plans. Really. We're going to start with a tearjerker, move to a rom-com, hit it with action, and end, if we last that long, with flat-out comedy. This right here? The perfect party for me."

He reached in the basket, took out a noisemaker. Blowing it, he made her laugh.

She sampled a petit four, and just closed her eyes. "Honestly, how does he do it?"

Reaching out, Jamie took her hand. "Let's acknowledge the elephant in the room so we can banish it back to the jungle. You hadn't lost that look in your eyes when you answered the door."

"I'm doing okay, honestly. No, there's nothing new. No sign of him, the car, he hasn't used the credit card again. Gideon thinks he realized his mistake."

"I'm glad he's honest with you. I'd hate if Nick placated me."

"I think he's stalled—like the story I'm writing. What churns in me, Jamie, is he'll kill someone else before they stop him."

"I picture him in a hatchback. I don't know enough about cars to pick a type, but it's an ugly poop-brown hatchback. The Hatchback of Destiny. And with him trapped inside, screaming, as it drives off a cliff, where it crashes far below and explodes in a raging inferno of hellfire."

She sipped some schnapps-infused hot chocolate.

"Wow, that's some picture."

"I try not to make enemies. Try not to wish harm on others, even the multitude of assholes who inhabit the world we live in. But let's be real, he deserves it."

She leaned over, kissed him. "The Hatchback of Destiny. I'm going to borrow that picture whenever the anxiety hits."

"It's all yours."

"Okay, elephant banished."

"Good. Now, drink some more adult hot chocolate, because I'm going to ask you for a favor."

"My prince, you don't need to ply me with schnapps for me to do you a favor."

"I want you to pose for me."

"To—ah . . ."

"Not a nude." He waved that away, and gave the dogs another treat. "This came to me at the last Sunday brunch. Zoey and Boone came, and you, Zoey, and Tessa were standing together, talking. It stuck in my head, how the three of you looked together. Blonde, brunette, redhead, all beautiful and striking in your own ways."

He offered her a little cupcake. "The Three Fates. I want to paint you as the Three Fates. It's an entirely new area for me, but I can't get it out of my head."

"You mean like in mythology? Greek mythology, right?"

"Exactly. The Moirai, three sisters who spin, measure, and cut the threads of life. I've actually done some research on them. I see Zoey as Clotho—the spinner—you as Lachesis—the allotter—and Tess as Atropos, who cuts the thread. I'd want you in white, but not like Grecian, not expected. A modern take. A smart white suit for Zoey, a flowy white dress for you, white jeans and a white denim jacket for Tessa."

"You've really thought about this."

Shoulders lifted, he held a hand palm up. "Obsessed with it. I know you're all busy, and I couldn't ask you to all be together throughout. If I could do some sketches of each of you, individually and together. Tessa's on board. I think Zoey will be, especially if you are. So say you are."

"I have no idea how to pose."

"It's my job to help you with that." Pushing the charm, he smiled. "More hot chocolate?"

She shook her head, laughed. "I'm seriously flattered, Jamie. You know I love your work." She sipped more hot chocolate. "So, you'll make me a goddess?"

"Baby doll, you already are."

"How could I say no?"

He blew the noisemaker again.

Chapter Twenty-Seven

While Arden spent her New Year's Eve as planned, Dubecki studied his new ID. The forger had price gouged him, no question, but he'd delivered.

Once he was good and settled with Arden in The Retreat, he'd find the best way to sell his mother's big fat diamond engagement ring. It would more than make up for it.

He'd check out of this dump of a motel in the morning, and Samuel Robert Lewis would check into a decent hotel. And, according to his calculations and route, would book another in Boise. He'd take a day to fix his accounts, two at the most, then head west again.

He should arrive, flush with money, and in his newly painted classy blue Mercedes by January fifth, maybe the sixth.

It couldn't take a day or two more to retrieve—he liked that word, *retrieve*—Arden. A few hours later, they'd be at The Retreat, where they'd snuggle right in for the rest of the winter while she learned her lesson.

By spring, she'd be tamed—another word he liked—and they'd be the happiest couple on the planet.

He picked up her photo, gave it a kiss.

"It'll take some work, but I don't mind. In fact, I'm going to enjoy it."

He picked up the newly purchased handcuffs. He'd gone with gunmetal gray instead of shiny silver. More, to his mind, dignified.

"We're going to have some fun with these."

As he'd worked until nearly three a.m., Gideon slept in. Arden started the New Year with a workout, and feeling righteous, considered seeing if she could give her stalled story a kick in the ass.

Before she could, her phone signaled a FaceTime request from Jen.

"Hey! Happy New Year, and safe travels."

"Happy New Year. We decided not to fly home today after all."

"Can't get enough of those California Pacific views?"

"It's spectacular." Travis angled his head in.

"Agreed," Jen said. "But we're actually driving back into Oregon. A house we liked where we liked just dropped the asking price. Doug thinks it's a sign. So we're all driving up to take another look. Zoey, Boone, and the girls are driving down. We hoped you would, too. If nothing else, we'll have a big family lunch somewhere and say goodbye in person again."

Arden decided she'd kick-start the story later.

"Text me the address, and I'll be there. It's the one in Myrtle Creek, isn't it?"

"That's the one." Now Doug stuck his head in. "Needs a little work, but a guy's got to keep busy."

"Then I'll see you in a couple hours."

"Gideon's welcome."

"The chief didn't get to bed until nearly four. I'll leave him a note."

She wrote out a note, added the time she left, then with Zorro headed out.

Gideon woke shortly after ten, and took a moment to wish Arden still slept beside him. They'd barely exchanged words the night before—make that this morning.

He'd crashed about thirty seconds after he hit the sheets.

He took a long, hot shower to help revive. He thought he might find her in her office, maybe in the library. But he didn't find her or the dog.

The unease hit hard even as he assured himself he'd have heard any sort of a break-in. His mind and body relaxed when he found her note in the kitchen.

Didn't want to text and wake you after the night you put in. I'm driving to Myrtle Creek to meet the family—all of them. Uncle Doug and Aunt Jen delayed their flight home to take another look at a house they liked.

Price drop. Leaving just before nine, should be back by three-ish. Take it easy today, Chief. I love you.

He said, "Huh." Calculated she'd be halfway there.

He made coffee, scrambled some eggs. Then decided what the hell, he'd take it easy for a few hours in Pop's workshop.

"Where's your girl?"

"Driving down to Myrtle Creek to meet the family. Doug and Jen are looking at a house."

"How about that?" Joe and Elvis walked out to the workshop with Gideon. "I thought that was happening about a year from now."

"Something set them off."

"I'd say that might be two more grandkids coming, plus the prospect of a wedding."

Gideon walked into the shop, drew in the scent. "I just moved in over there. That needs to settle in."

"Uh-huh. Since you were born, and that's literal, you've known what you want. When you know what you want, you aim to get it. Work toward it, and get it."

"So, say this is the work-toward-it stage."

"Uh-huh," Joe said again. "What're you going to make?"

"She's doing that basement, and she's already looking at furniture. She's got these nesting tables in her file. I can make them."

"Uh-huh. I can give you a hand with that. I need to get something from the house first."

Gideon considered his choices of wood. He wanted round, made up of four triangles, different tones. He could make them look rustic, but not too, give her serviceable and sturdy.

Since he'd already drawn them out, he chose his wood.

"I'm going with walnut," he said when Joe came back.

"Good choice. Here. When you finish working for it, give her this."

"Pop."

"In your own time, Giddyup." He opened the ring box.

Inside him, a fist squeezed over his heart. "That's Nan's ring."

"That's right. You may need to have it sized. It's not flashy, but it's damn pretty, and God knows it's good luck. She'd have loved that girl, Gideon. She and I want her to have this, if she wants it. I think I know she'd understand its value's not in the diamonds but the history and the sentiment."

They'd call it vintage, Gideon supposed, with the center diamond flanked by the tiny chips. No, not flashy, but simple. And he realized as he looked at it, if he'd gone out to buy one, he'd have gravitated to this style.

"She'd take it off and put it in that little dish when she made bread, so the dough wouldn't gunk it up when she kneaded it. Otherwise, she always wore it. Hell."

Gideon wrapped Joe in a hard hug. "Thanks, Pop. You're right, she'll know what it means. I'll give it to her when she's ready."

"Good enough for me. Well, let's get to work."

He got home minutes before she did, and stepped outside when she drove up.

"How'd it go?"

"First, hello!"

She threw her arms around him, kissed him. "First real kiss of a New Year. And I think I got my mojo back."

"What mojo is that?"

"Working out, on that really nice drive, why my book stalled. Tomorrow, we roll. As for the house? Big and sprawling so downsizing be damned. It's a good area for them, and has what they're looking for."

Zorro followed them in, went straight to the fire Gideon had started, and sighed as he plopped down.

Gideon thought while the dog looked tired out, Arden looked energized.

"So, yeah, the house is bigger than they'd talked about before, but—"

"Soon to be six grandkids."

"Exactly. And they're hoping we can all do a family dinner there every couple months, which could involve a stay over, so bigger. It looked good to me, but Uncle Doug says it needs work, so it must."

"And he likes that idea."

"Yes, he does. Aunt Jen made noises about paint colors and so on.

They made an offer, and wow." She snapped her fingers. "Bought a house."

"Fast work. Wine?"

"Why not? I think they gave this house a lot of thought over these past weeks, and when the price dropped? They're going back tomorrow, putting their house on the market. Lots of things to tie up, but they hope to be here, moved in, by summer. Way ahead of schedule. They're really excited. So." She lifted her glass. "Here's to that."

"Happy looks good on you."

"Feels good, too. The holidays made me realize how much I missed having them in the same time zone. Now, what've you been up to today?"

"Went over to Pop's, working on a project."

"I thought you'd sprawl out and watch—there are games on today, right?"

"I liked this better. I dealt with plenty of games half the night."

"I bet. Drunks, punks, and lunks."

Since he'd encountered plenty of all of those, he had to smile. "Good one."

"Why don't we sprawl out and you can give me the highlights?"

"A lot of lowlights mixed in."

They sprawled out in the living room and he told her about the drunks, the reckless, the giddy, the entertaining, and the belligerent.

"Kind of stupid to get mouthy with the man with the badge."

"You need people with badges because plenty get stupid. And plenty of them woke up today with hangovers, regretting the stupid.

"Did you follow through on the movie marathon?"

"I did, and enjoyed every minute. But before that I had a picnic right over there with Jamie, who brought hot chocolate laced with peppermint schnapps and a basket of delectables—of which I saved you some. Because I'm a very good girlfriend."

"You're not bad at all."

"And I agreed to pose for him."

"Pose?"

"Not naked—I can see your mind went there, and so did mine. And not just me. He wants Zoey and Tessa and me. As the Three Fates. They're—"

"I know who the Three Fates are, Legs."

"Of course you do. He wants a modern take," she said, and ran it through for him.

"Zoey said yes, too, so he'll do some sketches of us, separately, together. It feels weird but fun. I said I'd give him some time, once I pushed through the stall. All in all I had a good end to one year and a happy start to the next. Since you love your work, and love working in the shop, I'd say you did, too."

"You're not wrong. But since I missed you, this rounds out the start just fine."

With the story open for her again, Arden rolled right through, only stopping when Zorro nudged his head under her arm.

"Come on, go lie down. I'm cooking here."

When he made a sad sound, she glanced over, saw the time.

"Oh, wow, sorry! Lost track."

He raced down ahead of her and straight to the door—and zoomed out when she opened it.

Meanwhile, she went in, grabbed a tangerine, toasted the second half of the bagel she'd had that morning, and rewarded her productive day so far with a Pepsi.

Now back in her office, ready to work, with Zorro settled down with his afternoon treat, Arden set an alarm. She'd promised to meet the other two Fates at Jamie's studio at four-thirty for their first session.

It relieved her their first would be the group. Maybe she wouldn't feel as self-conscious that way. Maybe. Regardless, she'd work until four, or until she ran out of steam.

She ran out at three-thirty, and congratulated herself on a really good day.

She answered emails she'd ignored, gave a pleased nod at the text from her aunt and uncle. They'd arrived safe in Columbus, where they reported snow and temps in the twenties.

She looked out her window, where the sunlight came fitfully, but it came. And the temperatures hovered into the fifties.

"I'll take it."

While she didn't own a flowy white dress—and Jamie said wardrobe wasn't necessary—she changed into jeans and a T-shirt and threw a flannel shirt over it.

"Let's go out."

Thrilled with the idea, Zorro sprinted off.

The air smelled fresh and felt the same. Winter, yes, Arden thought, but it held no bitterness or bite today. When the rains swept back, and they would, they'd carry a shiver. And the fog would roll and spread.

But today, the sun peeked through clouds to sprinkle on the valley and add delicate hints of blue to the river.

She caught the scent of woodsmoke as she walked, as well as the scent of the damp that hid in the shadows.

She wouldn't pine for spring, for the warmth, for the blooming, not yet. Not when she wanted to embrace the moment.

Pines brought some green, and bare trees stood like sentinels. The breeze was a bracing kiss on her cheeks.

She arrived just as Zoey pulled up. Under an open gray trench coat, her cousin wore a navy dress that stretched over her baby bump.

She also, Arden noted, wore the perfect French manicure.

Glancing at her own nails, she winced. She really needed to do something about them.

Zoey took a garment bag out of the back.

"White sheath and jacket I saw at the maternity shop. I wanted Jamie to see if it works. Either way, it's mine."

"I have no flowy white dress."

"That will be remedied." Angling her head, Zoey smiled. "You look energized. Excited about trying on your artist's model?"

"No. But I had a really good day of writing. How's the next in line?"

"Active." After greeting Zorro, Zoey rubbed her bump. "Very."

With the privilege of friendship, Arden laid a hand on Zoey's belly, felt the kick. "Goal!"

"Shoots, scores. Boone says boy or girl—he remains adamant about not finding out ahead of time—this one's going to dominate the soccer field."

They'd just started toward the house when Tessa drove up.

"Hello, sister goddesses."

She bounced out of her truck on work boots. The tail of her hair spilled out under her cap, and her cargo pants and shirt bore some smears and splatters of her trade.

"Came straight from work," she said.

"So did we all."

Tessa looked up at Zoey, then shifted over to Arden. "Sister goddesses who work in very different trades."

"I'm going to need your trade in—Woody estimates—a couple months."

"I'll mark you down. When's he starting?"

"A week from Monday."

"Cool. Let me know when the drywall's up, and I'll come take a look. So, is this way weird or what?"

"Way weird."

Zoey shook her head. "Fun."

"If I had your face, I'd think fun." Tessa shrugged. "But Jamie knows what he's doing."

They trooped to the door. When Jamie opened it, he beamed like the rising sun.

"There's my beauties. And you, my man, Isis is ready to romp with you. Let me take you up. I have refreshments. The stairs aren't too much, are they, Mama?"

"Dude. I chase around after a couple of toddlers, and that's after working all day."

"But you'll tell me anytime you need to sit. This won't be a long one today, and I'm so grateful you could all do this first together."

In his studio, he had wine, water, a pot of tea, a fruit and cheese platter, and cookies unmistakably baked by Nick.

Tessa rubbed her hands together. "This is looking like a pretty good gig."

"I want you all comfortable and happy. So enjoy, relax a bit. What have we here, Zoey?"

"A white sheath and jacket I saw at my pregnant girl shop. You can let me know if it's what you have in mind. And since I want to know what you have in mind, I don't think Clotho, right? I don't think she was pregnant. Are you just going to work around that?"

"Absolutely not. We celebrate it," he said, lifting his arms. "You're the spinner of the thread of life, and you carry it."

He unzipped the bag, drew out the suit. Smiled with his sigh. "My fashion partner, this is perfect."

"I need more direction than white and flowing to find what you want."

"I'll take care of that."

"You're not buying me a dress."

"I'm buying my goddess her dress."

"I've got the jeans, the T-shirt," Tessa began as she bit into a strawberry.

"I'll find the jacket. And the red high-tops."

"I've got red high-tops."

"I'll look at them next time. Each of you will have that pop of red. Tessa, the shoes, Arden probably a belt or sash. Or if the dress doesn't work with one, the measuring tape. And with this outfit, Zoey, I think pendant. A big, bold red stone."

"Power color."

Jamie beamed at Arden now. "Just so. Now, don't mind me. Relax, enjoy, converse. I'm going to do some sketches, casual ones."

Tessa looked at Arden. "Weird."

Zoey just laughed. "Let me tell you about this tour group today." Obviously at ease, she entertained them until Jamie set aside his pad.

"All right, I want a few with you standing together. I have props."

"This is cute."

"Hand spindle. You'll hold it by the thread, the other hand cupped just below it." He held out a cloth measuring tape to Arden. "Both hands, held loosely."

"Because I don't measure until the thread's spun."

"You see what I see. And for you, scissors."

Tessa gave the slim, elongated scissors with gold accents a couple of snaps. "Pretty fancy ones."

"Why would you end life with kitchen shears? Arden, I'd love if you'd take your hair out of the braid for this."

"Sure."

"Cap off, Tess, and you on Arden's right, scissors right hand, and let's try left hand with the thumb hooked in the pocket. Zoey, Arden's left. Angle just a bit toward her, but look straight at me. Arden, lower your hands more, and relax them."

He gave them all bolstering smiles. "Talk amongst yourselves."

"Okay. Arden, that basement level. About twelve hundred square feet?"

"Um. Twelve hundred and thirty-six."

"How many colors are you looking for?"

"Well." Oddly, thinking about it relaxed her, and talking it through helped her visualize it.

Jamie didn't smile as he sketched now. He used an easel, a much larger sketch pad.

By the time he stepped back, the three of them had talked paint, dinner plans, Zoey's newest skin care obsession, and made a lunch date for the following week.

"You're brilliant, all of you. Perfect and brilliant. Would you like to see?"

"Bet your ass." Tessa hurried over. "Okay, wow."

Arden looked over Tessa's shoulder. "I'll second that *okay, wow*."

"I make it unanimous. I couldn't really see what you talked about, Jamie, but here it is. We look . . ."

"Like goddesses," Tessa finished. "But not all formal and old-timey. Like now. You put us in the outfits we don't have yet."

"I've seen Zoey's, and I have yours and Arden's earmarked. I wanted to see if this worked first."

Arden edged closer. "It worked."

They all looked straight out, as if aware of the onlooker, but the way they stood, the angles, made them a unit, and each with a task to do. Zoey's face, serene, almost dreamy, and hers? She supposed thoughtful, while Tessa struck her as coolly confident.

The varying heights and, yes, shapes, especially given Zoey's obvious pregnancy, added individuality.

"I'm buying the painting."

"Hey, wait."

Arden just gave Zoey a wide, closed-lip smile. "Dibs."

"Damn it."

"I haven't painted it yet, or said it's for sale."

"When you do. It's going in my new family room, over my new fireplace."

"I'll buy that sketch."

Zoey let out a frustrated breath at Tessa. "Damn it!"

"I'll need it for now, and when I don't, you can have it. No charge. I'll need to do at least one more," he told Zoey, "and that's yours."

Leaning over, Zoey kissed his cheek. "Thank you. Pregnant brain's made me slow off the mark. But not so slow I can't see this is going to be wonderful."

"The three of you inspired me. I can work with each of you individually when you have time for a sitting. And I'd like two or, better, three more sessions together, in wardrobe."

She hadn't expected to have fun, but she had. And, Arden thought, wasn't that the best kind of fun?

Nick got home before they left. When he walked into the studio, he studied the sketch, slid an arm around Jamie.

"I married a genius."

"So did I." Jamie tipped a head to Nick's shoulder. "Aren't we lucky?"

"I think I married a genius, because when he talks about his work, I understand nothing."

"Zoey, no one does."

"Exactly. What I do know is he's home from work, home with the kids, and he's making rosemary chicken for dinner."

"A guy who cooks doesn't have to be a genius," Tessa decided.

"True, and he's damn good at it. Which I'm going to prove by having you all over for dinner. We'll get the sitter to host a Girls Only Pizza Picnic in the bonus room. The kids will love it."

Zoey took out her phone, checked her calendar. "How about two weeks from Friday?"

"I'll check with Hawk. We're actually meeting up for pizza in . . . Oops, I'd better get going."

"My social calendar's open. I can't speak for the chief's, but I'll have him check."

"We're there," Jamie said at a nod from Nick.

"With dessert," Nick added.

"I was hoping. I have to get home. Jamie, this was a new and fascinating experience."

"Let's set up the next before you go. I'll come to you."

Arden walked home with a played-out Zorro. Evening had closed in with its deep, dark shadows, the creep of fog. She heard an owl call, and another, distant, answer.

Her phone signaled a text as she walked.

At Jamie's? I'll come get you.

I'm walking onto the driveway right now.

Instead of answering, Gideon opened the door. Light washed out from behind him in welcome. Zorro found the energy to desert her and run to Gideon.

He still wore his sidearm, which told her he'd only just gotten home. Even as he bent to rub the dog, those deep, delicious green eyes watched her.

And ridiculously, the way they did made her feel like a goddess.

She walked straight to him, framed his face in her hands, and kissed him.

"Somebody had a good time."

"I did, and a good day all around."

"I can add to that. I brought home dinner."

She stood where she was a moment, on the threshold, night at her back, the light and him before her.

"I love you."

He managed to look pleased and puzzled at the same time. "I love you, too."

She stepped in, and shut out the night.

In Boise, Dubecki ordered a steak dinner and a bottle of cab. He'd considered going out to a restaurant, as he'd grown tired of hotel rooms with only himself for company. But even with the darker, longer hair, the beard, some nosy asshole might recognize him. He was so close now, better to keep the lowest of low profiles.

He'd considered hiring a whore—you could always find a whore—

but though he wanted sex, he knew he couldn't settle for just that. He'd need the kill.

Unless, of course, it was Arden.

He couldn't afford to kill some whore in Boise, Idaho, when he was this close to what he wanted, needed, deserved.

So he settled for room service and a movie that contained nudity, violence, and adult language.

He really wanted all three.

Just to vent out some pressure, he thought as he ate. This trip put a lot of pressure on him. All the driving—hours most days—the fucking weather that kept him holed up in his room when it was impossible to drive.

The time, the expense, the fucking boredom.

She'd have to pay for that.

He'd cuff her to the bed, give her a taste of the belt before he took her from behind and made her like it until she begged for more.

And he wanted a goddamn blow job. He'd hold the knife to her throat so she didn't get any ideas and bite him again. Last time, his tongue had been sore for days.

He fantasized about the different ways he'd hurt her—to teach her a lesson. It gave him a nicer buzz than the wine.

He'd bought the zip ties and the duct tape, and he'd use them. Waste not, want not.

Once she'd learned her lesson, he'd bring them out again once in a while, just to refresh her.

She'd wear the clothes he bought her—he'd already picked up some things here and there. And nothing else.

Finally, he'd be in control. No one would ever tell him what to do or how to do it, ever again. Especially Arden.

She'd call him Sam, and if she slipped? Well, that's what a backhand was for.

He'd trash her ID. She wouldn't need new because she wouldn't go anywhere; she wouldn't need to buy anything because he'd provide what he chose to provide. And she'd better be grateful.

But maybe he'd give her a new name. Something more female, something softer. He'd think about it. He'd decide.

When he flew back to Ohio, say a year from now, to kill the others, he'd have to chain her to the bed. For her own good.

But he'd leave food and water close at hand.

She'd be so happy to see him when he got back from doing what he needed to do. She'd want sex right away, of course, and he'd give that to her. Then she'd mix him a drink so he could relax while she unpacked for him. She'd cook his favorite dinner before they had sex again.

He looked at her picture with a mixture of rage and lust and longing. She'd be who he wanted her to be, or by God, she'd be sorry.

He took a long breath, drank some wine. He needed to stay calm now, stay focused. Tomorrow, he'd drive to Riverbend.

Chapter Twenty-Eight

Gideon checked in with the state police in Oregon, and in Washington State. He spread it out to Wyoming, Utah, Idaho, circled back to Colorado.

Every single lead on Dustin Dubecki had petered out or dead-ended.

He went back to the routes, both to the target in the Olympic Mountains and to Arden. He worked out alternate routes, studied the weather patterns, calculated the timing.

The Jesse Flint ID—dead as far as Gideon could see. It hadn't been used in over a week. Again, backtracking, he decided Dubecki paid in cash often, but he'd also made use of the credit card. Hotels, gas. And, what chilled him, purchases of women's clothing. A few dresses, some boots, fucking underwear.

He debated sharing that with Arden, but what would it tell her?

He could have a woman with him, either willing or not. He could slip through the manhunt because they weren't looking for a couple.

Odds? he thought. Low, but still possible. Certainly as possible as a five-year obsession.

But he just didn't buy it.

He turned to his map on the wall, one with every known stop Dubecki had made, dated and pin-marked. And those pins stopped in the mountains of Colorado.

December twenty-seventh. They'd confirmed Dubecki had been in the cabin on that date. He'd left his DNA and prints all over the cabin. And he'd left his DNA inside his victim.

Since then . . . nothing.

"Chief? I'm off unless you need me for something."

"Give me five, will you, Hawk? Sit down a minute." As Hawk sat, Gideon gestured to the map.

"Dubecki used the Jesse Flint ID on the sixteenth, to buy a Mossberg 500 pump-action shotgun, and ammo, the Glock, also in Columbus, on the morning of December eighteenth. He used it to buy gas, and we know he stopped in Indianapolis, switched plates at the airport before he moved on to Chicago, switched plates at O'Hare. He got stuck in Chicago a couple of days. He purchased a men's sweater, thermal underwear, a woman's parka, sweater, and two dresses in Chicago, again using the same card."

Nodding, Hawk followed along the route. "Traveling alone at that time, as far as we know."

"Solo check-in at the Chicago Four Seasons, so yeah, as far as we know. Then he moved on to Iowa—weather bogged him down there an extra day. He bought gas, a hunting rifle with scope, road snacks, again using the card."

"He'd have cash, too."

"Which we can't track. We have him crossing Iowa and into Nebraska. Another dress, more gas, the hotel. Women's dress and underwear. Due west into Wyoming, where he bought a goddamn Stetson, Tecovas boots, and a pair of women's Frye boots. South from there to the cabin in Colorado, arrival Christmas Day, hit more weather, extended his stay. Probably paid cash for groceries. He killed Hailey Parkinson on December twenty-seventh."

"And hasn't used the credit card since," Hawk finished.

"It took him a week to get from Ohio to Colorado. Weather delays ate up three of those days. So we say four travel days. Unless he wanted to spend the night with a dead body, we figure he left the cabin on the twenty-seventh."

"Giving him a week to get here or up to Washington. Some weather, sure, but not like he hit in the Midwest or Colorado."

"If he figured out his mistake, switched to cash and kept going, he should have gotten where he wanted to be. But, you look at the places he booked. High-end. You can't check into a high-end hotel without ID, and they want a credit card on file."

"Hole up, wait for new ID. That'll take some time."

"Not that long if you pay enough. He would. He wouldn't like it, but he'd pay rather than stay in some cheap motel and delay any longer than he has to."

Now Gideon sat. "The accounts we dug out? Closed two days ago, and empty. He got what he paid for and he's on the road."

"You think here."

Though he'd gone over it from every angle, Gideon couldn't pinpoint.

"Toss-up. He knows, has to, Arden's going to resist. The place he's going needs to be stocked. There's a couple who open it when the family's coming, stock it, make sure there's firewood, fresh linens, all that. They haven't been notified."

Gideon paced. "He's got a blind spot with this place, that's my take. He knows law enforcement is after him, but he's got this blind spot. Like we can't reach him there, or won't look there."

"So the toss-up is he'd go there first, get everything ready. Then drive down—it's under three hours—abduct her, take her back."

"It's the logical choice in a batshit mind, so I don't count on it. I want to add another patrol on the house. I'd sit someone on it, but that makes it harder for her. She's careful, she's got the dog."

"I'll take care of that. We all know what he looks like, Chief."

"Keep a sharp eye."

Dustin drove by Arden's house. He eased off the gas to take it in, its situation, the neighboring houses, the front entrance, the car—make and model—in the driveway.

He had to force himself to drive on. He wanted, so desperately it brought tears to his eyes, to go to that front door.

He imagined it as unlocked, so he could walk right in. She'd be in the kitchen, one he visualized as roomy, up-to-date with cabiny touches, just like The Retreat.

She'd be surprised to see him, of course. But welcoming.

If she wasn't welcoming, he'd fix that right off the fucking bat.

He'd sweep her up and out. The thought of that had him trembling so he had to pull over, pull back some control.

She'd make noises about needing to pack, but he'd dismiss all that. He'd provide all she needed.

She'd resist. Yes, yes, she had that stubborn streak. He'd overcome that. If that required force, so be it.

He had zip ties, duct tape, and a nice roomy trunk.

No doubt she'd have softened up some by the time they got to The Retreat. But either way, he'd begin as he meant to go on. Teach the lesson.

Calm and confident again, he drove on.

He circled around one more time, noted a few lights on now as the sun slipped behind those western peaks. With considerable effort—and he congratulated himself on his willpower—he controlled the burning impulse to take her now.

The door might be locked after all, and he couldn't afford her—with that stubborn streak—to keep it locked. She could go bitchy and call the police.

He'd booked a room, so he'd go check in, order up some food. Low profile, he reminded himself. He'd check on her later, try the door, try windows, see if he could find his way inside.

Surprise her while she slept.

If Gideon had left the station even five minutes earlier, he'd have passed the blue Mercedes with Idaho plates, seen the driver—shaggy black hair, scraggly beard.

Very likely his cop instincts would've buzzed.

Instead, he finished up some paperwork, and though he scanned cars and faces as he drove through and out of town, he saw nothing and no one to give him that buzz.

As Dustin had imagined, Arden stood in the kitchen. Gideon came in through the mudroom, exchanged greetings with Zorro before he took off his jacket, secured his weapon.

He stepped into the kitchen, where she whisked something in a small bowl.

"Hello, Chief."

"Hello, Legs."

"I happen to have a very nice sauvignon blanc chilling."

"Why don't I open that?"

"Why don't you?"

He got out the bottle. "I thought it was my night to figure out dinner."

"It was, but I decided to try this. Glazed salmon fillets, which I'm determined will be fabulous—with rice and Broccolini—and felt it was above your pay grade."

"Maybe. But there's a grill out there I'm pretty handy with."

"Next time." Still whisking, she leaned into a kiss. "I had a good day. You?"

"Good enough." She smelled like peaches, fully ripe and ready. "Better now."

She set the bowl aside, picked up the wine he'd poured. "I had a conversation with my editor."

"Yeah? I take it that's part of the good day."

"A big part. They're pretty high on the book I turned in, which brings relief, joy, anxiety."

"Anxiety?"

"That they'll hate the next one. It's a vicious cycle, and I accept it as my lot."

"Okay."

Laughing, she sipped again. "It's smart not to tell me I have nothing to worry about."

"How would I know? Maybe this one sucks."

Laughing again, she punched him, lightly. "To move beyond the potential suckiness of my work in progress, they're high enough on the finished product they plan to give it a push."

He fed a delighted Zorro, then stepped back into the kitchen. "What kind of push?"

"Publicity, promotion, marketing, better exposure in major accounts. Part of that would involve me touring next summer."

"Like a rock star?"

"Not even remotely like a rock star. Possibly ten cities, Portland and Seattle to kick off. Signings, interviews, a book fair, and so on. It's an opportunity."

He studied her. "You haven't done anything like this before?"

"It hasn't been offered, but if it had, I'd have turned it down." She stepped over, measured out the rice to get it started. "I haven't been on a plane by myself in over three years. The only reason I've been on one at all, with my aunt and uncle, was to see Zoey, Travis, the families."

She huffed out a breath.

"And that was torture. The last time I flew alone, my friend Kyra from Brooklyn's wedding. When we were in middle school, we swore we'd be in each other's weddings. Not the main attendant—she had her sister—but we'd be in each other's wedding party."

She turned to him. "We lost touch when I moved to Columbus—my fault. We reconnected and stayed connected, so I flew to Brooklyn, and I rented a car to drive back because I nearly didn't get on the plane to go. The airport, all those people, then the plane. The confinement. I couldn't face it again, so that was that. I stopped doing signings, except at the bookstore where I worked, but even that was, well, horrible for me. I let him narrow my world."

"Bullshit. You didn't let him anything. The motherfucker beat and raped you."

She started to speak, but his fury came on so hot, so fast, it stunned her to silence.

"You didn't let him beat you, rape you, strangle you. Trauma's the big goddamn boulder dropped into the pond. The pond doesn't let the boulder hit. It doesn't have a choice. And the boulder causes waves and ripples that take as long as they take to subside. He's responsible, not you, so fuck the you-let bullshit."

"Well." She had to take a breath. "That's both comforting and logical."

"Fuck that, too. It's just truth. Jesus, Arden, you don't blame someone for PTSD, you blame what caused it."

"I've seriously pissed you off."

"Stupid pisses me off. Don't be stupid."

She thought about it. "I'm going to let that slide because comforting, logical, and oddly supportive. If they set the tour, I'm doing it."

"Good."

"Would you like to know why?"

"Because you're not stupid."

"No, I'm not. But more. I realized even inside the thrill of having this offered to me, my knee-jerk was to make excuses why I couldn't. Just shut it out, which struck me as the same thing as sticking a chair under the doorknob, and I'm not going back there. Maybe I opened my world moving here, but I've still kept it pretty narrow. That's done.

"The first time they put him away, it wasn't enough. My part in that was passive. Not my fault," she said quickly, "so don't trip the wire again. But this time, it's going to be enough, and the *enough* starts now. He's been in my head, lurking there, all this time. I'm pushing him out. Locking him out. Yes, I need him caught, put away, then he's done. He's in the Hatchback of Destiny."

"The what?"

"A visual I got from Jamie. He's trapped in a hatchback beater, screaming as it drives over a cliff and crashes in a fiery ball."

"Huh. Good visual. You're not passive." He gave her braid a tug. "You took steps all along."

"The best one was coming here. And because it was, I have something for you. Then I have to get these fillets on."

She opened a drawer, took out a box.

Curious, he took off the lid, then shifted his gaze to hers. "A key ring."

"You said ring, you didn't specify what kind."

He took it out, held it up. "A police badge."

"A chief of police badge, you'll note."

"Yeah, I see that." He pulled out his old key ring, worked the keys off, worked them on the new one.

"I take that as a yes."

"I'll be right back."

"But . . ." As he walked out, she looked down at Zorro. "Did you see that? I propose to the man, and he walks away. That doesn't bring joy or build confidence."

In sympathy, Zorro leaned on her leg.

"And the crazy? I love him anyway."

She got out a skillet, the fillets. She began to pat them dry when he came back in.

"Hold off on that a minute."

"I'm hungry, so—"

He tugged her around, pushed a box in her hand.

She knew a ring box when she held one.

"Oh" was all she could manage.

"You didn't do the one-knee thing. Don't look for that from me."

Because she didn't move, he reached over, flipped up the lid.

"Oh," she managed again. "It's beautiful."

"It was my grandmother's."

As her eyes flooded, she looked up at him. "That makes it even more beautiful."

"I take that as a yes."

"Make it official." She held out her left hand. "Put it on." When he did, she watched it sparkle on her finger. "It fits."

"I took that ring you wear sometimes with it into the jeweler. They sized it down a little. Not much. She had long, slim fingers, too."

He linked their fingers. "I love you, Arden. I want to spend my life with you. Make a life and a family with you. So." He held up his key ring. "That's a yes."

Tears spilled as she laughed, as she threw her arms around him. Her mouth met his. "That's a yes. We're going to frustrate each other."

"Looking forward to it."

"Me, too. We're a perfect match." Easing back, she framed his face. "After you kiss me again, I have to take a picture of the ring, on my finger, and send it out."

"Send it out where?"

"To Zoey, and Aunt Jen, April, Jamie, and absolutely to Joe."

"Why?"

"Reasons."

"I'm not sending a picture of my ring out to people."

She stroked his cheek. "Not even to Joe? Or Reg?"

"No." He had to admit, it was a pretty cool key ring. "Maybe," he muttered, and kissed her again.

That night she dreamed of dancing with him in the moonlight. She wore a billowy white gown and flowers in her hair. With the air perfumed with blooms and blossoms, and his eyes on hers, even the shadows held love.

As she dreamed, Dustin drove toward the house. He had the gun if he needed it, and anticipated using the zip ties, the duct tape.

He knew he'd want to make love to her the minute he touched her, woke her, but promised himself he'd wait until he'd finally taken her home.

He wondered if she slept naked. If she did, he couldn't be expected to resist. Maybe she slept naked tonight because, somewhere in her heart and mind, she knew he was coming for her.

He felt himself go hard as he passed the dark silhouette of her closest neighbor's house. Still a good distance, and no lights so no one to see him find a way in to Arden.

Her heart and mind might have told her to leave the door unlocked for him. But if not, he'd find a way.

They were meant to be together, so he was meant to find a way.

Switching off his lights—no point taking chances—he coasted the last few feet, started to turn into her driveway.

In the pale light of the moon, he saw the truck. The big pickup. A man's truck, just like he intended to have once they'd settled.

For an instant, his heart soared. She'd bought him a truck, just exactly what he wanted for their life together in the mountains.

Then it struck him, a thousand brutal fists.

The bitch wasn't alone in bed. She wasn't waiting for him. No, she was in there, in bed with some big yahoo with more muscle than brains.

She cheated on him like the whore she was.

The rage screamed through him so he gripped the wheel, shaking it so violently he expected it to snap off in his hands.

He'd kill them both. He had the gun. He'd break in, find them, kill them. Maybe the shotgun. He'd blow them to bloody pieces as they slept.

He eased out of the car, started back to the trunk to retrieve the shotgun case.

An owl loosed a long call, and made him jump.

What if they weren't asleep? What if the yahoo had a gun?

He didn't know where they were in the house.

Besides, a quick death? Too good for both of them.

"Need to teach her a lesson." He hissed it between his teeth, but he trembled as he got back in the car.

He'd return when she was alone.

She'd pay dearly for cheating on him with some truck-driving asshole. He had to keep her alive and make her pay.

The next morning, Arden made her latte while Gideon fried bacon.

"Do you want any of this? Bacon, eggs over easy."

"No. Listen, I don't want to be one of those crazy brides."

"Picture my relief."

"But I'd really like to set a date."

"Anytime's fine."

"Well, no, even non-crazy brides have tons to do before a wedding. And I want an actual wedding. Family, friends, flowers."

"Okay."

She rolled her eyes. Let the frustration begin.

"Your choice of suit or tux."

He slid his gaze in her direction. "Suit. Firm on it."

"I return your *okay*. I thought July. They're pushing my book to a June release so they can market it as a summer read, beach read. So July would give me a good buffer. Plus, both Zoey and April will have had their babies. Uncle Doug and Aunt Jen would be out here."

"I happen to have an open schedule in July."

"I thought here? The gardens in the back are well established, and we could add to that. A real wedding, but it doesn't have to be formal."

"I like here."

"I want Nick to make the cake."

"To that I say duh. Who else?"

Sipping her latte, she decided she'd find a dress that would blow that casual whatever right out of him.

"I want to get married in the sunlight—I'll take rain if it happens—and dance in the moonlight. You do dance, right?"

He pulled out the bacon to drain, cracked eggs in the pan. "Did you see my mother in *Foot the Bill*? Or *Enchanted Me*?"

"I did, both. Just because your mom can dance doesn't mean you can."

"What kind of dancing? Tap, jazz, ballroom?"

She grinned as she started to make her morning smoothie. "You cannot tap-dance."

"Can if I want. I don't want."

Truly stunned, she stopped. "Are you serious? This is a revelation even beyond the ability to make bread from yeast and flour. Prove it."

"No."

"Come on, come on. One little whatever." She did her version of a quick tap and made him grin.

"What was that?"

"I have no clue. Show me up."

To shut her up, he did a quick time step.

Her mouth dropped open. "Do that again."

"No."

"Maybe you could teach me."

"Maybe one night when we've had a lot of adult beverages."

"I'm going to make that happen." She snagged a strip of bacon.

"You said you didn't want any."

"I changed my mind. I'm knocking off work early today. I'm going into Riverbend, stopping in to see Joe. I want to thank him for entrusting me with Colleen's ring."

"He'll appreciate that." He slid eggs onto a plate, added the bacon, then the toast that popped up.

"Then I'm hitting the grocery store, so if there's something you want, put it on that phone app I told you to download."

"I can just tell you this was the last of the bacon."

"Download the app, Chief." She pulled her phone out of her pajama bottom pocket, added *bacon*.

"If you pick up some chicken, I'll grill it, and do the rest."

She added that.

"Get a receipt—the food's my bill."

"How about we just tally that up once a month?"

"That works."

"And so do I." She leaned down to kiss him. "I'm going up to do that. Be a good cop."

If he'd known how to be a different kind, he thought, he wouldn't be sitting here eating bacon and eggs watching the woman he loved walk away with her dog, and thinking July seemed like a fine time to get married.

Halfway through his shift, Brill called.

"Detective."

"Chief. I'm standing here with my partner, looking at a bunch of snow and mountains. We're in the Olympic Mountains."

"You got him?"

"No, sorry to say. We both had vacation time coming, talked to our captain about using it. He's as frustrated with how the search has bogged down as we are. We're out here officially for the next few days."

"Welcome to the Pacific Northwest. No sign of him?"

"None. We talked to the couple who take care of the place, and they haven't heard from him. It's a hell of a place and not a damn thing like a cabin. Cabins, in my experience, don't have butler's pantries and billiard tables."

"He won't have a chance to enjoy it."

"No, he won't. We thought we'd drive down tomorrow, maybe later today, brainstorm in person if that suits you. We'd like to see how Arden's doing."

"It suits me. I think she'd like to see you. She's doing fine. She'll do better when he's caught." What the hell, he thought. "We're engaged."

"No shit? Well, congratulations. I'll let you know when we head your way."

"You won't need snow gear, but expect rain later this afternoon through the night."

"We'll buy umbrellas."

When he hung up, he looked at the map on the wall.

The ones who'd taken Dubecki down the first time, he thought. He had a feeling, and it got stronger as he let it come, they'd be around when he went down this time.

And go down he would. They'd all but papered Riverbend with Dubecki's photo, the description of the car. He'd still had the Mercedes in Colorado.

Every hotel, B&B, the outlying motels had that picture, that description. Every officer on his force had their eyes peeled for him. Add the state police.

He wouldn't slip through again.

But because he had that buzz, he got up, walked out into his bullpen. "Hawk, I'm going to do a little cruising. Tap me if you need me."

"You got it."

Chapter Twenty-Nine

Arden walked into Riley's Hardware and straight into Joe's arms.

"Thank you. I'll treasure it all my life. Thank you."

"It was Gideon's to give."

"It was yours to give first. That means so much. I love you, Joe. Not just because you're his grandfather, but because you're you."

"I love you, sweet girl, not just because Gideon does, but because you're you."

"If I say any more, I'm going to embarrass myself and start crying right in the middle of the store." She breathed deep, drew back. "July seventeenth."

"That sounds like a fine day for a wedding."

"At home, maybe a little fancy, but not formal. One fancy I want, and don't ask me why, is an arbor. I want us to take our vows under an arbor. If I can get one in by planting time, I can plant a flowering vine. Then all the springs and summers to come, we can look at it, remember our wedding day."

"I'm going to build you an arbor." He nodded as he considered. "One that'll last."

"Really?"

"I like the idea of you and Gideon taking your vows under something I made for you."

"Oh, that makes it so much more special. Thank you! I have to get out of here before I do start crying. And I still have to get to the grocery store."

He took her hand, studied the ring on it. Then lifted it and kissed it.

"Well, that did it," she said as the tears spilled. "Come on, Zorro."

She dashed out, swiping at tears.

He saw her. Saw her rushing out of some store, with a dog.

She had a goddamn dog, a good-sized goddamn dog, and that complicated things.

But good to know, as he'd been on his way to the house she lived in, where she fucked around with that brainless yahoo in a pickup truck.

He could always put a bullet in the dog's head.

He caught the light, watching in the rearview as she walked to her car, put the dog in the back.

He'd need to turn around, since her car faced in the opposite direction. He fumed, cursed until the light changed.

He made the left, pulled into a driveway, seethed as he waited for a break in traffic to back out again.

He barely made the light, and saw—because it was meant—her just pulling out.

His heart drummed, drummed, drummed as he followed. One car between them, he thought, made it perfect.

She drove to the far end of town, made a turn, then another into a supermarket parking lot.

He drove past her, circled, found a spot where he could watch her.

She put the windows down about an inch before she got out. The dog watched her go, then must've lain down, as his head disappeared.

Dustin reached under the front seat to run his fingers over the gun before he pulled it out, holstered it on his belt.

"Take a nice nap, doggie. You'll take a longer one soon."

Gideon started at the first of Riverbend's two B&Bs. He didn't see Dubecki choosing the small and charming, but he needed to eliminate the possibility.

He'd already had his officers do a sweep of all hotels, the B&Bs, the motels outside of town, but this time he felt the need to do another himself.

The innkeeper, fortyish, sunny blond hair in a bouncing ponytail, and as friendly as a Lab puppy, offered him coffee and a slice of deep-dish apple pie.

"Thanks. Appreciate it, but this won't take long."

He showed her Dubecki's photo.

"Yes, Officer Betts brought that in. It's posted in my office. We don't have anyone like that in residence."

"He may have changed his hair, the color, the length. Maybe try to see him with some facial hair."

"Well, we don't have any singles—men or women. All our guests are couples or friend groups. That's most usual."

"Any single bookings for the rest of the week, into next?"

"I don't think so, but let me check. The idea that someone wanted for murder might stay here, it's unnerving, Chief Riley."

When she checked—no singles—he did his best to reassure her, then moved on.

After striking out at the next B&B with its offer of coffee and chocolate chip cookies, he started on hotels.

That took longer, with no offer of refreshments. As he headed for the last, on the far end of town, he contacted the station.

"Hawk, pass that list of Airbnbs and owners to Harley. I want him to run another check on Dubecki."

"Can do."

"I've got a few more stops. I should be back inside an hour."

"Take your time, Chief. Got a nice, quiet day going."

Gideon actually winced. "Sergeant, that's like saying *This is my last bank robbery before I retire to Martinique.* You're just asking for it."

"Hey, I have a black cat and I walk under ladders."

"Asking for it. I'm heading into the North Western Hotel."

"Fancy. Got a date?"

"Maybe later. After I check in at the station, I'll be hitting the motels out on Route 99, and out to I-5 if this craps out like all the rest. He has to sleep sometime and somewhere."

"I can send someone to check the motels, Chief."

"I've got it. Get Harley started."

Because the buzzing wasn't easing off, Gideon thought.

Arden ran into Tessa in Produce, and showed off her ring.

"Wow, suits you. So does he. And the ring's got that heirloom look."

"It was his grandmother's. Colleen, Joe's wife."

"Aw. Man, that's so sweet. I'm really happy for you. Now, watch out for Jamie. He's a major wedding freak."

"I got that, as well as a series of texts on area bridal shops and more."

"The thing is, you can't go wrong with him steering you."

As they talked, Arden selected fresh lettuce.

"How much of that rabbit food do you eat?"

"I like a variety."

Tessa held up a bag of salad mix. "Here's a variety."

"Nothing wrong with that. But." Arden added romaine to her basket. "Hard to make a sandwich with it all chopped to pieces."

"A couple slices of American cheese between two slices of bread, butter up the outside, fry it. Sandwich."

Arden sent her a pitying look. "Sister goddess, that's just sad."

"It kind of is. Okay, we're both here. What's your grilled cheese sandwich?"

"There are many, but for the basic? Any bread will do, but sourdough's the best. Then, mozzarella, for the stretch, pepper jack for the bite, and cheddar for the smooth. Butter that bread inside and out. You can elevate that basic with ribbons of basil, or some ham, some bacon, a nice thin slice of tomato—I recommend Roma. Either way, any way, don't use a press. Skillet, medium heat."

"You take sandwiches seriously."

"Oh, yes. Yes, I do."

"And you've made me hungry. Looks like we're having Arden's Grilled Cheese tonight."

"You'll thank me," Arden replied, and watched Tessa head for the cheese section.

As Arden walked through the store, she checked off her list, and thought how much more satisfying it was to shop for two instead of just herself.

She drank Pepsi, but the man stood firm on Coke, so buy both. They shared an affection for Oreos. Since he could bake bread, pick up yeast and more flour. Since she wanted to have Joe over for dinner—maybe a Sunday dinner—she debated mains.

Pot roast, what man didn't go for pot roast? She checked her phone for Jen's recipe, picked up what she needed.

She checked out, then started to steer her cart toward the exit when her phone signaled.

Another text from Jamie, she thought, and amused, opened it. He'd sent her a picture of a model wearing a wedding dress with a lacy corset-style bodice and flowing miles of skirt.

She paused to text back.

> It's gorgeous. But I thought, for a backyard wedding, I should go simple. Maybe street length.

Her phone rang before she got to the exit.

"Simple? Street length? You crush me. You're a queen! And don't say 'backyard.' *On the grounds*. Girl, if a woman can't be a queen on her wedding day, when?"

She remembered the dream she'd had, dancing with Gideon, the billowy skirt.

"Well . . ."

"Sweetie, whatever you decide will be perfect. And you won't order online—I have a few more, just for ideas. You'll want the experience of a bridal shop, trying on gowns. Champagne! Please invite me or I'll weep rivers. Don't let me browbeat you into something you don't want, but you're tall, willowy—and that hair! You can carry a gown like this."

She pushed the cart outside, stopped again. "I actually had a dream about a dress with a skirt like this."

"See! Simple's for third weddings at the courthouse. But no veil. You're not a slave, are you?"

She laughed, slowly pushing her cart to the car. "No, I am not."

"A tiara, or a crown of flowers. Gorgeous shoes. And since you're marrying that tall hunk of man, you can wear heels if you want to. Listen to me. I'm browbeating and interrupting your work. I need to come down when you're done. I'm making a wedding binder for you. Don't hate me. I can't help myself. And honestly, you'll find it useful."

"Jamie, would you consider coordinating my wedding?"

He let out what could only be described as a squeal. "Yes! You'll stop me if I go too far. But I won't. It'll be a struggle, but I won't. Text when you're done for the day, and I'll come down, we'll talk about all this. And I can do some more sketches—focus on face and hair."

"I'm actually about to load my car. I'm at the supermarket, so already done with work for the day. I should be home . . . by four," she said when she checked the time.

"Give me a few minutes more to put the groceries away."

"I'll help you with that. I'll watch for your car, and Isis and I will come to you. Think about your colors, my most beautiful bride."

"I should, shouldn't I? I'll think on the way home. See you soon."

Dustin watched her come out, finally! And just like a woman, with a phone at her ear. She wouldn't have to worry about phones once he took her home.

He frowned when he considered the cart of bagged groceries.

He realized he couldn't trust her to do the shopping once he got her home, so he'd have to handle that. Annoying, as food—shopping, preparing, serving—should all be her job.

But, no, he could hardly trust her there. In time, when she'd learned her lesson, but that could take months.

She finally finished blabbing, and dropped her phone into her purse.

As she loaded the groceries in the car, the dog watched her, tail wagging. She gave him some sort of dog treat.

Enjoy, Dustin thought. It'll be your last.

He waited until she'd backed out of her slot, turned toward the exit. He knew where she'd go, so followed at a safe distance.

And smiled, as he knew just how he'd handle the rest.

He could hardly wait to see the surprise on her face.

Gideon talked to the front desk clerk and the manager on duty. They had nine single male guests, three more coming in.

"We have the photo, Chief Riley," the manager assured him. "The staff's been briefed, and under orders to alert security if they see this man. Not to confront him."

"No one who looks like that has checked in while I've been on duty," the desk clerk told Gideon.

"And when you're off, who else works the desk?"

The manager sighed a little. "I'll get you that information."

"He has to know the authorities are looking for him, so he may have changed his appearance. Changed his hair, maybe a beard, glasses."

He took names, the single male guests he'd run, the other staff to talk to.

He pushed a little more, asked to talk to the housekeeping staff that would have cleaned the rooms of the singles.

Nothing popped there, but he took two more names of staff who had the day off.

He spoke with the concierge, and nothing.

He studied the lobby. Fairly busy—some wine club coming in.

Classy, Gideon thought. The lobby, a wine store, bar, coffee shop, gift shop. All leaned toward classy pulling up right at the edge of ornate.

Dubecki would want this.

I know you, you son of a bitch, he thought. You'd want this. Not the charming, cozy coffee in the kitchen, not the discount chains, the off-ramp motels.

No, Gideon thought, if Dubecki aimed here, this would be his last stop before The Retreat. He wouldn't settle for midrange. High-end, it had to be. With a day or two to stalk.

Frustrated, he crossed the lobby to the bell desk.

"Hey, Gideon."

Reg's cousin Mark gave him a quick salute. "Or should I say Chief?"

"I've got the key ring to prove it." Gideon dangled it.

"Sweet."

"Listen, I'm following up on the fugitive we're hunting."

"Got his picture right here." Mark reached under the desk, took it out. "We're all keeping an eye out for him, for the car."

"You've had some male guests, traveling solo, check in over the last couple days. He may look a little different from the picture."

Gideon went through the routine while Mark nodded. "I see what you're saying, wish I could help. Trust me, we don't want anyone like this guy around here."

"Let's try this. Black Tumi bags." The ones his mother had bought for him the day after his release. "Wheeled bags, pullman, garment bag, weekender."

"Well, jeez, Gideon, do you know how many bags we handle any given day?"

"New ones," Gideon pressed as another bellman came up—one that couldn't be old enough to buy a legal beer.

"Is this about that crazy killer guy?"

"Take it down, Jack, guests don't like hearing *crazy killer*."

"Just saying. We're all watching for him. Gives me the willies."

"New, black Tumi luggage," Gideon repeated. "Pullman, garment bag, weekender—all wheeled. He might not want it all unloaded. He'd have a laptop case, black leather. Driving a dark gray '25 Mercedes C-Class sedan."

"Wish I could say: *Hey, I know that guy*, especially if there's a reward. I took a couple of bags, looked new, I guess, out of a Mercedes yesterday. But a blue one. Pretty blue."

"Traveling alone?"

"Yeah, for a while, I think. But he had dark hair—really dark, like seriously black and sort of a beard."

Gideon felt the heat in his blood join the buzz. "Sort of?"

"Mostly like he hadn't shaved in a couple, three weeks. Needed some style."

Gideon pulled out a pen. "Look at this again," he ordered as he darkened the hair with the pen, scribbled on what passed for a beard.

"I . . . I don't know." Nerves shook in Jack's voice. "I guess. Maybe."

"Jack." Mark put a hand on his shoulder. "This is important. Take a couple of breaths, then think."

"Trying. I mean, we've been pretty busy, and he didn't look like the picture, and the car wasn't gray. Holy sh—cow, Mark."

"You'd have asked him where he came in from," Gideon prompted. "How was his trip."

"Um. There's been so many, but yeah. Yeah! He said he'd been traveling on business. I think . . . nearly done, he'd be heading home soon. He, um, he, um, wanted me to get some ice when we got up to his room, so I did, and he tipped me, like, I think twenty."

"What room?"

"Eighteenth floor. It has its own concierge and lounge. I think . . . 1804, it's a suite."

"Where's the car?"

"He didn't want to valet it. I remember that. Said he might need it later. I told him how he could call for it at any time, but he didn't want the valet. Parked it himself while I waited with the bags."

"Plates? Did you see his license plate?"

"I don't know. God, I feel a little sick. I carried his bags, and he kills people." Then his eyes popped wide. "Idaho!"

"Gideon." Mark kept his hand on Jack's shoulder. "I didn't get a good look, but black hair, scruffy beard, sunglasses. He walked out about an hour ago. I don't think he's come back."

"Call security, have them check his room. Now!"

He ran out to scan the lot. And pulled out his phone to call Arden.

She didn't answer.

Rain began to splatter as Arden pulled into her driveway.

"We didn't get lucky this time, Zorro. Hold on, let me get some bags out while I ask myself why I bought enough for two trips."

She grabbed her purse, tossed up the hood on her jacket. She slid out, ducked her head as she rounded to the back. Her phone rang as she opened the cargo area, grabbed two bags, one for each arm.

"You hold on, too," she muttered. Then moved to the rear side door to open it for Zorro.

"All right, okay," she said as he started barking. "Give me a second!"

She heard something, or felt something, turned.

Dubecki grinned. "Hello, Arden."

He hit her twice, not a slap, but with his fist. Right, then left.

It felt so good! Felt even better when she dropped, when groceries spilled everywhere. He kicked her purse with its ringing phone aside. She wouldn't need it. Then hauled her up over his shoulder.

Inside the car, the dog went wild. Barking, scrabbling at the window, leaping over the seat, and snarling.

Dubecki's grin only widened. He pulled the gun holstered on hip, pointed it, said, "Bang. This is your lucky day, pooch. I don't have to waste a bullet."

He hitched Arden more securely on his shoulder.

"We're going home, honey." He carried her to the car he'd left running on the side of the road at the edge of her driveway. He opened the trunk.

Someone shouted, and he jerked so hard he nearly dropped her.

He spun around, saw some man and another damn dog, one of those little yappy ones, running toward him.

"Die, bastard."

He pulled the gun, shot, but the man kept running.

Dubecki dumped Arden in the trunk, slammed it. As he ran for the driver's seat, he fired over his shoulder. And shaking with rage, fear, delight, punched the gas.

"Oh God, my God, oh God." With hands cold and shaking with horror, Jamie took out his phone.

His fingers betrayed him as he tried to open it, get to contacts, but he finally pushed Gideon's number.

"He's got her!" He shouted it before Gideon could speak. "He's got Arden."

"Where are you?"

"I—He—I was walking up to meet her at your house, and I saw . . . He had her, he was carrying her, she wasn't moving. He has a gun. He shot at me."

"Are you hit?"

"No, no. Zorro. I have to get him out of the car. He's still in the car. It wasn't gray. The car. Cerulean blue, a deep cerulean blue. I couldn't see the plate. I didn't think—"

"Which way did he go?"

"Um, um, it's away from town. West! That's west, I think."

"Get the dog, go home. I know where he's going."

"He put her in the trunk. He just, just threw her in the trunk, and I was too far away. I couldn't stop him."

"I will."

He was already in his car, and hit the sirens as he called the station.

"Dubecki's in a blue Mercedes sedan, Idaho plates. Heading west on Valley View Road. He has Arden in the trunk, unconscious, possibly injured. He's armed. Do not fire at the vehicle. Contact the state police, set up roadblocks. I'm in pursuit, but he has ten, maybe fifteen minutes on me. Send two officers to the North Western Hotel. It's room 1804. He didn't have his luggage, laptop.

"Roll out, we're going to cut him off."

He had to get through town, across the river. No way around that unless he took more time to bypass. The rain decided to pour instead of splatter. Gideon told himself it would slow Dubecki down.

Panic. He'd panicked, and driven the wrong way. He'd need to take back roads, work his way back around to I-5 to head north.

He hadn't killed her. Why put her in the trunk if he'd already killed her? No, he still had his eyes on the goal. Take her to The Retreat in Washington.

"You're not going to get there."

He snapped at his phone when it signaled. "Riley."

"We're on our way to you, Chief."

"He's got her. Son of a bitch," he cursed as he swerved around a car slow to pull over. "I'm in pursuit. Blue, not gray, Mercedes, Idaho plates. She's in the goddamn trunk. He's armed, shot at a civilian. Missed."

"We're on I-5," Brill told him. "GPS says sixty-eight minutes to Riverbend."

"Not anymore," Venmar said, and floored it.

"We'll contact the Washington State Police, get roadblocks, and we'll continue south on this route. He won't get past us, Chief."

He got past me, Gideon thought. By minutes. By goddamn minutes.

He crossed the bridge and raced on.

He took the curving road leading up at eighty, barely slowing when the car fishtailed.

The rain brought the gloom, and the fog. Dark would come early.

He took the next curve, cursing the need to ease off the gas. But he couldn't help her if he wrecked the damn car or dumped it in a ditch.

In the car. The dog in the car, so she'd been in the car.

Gone to see Pop, grocery shopping. Dubecki, either lying in wait at the house, or he'd spotted her in town and followed her back.

He contacted the station again. "Get me the name he used at the hotel. I didn't have time to wait for it. Get me the name."

New ID, had the car painted, switched plates again.

He had plenty of luck crossing the country. Too much luck.

"It runs out tonight."

Because Arden was alive, and she'd stay alive.

He wouldn't lose her. He wouldn't let her down.

He gunned it on the next straightaway as his beams cut through the fog and the spreading gloom.

He saw Jamie, standing in the rain outside his house, saw him cross both hands over his heart.

He didn't slow or stop. Instead, he thought, twelve minutes from Jamie's call to now. He'd made up some time, and he'd make up more.

Dustin drove like a madman. Each time the car shuddered or fishtailed, his fear came out in crazed giggles. They could chase him, for now, but they'd *never* catch him.

Homestretch, he thought. On the homestretch, and he and Arden would be where they were meant to be in a few hours. Less, even less, because fuck the speed limit!

The fog scared him, but he imagined cutting through it like a knife. Like the hunting knife he had strapped to his belt opposite the gun.

A man with a mission, and mission all but accomplished. He was a man who defended himself and his woman against anyone who came against them.

He hadn't had time for the zip ties—also on his belt—or the duct tape thanks to the interfering bastard with the stupid yappy dog.

He hoped the interfering bastard lay dead on the road in a pool of blood.

"That's what you get, what you get for trying to stop me from taking what's mine."

The dead guy couldn't stop him, and the dead guy couldn't call the cops. And they wouldn't know what the fuck when they found the dead guy, would they?

By the time they'd figured it out, he and Arden would be home, safe and sound, where no one could touch them.

The Retreat. His mountain home.

Reassured, he eased off the speed. His stomach still clutched and roiled, and he felt a near-urgent need to piss.

A few more miles, he decided. He'd pull over, take a piss, then use those zip ties. She could wake up before long and go hysterical as women did so he'd use those ties, and duct tape her hysterical mouth.

Arden drifted to consciousness. Her face burned as if someone had set a torch to it. She felt sick, everything spun and swerved.

At first she thought: Terrible dream.

Then she remembered.

Her eyes flew open, and the panic screamed through her until she could pull in air. She pulled it in too fast, gulping it so her throat began to burn like her face.

Every inch of her body broke out in a cold sweat, and her vision blurred, grayed.

She squeezed her eyes shut again, pushed, pushed against that helpless panic. The panic that tried to drag her under with sharp clawing fingers. Where she had no air, no light, no hope.

She heard her own breath, fast, labored. Second by sweaty second, she fought to slow it.

She would not lose control. She would not be a victim ever again. She would think, goddamn it. She'd think, she'd fight, and she'd survive.

Not a victim, not a victim, she heard Gideon tell her. *A survivor.*

On those slow, deep breaths, she opened her eyes again.

Dark, so dark, and rain pounding, and . . . movement.

She pushed her hands out, met resistance.

A car, in a car. In the trunk of a car.

That panic leaped back like a live thing, gripped her throat. She started to beat against the trunk, then stopped herself.

He'd hear her. And he'd make her stop.

Think!

He drove so fast, and when the back of the car slid from side to side, she closed her eyes, braced for the crash.

But it righted again, slowed a little.

Jamie, she thought. Coming when he saw her car, he said. He'd see Zorro inside the car. Please, please don't let him have hurt my dog.

Jamie would call Gideon, and Gideon would come.

Until then, she had to stay alive.

In the dark, she felt around, then remembered her Christmas gift. She'd left her phone in her purse, but she had the multi-tool and the tiny flashlight in her pocket.

She used the light, shined it around, focused it on the latch for the trunk. And there, as expected, the tiny glow-in-the-dark light on the inside latch.

She might not be good with tools, she thought, but she was hell on research. And she'd researched escaping from a locked trunk for her third book.

She breathed in, breathed out.

"Okay," she whispered, just for the comfort of her own voice. "You wrote it. You can do it."

She would do it, and she'd find a weapon. A trunk of a car had tools. A jack, one of those things that took the bolts off the tire. Maybe a wrench or anything she could swing or throw. And all of that? Under her.

She opened the multi-tool, did her best to curl up as small as possible. And got to work.

No, she wouldn't be passive, wouldn't be a victim. She'd survive, again, she'd survive.

And she'd either send Dustin goddamn Dubecki back to prison or to hell.

Chapter Thirty

Gideon swerved around an SUV as it pulled toward the shoulder, then screamed on. He punched the touch screen to take the incoming from Brill.

"Status?"

"We're coming up on the Corvallis exit. Staties in Washington are at the border."

"He'll jump on 5 if he gets where you are. Take the exit for Route 99, head south."

"Jesus, Venmar, you're killing me. We just did. Where are you?"

"I can't be far behind him. We've got rain, fog, and he doesn't know the roads like I do."

"Do you have backup, Chief?"

"It's coming. I'll get back to you."

Dubecki had made a mistake, Gideon told himself. Smarter, faster, if he'd turned around, backtracked, crossed the river, and taken the shorter route to the highway. Instead, probably panicked because of Jamie, he'd headed in the opposite direction.

Stuck on this road until he could cross over to 99, then ride that until he could intersect with 5.

And Gideon would be damned if he'd make it that far.

He streamed through the fog like a bullet.

He wanted off this stupid road, out of this goddamn fog. He wanted the clean mountain air, a drink by the fire.

Her fault, all her fault.

If he hadn't had to hurry, if she hadn't had some asshole—probably the one she was cheating with—shouting and running at him, he wouldn't have gone the wrong way.

Back roads could be useful, but he'd gone miles out of his way before he'd realized it, before he'd thought to tell the damn car to bring up the GPS and the directions to The Retreat.

Now he had to take this stupid road to another stupid road before he could take that to the highway and his straight shot.

Worse, she'd made him forget he'd left all his things at the hotel! Now he needed new clothes, a new laptop. He didn't have all his cash!

And would she appreciate she had made him forget the clothes he'd bought her? Would she apologize?

He'd fucking make her apologize.

She wasn't just going to learn a lesson. She was going to learn a hard lesson.

He had to slow down when he should've been on the highway doing a steady seventy-five.

He squirmed in his seat.

And he had to piss!

She'd screwed things up so bad he was going to have to pull over and take a leak on the side of the road, in the fucking rain. He'd end up drenched, and driving for three damn hours in soaked clothes.

He struggled to hold it, did his best to think of something, anything else. Just another couple miles. There had to be someplace to stop—gas station, mini-mart, some damn thing—where a man could piss civilized.

But he couldn't and, setting his teeth, decided that after he'd relieved himself, he'd open the trunk, give her a couple more good punches—less than she deserved.

He'd use the zip ties, the duct tape. That way, when he got on the highway, found some exit where he could pick up some dry clothes, she'd be quiet and secured.

With his bladder all but bursting, he shot to the side of the road, had the car rocking.

He shoved out, slammed the door.

She couldn't lift the lining enough to reach under, so she sawed through it. Her left eye throbbed like a bad tooth, and her hands cramped, but she used the knife to hack and saw until she could reach through the opening.

The car swayed like a boat in a storm, and she feared the growing nausea would win.

She felt the spare tire, some metal, shined her little light inside. Breathing labored, not from panic, but effort, she widened the opening. Despite the chill, her hands were slick with sweat, but her fingers closed around something metal, something slim but solid.

She had no idea of its usual purpose, didn't care.

Right now, she held a weapon.

Then the car swerved hard, rocked so her head rapped against the roof of the trunk.

And stopped.

She heard a door slam.

Twisting, she gripped the tool in both hands, prepared to swing when he opened the trunk.

Seconds passed, but she heard nothing except the rain.

She ordered herself to take one hand off the tool, open the safety latch inside the trunk.

She eased it open an inch, then two.

He stood a few feet away, legs spread, back to her, and, she noted with a kind of wild amusement, his dick in his hand.

She didn't hesitate. She shoved the trunk open, rolled out.

She had no war to wage against fight or flight. Fight had already won.

Long, aching legs carried her over. She'd started the swing when he turned his head. She had one glimpse of his shocked eyes before she connected.

It made a terrible cracking noise, and he made a sound like air escaping a balloon. He fell forward. She swung the tool over her shoulder, prepared to strike again. But he stayed down.

She stood in the rain, staring down at what had been her monster in the closet for nearly five years. Crumpled now, he looked so small. But he had a gun on one hip, a knife sheath on the other.

Numb, shivering, she realized he'd have used them on her. And the zip ties, he had zip ties on his belt.

But she'd stopped him.

"Move," she ordered herself. "Move, goddamn it! Get the gun, the knife, get his phone. Don't lose it now."

Before she could bend down, she heard the sirens.

"Someone's coming. They're coming for you, you son of a bitch."

She looked down at the metal tool. Blood, blood on the metal, on her hands. The rain was washing it away, but she had blood on her hands.

Gideon's headlights streamed over her. She stood shrouded in the fog, hair running with rain, her face pale and bruised. And a lug wrench in her hand.

He hit the brakes, the emergency flashers, then leaped out.

"It's you," she managed, swaying where she stood as she had in the trunk. "It's you. I think I killed him. Is he dead? The blood. I think I killed him."

He gripped her shoulders. "You're okay. You're in a little bit of shock, Legs, but you're okay. Go sit in my car."

"He has a gun, and a knife, but I think he's dead. I need to know. And you have to get his gun, right? Do that. Please."

Because she needed it first, Gideon checked for a pulse.

"He's alive."

"Not dead." Her breath whooshed out. "That's better. Killing him . . . I'd live with it, but this is better."

"Yeah, it's better. Go sit in the car, out of the rain."

"I don't want to. I hit him with this. You have to take this, too. For evidence."

Gideon took the gun, the knife, checked pockets. He cuffed Dubecki, still unconscious, and rolled him onto his side.

He left him there, walked Arden to his police car.

"Sit here. I have to call for an ambulance."

"I hear more sirens."

"Yeah, I hear them. It's my backup."

He called for an ambulance, then contacted Brill.

"I've got her."

"She okay?"

"Bruised up, shocky, but yeah."

"Dubecki?"

"She knocked him out with a lug wrench. Ambulance on the way. My backup's here. You should go straight to Riverbend Hospital. I'll meet you there."

"A lug wrench," Arden murmured as she studied it. "I couldn't think of the name."

"I'll take it now. Eyes on me, okay? Slow breath," he said when her hand stayed clamped around it. "Then let it go."

When she did, he brushed his lips over her bruised cheek. "I'll be back in a minute, okay?"

"Zorro. He was—"

"He's fine. He's with Jamie."

That's when she started to weep.

"Kim! Get a blanket for Arden, she's soaked. Stay with her," he added. "Let's get some road flares up. Hawk, bag this. She used it to knock him out. Bag these. He had them on him."

"She okay, Chief?"

"Banged up, and I want the medicals to take a look at her, but yeah. Dubecki's secure, and let's get something over him. We don't want him dying of exposure."

He looked over, saw Kim sitting with Arden, talking to her. Arden, tears done, nodding.

He wanted to gather her up, take her home, but doing that would let her down, and he had a job to do.

He walked over to the trunk of the car, shined his flashlight in, and saw the damaged lining, the colorful multi-tool.

"Jesus Christ, Santa." He had to press his fingers to his eyes. "Jesus Christ."

"She used that girlie multi-tool to cut the lining, get to the lug wrench." Beside him, Hawk shook his head. "Smart lady."

"Yeah, she's that."

"Ambulance is two minutes out, and he's coming around."

"Good. We're going to have a nice, long talk."

He walked over, crouched down. "Hey, Dustin, you awake?"

"Help me." The words came out garbled.

"I think she broke your jaw, nose, too. You're going to need a whole bunch of stitches. And that tiny little dick of yours? Pretty scraped up, some gravel stuck in there. Ouch."

"Attacked me."

"Is that right? Well, an ambulance is on the way, and in the meantime. I'm Chief of Police Gideon Riley. Dustin Dubecki, you're under arrest for the murder of Theresa Lester, for the murder of Hailey Parkinson, for the assault on and forcible abduction of Arden Bowie, for the attempted murder of Jamie Stuart. Oh, and deploying a firearm in a residential area. Plus, using false identification to obtain said firearm, and other related charges. You have the right to remain silent."

As he read off the rest of the Miranda, Dustin began to babble.

"You should save your breath until they wire up that jaw."

When the ambulance pulled up, he rose, called Jamie.

"We've got her. She's fine."

"Oh, you promise? You swear to all the gods?"

"I promise, I swear to whatever works for you. He banged up her face some, so we've got medicals on scene now. They'll take care of her. If they release her, I'm sending her home. I can't be with her yet. Can you go up when I let you know, take Zorro? She'll want the dog, she'll want you. And she'll want Zoey."

"Yes, yes. I nearly called Zoey a hundred times, but I knew I'd scare her. I'll call her now. We'll be there."

"I don't know when I'll get home. Can you stay with her tonight?"

"You couldn't pry us away. You saved her."

"No, she saved herself. She'll tell you about it. I'll call when she's on the way."

When Gideon walked over, Kim started to slide out. Arden took her hand. "Thanks."

"I'd say anytime, but let's not do this again."

"I need the ambulance guys to look you over," Gideon told her.

"I'm okay. He must have punched me. All I remember is turning around, groceries in my hands, and he was there. His face. Then I woke up in the trunk. You need a statement."

"We'll get to that. Plenty of time for that. If they clear you, somebody's going to take you home. First, Jamie's fine, not hurt. Are you listening?"

"Yes."

"He was coming to the house, saw Dubecki carrying you, dumping you in the trunk. Dubecki shot at him, twice. Missed twice."

"Oh my God. He could've been—"

"He wasn't. We wouldn't have been so close behind him if Jamie hadn't called it in. Jamie's bringing Zorro, and calling Zoey. They're going to stay with you."

He took her hand, held it in both of his. "I don't know when I'll get home. I've got chief-of-police shit to do."

"I get it. I'm a cop's girlfriend. Make that fiancée. I'm okay, Gideon. I heard your voice."

"My voice?"

"When I panicked. When I woke up in the trunk and panicked. I heard your voice. *Not a victim, a survivor.*"

Overcome, he brought her hand to his lips, held it there. "I love you. We'll talk about all the rest, but I love you."

He signaled to one of the paramedics. "I need you to take a look at my fiancée."

When Arden got home, both Jamie and Zoey waited under the portico. She'd barely stepped out of the car when Zorro came running.

She dropped down to hug him as he lapped at her everywhere, sang to her. "I'm okay, we're all okay. Were you scared? I was scared, too, but we're all okay. Let's go inside."

She grabbed Zoey's hand, wrapped an arm around Jamie, who put his head on her shoulder.

"He shot at you. Gideon told me."

"I was too far away to get to you. Oh, your poor, sweet face." He swiped tears away from his own.

"Jamie got your purse, your groceries, and most importantly, Zorro." Zoey squeezed her hard. "You dropped your keys, too, and we have them. We used them to get it all inside."

"I made soup, it's on the stove. And Nick's making the brownies you like, and—and there's fresh bread. He'll bring them down. I just have to let him . . ."

When his voice broke, he shook his head. "Sorry, I'm a mess."

"I could really use that soup, but before anything I need a hot shower."

"I'll go up with you." Zoey took her hand.

"I'll keep the soup on warm. Arden." Jamie stroked gentle fingers on her bruised cheek. "Just tell me he's locked up."

"Under guard at the hospital. I'll tell you everything after I shower and get dry clothes."

"We're staying," Zoey said as they started upstairs. "Jamie, Nick, and I. Gideon doesn't know when he can get back, so we're staying in your guest rooms."

"I know you're worried, but you don't need to worry now. I'm okay. I'm going to stay okay."

"That's right, you damn well are, but we're staying tonight. I was going to do a full family video call—they don't know yet—but I'll do it while you shower and change. Seeing you banged up will upset everyone. I want them to know he's in custody, and we're here with you."

Gideon met Brill and Venmar at the hospital.

"Hello, Columbus."

"Chief." Brill held out a hand first. "My partner and the newest contender for the Indy 500."

"Good to meet you." Venmar shook Gideon's hand. "What's the status?"

"He's in surgery. She broke his jaw, and he lost a few teeth. Plus, when he hit the road, he'd been taking a leak. His dick took some damage."

"No shit." Brill grinned. "How?"

"Why don't we have some crappy hospital food, and I'll tell you?"

Over a passable meal, he gave them what he'd pieced together on scene, then backtracked to the beginning and the identification at the hotel.

"Smart enough to have the car painted, keep switching plates, getting new fake IDs." Venmar shook his head. "But stupid enough to think, and he had to believe it, he could take Arden to the place in Washington State and, what, live behind some sort of force field that blocked out law enforcement?"

Gideon shrugged. "He got everything he wanted, one way or another, his whole life. Except whatever woman he decided he wanted at any given time of that life."

"The shrinks will have a field day," Brill commented.

Gideon's face went to stone. "He's legally sane."

"Bet your ass," she said, "and he won't slip through that crack again. Two women are dead who shouldn't be, and he did everything he could think of to cover his tracks."

"What we know," Venmar continued, "is that his mom's the one who pushed and convinced him to take that crack before. She's not alive to do that now. And what we've got? It wouldn't fly a second time."

"He's done. I'm hoping we don't have to work around you to take him back to Columbus. Matricide, it's the big one."

"If I pushed to keep him here, try him here for Arden over that, I'd lose. But I'd like a conversation with your prosecutor."

"Consider it done."

As Brill spoke, Kim walked up.

"He's in recovery."

"Will he be able to talk?"

"Doctor said in about an hour. They reset his jaw, his nose. She also busted his left eardrum."

"That's a fucking shame," Brill said.

"Isn't it? He'll need a couple implants." Kim tapped her teeth. "I didn't ask how many stitches, but they called in a plastic surgeon for that.

"Beck is taking first guard shift. Hawk went back to the station to deal with some of the paperwork. We thought you might want to call in Nat to get into the laptop. She's the best we've got on the cyber."

"I'll do that. You should go home."

"I'm heading back to the station, Chief, to work with Hawk. I'm invested. We all are."

"I'll be in after I talk to Dubecki." He glanced at his watch. "You've got time before closing to order pizza for whoever's in the house. It's on me."

"I hear that. Good work, Chief."

"Back at you, Officer."

"You've got a good team," Venmar commented.

"A good team, and Riverbend's a good town. Now, I hope I don't have to work around you to interview Dubecki on today's incident before you have a crack at him."

Brill lifted both hands. "We wouldn't dream of getting in your way."

Just over an hour later, Gideon stood looking down at the man in the hospital bed, the bandaged face, the blackened eyes that held nothing but rage.

Dubecki had to speak through his remaining teeth. "I'll have your badge."

"Right. Dustin Dubecki, this interview is being recorded. Do you understand your rights as were read to you?"

"I understand I have the right to tell you to fuck right off. I was attacked, viciously, and you have me cuffed to a hospital bed?"

"Who attacked you?"

"Arden Bowie. I want her arrested."

"Arden Bowie attacked you? Was that before or after she escaped from the trunk of your car where you dumped her after you attacked her?"

"I don't know what you're talking about. We were going home, to my retreat in Washington State. She went crazy, hit me with a hammer or something. She suffers from a mental imbalance."

"It was a lug wrench, which she retrieved from the trunk where you put her after you knocked her unconscious. Do you often take women home in the trunk of your car? Or, I should say, your mother's car. Which you stole after you murdered her back in Columbus, Ohio."

"Don't be ridiculous." Dustin looked away. "My mother gave me that car to make the trip, to pick up Arden and go home."

"Did she give you the car before or after you killed her?"

"Before—I didn't. You're trying to trick me."

"You attacked Arden Bowie before, again in Columbus, Ohio."

"That was a misunderstanding, nothing more than a spat, a lovers' spat."

"You admitted to the assault."

"Under duress. I had an incompetent, corrupt lawyer and an incompetent judge. Now, I've driven for weeks, through storms, and—"

"Like the one in Colorado where you killed Hailey Parkinson?"

"I have no idea who that is. I want to talk to Arden. I want you to take these handcuffs off me, arrest her for being such a bitch. And I want to talk to her."

"None of that is going to happen. You checked into the North Western Hotel in Riverbend using false identification."

Dustin made a *pff* sound. "Just a joke. I wanted to surprise Arden. Go get her. Now. Do your goddamn job!"

More rage, Gideon thought. Still in the eyes, but spreading so under the bruising, against the bandages, his face reddened with it.

Didn't like being told no. Being told no enraged him. So push on that button.

"You seem to be under the impression you can give orders. You can't, and, seeing you killed her, Mommy's not here to make it all better."

"You're an idiot. I never hurt my mother."

"You took her jewelry after you killed her. It's in the luggage she bought you, the luggage you left at the North Western."

"Moron! She gave me all that. She was done with that asshole Lester and didn't want the crap he gave her, so gave it to me. Somebody must have broken in after I left, strangled her. Lester! That asshole Lester because he realized she was leaving him.

"I never said she was strangled."

"Yes, you did! You did, too."

"The record will show otherwise. You beat and strangled your mother, stole her jewelry, her car. You hit her account up for a few thousand at an ATM the morning after you beat and strangled her."

"Did not. You can't prove it."

Gideon gave him a wide grin. "Wanna bet, Dustin? Or is it Jesse? Maybe you like Samuel now?"

Studying him, Gideon took a chance. "You really paid out the ass for those IDs, and now they're useless. The guy who made them? In custody and singing your name.

"We've got your laptop, your phone, too. We're getting all kinds of good stuff out of them. The kind that's putting you in a cell forever."

"You can't go through my personal property! I have rights!"

"That's not one of them. Jesus, you're stupid. You're not even pathetic, Dustin. You're nothing. You're finished. Arden's laughing at you right now."

"She better not be! She better not be or she'll be sorry." The cuffs jangled as he pulled against them.

"Who's going to make her sorry? You?" Gideon baited him with a grin designed to insult. "How?"

"I'll teach her a lesson, and she won't forget. A man takes charge, a man rules the house and the woman in it. A man provides and a woman is fucking grateful."

"You started teaching her a lesson today, with your fists."

"She deserved a good beating after the trouble she caused me. She put me in that hell after I brought her flowers? She's coming with me, and she's going to like it."

"But she didn't want to go with you, so you knocked her out, put her in the trunk of the car."

"She's lying about that. Typical."

"Dustin, not only will we find Arden's DNA in that trunk—blood, hair—we have a witness who saw you. You shot at him. Twice. Missed, twice. You're a crap shot on top of everything else."

"So he says. He's the one she's been fucking, cheating on me with. Thinks he can drive a big pickup, park it in her driveway."

Gideon just lifted his eyebrows. "Today's witness happens to be married, to another man. Are you stating you observed a pickup truck in Arden's driveway prior to today?"

"Last night, late. I saw it. Cheating on me with some fag? I was going to forgive her."

"You saw my truck, Dustin. Arden and I live together. We're engaged. We laugh at you all the time. We'll be laughing harder now."

"She's a whore!" He tried to shout it, yanking on the cuffs. "I should've killed you both that night, but I decided to forgive her."

"After you taught her a lesson or two."

Over the edge now, Gideon noted. His face bloodred, his eyes wild.

"A few good beatings, she'll learn. She'll learn or I'll choke the life out of her, because I don't take that shit from anyone, especially not a woman. There's always another whore to tame. You, you're a dead man. I'm a goddamn Dubecki, and I can buy and sell you. When my mother finds out—"

"You killed your mother, Dustin."

He lay, breathing hard, breathing fast. And those eyes ticktocking side to side.

"She can't help you now, Dustin, because you put your hands around her throat. You squeezed and squeezed and you choked the life out of her. How did it feel?"

"Orgasmic!" He snapped it out as best he could. "She didn't take care of me like she should have. She didn't keep our family together. I don't need her. I can hire the best lawyers. She was a bad mother, a bad mother. I'm not going to prison for killing her. She deserved it."

"And Hailey Parkinson."

"I don't know who that is."

"She came to the cabin in Colorado."

"Oh, that one. She pretended to be lost, tried to seduce me even though I told her I was married. Then she acted like she didn't want it. I gave it to her anyway. I don't take that crap from a woman."

"So you strangled her."

"So what? I'm a man, and I do what the hell I want. I'm done talking to you because I'm going to kill you anyway. I want a lawyer. Now."

"Good luck with that. We'll arrange for you to make your phone call."

He stepped out, where Brill and Venmar waited. "He wants a lawyer."

"Well, shit."

"Requested after he confessed." Gideon tapped his recorder. "To his mother—orgasmic—Hailey Parkinson—so what? Arden, she asked for it. Being legally sane doesn't mean he's not batshit."

"I hear that." Brill looked at Venmar. "We'd like to hear that interview."

"I need to get back to the station. You're welcome to join."

He didn't get home until nearly one. He knew there'd been times he'd felt equally if not more exhausted. But he couldn't remember when or why.

The whole group, gathered in the living room, rose when he came in.

"Pajama party?"

"She wouldn't go to bed," Zoey told him. "So—"

"Neither would they," Arden finished. "You look tired, Chief. Are you hungry, too?"

He shook his head, but crossed over, took the wineglass out of her hand, and drained the contents. "That'll do it. He confessed, to all of it."

Arden just sagged. "He confessed."

"Didn't take long to bait him into it, though it was a little tough on him, since you broke his jaw."

"I . . ."

"And his nose, and his left eardrum. Knocked out a couple teeth."

Zoey held out a fist. "Fist bump, goddamn it."

Arden obliged, then dropped down on the sofa. "I never hurt anyone before. It's . . ."

"In this case?" Jamie gripped Nick's hand. "You need to say *empowering*."

"That's the word," Nick agreed. "You took care of yourself, Arden. And more? Think about it. You stopped him from hurting more people."

"And he would have. Brownies." Despite himself, Gideon reached for one. "A man does what a man wants, and a woman has to fall in line, or pay for it. Always another whore to tame, and so on. They'll keep him, restrained and under guard, in the hospital for another day. Then Venmar and Brill will take him back to Columbus to stand trial for his mother."

"Venmar and Brill?"

"I haven't had time to tell you. They got into Washington State earlier today. They were already heading down here when all hell broke loose. He can hire all the lawyers he likes, but he'll go in for matricide, do life. If he manages to get out before he's dead, he'll stand trial for Hailey Parkinson, and then there's you, Legs. Add the shots he took at Jamie."

"Then it's done."

"It's done; he's done. I'll need your statement, yours, too, Jamie, but we can do that tomorrow."

"I wrote mine out," Arden told him. "It helped to write it out."

"I call this party over. I'm going up to bed." Zoey gave Arden another hug, then shifted to give one to Gideon.

"We'll get some sleep, too." Nick gave Jamie's hand a squeeze. "Isis is already down in there for the night, so if you don't mind, we'll stay till morning."

"Stay as long as you like." Arden rose to go to Jamie, kiss both his cheeks. "My hero."

"Don't make me cry again, it's embarrassing. Nick will be gone at dawn—the life of a baker—but I'm making breakfast." He walked over to Gideon, kissed him on the mouth. "My hero."

Gideon just shook his head, finished the brownie as Zoey went up, and Jamie went with Nick into the first-floor guest room.

"You really do look tired, Gideon."

"I had to get it done, had to close it up, do the job. Not just for the job, Arden. For you. I had to do that before I could do this."

He plucked her off the couch, lifted her off her feet, and held her, just held her, before his mouth found hers.

"I need to hold on a minute. I need it."

"Good." She recognized the trembling inside her, and him, as relief, and pressed her face to his shoulder. "That's good, because so do I."

"Christ. I've never been that scared before. I never want to be that scared again." He eased her back on her feet, laid a hand on her cheek. "He hurt you."

"I hurt him more."

"By Christ, you did. I'm glad of it, even if it meant I couldn't."

"Oh, but you did. You hurt him most of all. He confessed. He's going to prison. And you came for me. You came for me. You were there, right there when I needed you."

He started to shake his head, but she laid her hands on his cheeks to stop the movement.

"Everything was so sharp and clear when I got out of that trunk, when I hit him. I knew exactly what I had to do—and God, wanted to do. I did it.

"I looked down at him, Gideon, and I wasn't afraid. I knew I was done being afraid of him. Then it all went blurry and shaky and I couldn't seem to move. I saw the blood, and him lying there, and I couldn't move.

"Until you were there. Until I saw you."

"And I saw you, standing in the rain with a lug wrench in your hand. I got a little shaky myself."

"You took charge anyway, Chief." She linked her arms around his neck. "I'm going to marry you."

"You'd better believe it. Where do you want to go after?"

"After? Oh, honeymoon." It struck her they stood here, arms around each other, her dog leaning on her leg, and talked of a wedding and honeymoons.

After a nightmare for both of them.

"I don't know. I actually hadn't thought through that far ahead."

"Ever been to Ireland?"

"No. Have you?"

"Yeah. Let's go there. We'll stay in a castle."

"In a castle?"

"They've got them." He ran a hand over her hair. "And you don't mind the rain."

"No, I don't mind the rain."

"Right now? Let's go to bed. It's been a hell of a long day."

"Text the detectives first. Invite them to breakfast. How's eight-thirty?"

He looked at her, watched her smile. With a shrug he sent the text.

Hands linked, she walked upstairs with him, the dog at her heels, to end the long day, and start the rest of her life, in the safe and the quiet.

About the Author

Bruce Wilder

Nora Roberts is the #1 *New York Times* bestselling author of more than 250 novels, including *Hidden Nature, Mind Games, The Lost Bride Trilogy,* The Dragon Heart Legacy trilogy, and many more. She is also the author of the bestselling In Death series written under the pen name J. D. Robb. There are more than 500 million copies of her books in print.

BOOKS